THE CRYSTAL AND THE DRAGON

With a dramatic suddenness that you do not expect from a world in which you have lived for three months, and which has rained all day on the road you have to ride tonight, the dark arch of Claudia's tower window lit up with silver. The roiling depths of the golden globe stilled; the rich light dimmed to gray; and from a little spark of red in the globe's center there grew the stately form of a dragon. It grew to the size of the globe, to the outermost diameter of its glow; and stopped, before Ted had to decide whether he was going to leave the room, possibly dragging Ruth with him.

The wind rattled the windows. Ted could feel his heart thumping in his ears. He had a good side view of the dragon, which floated with its tail to the trap-door and its head toward Randolph, at the window. The dragon was bright red with touches of black. It was a very twisty, decorated dragon, with seven claws on each foot and a great many tendrils and spikes and whiskers.

Ted didn't want that huge, tapering head to look in his direction. It had black eyes with red pupils and could have looked at him, if it had wanted to, without turning its head. But its gaze was bent on Randolph. Randolph went down on one knee and bowed his forehead onto the other. It was the most extravagant gesture of respect that Ted had ever seen anybody in the Secret Country make.

FIREBIRD

WHERE FANTASY TAKES FLIGHT™

Birth of the Firebringer	Meredith Ann Pierce
The Changeling Sea	Patricia A. McKillip
Dark Moon	Meredith Ann Pierce
The Dreaming Place	Charles de Lint
The Ear, the Eye and the Arm	Nancy Farmer
Enchantress from the Stars	Sylvia Engdahl
Fire Bringer	David Clement-Davies
The Hex Witch of Seldom	Nancy Springer
The Hidden Land	Pamela Dean
The Kin	Peter Dickinson
I Am Mordred	Nancy Springer
I Am Morgan le Fay	Nancy Springer
The Outlaws of Sherwood	Robin McKinley
The Riddle of the Wren	Charles de Lint
The Secret Country	Pamela Dean
The Sight	David Clement-Davies
The Son of Summer Stars	Meredith Ann Pierce
Spindle's End	Robin McKinley
Treasure at the Heart of the Tanglewood	Meredith Ann Pierce
Westmark	Lloyd Alexander
The Winter Prince	Elizabeth E. Wein

THE WHIM OF THE DRAGON

PAMELA DEAN

FIREBIRD
AN IMPRINT OF PENGUIN GROUP (USA) INC.

FIREBIRD
Published by Penguin Group
Penguin Group (USA) Inc., 345 Hudson Street, New York, New York 10014, U.S.A.
Penguin Books Ltd, 80 Strand, London WC2R ORL, England
Penguin Books Australia Ltd, 250 Camberwell Road,
Camberwell, Victoria 3124, Australia
Penguin Books Canada Ltd, 10 Alcorn Avenue,
Toronto, Ontario, Canada M4V 3B2
Penguin Books (N.Z.) Ltd, 182-190 Wairau Road, Auckland 10, New Zealand

First published in the United States of America by Ace Books,
The Berkley Publishing Group, 1989
Published by Firebird, an imprint of Penguin Group (USA) Inc., 2003

1 3 5 7 9 10 8 6 4 2

ISBN 0-14-250161-1

Printed in the United States of America

To Patricia Wrede,
whose patience has been so sorely tried

ACKNOWLEDGMENTS

I am greatly obliged to David S. Cargo for the design of Heathwill Library; and to Michael Mornard for advice concerning the castle of the Dragon King.

As always, I owe more than I can say to Steven Brust, Nate Bucklin, Emma Bull, Kara Dalkey, Will Shetterly, and Patricia Wrede for providing kindness and censure in the appropriate doses.

Her Gentle and Fruitful Grace, Ruth, Lady of the Green Caves, formerly Princess of the Hidden Land and Lord of the King's Forests, to their Excellent and Estimable Lordships Randolph, King's Counselor, and Fence, Council's Wizard, greetings.

3 September 490

Dear Fence and Randolph,

I did try to write this in your manner, but I was afraid you would never unravel it. I am going to write in plain English, and trust to your perspicacity to understand.

I am not Lady Ruth of the Green Caves. Edward, Patrick, Ellen, and Laura are also not who you think they are. We come from somewhere else, where, for years and years, the five of us played a game. The game was you, The Secret Country. We had the characters, the people, right, except for Claudia. We had never thought of her. And we didn't have the story exactly right. But we would play the Banquet of Midsummer Eve, and Randolph's poisoning of the King, and the battle with the Dragon King; and in the end Edward found out that Randolph had killed his father, and so he killed Randolph in the rose garden. These events and people seemed strange and wonderful to us, and altogether different from the lives we led.

This summer we couldn't play. Ellen and Patrick and I were living about as far away from Ted and Laura as it's possible to be, and we were all very unhappy. But Patrick found a sword under a bottle tree. It glowed green. It's the one you called Melanie's. Ted and Laura found a sword under a hedge. That one glowed blue, and you called it Shan's. The hedge was the same as, or like, the hedge in front of the House by the Well of the White Witch. And that house was also in our world.

If you hold Melanie's sword and crawl under the bottle tree, you come out in a place called New South Wales. If you hold Shan's sword and crawl under the hedge, you come out in a place called Illinois. And if you begin in those places and crawl under with the swords, you find yourself in the Hidden Land. That's how we got here. Benjamin thought we were your royal children. And yours weren't around to contradict him. So we played our parts as best we could. You must understand that we did not, in the beginning, necessarily intend any deception. We were not certain that you were real at all; and yet you were the people we wanted most to meet in the world, and the Secret Country was the place we wanted most to be, and the princesses and princes you knew were the people whose parts we most dearly desired. We had doubts even then, and these doubts grew on us as we found our parts more difficult to play in truth than they had been in semblance; but by then we were entangled, and feared to do ourselves, and perhaps you also, more harm than good by a confession. Nor did we know what to confess. We thought we were in truth your royal children, or as near as you could get. It seemed to us that, if they were not back in our places contending with the strangeness of our lives, which we knew they were not, then they were nowhere except within us.

But when Ted was in the land of the dead, waiting for Lord Randolph and me to ransom him, he saw and spoke to all five of them. Edward told Ted that Claudia had killed them with a stratagem and a potion. This was not of our game. We grieve for your loss. If there were anything we could do to Claudia, we would do it. We think it best to go home, leaving you an account of what we know. We have left the swords, one under the hedge before the house, and the other under a bottle tree perhaps fifty yards to the right of it.

There is one other thing. Time flows in your world just as it does in ours. This startled us, because in the stories we've read, matters were better arranged. If we were a long time in the Secret Country, our guardians at home missed us and were angry, and if we were a long time at home Benjamin and Agatha missed us and were angry. So we bethought us of the Riddle of Shan's Ring, that it might blow time awry, so we could stay a long time in your country and be gone but a moment from ours.

Ellen and I took Shan's Ring to the hedge through which Ted and Laura had come into this country. And we tried diverse methods; and when we stood in our own world, and I stood outside the hedge, and Ellen stood in the yard of the house, I threw the Ring over the hedge to Ellen and said the verse aloud. There came a flash of purple light, and a gap opened in the hedge. I saw the Secret Country in it, so I came through back to this place. But Ellen saw the house light up, and a woman burst out of the door brandishing a broom and shouting incomprehensible things. This woman was the Lady Claudia, whom you know. Ellen ran for the hedge, and Shan's sword, which she held, pulled her down to show her where the Ring lay, and when she retrieved it, she came through the hedge back to this place and fell in the stream.

Now I thought that what had happened to Ellen had taken longer than what had happened to me. So I took Shan's Ring and went through the hedge. And I was in a strange country that looked like the Secret Country, in that it held the Well of the White Witch, and the plain, but that looked most unlike it in that the air and sky were glassy and felt altogether odd and unpleasant, and there was an army on the plain. So I came back quickly to the Secret Country. But you should note that this place in which I had found myself was the selfsame place in which Lord Randolph and Fence and I stood much later when we bargained with the unicorn for Edward Fairchild's life.

Now, once I had gone through the hedge with both the Ring and Shan's sword, I found myself back in our world again, and sat there for a little while, and came home. But for Ellen hours passed and the sun rose and she was greatly vexed. So we thought that Shan's Ring had changed the rate at which time passed, and we would be safe to stay here until the story's end.

But we find now that, knowing you and knowing Lord Randolph, we do not like the end of the story, and fearing to give you more pain than joy if we stay, we have gone.

Two more matters. First, in our game, Lord Andrew was a spy of the Dragon King; so have a care of him. And second, in sober reality, Randolph pledged his life for the return of Edward Fairchild. But he didn't get Edward Fairchild. He got Ted Carroll, whom he knows not and doesn't want. So you might try that on the unicorns if they get fussy.

We thank you for our sojourn in your country, which is one of the best ever we saw or heard tell of; and we repent of our deception; and we wish you well.

Believe me, good sirs, your most obedient,
most affectionate, most humble servant,

Ruth Eleanora Carroll

PROLOGUE

THEY had set free the fire of her house. That was nothing. Her house had been burned by the master of fire, and she had restored it. She had burned in such fire as made this a dance of sunlight on water, bright but harmless. But if they had intended not her destruction but their own escape, they had succeeded. And there were others in her house less inured to fire. She called the water-beasts without the proper forms of their names. They would match this discourtesy by coming without further preliminaries, and thus escape the fire. As she thought so, they surrounded her, bubbling and spouting. The faint smoke in the room was overlaid with damp purple mist, and the fire's crackling drowned in the rush and murmur of innumerable waters. She wished it were better than an illusion.

"Flee the fire," she said. "After the time it takes to boil six kettles, I will requite this barbarous rudeness."

They hissed like a gallon of water spilled on a giant's griddle, and were gone. The smoke grew thicker. She could not remember how many cats were in the house, and cursed the humor that made them all black cats. She called each cat's six names, and in a little time had all nine of them climbing her skirts. No cat that had lived with her feared fire. But they were indignant, and disposed to be intransigent. She crouched and gathered them in, grinning. So those children had broken the mirrors in her house. Who would break the mirrors in her mind?

She spared a moment to look into one that offered no

escape: not for her, and not for those she looked at. She saw Fence and Randolph, in High Castle, in its Mirror Room. They did not know what its mirrors could accomplish, and in any case were occupied with other matters. It pleased her to see them standing there as the outline of their doom took shape, surrounded by salvation and thinking it ornament.

Randolph was thinner than when she had danced with him at Midsummer Eve, his face sharper, his green eyes darker, his wild black hair limp and his bewitching voice hardly better than a croak. He looked as if he had been ill a fortnight.

"Truly I felt such nudgings and nibblings as thou explainest thus," he said, "but I tell thee, Fence, not once did I feel them regarding King William. That foul crime I did of my own will."

She had never seen Fence look like this. Nothing she did could make him suffer so. Randolph could make him suffer worse, and, before the end, no doubt he would.

"Will you, then," said Fence, "tell me why?" His round green eyes and innocent face beneath the untidy brown hair were not amusing, and his shortness was no cause for contempt. He was formidable.

"That you might be here to reproach me," said Randolph. He suffered Fence's look and countered with mere steadiness. He seemed to be bearing some pain so great that he dared not attend to it. She had never seen Randolph look so, either.

She reached out a hand, and frowned. Her mind-mirrors were but doors or windows; they were not, as the mirrors of her house had been, instruments of her will. She could work no nudgings and nibblings from here.

"Better far that I were dead, having had no doubt of thee while I lived," said Fence, still looking up at Randolph.

"What? Dead, the truth undiscovered?" said Randolph. The mockery in his voice was mild, but she felt it in her bones like a curse. So, it seemed, did Fence.

"You made this truth!" shouted Fence. "Spare me your convolvings."

"I had thought to," said Randolph, and the mockery now was leveled at himself. "Edward, I thought, had killed me long since."

"Edward," said Fence, as though he still did not believe it, "is dead. You are the Regent."

"I am a regicide."

"A perfect jest, then," said Fence. "Having killed King William, his heir dead already, you must take William's place."

"That is madness."

"No," said Fence, "it is justice."

She laughed. She would not have thought of this. Had those children done it? Both men started at the laugh; Randolph drew his dagger. She chuckled, in her mind only, as they snatched back the tapestries covering the mirror. Their arts could not discover her, unless she continued so careless.

"An the very air laugh at us, is that not justice also?" said Randolph.

Fence's mouth quirked, but he said nothing.

"Fence, it is not justice to make me king. What of the country? I am a poison as potent as that wherewith I struck down William, the only antidote thereto being my death."

"If that were all, all would be easy," said Fence. "You are not the poison. Your act is that. Though you die and enter the shadows and forget what you have done, yet you have done it, and all our history to come is poisoned thereby. At least stay and see your handiwork."

"Stars in heaven," said Randolph. As he had in the event, he looked far more poisoned than had the dying King.

"The lesson of Melanie was ever bitter to your mind," said Fence. "Learn it now with your heart. Life gained by treachery is a pain sharper than death."

In her fury at this statement, though it was an old axiom in the teachings of the Blue Sorcerers, she almost spoke aloud to them. But a brisk blow on her cheek brought her back to the burning house, where an unhappy cat resented her neglect.

"Quite right, small one," she said to it. "All attend."

She found in her mind a mirror that was a door, and sent three cats where they would be most useful. She found the second door, and pulled herself and the other six cats through it, to her House in the Hidden Land, four leagues from where Fence and Randolph turned and turned in the maze she had made for them. She must consider now whether it was still possible to bring them to the trap at its heart.

Chapter 1

"That was good," said Laura mournfully, and licked an escaped drop of ice cream from her elbow.

"You don't sound like it," said her brother. The lock of hair on the right side of his face was sticky with chocolate ice cream, but he managed to look and sound superior just the same.

"I thought," said Laura, who was used to this, "that maybe I wouldn't like ice cream anymore."

"You wanted the Secret Country to leave its mark, huh?"

"Well—"

"You just look at that scar on your knee if you want to see a mark," said Ted.

Three small children pushed between them, and they moved slowly away from the drugstore and down the dusty summer street. Laura had never before thought it possible to be tired of summer.

"Let's go home," said Ted.

"I'm not used to it yet. If we get home before dark they won't be *too* mad."

"Oh, my God!" said Ted, stopping dead before a gas station.

"What's the matter?" Laura said, looking at him carefully. It was hard to concentrate on his expression. He looked so peculiar in his too-short jeans and his too-tight shirt, with the thick, light brown hair down past his shoulders. Laura supposed she looked peculiar too. Her shorts fit well enough, but her blouse was too tight across the shoulders now and too short to tuck in.

"Shan's Ring didn't work," said Ted, in a tone of outraged disbelief. "We've been gone for *months*."

They *had* been gone for months, struggling through an imaginary world come gruesomely to life. Hence their old clothes no longer fit them, and Ted's hair was too long.

"Looks like summer to me," said Laura, taking in with a gesture the violent blue sky, the deep green of the oak and maple trees, the daisies blooming in the yards of old houses, the drooping peonies with their petals showered to the ground.

"Remember when we left?"

It seemed a very long time ago. Laura scowled. Sneaking down the stairs, she had fallen over her shoes; the refrigerator in the moonlight had looked like a polar bear; they had argued over whether, since they had deserved to be sent to bed without supper, they could take any food with them now; they had argued over whether it was right to bring a flashlight to the Secret Country, where such things were unknown—

"It was *night*," said Laura.

"And it's not night now. Shan's Ring was supposed to bring us back within *five minutes* of the time we left."

And from the scanty and anonymous evergreen shrubs that failed to decorate the ugliness of the gas station, a cardinal whistled its ascending song.

"I *told* you," said Laura. From a distance of perhaps three feet, careful to make no sudden move, she addressed the cardinal. "Mysterious servant of unknown forces; minion of the Secret Country. What's going on?"

"They can't talk!" said Ted, with an enormous and hurtful scorn.

Laura looked sideways at him and decided that half of it was fear. She was frightened herself. "Can you take us to someone who can tell us what's going on?" she said to the bird.

It flew halfway down the street and alighted on the wrought-iron arm of a bus-stop bench.

"Come on," said Laura. She grabbed Ted's hand. "How else are we going to find out what's wrong with the magic?"

"We're *finished* with magic," said Ted.

The cardinal began to sing again.

"Maybe," said Laura, in the manner of the Secret Country, "magic hath not finished with us."

This had sounded merely clever as she said it, but watching Ted hear it she thought it had an ominous ring, and wished she had kept her mouth shut.

"You know what Shan said," she offered. "If say No you will, then say it as late as may be."

"Where did you get *that*?"

Laura gulped. It had come from the back of her mind, the part that knew more than she, and recognized things she had never seen. "I guess Princess Laura read it somewhere," she said.

"You've still got Princess Laura? Because Edward's gone."

This was extremely disconcerting. Laura had Princess Laura still in the back of her mind, and Laura thought the cardinal meant something more than natural. Ted no longer had Edward, and Ted thought the cardinal was just a cardinal. "So," said Laura, with a hideous feeling in her stomach, "I better go by myself."

Ted stared at her and gave a most unpleasant laugh. "Serve you right if I let you." There was a monstrous pause. "Feel free," said Ted.

The cardinal hooted at them and rose fluttering from the bench. Laura was not sure she could move. She looked at Ted. He was looking at the cardinal, with about the same expression as he had worn long ago when he found out that Laura, reading his enormous copy of *The Mysterious Island* in the bathtub, had dropped it in the water.

"By the mercy of Shan," said King Edward, between his teeth, "may we not all rue this day. Come on, Laurie."

The cardinal had an upsetting understanding of traffic lights, sprinklers, children playing softball in the street, unsteady fences, unfriendly dogs, irate bicyclists, and the other hazards encountered by two people following a bird through unfamiliar territory. It led them through the little business district where they had bought their ice cream, past streets of huge old houses and huger older trees, through empty back yards and down crooked alleys, across a busy street, under a freeway, down a clean, white, empty road and into a housing development so new that half the houses had no lawns yet. The houses were very large, somewhat odd, and extremely expensive-looking. The cardinal shot past them all, waited in a little stand of trees the bulldozers had missed, and with one last triumphant whistle perched on a mailbox and folded its wings.

Ted and Laura panted up, sweating and red-faced. They stared past the cardinal over a long slope of blowing grass, at the top of which stood a house. It was like a stack of wooden blocks that somebody had brushed against: untidy and lopsided, but not actually fallen over. Its windows were round or triangular, its winding flagstone walk absolutely bare.

"Gah!" said Laura. "What an ugly house!"

"Lucky for us, maybe," said Ted. "You liked the Secret House. Remember who lived in *that*."

Laura looked at the mailbox, which said, in gold letters, APSINTHION. "The name's ugly too," she said.

"Maybe the Apsinthions won't like ours, either," said Ted.

They walked up to the blank wooden door and pushed the button beside it. Inside the house they heard a melodious but disorganized rattle, as if somebody had poured a handful of marbles into a glass jar.

The door opened inward, and a man from one of Laura's visions stood smiling at them. No, magic had not done with them.

Beside Laura, Ted jumped. Laura went on staring. The

man, glimpsed so briefly in a vision she had hoped she wasn't having anyway, really did, under this more leisurely examination, look like Fence and Randolph. He was short, as Fence had been. He had Fence's straight brown hair, better cut; but Randolph's sharper face. The long hand that held the edge of the door was Randolph's. The grin was Fence's, and so were the round green eyes. Randolph had had almond-shaped eyes, usually narrowed. In Randolph's face, the eyes of Fence looked less ingenuous.

Stop thinking about Fence and Randolph as if they were dead, Laura told herself. She looked at the man's eyes again for reassurance. They held a tiny spark of red. Perhaps, Laura thought hopefully, it's just the way the light hits them. But he wore a red robe too. In style it was like the ones they had grown accustomed to at High Castle. But it was red, and so were his boots. Nobody at High Castle had worn red, except Claudia.

The man watched them looking him over, and the glint in his eyes deepened. He was still smiling.

Ted cleared his throat. Laura wondered how long they had been staring. "My lord," said Ted, "the cardinal brought us."

"In his name, be welcome," said the man, and he stood aside to let them in. His raspy voice was only vaguely familiar.

Ted took her by the hand, and they walked boldly past the man into his house. Pale polished floors stretched all around them, gleaming in the light from high windows. Out of the corner of her eye Laura saw red cushions, and black, and white; and dark wooden tables.

The man in the red robe shut the door behind them with a hollow boom. Laura, starting, saw Ted jump too.

"Who are you?" said the man in red.

Ted hesitated. "Edward Carroll," he said, and, defiantly, "crowned King of the Secret Coun—the Hidden Land. This is the Princess Laura, my sister, as royal as I."

The Princess Laura, alerted by his tone, worked this out and grinned.

The man in red stood still, as Fence would do if you startled or intrigued him. "The name of the royal house of the Hidden Land," he said, "is Fairchild."

"So it is," said Ted.

Laura saw him trying not to grin, and worked that out too. Apsinthion *didn't* like their name.

"Oho," said the man. "Sits the wind in that quarter?"

"Did you expect this?" Ted asked him.

"Expectation," said the man in red, "foils perception."

"What do you perceive?" said Ted. Laura admired this response.

"That you are of two minds, to go or stay."

"Did you send the cardinal for us?" said Ted. Laura recognized the resigned determination of the voice he used in Twenty Questions, a game he despised.

"I send the cardinals to bring me news," said the man in red. "I have had stranger news than you in my time, but not in this place."

"The news isn't *about* this place," said Laura, when Ted was silent. "Did you send the cardinal before?"

"Where?"

"In this place," said Laura, realizing that "The Secret House" would mean nothing to him. "To One Trumpet Street," she added. She wondered if addresses meant anything to him either. There had been none on his mailbox.

"Oh, criminy!" said Ted. "Laura! One Trumpet Street?"

Laura scowled at him. She knew that tone.

"One trumpet—one horn. Unicorn!"

"What a stupid joke."

The man in red took three steps forward and laid a hand on Ted's shoulder. Laura wondered why he flinched; the man was hardly touching him.

"What knowest thou of unicorns?"

"What should I know, if I'm King of the Hidden Land?"

"What thou shouldst know hadst thou been heir thereto, is no matter; what thou dost know as a stranger, I would be told, and quickly."

"Why should I tell you anything?"

"We've *been* telling him, Ted," said Laura.

"Well, maybe we should stop."

"He's been telling us, too."

"A just observation," said the man in red, letting Ted go. "And yet perhaps what you wish to know, I have not told. Will you tell me, what beast is it the dwellers of High Castle pursue each summer?"

"The unicorn," said Laura, pleased with herself. She felt Ted glaring at her.

"What beast flees not the winter?"

"The unicorn!"

"And what beast hath given its voice to the flute?"

"The unicorn," said Laura, desolately.

"Well done. Now. What beast is it the unicorns pursue each summer?"

Ted and Laura looked at each other.

"Before what beast doth winter flee?"

Ted made an angry noise between his teeth.

"What beast maketh that which putteth the words to the flute's song?"

Ted looked thoughtful for a moment, but said nothing.

"Well," said the man in red. "When you know these things, then what manner of thing I am you will know also."

"*Did* you send the cardinal to One Trumpet Street?" asked Laura.

"Tell me what it did there, and I will tell thee if 'twas of my sending."

"Laura, shut up," said Ted.

"It made me trip," said Laura, recklessly, "and fall through a hedge."

"Shut *up*!" said Ted. "As your sovereign lord, I command you!"

"That," said Laura, bitterly, "is a dirty trick."

"But needful, perhaps, to kings," said the man in red, with surprising mildness. He cocked his head, studying them. "Thy sister is wise," he said to Ted. "By the terms of my most carelessly offered bargain, I must tell you that, indeed, the cardinal was of my sending."

"Did you mean—" said Laura; then she remembered her oath of fealty and the order just delivered, and closed her mouth hard.

"I think," said the man in red, "that we must endure long speech with one another. Will you sit down?"

Laura hesitated, a hundred parental warnings about accepting hospitality from strangers coming tardily to mind. If Ted remembered these, he showed no sign. "Thank you," he said, rather grimly.

They followed the red-robed man across the room and sat down on cushions.

"Have you drunk of the Well of the White Witch?" said the man.

"What will you tell me if I tell you that?" said Ted.

"Only that it is therefore safe for you to drink the sole refreshment I have to offer." He looked them over and smiled again. "My messengers set perhaps too swift a pace for the wingless."

"Thank you," said Ted. "We'd like some water."

The man in red left the room.

"Do you know him?" whispered Ted.

"No. I saw him in a vision. He was reading the book where the dragon burned down the Secret House."

"And now we've burned it down again," said Ted.

"He looks like Fence and Randolph."

"Maybe he's an ancestor. Are Fence and Randolph related?"

"'Wizards have no kin,'" quoted Laura.

"They've got to come from somewhere."

"I know. I just meant it might be hard to find out."

"It's impossible to find out, here. Unless he tells us."

"Why shouldn't we tell him stuff?" said Laura.

"Because we don't know whose side he's on, dimwit!"

When Ted started calling names, you could continue on into a satisfactory quarrel, but you were unlikely to actually get anything accomplished. Laura kept her mouth shut, and the red man came back into the room carrying a tray.

It was lacquered a brilliant blue, and as the man took from it the thick familiar mugs of High Castle, Laura saw on its flat surface the stylized figure of a red running fox. The emblem of the Fairchild family, the royal sigil of the Hidden Land.

"Have you a right to that?" demanded Ted, sounding very like King Edward.

The man turned his head and looked quite fierce for a moment; Laura was glad he wasn't looking at her. Then he let his breath out and took a drink from his mug.

"More right than thou," he said, amiably.

"I'm bound by an oath, at least," said Ted.

"I also," said the red man.

"Look," said Ted. "This isn't getting us anywhere."

"I," said the red man, "need go nowhere. It is thou, and thy sister, that must needs go."

"Where?" said Laura.

"To the Hidden Land, to finish out thy tale."

"We don't want it to finish," said Ted.

"It will finish without you," said the red man. "All you have striven to abolish will come to pass, while you dally and eat sweetmeats." His tone stung like dust blown on a high wind.

"The cardinal showed us the sweetmeats!" said Laura, hotly.

The man smiled, and drained his mug. "The cardinal hath his humor also," he said.

Laura took a drink from her own mug. Clear, icy, piercing, the water of the Well slid down her throat. She remembered the baked-grass smell of the plain, the heat in the air wavering like water, the sun striking awful visions from the distant windows of the Secret House, her cousins squabbling, Benjamin riding over the horizon with the dreaded horses. She desired more than anything else to be back in the Hidden Land.

"Will all we want to abolish come to pass," said Ted, who had been staring at the floor for some time, "if we go back?"

"You are able to prevent it."

Ted and Laura looked at each other. That they were able did not mean that they would.

"Why should we believe you?" said Ted. He took a swallow of water, and Laura saw him blink. "Can you prove this? Who are you?"

"Come upstairs," said the red man.

CHAPTER 2

SHE stood in a dusty room and scowled. The cats sat on the floor and sneezed. The water-beasts, whose notion of tidiness was that one spoke to them properly, oozed and burbled in a mild discontent caused by having been moved.

She strode across to the window, stumbling slightly on a clutter of bones. The cats, flowing after her, stopped and began to circle the pile, sniffing. Claudia looked through the grimy glass. Where she should have seen the tops of trees, the vanishing and reappearing slide of the little stream, the round pink dot of the Well and a vast stretch of baked brown grass, there lay the enigmatic expanse of the Gray Lake. Its flat dark surface took the peaceful evening sky and mirrored it into the semblance of an approaching storm. Its long shape was lavishly fringed with goldenrod. Beyond it, steep yellow-clad slopes wandered away, and above them mountains lost themselves in mist.

The air was full of voices. "Something's amiss," she said, to make sure, and instantly they echoed and answered her.

Nothing comes amiss, so money comes withal. All is amiss. Love is dying, Faith's defying, Heart's denying. Nothing shall come amiss, and we won't come home 'til morning. Mark what is done amiss.

She fixed her eyes on the red gingham cuff of her dress, where the machine-made lace staggered like a badly drawn rune; and the voices stopped. She had found them useful and pleasant once; but they were mockery as often as they were counsel, and there was no manner of telling which from which.

She turned to the mirrors in her mind, but their power was dimmed. She had been bound here once. And in any case, the blue flame, whereby she knew the hearts of the children, burned here also, but like the conflagration of a summer forest after lightning. Even if they had seen or heard tell of this place, the children's little flicker, that gave her the best part of her power, would be lost in the larger burning. To tamper with this greater fire would give notice to those she wished, for a while yet, to avoid.

I have seen the moment of my greatness flicker, said the voices.

"So, my old enemies," she said, and chuckled.

She stepped around the fascinated cats, avoided the water-beasts, and walked down the long hall to the rooms at the back of the house. Faintly beneath the smell of dust and water, the scent of cinnamon still lingered. The voices said, *A man cannot be too careful in the choice of his enemies.*

She laughed; and, as often happened, this silenced them.

The room of mirrors was glittering clean. She moved from one little diamond pane to another, until she found what she sought. The youngest girl and the oldest boy, staring in awe, fear, and suspicion at a man in a red robe.

"And my old friends too!" said Claudia.

Once more unto the breach, dear friends, once more; Or close the wall up with our English dead! She scowled again, considering that. Some of the voices spoke mere gibberish, and not any foreign tongue she knew the sound of. But even in those that spoke most clearly, odd words would surface from time to time. English dead. What sort of dead were those? The sort that walked, perhaps. As she did, and the man in red also.

She laid her hand upon the glass. "Burning one," she said, "knoweth Chryse what thou art about?"

The children did not hear her, but he did. He only smiled.

With the spatter and drum of rain on a roof, the water-beasts rampaged into the room behind her and demanded the explanation she had promised. She smiled too.

"That one, children," she said, and showed them the man in red. "Not the little ones whom you have seen before. That one."

CHAPTER 3

UPSTAIRS in the house of Apsinthion was a room of mirrors. They were everywhere, in frames carved and gilded, or plain and unstained, or worked silver, or jeweled gold. Little ones lay on all the furniture. Large ones swung gently on stands of wood or metal. They held a hundred copies of the red ceiling, the polished wooden floor, the sunshine falling through the windows, the summer sky of Illinois that lay flat against the glass of the skylight like a layer of paint.

"Oh, God," said Ted to Laura, as they stood arrested in the doorway. "Is he like Claudia?"

Laura pointed silently at the mirror they stood before. It showed only themselves. They walked into the room, avoiding the first mirror and finding themselves again in a larger one. Their host appeared behind them in that mirror and waved his hand at it. A wash of blackness went down its surface, and they saw, as if they rode across the plain at a distance, High Castle with the mountains at its back. For a moment Ted thought they were looking at a sunset, and then he knew. High Castle was burning. Fire leapt from every wall, and met itself in the moat as half a tower fell hissing. The outer walls that should hide the moat from view were down already.

"Did we do that?" said Laura. She sounded as if she were sure of it. Ted supposed that if you spent your whole life breaking things without meaning to, you might easily believe that any catastrophe was your fault.

"Your absence will do't," said Apsinthion.

"How?" said Ted. He felt Laura looking at him, probably admiring his composure. Never mind that his hands were shaking.

"Lord Andrew hath his suspicions even now," said the man in red. "Think you what he will tell the council: What is easier to believe, those things writ i'the letter Fence hath, or that Fence and Randolph plot against all the royal house?"

"Benjamin'd have better sense—" said Ted.

"Oh, aye," said the red man, in Benjamin's manner exactly. "Benjamin, and Agatha, and Matthew. Hence civil war, and Randolph's death; a land divided, and no certain heir."

"Can you send us back?" asked Ted.

"I can." He met Ted's eyes in the mirror. The little flame in his obscured the pupils. "But know that other powers may so sort themselves that I cannot send you home again."

Laura's face grew shocked, and she stared into the mirror. Apsinthion tucked his hands up in the sleeves of his robe and seemed prepared to stand behind them as long as was needful.

Ted tried to think. He looked around Apsinthion's house, which was congenial to him in a remarkable degree. You could have a place like this yourself, he thought. After college. He had just started junior high. Ted sighed.

He thought of his one or two brilliant teachers (usually in subjects he didn't like or wasn't good at), one or two cruel or foolish ones, the rest amiable and forgettable; the other kids, with their peculiar preoccupations: television, video games, sports, clothes; nothing that was both real and beautiful. Vacations: reading, hiking, bicycling, watching television to see if it had gotten any better, quarreling with Laura, plotting with Laura new twists for the Secret Country, and waiting, waiting for the summer when they could return to their best reality. This summer, as blank as the television screen when the set was off, and promising even less.

If he went back, he could be a king (falteringly, and for a little while), rescue five children from the land of the dead (perhaps), save Randolph from the unicorns (how?), live in High Castle (until they threw him out because he wasn't real). If you want to save people, join the Peace Corps, he thought. If you want adventure, be an astronaut.

No. The Secret Country was smoothed to the contours of his mind (or they to it). However he balked at its refusal to conform to his plot, however bizarre the vistas it had yet to reveal to him, whatever the Outer Isles and Fence's Country were really like, they would speak to him (or he to them) in ways that the Moon or Mars never could. Even if he became a doctor and cured everyone in sight, the accomplishment would be hollow beside dragging five royal children from the shadows to which he himself had, perhaps, consigned them. That was the point. He was responsible for the Secret Country.

He turned to his sister, who was chewing the end of her left braid and looking close to tears. She hated being at the Barretts' more than he did. She hated school more too. She was not stupid, and could have been perfectly happy sitting at the back of some classroom, reading and writing and spelling and learning the names of all the presidents of the United States before anybody else had figured out what a president was. But when they tried to teach her spelling with a modified Bingo game that required you spell your word at the top of your voice, she was doomed. Laura, thought Ted, wouldn't shout in front of twenty-five other third-graders if it would win her a million dollars.

Had the Secret Country been even worse for her? She had been endowed with peculiar powers, and required to shout about them, but perhaps Fence and Randolph were an easier audience than her peers.

Oh, hell, thought Ted. He had forgotten their parents. They might have gone off to Australia without him, but that was hardly comparable to vanishing into an imaginary country without leaving so much as a farewell letter. And if he and Laura did leave a farewell letter, everybody would think they had gone crazy, or been kidnapped, or both.

"Shan's *mercy*," he said.

"Not yet," said the man in red.

Laura jerked her head around and fixed wet eyes on Ted. "We have to go back," she said.

"Don't cry about it!"

"I'm not crying at *you*," said Laura, with dignity. "I *saw* something in the floor."

The man in red took two paces away from them, frowning. Laura said, "I saw Fence killing Randolph."

"I suppose you'd rather see me doing it?"

"You show him," said Laura to the man in red. "It sounds stupid when I say it."

"That is a grave failing," said the red man, clinically.

You creep, thought Ted. "You'd better show me," he said.

The man shrugged once, like Fence, and walked across the floor to the most ornate of the wall mirrors. Its carved wooden frame was six inches wide, showing the story of an old man and a young man and a group of animals: cat, dog, eagle, horse, unicorn. In the center of the top piece was a gilded sunburst.

Ted and Laura looked at each other.

The man in red tilted his head at the mirror, which abode unchanging, giving them his slight form and enigmatic face, Ted's tousled head at his shoulder, and at Ted's shoulder Laura's fraying braids and wet blue eyes.

"Purgos Aipos Autika," said the man; or something like it.

The interior of the mirror wavered and steadied. Fence and Randolph faced one another in the rose garden. It was late autumn and early evening, and the rain poured down around them, so that the scene was blurred as if the mirror needed dusting. But their swords blazed, blue and green, and springing back from the blades the raindrops sparked like fireworks.

"No, never mind," said Ted, reflecting that he would rather trust Laura than the red man, and not caring to see more.

"But, Ted—"

"It's okay, I believe you. But what if we can't get home?"

"He didn't say we couldn't get home," said Laura, violating one of the tenets of good manners by referring to their host as if he were not present. "He said he couldn't send us home again. There's still the swords."

"That's true," said Ted. "And now that we don't have to pretend anything, we should be able to get Fence to let us use them." He turned to the man in red. "But how do we prove anything to Fence and Randolph?"

"Ask them the three riddles," said Apsinthion. "They will have more need than you to find the answers. Also," he said, slowly, "tell them this. To Fence, 'All may yet be very well.' And to Randolph, 'La Belle Dame sans Merci hath thee in thrall.'"

"Claudia?" said Ted.

Their host smiled. "I'll set you on your journey," he said.

"Wait a minute," said Ted. "The last time we left, we set up magic so we'd only be gone five minutes here. But it didn't exactly work. And we can't just disappear. Our parents would worry."

"What manner of magic?" said the man in red.

"Shan's Ring."

"*Thou?*"

"Well, Ruth, actually."

"Lady Ruth of the Green Caves?"

"Uh—"

"Another changeling?"

"Well, yes."

"*Now* who's telling too much?" demanded Laura.

"We're trusting him to send us back."

Laura was silent.

"I'll strike you a bargain," said the red man. "By your oaths to the Hidden Land, use not Shan's Ring even in direst peril. And I'll blow time awry for you, that you be not missed."

"What's wrong with Shan's Ring?"

"All too little," said the red man, with a wry face, as if he were making a joke. "It doth wake powers that are better sleeping." He frowned. "How often hath this thing been used?"

Ted thought about it. He couldn't remember exactly what Ruth had done to change the time. "Two or three times, I think."

"Three will do't," said the man in red. "Walk warily." He frowned again. "It may be," he said, "that that use did but awaken me. But wake not the others; in especial, wake not more than one. If they confer together, touching the disturbance, they will seek you to your peril."

"Okay," said Ted, "I promise."

"And thou, Princess?"

Laura hesitated, frowning. Then her face cleared. "Yes," she said. "I promise, by my oaths to the Hidden Land, not to use Shan's Ring."

"Then come away," said the man in red.

Ted wondered what Laura was thinking about. If it had been Ruth or Ellen or Patrick, he would have wondered what she was up to, but Laura was not a schemer: the trouble was to get her to do anything, not to keep her from doing too much.

The man stopped beside a tall, narrow mirror with a plain silver frame. They walked over to him, a little slowly. He smiled. "Purgos Aipos Nun," he said, and then, to Ted, "Go quickly."

Ted turned sideways and stepped carefully into the mirror. It gave before his shoulder like cloth, and he put his head out into cloth-smelling dimness and the sound of weary voices. He stepped through and was instantly entangled in heavy material. He pushed at it, and it parted for him. He was behind the Conrad tapestry in the Mirror Room at High Castle. Fence sat on Agatha's sewing-table, and Randolph sat on the floor. They did not look at one another.

Laura bumped Ted from behind and said frenziedly, "The house is flooding! Purple water!"

"Shut up!" Ted didn't care what was happening back at the stark house. Their business was with Fence and Randolph, who now knew a great many awful things about them.

Fence and Randolph looked up, and then stared. Randolph stood up. There was no expression on his face at all, but Laura stopped trying to talk.

"Edward?" said Fence.

"No," said Ted, his throat hurting him. "It's just me."

"Wherefore," said Randolph, as if he were demanding an explanation for the back gate left open and the dog lost, or perhaps a large hole dug in the back yard without permission, "art thou returned?"

CHAPTER 4

LAURA was so shocked by Randolph's tone of voice that she forgot about the purple water. There was a calculation in the way Fence and Randolph looked at her that had not been there before. They knew who she was now; or, no. They knew who she wasn't.

Ted said, "We were sent back, by a man in a red robe."

Laura saw Fence's head come up, like that of a cat who hears you open the refrigerator. But Randolph said, in the same unfriendly voice, "Wherefore did you let him do so?"

"He said that if we didn't, everything we strove to prevent would come to pass."

"Who was he?" said Fence. His voice was merely neutral, but in him this was as great a change as the hostility in Randolph.

"The mailbox said Apsinthion."

"That's wormwood," said Fence, with a kind of skeptical surprise. "What manner of man was he?"

Laura wished they could all sit down. But the room contained one sewing-table, on which Fence was still sitting, and Agatha's high-backed chair with the tapestry cushions, on which she would have felt wrong sitting even before they left.

"He looked like you and Randolph," said Ted, "only mixed together. He had a house full of mirrors."

Fence and Randolph turned to one another; for a bare instant everything seemed familiar. Then Fence looked away, sharply, and said to Ted, "What else?"

"Okay," said Ted. He began with their encounter with Claudia in the yard of her house, in their own world; and ended with their stepping through the mirror into this room. At no point in his narrative did Fence or Randolph ask for any clarification. Randolph, in fact, showed no reaction whatsoever. Fence took the story in as though he were judging it for a contest. Ted saved the three riddles and the messages for last. The riddles evoked no response. "All may yet be very well" made Fence roll his eyes. "La Belle Dame sans Merci hath thee in thrall" produced, finally, a reaction from Randolph.

"What tongue is that? What mean those words?"

"French," said Ted, gloomily. "I don't know."

"Two unhandily returned is already two more—" said Randolph; Fence glanced at him and he stopped.

"It *sounds*," said Laura, "like it means 'the beautiful lady who never says thank you.' "

Fence actually smiled at this, but Randolph went on looking at the floor. Fence said, "Wherefore may we regard these words if we know them not?"

"It's Randolph who's supposed to regard them," said Ted. "You're supposed to regard Shan's. All may yet be very well."

"Anyone may quote Shan," said Fence, "and most have."

The devil, thought Laura, can cite Scripture for his purpose. But Shan wasn't Scripture—was he?

Ted must have been thinking something similar; he said, "I am made all things to all men, that I might by all means save some?"

Fence slid down from the table and strode across the room in a swirl of black. He stopped in front of Ted, and the smell of burning leaves engulfed Laura two feet away. If Ted grew a little more, thought Laura crazily, he would be able to look Fence right in the eye. Fence appeared merely intent, but his voice was furious. "Where read you that?" he said.

"*I* read it in the First Epistle of Paul to the Corinthians," said Ted. "But Edward's remembering it."

Laura did not know what Ted had hoped to achieve with this revelation. She herself was relieved; she thought of the dead Prince Edward as an ally. Fence said, "Dear heaven," in the tone of a man whose child has brought home a stray python.

"What's the matter?" said Randolph.

"Edward speaks to him," said Fence, without looking around.

"How?" said Randolph to Ted, not altogether as if he were prepared to believe him.

"In the back of my mind, somehow, or underneath."

"I suppose," said Fence wearily to Laura, "that the Princess Laura speaks to thee also?"

"Yes," said Laura.

"That's why I thought we might be able to get them back," said Ted. "We seem to be connected."

"Fence?" said Randolph; Laura concluded that, whatever Fence understood, Randolph did not.

"You have not read in that book either," said Fence, turning and staring at him. "But Edward hath."

"What book?" said Ted.

"This speaking of Edward in the backward of your thoughts," said Fence, "is a devising of Melanie, that she worked on Shan without his will. He wrote on it in his reports to the Blue Sorcerers, saying, 'I must be all things to all men, that I might by all means save some.'"

Laura doubted that that was what Saint Paul had been talking about, but this was no time to say so.

"What bearing hath this on the present issue?" Randolph said.

"A moment," said Fence, and to Ted, "A cardinal did deliver you to this man in red?"

"Then let his minions have the care of them," said Randolph.

"Randolph, for the love of heaven!" said Fence. "There's no blame on the children."

"Is there not?" said Randolph. He jerked a wad of paper out of the long jacket he wore and flung it down on Agatha's table. The top sheet was covered with Ruth's round, back-handed writing. She wrote that way because a teacher had once chided the left-handed Patrick for doing it.

"Didn't Ruth say we didn't know?" demanded Ted.

"Evil done unknowing yet hath evil effect," said Randolph.

"Randolph," said Fence, "that is ice so thin thy feet are wet e'en now. Let be."

"We thought we might be able to make it up to you," said Ted.

Scorn drew itself along Randolph's face like ink spilling on the white tiles of a bathroom floor, and Laura felt cold.

"Randolph," said Fence; and Randolph shut his mouth. "How?" said Fence to Ted.

"Have you told anybody about that?" asked Ted, pointing to Ruth's letter.

"No."

"All right. So we can prevent the civil war by pretending we're the real royal children. And maybe we can tell you enough about our game for you to figure out what Claudia's doing and why. And maybe we can get your royal children back for you."

"It was bravely done," said Fence, in the kindest voice he had used yet. "But we will do well enough. Do you go to your homes and regard us not."

"You have got to be kidding," said Ted. Laura recognized the signs of a monumental fury, and could not decide if she wanted to keep quiet or help him out. "How in the hell," said Ted, "do you expect us to regard you not? We've lived with you for three months; and we lived with you for years before that, really. You're part of our lives whether you like it or not. And I promise you," finished Ted, in a dire tone Laura had seldom heard out of him, "that we'll use whatever power we have to make your lives miserable if you don't let us stay and help."

"Oh, that's logic indeed," began Fence, in a tone of exasperated amusement; but he was overridden.

"That," said Randolph, not loudly at all, "is the outside of enough. Begone from here and do your worst, or stay and regard ours. There are dungeons in High Castle deep enough for the likes of you."

Laura thought that Ted should have known better than to threaten Randolph.

"All right," said Ted. "All right. May I remind you of something? You—both of you—swore me an oath."

Randolph's face was so terrible that Laura looked away from it. But Fence, after a moment of anger as monumental as Ted's, simply sat down on the floor in the midst of his black wizard's robes and laughed until he cried.

There was a petrifying pause. Laura looked only at Fence. His giving up of dignity hurt less than Ted's dirty tactics or Randolph's loss of control. He had never been very dignified anyway. When he stopped wheezing and pushed his hair out of his red face, Laura, greatly daring, edged around Ted, sat down beside Fence, and offered him her handkerchief.

"Shan's mercy," said Fence, taking it and blowing his nose vigorously. "Shan's mercy on the lot of us, it's better than we deserve. Thy lessons from Edward were well learned, my lad."

"Faugh!" said Randolph, still not loudly. "Had they been well learned, I were dead long since."

Fence looked up at him, all hilarity gone. "No," he said. "Those were your lessons. Not Edward's. And not mine."

They were going to start arguing again. Laura looked hopefully at Ted.

Ted took a very deep breath and pushed his fists into the pockets of his jeans. Laura knew he wanted to yell. But you didn't yell at Fence and Randolph. As King Edward, Ted might have come to it in the next few months; and they might have let him get away with it. But as Ted, he had to start all over; worse than that, because they didn't want him. All the kindness and trust he had had from them these three months had been for Edward, and the actions that they had approved of were not, now, marks in his favor but rather evidence of betrayal.

"You'd better go," said Fence again. "And of your courtesy, save your ill-wishing for more worthy foes."

"Now look," said Ted, not yelling. "I didn't come back here for my health. A sinister man came close to *making* us come back. He asked three riddles you haven't even considered, and he gave us one quotation from your world and one from ours. You're not thinking. All you want to do is get rid of us. I wouldn't want to look at us either, if I were you. But *we* didn't kill those kids. Claudia did it. And she did to us the exact same things that we did to you—but she *knew* it. We're as mad at her as you are."

Laura admired this logic. He should have tried it before the threats.

Fence quirked the corner of his mouth and looked at Randolph, who, without noticing, slapped his hand down on Agatha's table and started to speak. Fence, with his habitual gesture, put a hand on Randolph's wrist. Randolph turned on him with a ferocious expression. Fence took his hand away.

"I would cry you mercy," said Randolph to Fence, "were there mercy in the universe to nick the edge of my iniquity."

"Take less pleasure in thy mouthings," said Fence, in an astonishingly deadly voice, "and thou shalt have mercy enow."

There was a pause worse than the last one. Then Randolph said, "What, a villain that mouthes not?" and without waiting for an answer, turned to Ted. Laura saw that Fence looked more relieved than otherwise.

"Do we grant," said Randolph to Ted, in a cooler voice than he had used with Fence, "that until we have studied what to do, 'tis better for the country that nothing seem to be amiss, will you in turn agree that you are nowise trained for statecraft and that for you to take up your duties would be disaster?"

"Well," said Ted, "I don't know about disaster, but I don't really *want* all my duties. What do you propose to do?"

"Randolph is Regent," said Fence.

"I have told you, no," said Randolph.

"What about you, Fence?" said Laura. "Can't you help Ted?"

"In the end," said Fence, "what Edward orders, that must we accomplish. But if you will agree to take my guidance, Edward, and to gainsay my advice only under desperate conditions, I think we will deal very well."

"That's fine with me," said Ted, quickly.

"Excellent," said Fence. "Now. For all to seem as it was, it is needful that we retrieve your companions from their exile. They are gone by way of the green sword under the bottle trees, and may be recovered by that means?"

"Well, yes and no," said Ted. Laura was rather taken aback by the speed with which plans were being made, but Ted seemed to be following them well enough. "We can get to where they are that way. But then we'll have to persuade them to come back."

"It liked them well enough before," observed Randolph.

"It didn't like Patrick," said Ted. "He's like Andrew—he doesn't believe in magic. Being here just drove him crazy."

"Well, we will try what persuasion we may," said Fence. "And in any case 'twere folly to leave so potent a weapon lying about in the woods like an abandoned doll."

Laura thought this was unfair, given all the trouble they had taken to make sure Fence knew where the swords were.

"What means of persuasion do you suggest?" said Ted.

"I had thought to come with you," said Fence.

Laura let out a delighted chortle. Ted started at Fence for a moment. "Be warned," he said, "that Laura and I have never been to Australia. We won't know how to act, necessarily."

"How to act," said Fence, "will be to find those three privily and speak to them so. Where cometh out this path to Australia?"

"I think Patrick said the back forty."

Fence looked patient.

"It's on a farm," said Ted, who had only the faintest idea of what a back forty was himself.

"Well enough," said Fence. "I was born on a farm."

Ted and Laura both stared at him. He picked up Ruth's letter from the table where Randolph had thrown it, and held it out to them. It did not take them long to read it. Laura admired the style. They handed it back to Fence, and he stood up shaking out the folds of the absurd starry robe he wore. "What do we stay for?" he said.

They left Randolph sitting in the dim room among the glints of polished wood and glass and the muted colors of the tapestries. Laura preferred not to wonder what he was thinking.

At the head of the stairs Fence paused. "Garments," he said. He fingered the shoulder of Ted's shirt, and smiled very faintly. "You never had these from the West Tower," he said. "Men go garbed thus in your country?"

"Yes," said Ted, smiling back.

"Well," said Fence, "to the West Tower we must go, all the same, and find somewhat more suited to a farm."

The warm, cinnamon-scented air of the West Tower enclosed them comfortingly. Late sunlight blazed in through its nine windows, some gold as it ought to be, and some a violent pink reflection off the outer walls of High Castle. The room was piled and heaped and hung with clothes, most even less suited to a farm in Australia—or anywhere else—than Fence's robe.

Fence seemed to know his way about, and quickly found a plain muslin shirt. But they could not locate anything resembling trousers. Ted, appealed to, said firmly that a shirt and hose would be even odder than the starry robe.

Laura remembered suddenly that, if it were June in Illinois, it would be winter in Australia, and that even in the twentieth century some people wore cloaks in winter. Fence received this information dubiously, but said he'd as lief swelter in a cloak as rummage here any further. They found a black cloak for Fence, and a red one for Laura, who remembered Claudia and wished it were any other color, and a green one for Ted, and went down to the stables, where the grooms had looked at them oddly but consented to pack the garments into saddlebags and saddle two horses.

"Why not three?" said Fence.

"Laura can ride with me," said Ted, climbing onto Edward's horse. "Can you give her a boost?"

Fence did as he was asked, but looked at Laura once she was safely behind Ted. "Wherefore this unaccustomed shyness?"

"I *hate* horses," said Laura, with violence. She hated horses, and Princess Laura loved them, and it was an enormous relief to be able to tell the truth for once.

Fence's face closed up like a brand-new paperback. Maybe, she thought, they should just keep on playing their parts.

The day was cooling into evening as they rode away from High Castle. The distant eastern sky was piled with little round clouds, and above that was an improbable dark blue. It was too early for stars. Three crows flapped slowly over their heads, and some little bird whistled and piped in the grasses. The huge plain still gave off its scents of baked grass and dust. Laura felt very odd. Not four hours ago she and her brother and their cousins had ridden this way, resolved to give up the Secret Country. It seemed beyond the bounds of reason that now she and Ted were going to Australia with Fence. For the first time since she came to this country, the power and presence of magic, the difference it made in plans and actions, became clear to her.

When they came to the Well of the White Witch, the western sky was still spilling color, but it was dark enough for them to see the Well's glow. Like those unexpected and disconcerting walls of High Castle, it was a vivid pink granite. It lit the tall grass around it as if it were a bonfire.

"Fence!" called Ted. "We usually leave the horses here." He persuaded their own horse to stop. Laura wondered if the horses they escaped on had managed to get home yet.

Fence had turned his horse back to them and dismounted. He came over and held up his hands for Laura, who slid down and managed to land on her feet. Ted dismounted. "Oh, hell," he said. "Ruth always whispered sorcerous words at the horses."

"Well, my powers are other," said Fence, "but I have speech enow for that." He laid his hand on the neck of Ted's horse and said, "Thou, my steed, may graze thy fill, for I must dismount and walk." He went over to his own horse and repeated it.

Ted and Laura stared at each other in the glow of the well. Their mother had sung that song to them.

"What spell is that, Fence?" said Ted.

"One of Shan's," said Fence. He pulled the three cloaks out of the saddlebags and handed them around. He put his own on, so Ted and Laura followed suit. Fence said, "Now lead on."

They climbed the bank above the Well, and went lightly along the wooden bridge over the little stream, and slid and scrabbled along the stream's edge until the bottle tree bulged out of the darkness at them.

Fence put both hands on its smooth bark and whistled

under his breath. "I can well believe," he said, "that where this tree is native, all the seasons are upsodown."

Ted rummaged cautiously in the hollow made by the bottle tree's many trunks, and drew up Melanie's sword by its jeweled hilt. It was not glowing.

"I am tame," said Fence, as Ted hesitated. "Pronounce."

"We all need to hold onto the sword," said Ted, "and then somehow duck under this mess and come out the other side."

"We're none of us so large as we might be," said Fence, cheerfully. "Do you lead the way, and we'll set the Lady Laura between us." His voice faltered a little on Laura's title, and Laura thought that Fence had almost forgotten that they were not his own royal children.

They arranged themselves as he had said, wound their hands around the hilt of the sword, and ducked awkwardly under the bowed branches of the bottle tree. Then they were squelching over short grass that soaked Laura's tennis shoes, and blinking in a gray light, and shivering in a straight, hard wind that whipped her hair back so fast it hurt as if Ted had pulled it.

Compared to winter in Pennsylvania this was paltry. The grass was still bright green, almost the color of Melanie's sword when that weapon chose to display its light; and in this colorless world, the grass seemed to glow itself. The squelchy land rolled away before them, up and down and up again in a towering slope touched here and there with shapely pale trees. Their bark was peeling off in long strips, as though the wind were tearing them to pieces. A fence, also shaking in the wind, and rattling a little, ran down the middle of the slope and then bent sharply away from them.

"It isn't just winter," said Ted, tipping his head up at the gray sky and shaking the hair off his face. "It's *morning*."

"That's tidy," said Fence, a little absently. "How late do your cousins arise?"

"I don't know, in the winter," said Ted, and then, catching Laura's appalled glance, "Oh, hell."

"*School,*" said Laura. "What day is it?"

"By my reckoning," said Fence, gently, "it is the fifth day of September in the four hundred and ninetieth year since King John threw o'er the Dragon King."

A red bird flew out of the bottle tree, circled the three of them, whistling, and took off over the hill. Well, thought Laura, that's that.

"That'll fetch them," said Ted, somewhat too smugly.

Fence caught hold of Ted's cloak. "What knowest thou?"

"We keep being rescued by cardinals."

Fence let his breath out and shook the fold of the cloak a little. "What art thou?" he said.

"Ask Claudia," said Ted.

A maniacal barking made itself apparent, the persistent yap of a collie. A black-and-white streak, flapping behind it a long yellow leash, shot down the hill and halted three feet away from them, growling like a cageful of tigers. Laura stared. Shan was a lazy dog who wouldn't even run races with you.

Fence stood quite still, keeping hold of Ted's cloak. "Is this thy rescue?" he said.

"It's just Shan," said Ted. "Good dog, Shan, good boy." The dog, a nondescript, sharp-nosed, shaggy creature who had looked much more like a collie when he was a puppy, wagged his tail and went on growling. Laura supposed he remembered her and Ted, but didn't care for Fence.

Fence said, "Thy dog's called Shan?"

"It's Ruth and Ellen and Patrick's dog."

"They weren't allowed to call him Prospero," offered Laura.

Fence turned and stared at her; Shan growled louder and Fence took no notice. "*Prospero?*" said Fence.

"Prospero," said Laura, bravely, "is a magician in a play."

"Thy play? Thou hast made him up also?"

"No, William Shakespeare did."

"Shan!" yelled a distant and familiar voice.

"Here they come," said Ted.

Three figures came over the hill, two short and one tall. Ruth was not wearing a skirt, as had been her wearisome custom when they played together, but she was, to Laura's eyes, very oddly dressed in gray corduroy pants, pink leg-warmers already splotched with mud, pink-and-gray running shoes, and many layers of shirts of pink or gray or white whose tails hung out at varying lengths and made her look as if she were wearing a jester's costume. Laura thought she ought to tie bells to all the hems.

Patrick and Ellen, on her heels, were dressed reassuringly in brand-new jeans—Aunt Kim must have noticed that the old ones were too small—battered red corduroy jackets, and dirty tennis shoes. Ellen had found, somewhere, a black wool beret like the velvet caps the pages wore in High Castle. Patrick had a blue stocking-cap falling out of his jacket pocket. Ellen's and Ruth's cloudy black hair tangled in all directions in the wind. Patrick's pale brown, straight hair was only a little ruffled. All three of them wore bulging knapsacks.

Ellen caught Laura's glance immediately, with a look half of greeting and half of alert bewilderment. Patrick was so expressionless Laura knew he was upset. Ruth looked the way she used to if you burst into her room without knocking when she was writing her journal.

"What are you *doing* here?" demanded Ruth, stopping next to the dog. Her harried glance brushed Fence, faltered, and settled firmly on Ted.

Patrick got down on his knees in the wet grass and laid an arm across the dog's back. Shan stopped growling. Ellen grinned at Fence, but Patrick did not look at any of them. Laura supposed that seeing Fence in his own back yard was upsetting all Patrick's theories.

"That's a fine greeting," said Ted to Ruth.

"We're going to miss the school bus."

"Ruth," said Ellen. "They brought *Fence.* Forget about the school bus."

"You have to come back," said Ted.

"No way in hell," said Patrick, still without looking up.

"There's a fine, open spirit," said Fence. All three of them jumped at the sound of his voice.

"Fence, is it really you?" said Ellen, peering at him from under her hat.

"Turn that question on thyself," said Fence, rather sharply.

"Oh, *hell,*" said Ruth. "You read my letter."

"Wherefore writ, if not to be read?"

"Well, but I didn't think I'd see you again."

"It sounded fine," said Ted.

"It sounded *stupid,*" said Ruth. "I was in a terrible hurry."

"It was well enough," said Fence.

"Fence," said Ruth, "I'm sorry."

"Thou hast said so already, in the letter," said Fence, and smiled. "Be of good cheer. The fault's not yours. But in good earnest we desire you back, to play your parts yet for a little while."

"Ellen has now missed her bus," said Patrick, "and Ruth and I will miss ours in ten minutes."

"You'd better tell us," said Ellen.

It was beginning to rain, but nobody suggested finding shelter. They stood there with misty drops gathering on them while Fence told Ted and Laura's story.

"Good," said Ellen, when he had finished. "Let's do it. I knew it was wrong to leave."

"Good?" said Ruth. "Claudia can look at a piece of glass and make Randolph do what she likes, Claudia did make us do what she liked, and you say good?"

"So let's get her," said Ellen.

"You won't make Ted fight Randolph?" said Ruth to Fence.

"Stars in heaven, lady, why should I meddle so?"

"*Randolph*'ll make Ted fight Randolph," said Patrick.

"I'll strive to prevent him," said Fence.

"Well, I'm willing to risk it," said Ted. "Do remember, can't you, that the red man said everything we were afraid of would happen if we *didn't* go back?"

"It can't all happen," said Patrick. "You can't kill Randolph if you aren't there."

"Ruth's letter told Randolph how to get here," said Ted.

Ellen stood up. "Well, let's go," she said.

"I'm in the middle of an experiment," said Patrick.

"Does he *have* to come?" said Ruth to Ted. "If he was missing, wouldn't that be an excuse to go after Claudia?"

"We have been after Claudia," said Fence, poking one arm out of his cloak and wiping rain off his forehead. Laura stared at the shift and glimmer of his starry sleeve, waiting for one of the points of light to swell into vision. Nothing happened. Fence went on talking, in a tone of wry patience. "We have accusations. Mind you that she tried to stab me on the stairs."

"Besides," said Laura, "won't your parents miss you and Ellen?"

"Sure they will," said Ruth, grinning maliciously. "Pat can explain to them."

"You better watch it," said Patrick. "Our parents aren't suspicious, but Ted and Laura's are."

"That's true," said Ruth, sobering at once. "Mom just thought we'd grown and she hadn't noticed until now; she's been awfully busy trying to run this blasted farm. And we'd have to dye our hair green and put safety pins through all our finger-joints before Daddy would notice. But your mother called me Mary Rose, and your *father* called Patrick Thomas the Rhymer."

Laura thought that Patrick was about as unlike Thomas the Rhymer as anybody could get, and just managed to turn her laugh into a snort.

"It isn't funny," said Ruth, undeceived. "*They've* read all the right books. They think we've been in Elfland, and that's really not so far off the mark."

"It is," said Patrick, in his most annoying voice, "about as far off the mark as you can get. Time stands still in Elfland and goes along as usual here. By that definition, *this* is Elfland."

"Well, it is for Fence," said Laura.

"Don't think about it," said Ruth, a little wildly, not to Fence but to the rest of them. "I just meant Patrick's right. They're suspicious."

"They were joking," said Ted. "They do it all the time."

"Not just joking," said Ruth. "Believe me."

"Well, okay, so it's all or nothing," said Patrick. "So persuade me to come back."

"Patrick," said Ellen, "you can't get anything done while we're gone anyway, because we'll have to fix the time again."

"I *told* you," said Patrick, "we didn't fix it last time."

"No, that's right," said Ted. "Laura and I left home at night, and when we got back home it was afternoon."

Patrick said, "We left here in the daytime, and when we got back it was night. We'd lost twelve or thirteen hours."

"Well, that's not so bad," said Ellen.

"You've got a remarkably selective memory," said Patrick. "Shall I recite for you what Dad said? And what Mom did?"

"It doesn't matter," said Ted. "The red man fixed the time for us, and I bet that holds for the whole planet."

"That's really persuasive, Ted," said Patrick.

"What's the *matter* with you?" said Laura. She had to say something violent to squash her impulse to run over that hill, or in whatever direction was necessary, and find her parents, and forget about adventure and philosophy and riddles. She went on, loudly, "So what if we get in trouble? Isn't it worth it to save the Secret Country? Why don't you worry about the rest of this when we've done the important stuff?"

Ted looked at her; he knew what was wrong. "Well?" he said to Patrick. "What *is* the matter with us?"

"*You* are soft in the head," said Patrick. "*I* am practical. Why should I want to save the Secret Country?"

Fence stared down at Patrick, who still knelt with his arm around the dog. "Consider it," said Fence, in a light and very terrible voice, "the price of thy fencing lessons and thy room and board these three months."

"I'm not at all convinced," said Patrick, perfectly coolly, "that you roomed and boarded anything except my imagination."

Laura felt a shiver go over her skin. When all this was only a game, Patrick had played Fence, and he had used just such a tone and just such a level look from cold blue eyes as he was turning on Fence now. Fence had an altogether less alarming face, but his demeanor made up for it.

"The lunatic, the lover, and the wizard," said Fence, "are of imagination all compact. What art thou, then, that setteth the housing of thine so low?"

"Jesus Christ!" said Patrick, passionately. Nobody reproved him for swearing. "Don't quote Shakespeare at me! All right. All right. I'll come back. But I promise you, I am *not leaving again* no matter who doesn't want what to happen until I *have figured out what the hell is going on.* Is that clear?"

"Abundantly," said Ruth, in her dryest tones.

"And *also,*" said Patrick, "I want to test whether time stands still here while we're in the Secret Country."

"Okay," said Ellen. "You just take off your nice watch and leave it out in the rain, and we'll come back tomorrow and see what time it says."

"It's good to two hundred meters," said Patrick, calmly. He unbuckled the strap and laid the watch down in the vivid grass, where it said, in evil red characters, 8:45.

"Is it a bargain, then?" said Patrick, looking up at Fence.

"Oh, of a certainty," said Fence, still in that voice. "For I most earnestly desire these discoveries also."

"All right," said Ted, whom this exchange seemed to have made extremely uneasy. "Send Shan home, Patrick, and let's go." Laura remembered other bargains and their outcomes, and didn't blame him. He caught her glance, and shrugged resignedly, as their mother would do when their father got silly. Then he said to Fence, "Let's get out of here."

CHAPTER 5

IT was dark when they got back to High Castle. They had missed supper. Fence spoke to the yellow-haired boy who was stationed in the stables for just such emergencies, and then hustled them up the two hundred and eight steps to his rooms in the South Tower. Their way was lit by purple torches that made everybody look a little sick.

Fence had added what Patrick would have called security precautions since Ted was last here on Midsummer Eve. Then Fence had used one plain key. This time he had one plain and two jeweled. He was slow with them, as if he were not yet used to the arrangement.

Ted stood pressed against the cool stone wall with Laura and the others crowding the steps behind him, and considered the door itself. Its dark wood was carved with one of the puzzles of High Castle: eight scenes starting at twelve o'clock and proceeding clockwise to an enigmatic conclusion. They showed a young man with decided eyebrows talking to a wizard. Then, wearing a wizard's robe himself, he captured or cajoled a cat, a dog, a horse, an eagle, and a unicorn. In the last scene, the unicorn was gone but all the other animals and the man stood looking at an object like a stylized sun. This story was repeated all over High Castle in carving and tapestry and even around the border of Fence's dishes. But sometimes it had this ending, with the sun, and other times ended with an irregular patch like a flaw in the piece in question, from which all the animals were running away.

Ted remembered that he was not playing Edward, who had known this story all his life. "Fence?" he said. "Who is that in the carving?"

Fence pulled the last key out of the door and pushed it open. A rush of warm air laden with the smell of old ashes and snuffed candles slid past them.

"That," said Fence, leading them into his parlor, "is Shan, as you must well—" He broke off, and made a sign in the air with his hand. Light, good wholesome yellow light, bloomed from three lamps on the walls, and flames crept up under the logs in the fireplace. The fire caught better than it should have; there was no kindling.

"Sorry," said Ted to Fence.

"I know it," said Fence. "There's no help."

"He looks like Shan, but our story about him is different."

The others surged into the room behind them, unwontedly quiet. Fence stood in the middle of his parlor, on the bearskin, and looked at Ted with a pained expression that verged on the desperate. "Is there no end to this?" he said.

He ushered them to seats around the table, in the plain dark chairs with their blue cushions, Ruth and Ellen and Patrick on one side and Ted and Laura on the other. He sat down himself at one end of the table, with his back to the fire and his face to the door. Then he looked them over one by one, with the expression of somebody who is searching in the lost-and-found, among a dozen red mittens, for his own with the frayed right-hand thumb and the chocolate stain on the left cuff. Nobody would look at him except Ted.

"So," said Fence. "You're very like them. But the copyist hath erred, here and there."

"Who *is* the copyist?" said Patrick.

"Claudia," said Laura.

"Not Claudia alone," said Fence. "She hath too few years, for so much knowledge. That she doth is forbidden, or not yet arrived at in the careful labors of the true wizards. Hath trod a hard path and a long, that would take the road less traveled by."

"And that," said Ellen, as if she couldn't help it, "has made all the difference."

"Stop showing off," said Ruth, sharply.

Fence looked at her quickly. "Showing off what?"

"You sound to us," said Ted, "as if you're quoting poetry half the time. Not just you—not just thou, but all of you."

"This thy William Shakespeare was a poet, then, and I did presently recite from him?"

"Yes; but you just recited from Robert Frost," said Ruth.

"I do not know," said Fence, with considerable emphasis, "to read this riddle."

"Well," said Ted, "that's the least of our worries."

"Save that, 'til it be solved, we bear the millstone of Prince Patrick," said Fence, quirking the corner of his mouth in the way he had.

"Not prince," said Patrick.

"Amend me not," said Fence. "Thou art the prince to all save me and Randolph, and mayhap some few others 'twere good to tell't."

"What all," said Ted, "do we have to do?"

"Two matters strictly of the Hidden Land," said Fence, looking to his right at Patrick, who looked blandly back at him but turned rather red, "we must not neglect, for they are pressing: the embassy to the Dragon King; and the messengers to Chryse and Belaparthalion, trying whether, in change for these swords of yours, they will put some rein on the plunging ambition of that prince."

"Can you do them without us?" said Ted, leaning forward a little to see beyond Laura's head, which she had propped on both hands. Nobody seemed likely to care that she had her elbows on the table. "Because what we need to do is to track down Claudia and find out how she found us and brought us here and what the connection between our country and yours really is."

"We also," said Laura, "need to find out who the red man is."

"And we need to get your kids back from the dead," said Ellen, "so we can go home again."

Fence bit his lip, and then seemed to give up, and grinned. "All our ways may lie together. To discover the red man, 'twere best to read in the library in Fence's Country. And that lies between here and the haunts of Chryse and Belaparthalion. To consult with the dead while being still alive, some must travel to the Gray Lake. And that lies between here and the realm of the Dragon King."

"That's easy," said Ellen.

"Too easy," said Patrick.

"How so?" said Fence. "Power and knowledge are two, but as twin compasses are two; one makes no show to move, but doth, if th' other do."

This baffling utterance, with which Fence seemed rather pleased, was accorded a blank silence. Ted realized that he, not Fence, had asked the last pertinent question. He looked at Fence, who appeared expectant.

"I would like," said Ted, "to get it into everybody's head that it's essential to go on pretending we're the royal children. Is it true, Fence, that they say, 'Walk not in the Hidden Land, it will take all you have and laugh you to scorn for having nothing?'"

"Travel not," said Ruth.

"Oh, aye," said Fence. "They say so. Fence's Country and the Outer Isles do have a better welcome for strangers; but 'tis not as strangers that you'll be chastised, if matters run amiss, but as usurpers."

"Usurpers do away with the rightful claimant," said Patrick.

"By some accounts, you have done so. If you have power

o'er matters in this land, is not Claudia but another of those matters?"

"But she wasn't in our game at all," said Ted.

"Fence," said Laura. "The night of the Banquet of Midsummer Eve, I asked you, who is that snake lady. And you said you thought I knew her. I didn't." Fence regarded her steadily, and she added, "We didn't like her, either."

"Child," said Fence, "fret not on me. But there are others will say, on the heels of such dissembling as the five of you have performed this summer, what is that, or any tale of thy ignorance, save another instance of't?"

Laura put her head down and stuck the end of one braid into her mouth. Fence turned his innocent gaze upon Ruth, who was scowling, and said, "My lady, thou in especial art endangered."

"Don't I know it!" said Ruth.

"Canst thou then think of putting off thy duties for a while?"

"Well, *I* don't mind," said Ruth. "My duties would make it hard for me to go anywhere. But is it fair to Lady Ruth?"

"If Lady Ruth should walk again where fair or unfair concerns her, I'll see to her reinstatement," said Fence.

Ruth made a face. "Now I just have to manage Meredith."

"I'll speak to her," said Fence.

"Thank you."

"Do we want to get cut off from the Green Caves like that?" said Patrick. "If the cardinals are minions of the Green Caves, and the Green Caves people are stingy about sharing their knowledge—" He looked at Fence, who nodded. "Well, then, unless Ruth is one of them, we may not have much chance of solving that part of the mystery."

Ruth said, "I don't have to resign *immediately.*"

"We'll do't when the time is right," said Fence.

There was another silence, broken by the sound of footsteps and breathing and a thump on the door as of somebody kicking it. Fence got up and unlocked it, and let in Randolph and the yellow-haired page, both carrying trays and panting. They set the trays at the end of the table. The boy started to fill mugs from a large jug, and Randolph said, "I thank thee, I'll do the rest." The page gave him a startled look and left.

Randolph poured for all of them, with extreme care. It occurred to Ted that he wanted to defer the moment of greeting. Ted looked at Ruth, who was staring at the table; at Ellen, who was trying to catch Randolph's eye because she was genuinely glad to see him; at Patrick, who was gazing fixedly at Randolph as Shan had stared at Fence. Ted didn't blame Randolph for stalling.

Randolph finally sat down at the other end of the table, with Laura on his right and Ruth on his left, his back to the door. He raised his mug. "To deception," he said, "and to its confounding." He drank without offering to click mugs with anybody. The rest of them drank too. It was the Secret Country's version of lemonade, too full of cinnamon and nutmeg for Ted's taste.

Fence put his mug down and said, looking hard at Randolph, "In your true guises, you are all welcome to High Castle."

Randolph sat without responding. His hair and the dark blue of his clothes swallowed the lamplight; only his eyes, greener than Fence's, the green of Ruth's or Ellen's, gleamed a little, and the golden contents of his goblet as he turned it between his palms. Ted suddenly realized that Randolph was wearing no jewelry. It had all been connected with his study of magic, and he was no longer Fence's apprentice. Randolph finally said, in a much quieter voice than Ted was used to from him, "What others must we doom to this conspiracy?"

Down the length of the gleaming table, over the plates of meat pies and cheese pies and spinach pies, over the bowls of grapes and peaches and the little hard yellow apples of the Hidden Land, Fence's eyes met Randolph's and held them. "Benjamin," he said.

And Randolph flinched. His voice was perfectly even. "Have we not broke sorrow enow to him to last a lifetime, without this burden also?"

"Consider his lifetime," said Fence. "I'll tell him; don't trouble yourself. Who besides?"

"If there's a learned pane in this window we piece together," said Randolph, " 'twere best have Matthew."

"That is to have Celia also," said Fence.

Randolph nodded.

"What about Agatha?" said Laura.

"They were very dear to her," said Fence.

"She doesn't act like it!" said Ellen, in astonished tones.

Fence looked at her briefly, but did not answer. Randolph, Ted realized, was acting as if he were having a private conference with Fence, and did not want to acknowledge the remarks of the five of them. Ted couldn't blame him, but that did not make this treatment easier to take.

"Agatha's so hard to fool, you see," said Laura.

"You need deceive her a bare sennight," said Fence. "We must away."

"Well, okay, then," said Laura.

Ted removed his startled gaze from his sister; nobody had asked her opinion, and it was usually hard enough to get it out of her when she was asked. He addressed Fence, who was still looking at Randolph, and rather as a nearsighted person will look at the chart in the eye doctor's office. "Can we manage with so few?" said Ted.

"I do believe it," said Fence, without moving. "If Randolph can sift the riddles of the Gray Lake, Matthew and I shall do what we may with the Library of Heathwill."

"Who do we go with?" asked Ellen.

"I fear me you must be separate," said Fence.

There was a chilly silence.

"Well, who gets to decide?" said Ellen.

Fence said to Randolph, "Which wilt thou have?"

Ted was reminded of choosing sides for gym class, and hoped absurdly that Laura would not be the last one picked.

For the first time since he had entered the room, Randolph looked at the five of them, one by one. His face was judicious. Patrick scowled at him, and he did not react. Ellen grinned, and he raised an eyebrow at her. Ruth lifted her chin and returned a good imitation of the judicious expression. Ted, when his turn came, tried to look reliable. Randolph's gaze lingered on him.

"Are you right-handed?" said Randolph.

"Yes, my lord." Ted remembered with uncomfortable vividness their first fencing lesson. Randolph, however, who must have had it in mind also, looked vaguely satisfied, though there was no warmth behind it.

"For an embassy to the Dragon King," said Randolph, "'twere best have our own King."

Ted did not think this a good plan to ensure that he didn't kill Randolph, but Randolph was right; if they were going to continue this masquerade, the King belonged with the embassy wherein courtesy and preserving the forms mattered most. He doubted that Belaparthalion or Chryse would be half so impressed by the King of the Hidden Land as they would be by Fence.

"True enough," said Fence. He turned his head to Laura. "I think I must have thee," he said. "In the sorcerous library, we may find news of thy talent. Randolph?"

"Lady Ruth," said Randolph, in rather an odd voice, "you have spoken once with the Judge of the Dead; will you so again?"

"An it please you, my lord," said Ruth, in an equally odd voice, "I will."

They had spoken with the Judge of the Dead in order to return Ted himself to life. Ted wondered what had happened then that remembering it now should make them sound so strange. The memory made him feel odd too, but he was the one who had died.

"Well, what about the rest of us?" said Ellen.

"A moment," said Fence. "When entered you this country?"

"We came in the first week of June," said Patrick, "but we didn't do anything except wander around the Well of the White Witch until Ted and Laura showed up, on the fourteenth. Benjamin came looking for the real kids, and found us."

"So she did it then," said Randolph, "and all our dealings thereafter were with you five."

They all nodded.

"What," said Ellen, "about the rest of us?"

"I'll take you," said Fence, smiling. He was probably relieved to be able to change the subject. "Fence's Country will like you greatly."

"Is that where you're from, Fence?" said Laura.

Fence went on smiling, but Randolph's face grew utterly blank, and then he pushed the still-full goblet away from him until it clinked against the nearest platter. Fence said placidly to Laura, "Nay, I am but named for him that gave's name to the country. I come from the Outer Isles."

Randolph stood up. "I cry you mercy," he said to Fence. "I have yet some business that awaiteth me."

"This won't serve," said Fence, with no particular emphasis.

Randolph leaned the heels of his hands on the table and said, "I do beg you, then, hold to the affair we are bent on and start not aside for these trivialities."

"Any knowledge," said Fence, "is armor 'gainst their discovery."

Randolph sat down again. It turned out that more planning must wait until Benjamin, Matthew, and Celia had been informed of what was going on; and until Andrew had been told that the King would be joining his party. Ted thought that this might cause trouble, but he meant to let Fence worry about it. For all the discussion they got done, Fence might as well have let Randolph leave; unless he had meant not to continue the discussion, but to make Randolph eat with the five imposters.

Which was probably in theory the right thing to do; but nobody had much of an appetite.

Chapter 6

Laura lay in the breezy darkness of the room she shared with Ellen, under linen sheets and silk quilts and, square on her chest, the hot, solid weight of the black cat, which had decided suddenly after months of ignoring them that Ellen and Laura were the only people it could stand to look at.

She was not exactly asleep, or exactly awake. A blue wash of moonlight swept in the unglazed window, struck the silver pitcher that sat on their dressing table, and fell muted into her face. She wished Ellen snored. She wished for a thunderstorm. She was afraid of what she would see if she dozed, and terrified of what she would dream if she slept. She was not the Princess Laura and she had never even laid eyes on the Princess Laura's mother; but Fence had told her that the visions she saw and the oddities she dreamed of were a legacy of that mother's family. She did not mind playing Princess Laura, but she minded this.

Ellen did not snore, and the night was clear. The moonlight fixed her with its glittering eye, and she saw what she was meant to. The evergreen trees of the forest were enormous; their branches began yards above her head. Between their widely separated trunks were only piles and heaps of discarded brown needles, and fallen branches, and an occasional seedling, growing hopefully upward. The air was very cold and smelled damply of pine and cedar. There was also a fainter smell that Laura associated with Christmas. Blue spruce. Laura was confused by this sudden collision of her memories and Princess Laura's. It was she who remembered Christmas, but Princess Laura who knew that that smell meant blue spruce.

"Deck the halls with boughs of holly!" shouted Laura, afraid that Princess Laura would move her to say something peculiar.

Her voice was frail and faint in this vastness of air and branch. Very high up, a sharp wind drove long clouds across a thin blue sky. She could hear crows quarreling.

Laura was cold and puzzled, and beginning to be bored. She listened to the inside of her mind, but nothing unusual was there. Princess Laura wasn't going to be any help. Laura hunched her shoulders against an eddy of wind, and realized she was wearing a pack. She shrugged it off and knelt gingerly in the needles to open it. It was made of green nylon, and the tag said "Caribou." Inside it were a squashed apple, a little ivory unicorn with green eyes, a pocket-sized copy of *Peter Rabbit*, with the original illustrations, and a silver flute that made her tentative hand shiver as if it were falling asleep. She had felt it before. This was the flute of Cedric.

Laura stared at this collection for some time. The unicorn was hers, a present from Fence. The food might have been anybody's. She opened the little book, and encountered Ellen's determined black script on the flyleaf. "EX LIBRIS ELLEN JENNIFER CARROLL. THIS MEANS YOU."

The flute was Laura's too. Somebody who had seemed to know what he was doing had given it to her, when Princess Laura was already dead. Fence said there was a saying that Cedric's flute would save them at the end. Ruth, who had had flute lessons for eight years, couldn't get a single decent note out of this flute. Laura, who couldn't even play the piano, let alone coordinate her breath and her fingers at the same time, could play this flute to perfection.

She supposed she might as well play it now. It was very cold to the touch. She put it to her lips and blew a few experimental breaths. She played "The Minstrel Boy," which had once summoned her a unicorn. This time it summoned nothing. She played "Sir Patrick Spens," which had pricked Randolph's conscience. Only her cold fingers tingled where she held the flute. She played "Matty Groves," which she did not like. Whatever she hoped to wake up did not care for it either.

"You could at least let all the wild animals come and listen and be tamed," said Laura, removing the flute from her mouth and addressing it severely. She gave up on Secret Country songs and, defiantly, played "James James Morrison Morrison."

She was playing the last line when the tree nearest her burst violently into flame. A rush of hot air drove her backward. Laura considered running, but saw that neither nearby trees nor the needles at the foot of the burning one had caught. The flame was very clear and yellow. Laura looked at it hopefully; but the tears ran down her face from the heat and the brightness. She blinked them away, and when she opened her eyes again she was staring into a shaft of moonlight, and the cat had jumped down from the bed.

Ted and Patrick got up in the morning and found a note from Fence stuck to the inside of their heavy wooden door by no agency that they could discover. It peeled off neatly. It was folded in three and sealed with a blob of blue wax on which there was no imprint of a seal. Fence's handwriting was round and earnest, like his face.

His sentences were more brisk and businesslike, and required Ted and Patrick to meet him after breakfast in the Council Room. This gave Ted an uncomfortable sensation in the stomach; but Fence had added a line at the bottom of the page to say that he would already have apprised Benjamin, Matthew, and Celia of Ted and Patrick's true nature. Ted felt better, until Patrick said, "What do you suppose he thinks our true nature is?"

"Thanks a lot," said Ted. Patrick just stood there on the stone floor in his white nightshirt, with his pale brown hair sticking up, and grinned at him.

"What are you so pleased about?" said Ted.

"I'm just looking forward," said Patrick, serenely, "to being myself once in a while."

"We agreed that we need to keep up the masquerade."

"But not with anybody who knows."

"Pat, come on, we're only here on sufferance."

"That's right," said Patrick. "Mine."

Ted said, in as close an imitation as he could come to Benjamin's abrupt tones, "Pride goeth before a fall."

Patrick regarded him with the intent, blue, merciless stare he had used when he played Fence. Ted had never thought to ask him what he thought of the harmless-looking, untidy, abstracted reality that was High Castle's resident wizard. He did not ask him now. "Let's get dressed."

"I hoped," said Patrick, crossing the huge room to the six oak chests lined up against the wall, "that I'd never have to wear those damn stockings again."

"Don't we have any robes, like Fence and Benjamin wear?"

"I don't want one like Fence's," said Patrick, rummaging. "I don't want one at all. They're probably as hot as the hose."

"Well, it's fall now. The hose won't be so hot."

Patrick looked over his shoulder, his hands full of embroidered silk, his face holding its most distant calculating expression. "It's fall," he said, "and it's a hell of a lot warmer in here in the morning than it was all summer."

"Maybe we burned Claudia up with her house," said Ted, savagely.

"I hope not," said Patrick. "What if the only way to find out what's going on is to ask her?"

"No problem," said Ted, still savagely. "You just go to the land of the dead."

Patrick hauled the nightshirt over his head, flung it into the middle of their bearskin rug, and disappeared into the violet folds of the silk shirt, still with the calculating expression. He had lost track of what he was holding; he would never have put that shirt on if he had looked at it first. Ted put on one of the linen shirts Patrick had strewn on the floor.

"And ask her?" said Patrick.

"The ghosts don't remember, unless you nudge them."

"The sight of you ought to nudge her all right," said Patrick, crossing the room and picking his jeans up out of the rocking chair. There was something strange in his tone. After a moment Ted recognized it as admiration. Admiration from Patrick was rare, and, just now, unnerving.

"When's the council?" said Patrick.

"Eleven. We should go now."

"Oh, Lord," said Patrick, standing up abruptly. "I have to go check my watch."

Well, thought Ted, Patrick would have to get the sword from Fence, who would say something to keep him in line. Ted waved him cheerily on his way and ran down to the Council Room. Randolph was there already, with the three girls. Ruth was wearing the sort of white flowing dress she had always worn in this country. Ellen and Laura had apparently, like Patrick, suffered a rebellion against the garments of the Hidden Land; they had put on their boys' clothes from the battle.

Randolph was wearing blue as usual, although he was no longer of the school of Blue Sorcery. In the late morning light he looked, if not all right, at least better than he had. The table in front of him was piled with books and scrolls and maps. Most of them were dusty. Ted was nerving himself to ask what they were for when Celia and Matthew came in, also piled with books and scrolls. Matthew, a long, thin young man with red hair and a sardonic eye, looked at the children with an expression of uneasy reproach and said nothing. Celia moved briskly past him, dumped her burden on the table, and smiled. She was taller than Matthew; she had sleek yellow hair braided down her back, and pale eyes that might have been blue or green or gray, and a long, puckered scar on her forehead.

"Give you good morrow," she said. "I am Celia, called Lady for my service to the last Queen; but in this company we dispense with sugary courtesy. Matthew is my husband, and the three yellow bees you've marked buzzing hither and yon making an upset are my children."

There was a muddled silence. Ted collected himself and said, "Thank you. You know our names and we don't have any sugary titles. Laura is my sister. Ruth and Ellen are my cousins. The Patrick with the superior smirk who isn't here is their brother."

Celia said, "You are welcome to High Castle."

"I doubt it," said Ruth. "But it's kind of you to say so."

Matthew grinned; Randolph actually looked at Ruth as if he were seeing her; Celia made a disapproving frown and then smiled too. "So," she said. "Let plain speaking be the order of the day."

There was another silence, less uncomfortable, broken by the arrival of Fence, who sat down in the chair to the left of the one that had been King William's. Celia and Matthew sat down too, and Ted gathered his courage and sat in the King's chair.

"Where's Benjamin?" said Ellen. Ted knew that she was, as always, enjoying herself. He and Ruth and Laura, because they were not, would never have asked Fence that question.

"Recovering himself," said Fence, sitting down and exchanging some look with Matthew.

"Is he terribly grieved?" said Ellen. She didn't sound eager, but like somebody dispassionately in search of information.

"He is so," said Fence. "More to thy purpose, he is wroth. A saith, if a should lay eyes on one of you before the day is out, a will break that one between his two hands."

Ellen sat back abruptly. "We didn't *do* anything."

"You cozened and deceived him, and all of us; if there was a necessity in't, yet thou shouldst give Benjamin some little time to see it clearly."

"Can we *have* a council without Benjamin?" said Ted.

"Well enough," said Fence. "He hath told me his desires; and given leave for all of you to accompany what embassies we have chosen for you."

"Well, good." Ted decided that this time he would outwait Fence. Fence had called this council.

Fence said, "I have spoken also to Andrew. I'd thought to have some small difficulty in the persuasion, but he seemed well pleased to have thee, my prince, and Randolph also, in his train. So have a care."

He looked at Ted until Ted nodded, and then looked at Randolph until Randolph put his head back and said to the ceiling, "Fear me not."

Ted remembered, suddenly and unpleasantly, that there was another secret here they had not spoken of. Only the five children, Randolph, and Fence knew that Randolph had killed the King. Andrew suspected it, but had seemed unwilling to enter any accusation because of some plot of his, or of his sister Claudia, that he did not want to call attention to. Matthew and the other members of the King's Council had all the information they needed to discover Randolph's crime, but they had not discovered it yet.

"How," said Ruth, rather diffidently, "did Andrew like the notion of having me along?"

"That pleased him also," said Fence, "that thou, and Randolph and Ted, that he thinks are both besotted on thee, should be made to travel all together and endure one another's company."

"Do we have to keep up *that* masquerade?" demanded Ruth.

"In small things only," said Fence. "A hasty withdrawing on thy part, or a gaingiving in thy look, those will serve."

"I can hardly wait," said Ruth, gloomily.

Ted could not look at Randolph, who had been betrothed to a girl he now knew was dead; and who had, when the present Ruth appeared, been treating Lady Ruth with distant courtesy and dancing every dance at the Banquet of Midsummer Eve with Claudia. Then Claudia tried to kill Fence, and Randolph avoided both her and Ruth. On the journey back from the battle, Randolph began, cautiously, treating Ruth as an affianced bride who had reason to be angry with him. Ted thought that Randolph hoped that Lady Ruth, who unlike their own Ruth had great pride and a hasty temper, would refuse to take him back after his dallying with Claudia. Randolph had told Ted that he did not, as a regicide shortly to be so proclaimed before the court, wish to encourage anybody to marry him. Ruth had been driven almost to distraction by this state of affairs. At least now both of them would be playing a part.

"Andrew," said Fence, having considered Ruth and apparently decided not to comment on her remark, "doth require that those accompanying him be prepared to depart four days hence."

"Oh, good," said Ruth. "There's an enormous Green Caves ceremony six days hence."

Fence frowned. "'Twere better not delay our speech to Meredith," he said. "She'll need one can take thy place."

"Give me today to poke around," said Ruth, "and then you can tell her I'm resigning. I'm still in disgrace, you know, so the place she'll have to fill won't be very exalted."

Fence nodded. "Well," he said. "Matthew and I will also make ready to depart four days hence. We must devise some means of exchanging news." His glance brushed Randolph and moved to Ruth. "What training hast thou?" he said to her. "Canst read a message in the grasses, or the stones along thy way?"

"Of a certainty I cannot," said Ruth; she did not sound sorry.

"No matter," said Fence. "We will send by music. Laura, wilt thou bring thy flute?"

"Yes," said Laura, staring a little but seeming more pleased than otherwise.

"Dost thou play also?" said Fence to Ruth.

"Pretty well," said Ruth. "On an ordinary flute."

"Excellent," said Fence. "Celia, who goes north with us, will aid Laura, and before we depart also will instruct thee."

"On the subject of instruction," said Celia, "we have brought somewhat. Edward, hand thy lady cousin the undermost book. 'Twere best she read it before the Green Caves are barred to her. Thou and Patrick will profit most from the scrolls and the blue books."

Ted slid the dusty volume from his stack and handed it down the table to Ruth. Its dark green cover was stamped in silver: *The Book of the Seven Wizards*. It sounded like something they would all have enjoyed reading, before they got into this mess.

"Now," said Fence. "If aught's unclear to our visitors, let them ask us not to unmuddy them. And if aught's unclear to you, Randolph, Celia, Matthew, ask now."

All of Ted's relatives looked alarmed. He could at least postpone the inevitable. "Can you tell us," he said, "the story of Shan?"

"'Tis in the thicker blue book," said Celia.

So much for that.

"Can you tell us," said Celia, "of Andrew? This report of his spying mislikes me. What, as such, did he accomplish?"

"Nothing," said Ellen. "He was always thwarted."

"Was he so foolish, then?"

"No," said Ellen, "but he was *wrong*. He didn't believe in magic."

"Which was a considerable handicap," said Ruth dryly.

"Fence," said Matthew. "The antidote is hereby explained."

Celia said, "But how knew he one would kill the King?"

"And who did so?" said Matthew, gloomily.

Celia turned back to Ellen. "What hath Andrew yet to do?"

"Nothing, I think," said Ellen.

"He betrayeth not this embassy?"

"We don't know," said Ellen. "The embassy wasn't in the game."

"How not?"

Ted said quickly, "We ran out of time. It was September by then, and we had to go back to school." It seemed to be the outsiders' turn again, so he said, "What about Laura's visions? They can't really be a talent of her mother's house."

"*Did* Princess Laura have visions?" said Laura.

"She had dreams that would have grown so," said Celia, "but was too young for visions." She looked intently at Laura. "What age hast thou?"

"Eleven," said Laura.

"The Lady Laura was but nine," said Celia.

Celia and Matthew looked at one another. Nobody said anything. Ted thought what a strain this must be for all of them, confronted with the lying doubles of children they knew in their minds, but surely not yet in their hearts, to be dead, and to have been dead for three months. Ted remembered Laura's vision, that Claudia had buried the bodies in the cellar of the Secret House. *But keep the wolf far thence, that's foe to men,* he thought, *for with his nails he'll dig them up again.*

Ted made a sharp movement, as if he had found a spider walking up his arm, and both Fence and Celia turned inquiring faces his way. "Fence," he said, "Edward says to keep the wolf far thence, that's foe to men, for with his nails he'll dig them up again."

"That's another spell of Shan's," said Fence.

"But why's it in the back of my head? Are Laura's visions another manifestation of it?"

"Have all of you this affliction? Hath Patrick?"

"Oh, yes," said Ted. "But it's not words, with him. It's muscle memory. All the prestidigitation."

"But not the bladework?" said Fence.

"No. And Laura has the visions, but she can't ride a horse."

"I don't have much," said Ellen. "The name of a flower, or knowing that the pies have bones in them."

"The devising of Melanie," said Fence, "was that some dear to her, whom Shan had killed, should speak to his lightest thought, as do the unicorns in the places of their abiding."

"What's Melanie got against us?" said Ellen.

"Could Claudia have learned it from her?" said Ted.

"Or from another," said Fence. "Or it may be that, being so like your others, wearing their clothes, sleeping in their beds, answering to their names and observing all their ways with the very comment of your souls, that you be not found out, you are like enough to them that you hear them speaking. For sorcery makes nothing happen that may not happen left alone. It can turn a trickle to a sea; but there must first be a trickle."

"Your turn," said Ellen.

"In your game," said Celia, "who did murder King William?"

Ted's whole interior recoiled like a snapped rubber band. Fence was actually managing to give Celia an admiring glance, as if to say he should have thought of that question himself. Randolph was extremely pale, but that wasn't much of a change. Ellen looked thoroughly shocked, which would be good for her. Laura appeared to be going to say something, and Laura was not good at improvising.

"It depended," said Ted. This was just short of a lie; in the early days of the game, it had depended. "Sometimes," said Ted, "it was Andrew; sometimes it was an evil castle magician that we got rid of later; and sometimes, when we got tired of the obvious, it was Randolph; and once it was Agatha, and—"

"No profit there," said Celia.

"Well thought," said Randolph, to the tabletop.

"*Our* turn," said Ellen, quickly. "Why didn't breaking the Crystal of—"

"What do you know about Claudia's sorcery with the windows?" Ted overrode her loudly. It was, of course, too late. When people in the Hidden Land heard "breaking the Crystal," there was only one interpretation they would give it.

"Edward," said Fence, in a less terrible voice than Ted had expected. "Tell the tale."

Ted felt put upon; why should he have to guess Patrick's motives or, where he knew them, decide whether to betray them? But he told the story. The Crystal of Earth was no part of their original game, but Patrick had dreamed about it: a globe like a gigantic snowflake paperweight, which had a magic in it that, let loose, would destroy the Secret Country. Fence had confirmed this, more or less, by listing for them the three things that were dangerous to the Hidden Land: the Border Magic, the Crystal of Earth, the Whim of the Dragon. So on Midsummer's Day, Patrick, infuriated by Fence's taking from them the swords of Shan and Melanie, their only way home from this country, had decided that he would break the Crystal and set them all free. Ted had followed him to the North Tower, protesting. Patrick had broken the Crystal. And for the barest moment, they had seen home. Then they were back in a Secret Country none the worse for this wavering. They gathered all the colored fragments up and hid them in Ruth's room.

Ted looked over at Fence's intent face, and said, "There's an awful lot Ruth didn't think to tell you in that letter!"

"Well, she was hard-pressed," said Matthew.

Fence said nothing, but only waited. Ted would have felt

better if he had been angry. None of them looked angry. He supposed they were waiting for Patrick.

"All right," said Ted. "I noticed, during the Unicorn Hunt, that the ground in the Enchanted Forest sometimes feels like the magic swords—there's that tingling. So I thought we should try standing there and changing things around, the way we used to do in the game. So I tried it, saying that Patrick and I had never practiced with the magical swords, and therefore you and Randolph took them not. And that didn't work. But Laura said, 'Let's say Prince Patrick broke not the Crystal of Earth.' And *she* felt the ground tingle. So we went back to Ruth's room and looked in the towel; and all the fragments were gone. We went to the North Tower, and there was a floating globe, much larger than the one Patrick broke, and having inside it sparkles of all colors, but giving off a deep gold light like nothing I have seen. And that," said Ted on the last of his breath, "is the tale of the Crystal of Earth."

"What appearance had the Forest, when this was done?" said Fence.

"Very different from during the Hunt," said Ted. "The hedge of roses had grown wild, and the stream was much deeper."

"But there were roses?" said Celia. "That was the true power of the unicorns, then, and not some meddling of Claudia's."

"Okay, but why was what Patrick broke not the Crystal of Earth?" Even as he said the last few words, Ted realized what the answer was. "Because we were going to stand in the Enchanted Forest and say, 'Let's say Patrick broke not the Crystal of Earth,' the Crystal of Earth wasn't there for Patrick to break?"

"What *did* he break?" said Laura. "*Something* happened when he did it."

"Now that may be some meddling of Claudia's," said Celia.

Somebody rattled the door. Matthew got up and let Patrick in. Patrick was flushed, and his eyes gleamed. Ted realized that he was excited, not tired. The things that got Patrick excited were always either incomprehensible or troublesome.

"Did it work?" said Ellen. "Where's your watch?"

"It worked," said Patrick. "When I got back there, the watch said it was eight forty-five on June seventeenth. That's when we left. But that's not the half of it." Patrick shouldered himself out of his knapsack, opened it, and began piling books on top of those already on the table.

"Now," he said. "These books are about a lot of things that must be just as impossible here as digital watches. This used to be my digital watch." He pushed back the violet silk sleeve of his shirt, thick with embroidery in black and white, and showed them the watch he wore. It had a plain leather strap, a round crystal, and the usual twelve numbers picked out in gold. The hour and minute hands were gold too.

Laura remembered the serviceable black plastic watch with all its baffling buttons and its red characters in twenty-four-hour time that would show you the date and the day of the week if you knew how to ask it, and was safe underwater to two hundred meters.

"That's *your* watch?" she said.

"You bet it is. This happened once before, remember? And I think you must have been right, Laurie. Your flashlight did turn into a lantern. Now, just what happened when it did?"

Laura looked at Fence, who nodded at her. Ted decided that they were letting Patrick dig his own grave, and then they would push him into it.

"It *stayed* a flashlight," Laura said, "until Ted tried to turn it on. Then there was a flash of blue light. Ted dropped it in the stream. There were a lot of sparks, and then the blue light went out. And all we found in the stream was a lantern."

"I got a green flash from the watch. Now." Patrick lined the books up on the table. *The Handbook of Chemistry and Physics, Elements of Programming Style, The Communist Manifesto, An Outline of Intellectual Rubbish*, and a science fiction novel called *Inherit the Stars*. "I went through these and marked passages contrary to the way reality works in the Secret Country," said Patrick. "And they are all still here. Nothing whatever has happened to these books. Whatever makes these things happen alters artifacts, but it leaves books alone."

"Touching the alteration of artifacts," said Celia. "What is this tale we hear of the Crystal of Earth?"

"Who told you?" said Patrick, in a dangerous tone. His face had not changed.

"Never mind," said Fence, to Laura's profound relief. Ellen would feel bad enough without Patrick's hollering at her.

Matthew said, "Why broke you that Crystal, knowing what fate you doomed us to?"

"I wanted to go home," said Patrick, pale but still calm.

"Patrick," said Fence, "there must be no more of these trials and testings, neither out of temper nor out of thy cooler speculations. Thou knowest nothing; thy proddings are perilous. Have I thy word?"

Patrick's calm face moved swiftly into stubbornness. He said, "I prefer example to authority."

Randolph stood up, his face furious.

"No, wait," said Ted. He looked at Patrick. "You swore me an oath," he said.

"Oh, no, you don't," said Patrick. "You may be my King, but you're not my superior officer."

"He is more," said Randolph. "He hath the power of life and death o'er thee, without counsel or appeal. Thy officer is answerable to his, and to his King; the King is answerable to himself, and to powers so fickle 'twere better none awakened them. And thou didst swear."

"I said faith and truth," said Patrick, "and you'll get more of both of them if you let me go my gait."

"Patrick," said Ted, "remember where you are. The oath means what it means. Words have power here."

"Say some, then," said Patrick, his face flushed again but otherwise unreadable.

"Don't go performing private experiments like breaking the Crystal of Earth. Don't do anything without consulting us."

Patrick looked from Celia and Matthew, who were a little tense but clearly amused, to Randolph, who was still angry, to Fence, whose face was as uninformative as Patrick's own. Then he looked at Ted. "It's as bad as having a government grant," he said. "All right. No unauthorized research. I hope you won't be sorry."

"Thy hopes commend thee," said Fence, dryly.

Patrick sat down in the chair to the left of the King's, looking as if nothing out of the ordinary had happened. If those four people had ganged up on Laura, she would have been in tears.

"Whose turn is it now?" said Ellen, without much vigor.

"Yours, yours," said Fence, "for we have just put Patrick to the question."

"Pat?" said Ellen. "Ask them something you want to know." And that, thought Laura, was Ellen's apology for what Patrick didn't know she had done.

"Tell us," said Patrick, "about Shan's Ring."

"Nay, do you tell us," said Fence. "Shan says in his journals that he had it from the unicorns, and that it did greatly magnify the power of his mirrors."

"What was the power of his mirrors?" said Ted.

"To see matters far off, as ours show us still today," said Fence. "Mayhap also to see things that shall be an certain conditions be met; we are not agreed."

"Because that's what Apsinthion could do with his mirrors," said Ted, "and I don't think he had a ring."

"Well, *does* Shan's Ring magnify the power of your mirrors?" demanded Patrick.

"Not ours," said Fence. "Shan's were, it may be, made differently."

Patrick scowled. "What about the riddle?" he said.

"We solved that," said Ruth.

"I don't think so," said Patrick. "I think that was fortuitous. I think blowing time awry is a side effect, and every time we use Shan's Ring we do we don't know what."

"The red man," said Laura, "said it worked too well and woke up powers that were better off sleeping."

"What powers?" said Fence. "Only the Outside Powers do sleep."

"But Benjamin said they were rising," said Ellen, "before we ever found Shan's Ring." She seemed to give up. "Your turn," she said to Fence.

"This matter's too long for talk," said Fence, "but I would you'd write me the story of your game as you did most commonly play't out. In its departures from our history we may find answers."

Laura thought this would be tedious; but it was clever of Fence to avoid asking them to talk about the game, in front of people who didn't know what Randolph had done. "You should get another question, then," she said.

"In this game," said Fence, "how were events ordered?"

They all looked helplessly at one another. Fence said, "Tell me of a small thing only."

"Fire-letters," said Matthew. "Had you those?"

Ellen laughed. "Oh, yes," she said. "That was my fault. Ted and Patrick sneaked off and built a bonfire without me, and I got so mad they had to make up the fire-letters on the spot."

Matthew looked as if he wanted to withdraw the question. Randolph said, "*This* is how our very lives are ordered?"

"Or the other way?" said Laura, quickly.

"Yes," said Patrick, with an approving glance. "*Because* in the Hidden Land there are fire-letters, when Ted and I needed to calm Ellen down with some intriguing thought, fire-letters came into our minds."

Ellen started to say something; Laura shook her head, hard; and Ellen closed her mouth. Laura was relieved. This was no time for the old argument about who had put what into whose head. However distasteful it might be to the five of them to think that their wonderful game had been slipped into their heads by Claudia, it was far worse for the characters of the game to think that all their actions and all their history had been dictated by a bunch of children in unwitting collaboration with a renegade sorcerer. Until they knew which way—if either—it had gone, it would be better for the people who had to live in the Hidden Land to think that power flowed from them to Laura's world, and not the other way around.

"I think we should take a break," said Ted.

"Well, we must all to our studies," said Fence, pushing his chair back. "Bear yourselves meekly, I beg of you; and should you see Benjamin, stand aside from his path."

CHAPTER 7

SHE dozed in the dusty house. The windows of her mind were open. If anything happened that concerned her, she would dream of it. The six cats dreamed now, twitching, and gave her sleep a faint background of breathless rushing and the taste of blood. The water-beasts were lavishly entertained by the courtesies of the man Apsinthion; their smugness mingled with the cats'. The voices that abode in this place sang lullabies. This did not mean that they had forgiven her, but that they could, for a time, forget.

The music that summoned her burst in like a shower of hail. She had sprung to her feet before her eyes opened. No echo drifted in the sun with the dust motes. The cats slept on. The voices altered and proclaimed, *The way was long, the wind was cold, the hemlock umbrels tall and fair, whilst we have slept we have grown old, his house is in the village there.*

She looked intently at her left ankle, with the cat scratch, and the smear of dirt on the bone, and the little faint scar from the unicorn's hoof. The voices ceased. One instrument could reach so into her sleep; and one person knew what music to play on it. The music was old and well loved; anyone might play it; that might be chance. But play it on that flute? She stood up and went along the dim hall to the back room, and found after a moment's thought a pane on the upper right of the back wall.

"Cedric," she said. "Thy playing troubleth me."

Her second lover had long, dark hair and green eyes and

looked more like Randolph than she had remembered. He gazed out of the little diamond pane at her, and the red stone in the ring he wore glared at her like the eye of an angry wolf. He said, in his snug, deep voice, "When art thou?"

"In September of the four hundred and ninetieth year since King John defeated the Dragon King."

"In August of that eventful year," he said, laughter limning his voice, "I did give my flute away. Look elsewhere for the source of thy discomfort. I'll trouble thee no more."

"You will trouble me always," she said; for what use, after all, could he make of this weakness now?

"Thou troublest thyself," he said.

"Who had the flute from thee?"

"Laura," said he. "Princess of the Secret Country."

"Thou fool," said Claudia. "The Princess of the Secret Country died in June. That was a creature of mine."

"I do not think so," he said. "Look again." And he turned and walked away from her. She leaned her forehead on the soft, warm glass and stared at him with all her strength. The clearing in the forest where he had stood formed itself for her, each dead brown needle as precise as a jewel on the merchant's velvet. But she could not bring him back.

To think of following him into the dark backward and abysm of time, leaving her plots half-woven, strings dangling from the loom, was foolish. But her smile was not for its foolishness. She was tired. The tools she had brought to finish out the pattern were rebellious. One of them had the flute of Cedric. It was too late to make improvisations in the pattern. They would look like mistakes. They would be mistakes. Unless this should be not the weaving's border, but its middle.

"Look again," he had said. She laid her hand on one of the larger panes in the left-hand wall. "Purgos Aipos," she said. She could not step through, but she could see. The creature Laura was afraid of the water-beasts; but she loved cats.

CHAPTER 8

WHEN the council was over, Ruth took her green-bound book up to her own room, where she locked the door and curled up in a tall, carved chair liberally supplied with cushions. She had filched the cushions from around High Castle. Lady Ruth must have enjoyed being uncomfortable.

Ruth opened the book and was disappointed. The section concerning the Green Caves was a collection of translated extracts from works she had already, painfully, read in their original tongues. Celia had been kind, but she couldn't have been thinking. How did she suppose Ruth had gotten through three months as an apprentice?

Ruth laid the book down and sat looking at the room. Lady Ruth had a huge rag rug in green and red and blue; an undersized bed covered with a silk quilt in the same colors, with blue wool curtains; twelve narrow tapestries depicting the plants most precious to the Green Caves in excruciating and, given the medium, unbelievable, detail; three deep, narrow windows overlooking the vegetable garden; the chair, the table, a hanging cabinet full of glassware, and two chests in dark wood. Unlike the Princesses Laura and Ellen, she had no dolls, musical instruments, or abandoned sewing projects. Whatever Lady Ruth did besides sleep and dress in white, she did it elsewhere; and whatever she owned that was not practical, she kept it elsewhere.

Ruth had never bothered to find out where, if anywhere,

Lady Ruth kept the appurtenances of her life. But it was with this in mind, rather than the useful intention of finding out what she could before she was barred from the Green Caves by her resignation, that she went downstairs again.

The actual Green Caves were far to the west in a place called, predictably, the Cavernous Domains. The members of the school of Green Sorcery in High Castle had possession of the original wine cellars, the ones built for the inner white castle. These were naturally rather damp, but it was the skill of this branch of sorcery to turn such attributes to an asset. Ruth wended her way down and inward to one last cold, dusty stair, pushed open a wooden door stoutly bound with iron, and entered into a warm place of light and greenery, a circumscribed botanical garden.

Ruth went briskly past all its riches, through another iron-bound door, and into a long corridor carpeted in yellow and lavishly lit with golden lamps. There she stopped, considering. The first room on the right was the apprentices' library; the second was Meredith's study; the third was the journeymen's library; the fourth was a refectory. The first room on the left was the potting room; the second was where they dried the herbs; the third was where the artists worked; and the fourth led to a suite of guest chambers for visitors who preferred to sleep underground. If the game and reality ran together in this instance, those chambers had been furnished for the Dwarves.

Ruth walked down the hall and put her hand to the door of the guest-chambers. It opened readily and she stepped inside and shut it. There were two dim purple torches here, one to either side of the doorway; and one of the golden lamps at the far end of the room. It had been meant for Dwarves, all right. Ruth tried all the chairs and benches, one after the other, like Goldilocks. The room was tidy, but smelled of damp and stone and some odd medicinal thing that might have been the torches burning, or might not.

Ruth tried the door at the other side of this sitting-room.

It also opened, and showed her a square hallway off which opened three more doors. Two of these led to sleeping rooms, each with four small beds and four chests and four purple torches. The third led to a larger room lit powerfully with a dozen golden lamps. Ruth took one look, bolted inside, and shut the door hard. On the hearthrug was worked a large and perfectly recognizable cardinal.

All the walls were lined from the floor to the twelve-foot ceiling with shelves, and all the shelves were crammed with books. There were books on the floor amid the cushions. There were books on the table in the center of the room and on all chairs around it. If this library was like the others in High Castle, there was no card catalogue. If you were lucky, there would be an index, arranged by some useless criterion such as the date on which the book had entered the library. Any index would be in the charge of Meredith, who would, presumably, hand it over to her guests.

She wouldn't hand it over to Ruth. Ruth had disgraced herself back in June, when she had, to all appearances, revealed to Ellen and Patrick one of the protective sorceries the Green Sorcerers had planted around High Castle. Meredith had demoted her to apprentice and kept her there.

Ruth leaned on the door. What was it that had made her think to come here? Lady Ruth knew; but Lady Ruth's knowledge, like this library, had no card catalogue. Ruth could read the old language the books of the Green Caves were written in, with frequent recourse to a dictionary. She could, when trapped into some ceremony of the Green Caves, make any responses that Lady Ruth had once been assigned. She couldn't remember them beforehand and spare herself apprehension. And she could not, now, call into the lighted spaces of her mind the reason she had come to this library.

She walked forward into the room and began turning over the books on the table. She thought doggedly about other things: the Australian accent that made even the plainest of the boys at school worth listening to; the fact that she had forgotten to sew the middle button back onto her denim skirt; how Shan had chewed up her copy of *The King of Elfland's Daughter.* Finally, in desperation, she began reciting poetry. She didn't know much, unlike Ellen, who memorized it with the same speed and dispatch with which she ate chocolate. "With blackest moss the flower-plots / Were thickly crusted, one and all," she announced to the cold, swept fireplace. "The rusted nails fell from the knots / That held the pear to the garden-wall."

And with the same thoughtless assurance, the same swift walk of habit, with which she used to make for the science fiction shelf in the library at home, Ruth walked to the shelves on the right of the fireplace, knelt down, and extracted from the middle of the bottom shelf three small volumes bound in red.

"Bingo!" said Ruth, unpoetically; and she sat down on the hearthrug, folded her legs up under the full white skirt, and began to read.

The books were written in a relatively plain English. The spelling was abominable. They were titled *A Short History of the Dwarves*; but the Dwarves, Ruth thought, might have found it a rather narrow and unrepresentative history. They were really the story of the impingement of the sorcerous methods of the Dwarves on the philosophy of the schools of sorcery in these central lands: the Hidden Land, Fence's Country, the Dubious Hills, the Great Desert, the Kingdom of Dust, and the Forested Slopes. The Dwarves had chosen three animals, the raven, the marten, and the sunfish; and by some combination of magic and what sounded to Ruth like genetics, had bred them to be magical beasts, capable of acting as spies and messengers but having in them, like the dragon or the unicorn, an unchancy element that would play you false when you could least afford it.

The Dwarves, who had a fondness for green growing

things but a dislike for living aboveground, had traded knowledge with the sorcerers of the middle lands. So now the Dwarves had botanical gardens under the earth, and the Green Caves had the services of snakes and fishes and the little burrowing mouse; while the Blue Sorcerers, like Fence and Randolph, could call upon the cat, the dog, the horse, or the eagle. The Yellow Sorcerers might tame the lesser hawks, the squirrel, or the black bear. And the Red Sorcerers had made intelligent, useful, and unchancy the red deer, certain finches, and the cardinal.

Ruth stuck her feet, which had gone to sleep some time ago, ungracefully out in front of her. "Oh, *Lord*," she said. She had thought the cardinals were servants of the Green Caves. The Green Caves people, however mysterious and testy, were benevolent. The Red Sorcerers were another thing entirely. Several centuries ago, they had made themselves so unpopular that the quarreling, backbiting, bitterly independent members of the other three schools had ganged up on them and tossed them out of the middle lands. Red Sorcerers were said to infest the seacoast countries, and to be allowed grudgingly in the Outer Isles. But not in the Hidden Land.

But Claudia wore red. Ruth jumped up, scattering books; and then made herself sit down again. Fence and Randolph must know this already. And Benjamin; what had Benjamin said to Ted? "I would not come between the cardinal and its charges. If thou art one." Those were not the words of someone who had discovered that the messengers of an outcast school of sorcery were abroad in his adopted country. And Randolph had said to Patrick, when a cardinal's interruption saved him from having to practice fencing, "I knew 'twas folly to allow rival magics in this castle." But the rival magics were the Green Caves and the Blue Sorcery. And these rooms were for Dwarves, who were not Red Sorcerers; and yet there was a cardinal on the hearthrug.

"You are about as dumb as they make them," Ruth said aloud. There was no need to sneak around like this. All she had to do was ask Fence and Randolph.

Except that Fence and Randolph either had not known or had not wanted to tell her. To her suggestion that she prowl around a little, trying if she might discover more about the cardinals, they had returned only the bland silence that implies consent.

"Jerks," said Ruth, bitterly. She shoved the three books back into their place, stood up, and, leaning on the marble mantelpiece with its useless candles in their silver holders, she said, "O'Driscoll drove with a song / The wild duck and the drake / From the tall and the tufted reeds / Of the drear Hart Lake. / And he saw how the reeds grew dark / At the coming of night tide, / And dreamed of the long dim hair / Of Bridget his bride."

And walked, with the brisk thoughtless stride of habit, across the room, and stretched her arm up as far as she could, and tipped down a thin volume minus its binding, tied up with blue ribbon.

All of the books were copied by hand; the Secret Country had not yet discovered the glories of moveable type. The copyists, for the most part, had a tidy and invariable script; you often forgot, reading it, that somebody had painstakingly traced every letter with the sharpened quill of a goose feather. But this book was written in longhand, rather cramped and spiky. Ruth sat down in the nearest chair and began to read.

It began in the midst of a sentence. ". . . air is fulle of Voyces," it said. The spelling was abominable here, too, but it was consistent. If the writer spelled "only" as "onlie," he did so every time.

Ruth found neither enlightenment nor much entertainment in this work; but she plodded through all of it. "To banish such Voyces," she read, "it is above all Else necessarie that thou banishest wordes from the threshold of thy mind and heart. These Voyces do gain their powre from chance wordes thy mind or mouth shall let fall."

As she read on, it seemed likely that it was some lesson of the Blue Sorcerers; it spoke of the habits of cats and dogs and horses and eagles, and how to address them with one's Inmost Voice. That subject exhausted, the writer began a dissertation on the nature of enchanted weapons, and ended suddenly in the middle of a paragraph.

"Bother!" said Ruth, and slammed the book back into its place. There was nothing in its vicinity that looked like what had come before or after it. "Well," said Ruth, "let's hope third time pays for all." She scowled at the rug; she was running out of poetry. She cast around in her memory, and grinned. "Egypt's might is tumbled down / Down a-down the deeps of thought; / Greece is fallen and Troy town, / Glorious Rome hath lost her crown, / Venice' pride is naught. / But the dreams their children dreamed / Fleeting, insubstantial, vain, / Shadowy as the shadows seemed, / Airy nothing, as they deemed, / These remain."

And thoughtlessly she took from the table before her, from under five or six tumbled volumes, a fat black book stamped with gold lettering: *On the Mingling of Sorceries as They Had Been Paints on a Palette, its Benefits and Disasters.*

"Well, hallelujah!" said Ruth. Having no hat, she flung her handkerchief into the air and, when it fell back down onto her head, burst out laughing.

Fence did not laugh. Fence, whom Ruth sought over all the first two levels of High Castle and finally found, resignedly, in his own room at the top of his two hundred and eight steps, was appalled. He knew the book, but he had not known that the sorcerers of the Green Caves possessed a copy. Nor had he known that the short history of the Dwarves existed, or that the origins of his own knowledge might be as those red volumes claimed. It was hard to say which discovery upset him more.

"I'd thought there was one copy only," he said, holding the fat black book in one hand and absently pouring wine for Ruth with the other.

Ruth pushed her glass under the effervescent pale stream and said, "Thank you, that's enough. Why are you so surprised? Didn't you tell us that those purple water-things were the result of combining Green and Blue sorcery?"

"No," said Fence, putting the bottle down and looking up sharply, "you told us."

"You didn't deny it," said Ruth.

"It's true," said Fence, paging through the book. "But look you, we had thought that was the only instance of such meddling, for that the results were so ill. Claudia's knife wherewith she made to stab me below was also of that combination, wherefore we knew her to be renegade. But that the cardinal began as the Red Magicians' servant is ill news, and fresh. More's amiss than Claudia." He shut the book. "Read you aught else?"

Ruth described the fragment bound in blue ribbons. Fence's face darkened. "That," he said, "is the journal of Shan. If they came by it honestly, they had given it into our keeping." He stood up. "Rest here. I think I must speak with Meredith."

"Fence, you can't! She'll kill me!"

"Well," said Fence. "What keys and knowledge are needful, to find this library?"

"No keys," said Ruth. "It's in the old wine cellars."

"I might wander there, as well as anyone," said Fence. "Fear me not, I'll contrive some tale." He grinned. "And this also may serve as the reason whereby I shall remove you from their influence. You need not resign, lady; we'll forbid you their company."

Ruth, full of profound misgivings that she could barely articulate even to herself, got up quickly. "Fence, is this wise? Do you want to start a major fight between two schools of magicians on the eve of your departure?"

"Better late than never," said Fence, grimly for him. "I'll see you at supper." And he tucked the book under his arm and went out, slamming the heavy door behind him.

CHAPTER 9

AFTER the council, Ted and Patrick retired to their room, where Patrick lay on the rug and read *Inherit the Stars*, and Ted sat in the window seat and read the book Celia had given him.

Its framing narration was written for ten-year-olds; but it quoted copiously from Shan's journals, from later commentators on them, and from a variety of other sorcerous and historical works that were hard for Ted to puzzle out and would have been far too much for a ten-year-old. Maybe you were supposed to begin with the framework and grow gradually into the quotations. Ted plowed doggedly through them whether he understood them or not; maybe they would wake up Edward's knowledge, or spur Edward to make some enlightening remark.

He was reading the story of the wizard and the animals. The old man in all the tapestries and carvings was Prospero, who had been Master of the Red School, where Shan had started out as an apprentice. In pursuit of his studies, he had been sent to a place called Griseous Lake, to watch a song happen. This made no sense to Ted, but there was no explanation. He had lost his horse and arrived too late for the song, as the result of which a young Blue Sorcerer had died. At Griseous Lake, he had met Melanie, and after a time had quarreled with her because she had made him immortal. Ted, remembering that immortality came from the blood of a unicorn killed by treachery, could understand a reluctance to profit from such a deed; but Shan, besides that, seemed also to object to immortality itself.

The Red Sorcerers all had animal companions, whom they called fellows. One of the early tasks of an apprentice was to find his inner ear, wherewith he could understand his fellows, and his inner voice, wherewith he could speak to them. Shan, who had been clumsy and backward in this regard, achieved both voice and ear suddenly in the course of gaining his immortality. He had not meant to cheat, if you could call that cheating, and he did not want the immortality anyway. But the Red School dismissed him from its service.

He had taken from the body of the dead Blue Sorcerer anything he thought the man's friends might find valuable. He accordingly took this collection to the Blue School, which welcomed him happily and invited him to join its ranks instead. His first task was to discover exactly what had happened to the Blue Sorcerer. That was a separate story, which Ted reluctantly skipped because it had little to do with Shan.

The discovery took Shan about ten years, during which he made up his quarrel with Melanie. He still had his fellows with him, cat, dog, horse, and eagle. He had refused to tell what few secrets of the Red School he knew to the Blue Master, but he found himself telling them to Melanie. Melanie, who had a long-standing grudge against the unicorns, enlisted the aid of a dragon and managed to turn a unicorn into a fellow. When Shan found out, he was outraged; Melanie refused to release the unicorn, and moreover had told the Blue School about her achievement. The Blue School was half fascinated and half horrified; it was certainly very pleased to get the information it had wanted about the methods of the Red School. Shan spent much fruitless effort seeking a way to free the unicorn, and finally, at the unicorn's request, killed it. Then he resigned from the Blue School before they could kick him out.

"What a hideous story!" said Ted.

"It's suppertime," said Patrick.

Ted told him about it on the way downstairs, and had the satisfaction of seeing Patrick blanch. They found their respective sisters in the crowded hall. Ted sat down next to Ruth and requested that she pass the salt.

"Do *you* know where Fence is?" she said, pushing the heavy cut-glass salt cellar in his direction so carelessly that she spilled its silver spoon and a good pile of salt. Ellen made an exasperated noise and began spooning the spilled salt back into the cellar, along with a few crumbs and some cat hair.

"I haven't seen him since this morning," said Ted, looking away from this operation and concentrating on Ruth's face. She seemed to be trying not to cry, and Ted felt it necessary to justify having lost track of Fence. "I've been reading."

"So have we all," said Ruth, darkly. "Fence has gone to beard Meredith in her den, and he said he'd see me at supper."

She explained what had happened. Ted couldn't blame her for worrying. It was Fence's nature that, if he said he would see you at supper, then he would see you at supper. Ted said, "Where's Meredith's den, Ruthie? Should we go rescue him?"

"What do you suppose we can do against a bunch of sorcerers?" said Patrick.

"Quite a lot, probably," said Ruth. "They're sworn to abjure violence, and there are five of us. But we aren't supposed to know anything about it."

"Where's Randolph, then?" said Laura.

They all looked around; it was crowded in the Dragon Hall, and all the red and pink light made it hard to recognize people. Ellen finally located Randolph by standing on the bench. He was sitting with Matthew and Celia at one of the shorter tables to the right of the fireplace.

"Benjamin's with them," said Laura, also standing, rather precariously, on the bench.

Ted got up. Sure enough, between Randolph's wild black head and Celia's smooth, braided one loomed, six inches higher than either of them, the graying, dark head of Benjamin and his big, brown-clad shoulders. Matthew, sitting across from the three of them, caught Ted's eyes and favored him with a steady, if blank, look, probably intended to tell Ted to behave without attracting Benjamin's attention.

"Well, he's got to look at us sometime," said Ted, and started to climb over the bench.

Ruth caught hold of the hem of his shirt and dragged him back down, upsetting her ale into her plate. "Not today," she said. "We were specifically ordered to leave him alone today."

"Do you want to help Fence, or don't you?"

There was a furious silence.

"Well, for heaven's sake," Ellen said. "You're the King, aren't you? Get a page to fetch Randolph."

At a formal banquet Ted would have thought of this himself. There would have been pages everywhere, and he would have been stuck up at the head of the table feeling silly. But in this hall you served yourself and sat where you pleased. "Seest thou any pages?" he said.

"I see John," said Ellen.

"Well, wave to him and then get down off that bench before Benjamin sees you. Laura, get down before you fall down."

Laura got down. Ellen also did as she was told with remarkable meekness. John came up to them smiling, leaned over the table, and said to Ted, "How may I aid you?"

"Could you, of your courtesy, go to Lord Randolph and tell him—privily," added Ted, "that I need to speak to him?"

John looked not as if he were going to refuse, but as if he were puzzled. Ted said, on impulse, "Benjamin is vexed with us."

John grinned a grin of perfect comprehension and said, "As Your Majesty wills it," in a tone that any one of the five of them might have used, playing. Then he charged across the crowded room to Randolph. Randolph got up promptly, crossed the room, sat down next to Ted with his back to the table, and said, "What is your gracious will?" in a perfectly serious voice.

Ruth told her story for the fourth time. Randolph frowned all through it. "You have been with the cavernous magicians these three months, and knew not sooner?"

"How was I supposed to know sooner?" said Ruth, so sharply that Ted blinked. Randolph seemed unaffected; and also unconvinced. Ruth said, "I spent those months as a disgraced apprentice; because of the Nightmare Grass."

"Oho!" said Randolph, as if something had suddenly become clear to him.

"Yes," said Ruth. "So I didn't know. But your Lady Ruth knew right where those books were."

"The next question," said Randolph, slowly, "is, knew Meredith that she knew?"

"You think she might have been as sneaky as I am?"

"Sneakier by far," said Randolph, looking her in the eye until she turned red.

"Shouldn't we all do some sneaking?" said Ted, impatiently. "You don't know what may be happening to Fence."

"But look you," said Randolph. "Ruth must not seem to have betrayed her to Fence."

"Well, you won't find out by speculating," said Patrick. "Let Ruth stay here."

"Come on, then," said Ellen, jumping up.

Randolph stood up from the bench and surveyed them. "All of you?" he said.

"Say Fence asked you to come for him if he was late, and we were all with you and would not be gainsaid," said Ellen.

"And that's no more than truth," said Randolph. He stopped in the act of turning away, and looked at Ruth again. "Will you guide us so far as the door?" he said.

"Good heavens, don't you know where Meredith's study is?"

"How should I?" said Randolph.

Ruth stood up and shook crumbs from the white folds of her skirt. "It's in the old wine cellars." As Randolph simply went on standing there, she added, "*Fence* knew where those are."

"Shut Fence in a wardrobe," said Randolph, precisely, "and he'll find the loose plank i'the back before thou'st turned the key i'the lock."

"I'd think," said Ruth, exasperated, "that rival schools of magic would spy on one another."

"So they have," said Randolph, in extremely grim tones. "But one of 'em hath been o'er-trusting. Come your ways."

They followed him out of the noisy hall. Ruth then led them to the back of High Castle, out of the regions Ted was familiar with. Nobody said anything until she marched down the last narrow stairway and flung open the door into a dazzle of gold light. It smelled of flowers and greenness and grass baking; it smelled like the soul of summer; it smelled as the whole outdoors had smelled on the day of the Unicorn Hunt. Something stirred and stretched in the back of Ted's mind, and, incomprehensibly but with a pleasing rhyme and rhythm, Edward said, "The fieldis ouerflouis / With gowans that grouis, / Quhair lilies lyk lou is, / Als rid as the rone."

"I never knew this was here!" said Ellen, indignant.

And Patrick said, "They *can* grow trees underground. One point for us."

"What're you doing," said Ted, irritated, "keeping a list of everything we got right in the game?"

"Shut up," said Ruth, from the far door.

Randolph had already joined her there; the rest of them hurried up. "Now, then," said Ruth to Randolph. "Meredith's study is the second door on the right." She took him by the elbows and shook him slightly, as if he were Patrick. "Now *watch out*," she said. "Meredith is a *demon*. She'll say awful things that go around in your head for weeks afterward."

Randolph said, "We'll heed your warnings," and Ruth let go of him. He opened the door softly, and they followed him through it.

CHAPTER 10

RUTH stood in the green smell and waited. She leaned her back against an oak and thought very pleasantly about almost nothing. In the far spaces of her mind somebody said, *The fieldis ouerflouis / With gowans that grouis, / Quhair lilies lyk lou is, / Als rid as the rone.* She looked thoughtfully at the lilies at her feet, which were certainly the color of rowan berries, although she would not have called that red. She blinked; the tangled, half-familiar language drifted away.

The far door burst open and the rest of them tumbled back in. Ellen and Patrick bolted up to her and began talking about broken glass and people in white.

"Not here," said Fence. "Come to my chamber."

"Oh, Fence, for the love of mercy," said Ruth. "Not all those stairs. Come to my room. I think Lady Ruth might even have kept there somewhat for our refreshment."

They came with her docilely enough.

It seemed to Ruth, ushering her six guests into her room, that she had done nothing since returning to the Hidden Land except gather in odd places for uncomfortable conferences. Her three younger relations piled into the room and took over the bed. Ted lay on the rug. Fence, refusing her offer of the one chair, sat on the table. Randolph came past her last of all, and Ruth felt suddenly peculiar. He was much taller than the rest of them, and his constraint and the signs of stress on his face made him seem by far the most adult. Fence was as grown-up as they came, but Fence seldom looked it. How old were they, anyway? Younger than her parents? Ruth consulted the back of her mind, which was silent; and then blurred her thoughts, whereupon she knew that Randolph was twenty-six and Fence three years older.

Ruth shut the door. Randolph sat down on one of her chests, beneath the tapestry depicting the double white violet that blooms twice a year. Ruth felt it necessary to take the situation in hand. She took from the little wall cupboard a tray containing eight rather dusty goblets in red glass and a large red glass decanter. She put the tray down beside Fence, twisted the stopper out of the decanter, and poured into one of the goblets a thick, dark fluid. It clung to the sides of the glass and gave off a potent smell of blackberries. Ruth handed the glass to Fence, who was looking bemused.

"There," she said. "Is that fit to drink?"

"It's one of Agatha's cordials," said Fence. "Sweet but wholesome."

Ruth accordingly distributed glasses to everybody, and sat down in Lady Ruth's chair. "Now will somebody tell me coherently and in a decent order," she said, "what happened in there?"

"Fence first," said Randolph, in a stifled tone as if he wanted to laugh, "for great events transpired e'er we arrived."

Fence snorted, and ran both hands through his hair, flattening it again. "Oh, great," he said. "Two sorcerers with more wit than to use their powers; the one barred from any effect of violence by the lack of his weapon and a disinclination to do harm, t'other by her sworn oath. A tussle of children."

"What made you so mad?" said Ellen.

"Me, thou knowest," said Fence. "What did so enrage Meredith was, first, that any dare meddle in her affairs; second, that I should presume to remove the Lady Ruth; third, that I demanded to read o'er the indices of her libraries. She soon minded her that should she ope her indices to me, my presumption would then be revealed to me regarding the Lady Ruth."

"I don't like the sound of that," said Ruth.

"You shouldn't," said Ted.

Fence looked at him, and then at Ruth. "Indeed, she said she'd speak to you herself, and I could not gainsay her."

Ruth experienced the swooping dread of a person who wakes up on a lovely summer morning and remembers that she has to go to the dentist. "Shan's *mercy*, Fence! You told me not to trouble myself! Now she's thrice as stirred up as she'd have been had I braved her, and you've left her to me?"

"What am I to the Lady Ruth," said Fence, rather sharply for him, "that I might meddle so in her affairs?"

"How should I know? You *said* you could meddle!"

"Forgive me," said Fence, more quietly. "I did in some wise mistake the Lady Ruth's commerce with Meredith."

"She hasn't—I haven't *had* any commerce with Meredith all summer, not to speak of."

"That, I think, is for your punishment. She hath withdrawn her custom of friendly confidence, thinking to wound you."

Ruth found this reasonable, but could not refrain from saying, "Oh, that's wonderful. Now I get to go be wounded, I suppose, and hope that's excuse enough for leaving her tutoring?"

"Wait," said Randolph. "Fence, thou hast no power o'er the Lady Ruth, but I have. I'll remove her, as my betrothed, from a malign influence. Meredith will be choleric, but she'll have little recourse."

Ruth struggled with contradictory impulses. Having scolded Fence for saying he would help her and failing, it was foolish, not to mention ungrateful, to refuse the selfsame help when Randolph offered it. And yet she was indignant that he should choose this way out, as if he were certain she would never manage the matter on her own.

"Ruth doesn't like it," said Ellen, who was acute, if not discreet.

"Nor I," said Randolph, promptly. "Yet meseemeth the handiest way from out our difficulties. My lady?"

"I'm not anybody's lady," said Ruth. She had figured out what bothered her. She disliked Randolph's calling attention to the betrothal just when breaking it off would save them both embarrassment. But Randolph was right. She said, more calmly, "Yes, it is the handiest way out. It's just not very savory."

Randolph stood up. "No," he said. "It is of a piece with all our business this summer. By your gracious leave, I'll go rant at Meredith."

"Shouldn't you wait until she's calmed down?" said Ted.

"No, I think not," said Randolph. "In the wake of calm cometh thought; the less she thinks while yet she hath Ruth in her grasp, the better." He paused on his way out and said to Fence, "I'll make report to you."

"Make it here, to all of us," said Fence.

Randolph said, "As you will," and left, closing the door with a certain force.

"What else happened?" said Ruth.

"'Twas Claudia," said Fence. "Like me, Meredith taught her, and did presently refuse to teach her; yet she learned more than Meredith knew, and did, it now appeareth, some little mischief. She did strew about the open library library works not rightly the Green Caves', or rightly theirs but secret. We know not whence she had Shan's journal. The book concerning animals they had most properly from the Red Sorcerers, before the war; and they do use it to subdue the cardinal to their will, and for naught else. The third book, the history, they had from the Dwarves, though it differeth from our own accounts."

Ted listened earnestly to all this, as if he were trying to commit it all to memory. The three younger ones, having heard it twice already, bounced gently, trying out the bed.

"All right," said Ruth. "Now, almost nobody at High Castle wears red, except Claudia, who wears it all the time, and Benjamin, who has a red cape. How does this fit in?"

"We shy from red, for the reasons you saw in the book," said Fence. "This is no law, nor hath it truly the force of custom. Claudia, methought, did wear red to be rebellious at little cost. Benjamin wears it because he is of Fence's Country, where all the wars were fought. It is their reminder of what transpireth when sorcerers strive one with another."

"Fence," said Ted. "The man who sent us here wore red."

"Good grief," said Ruth, jarred. "I'd forgotten. So is *he* a Red Sorcerer? Is this all some complicated trap?"

"I know not," said Fence, fixing her with a very sober expression. "But this matter, as it so far unfolds itself, hath not quite the smell of those Sorcerers. What smell it hath is strange to me."

"Could *Claudia* be a Red Sorcerer?" said Laura.

"No doubt," said Fence. "Insofar as she is a Blue Sorcerer, and an initiate of the Green Caves. She might have traveled, and cozened one of them also."

"I couldn't help wondering," said Ruth, "why the mixture of Blue and Green sorcery should produce purple beasts. What if it's a mixture of Blue and Red?"

"She had one blue and one red stone on her dagger," said Ellen.

"Are the Red Sorcerers plotting a comeback?" suggested Patrick.

Ruth looked at Fence, who was leaning back, supported by his hands, and looking half-thoughtful and half-amused. There was a pause, as that line of discussion died for lack of knowledge. Ruth wondered if Fence could have supplied it.

"Benjamin," said Laura, after a moment, "said red was the color of the Outside Powers."

"That is so," said Fence. "From them the Red Sorcerers did draw their power; they trifle not with the elements, as we other schools all do, but reach beyond them to their origins."

"Sounds dangerous," said Patrick, in a tone relatively free of sarcasm.

"It is so," said Fence, looking him straight in the eye.

Patrick didn't look away, but he did shrug in the way he would when he thought you were taking something too seriously. Fence smiled at him, started to speak, and stopped.

"What's the matter?" said Ruth.

"You're very like," said Fence to Patrick. "Very like Prince Patrick."

"That's a pity," said Ruth, tartly, over the ache in her throat.

"Fence?" said Ted. "What about the rest of us?"

Ruth turned and glared at him; he was only making things worse. Ted lifted his chin and gave her a level, slightly arrogant stare from under his thick brown bangs. It was a very Edward-like look.

"Well," said Fence. "Ellen is like the Princess Laura, and Laura like the Princess Ellen. Thou, my prince, art very like Edward overall, but hast some relish of contention in thee, that I do welcome, and did wish to find in Edward. Thou hast also less of maturity."

"I'm only fourteen," said Ted.

"Well for you," said Fence, his mouth quirking, "that Edward is—that Edward was someways behind his age."

Ruth, fuming, saw that Ted had indeed made things worse, making Fence think about Edward, whom Fence had been particularly fond of. "What about me?" she said.

Fence gave her a considering look, and she wished she had not tucked her feet up under her skirts. Lady Ruth was dignified. "And thou," said Fence, unsmiling, "hath an outward show very like thy other, but art somewhat softer i'the'center."

"I am not," said Ruth, severely, "a chocolate-covered marshmallow cookie."

Ellen choked.

Fence made a face. "'Tis too sweet a combination," he said. "You mistake me. The Lady Ruth made never a sweet show."

"No wonder she and Meredith got along," said Ellen.

Fence did smile at that.

"I can't wait to get out of here," said Ruth.

"I would be gone also," said Fence, "but there are preparations cannot be hurried."

"It's just that between Benjamin and Agatha and Randolph—and this betrothal—"

"Is Andrew better?" said Fence.

"Yes!" said Ruth. "Andrew doesn't love us; we never even pretended to love Andrew."

"*Ruth,*" said Ted, with an appalled gaze that had nothing of Edward in it.

Ruth gulped. Now *she* was doing it. You jerk, she thought to herself. It must be the mental equivalent of wanting to pick off a scab; except it isn't *your* scab.

"Trouble not," said Fence, kindly.

"You keep saying that," said Ruth.

"Well," said Fence, "you are all so sensible that, did it not sort so ill with my presentiments, I'd think you conscience-scathed, and eager to amend it."

Sensible? thought Ruth. Sensible to sight as well as hearing? Sensitive? She opened her mouth, but Ted was quicker.

"We *are* conscience-scathed," said Ted. "Claudia made it sound as if we had some hand in all your misfortunes. We didn't know we were affecting real people, when we played our game; but we did play it. It's as if," said Ted, suddenly inspired, "we had shot an arrow o'er the house, and hurt our brother."

"No more but so?" said Fence.

"Well," said Ruth, in response to Ted's helpless glance, "it argues a sort of carelessness in us, doesn't it?"

"It's not just *conscience*," said Ellen, suddenly. "We're *sorry.* Not because we did it, but because it pains us to see you in evil straits."

"I know it," said Fence. "Why?"

"Because we're so sensible, I suppose," said Ruth, dryly. "Don't the evil straits of strangers pain you, Fence?"

"Of a certainty; but not in this wise."

"That's it," said Ted. "You're strangers, and yet you aren't."

"And you," said Fence. "So are you to us."

"And that," said Ruth, "is why I want to go. We'll be doing something to make restitution."

Randolph came in without knocking, shut the door, and leaned on it. He looked harassed.

"What did I tell you?" said Ruth. "Around and around in your head for weeks afterward."

"Nay, hours merely, I'll wager," said Randolph, with a very brief smile.

"Do you want some more cordial?" said Ruth, offering him her untouched glass. "You look as if you needed strengthening."

Randolph smiled again. "I thank you, no. The deed's done; you are free of the Green Caves. But free upon condition." He exchanged a long look with Fence, the meaning of which escaped Ruth. Randolph seemed resigned; Fence, after a blank moment, cast his eyes to the ceiling and let his breath out in a sound that might have been a snort, or an aborted chuckle.

"Don't be so *dramatic*!" said Ruth, losing patience. "What do I have to do? Dress in sackcloth and ashes? Promise her my firstborn son? Set the sun, the moon, and the stars in the sky? Sort innumerable bushels of mixed wheat, barley, and rye into their separate piles? What? I can't wait."

Randolph, grinning as Ruth had never seen him grin, came forward and knelt at her feet. Ruth wished he wouldn't.

"No," said Randolph. He looked up at her with a face not much altered from the one she saw in her mirror every morning. If she had had a brother who resembled her, instead of taking after her father's side of the family, he would have looked like Randolph. "No," said Randolph again. "If that's what thou hast stomach for, this stricture is bare of substance as the air."

"Begot of nothing but vain fantasy," said Ruth, unable to resist.

Randolph frowned, and looked at Fence, who said, "Is this thy play-maker again?"

"Yep," said Patrick from the bed. "Shakespeare. *Romeo and Juliet.* And you know what he said right after that? 'My mind misgives / Some consequence yet hanging in the stars / Shall bitterly begin his fearful date / With this night's revels and expire the term / Of a despised life closed in my breast / By some vile forfeit of untimely death.' "

This precise and unemotional recitation was accorded a polite silence. Ruth glared at her brother. That was Romeo's speech, just before he went off to crash the Montagues' party and meet Juliet and begin the love affair that would kill him. Patrick thought she needed a warning. He was an idiot.

"Would you mind telling me, my lord," she said to Randolph, "what is this stricture?"

" 'Tis merely," said Randolph, "that we wed before a year is out."

"Well, you're right, that's no problem," said Ruth, over a very uncomfortable jolt in her stomach. "We should be finished with this business, one way or the other, long before a year is out." Oh, Lord, she thought, what a thing to say. He'll probably be dead.

"Did you give her your word?" said Fence to Randolph.

There was another silence, not a polite one. Ruth was amazed. She watched Randolph turn red and then extremely white, and then sit back on his heels and look squarely at Fence.

"I did so," he said. "So you see, my lord wizard and my lady play-maker, you need have no fear of me; for that I promise, I do not perform. I beg your gracious leave." And he stood up, with considerable grace, and went at a measured pace out of the room. He closed the door so gently that all they heard was the little click of the latch.

"Well!" said Patrick. "Tact isn't *your* middle name, is it?"

"Shut up," said Ruth. Had Fence known what he was saying? By killing the King, Randolph had broken the most solemn oath he would ever take, and he was painfully conscious of it. Could Fence possibly have made such a wounding remark by accident?

"I meant Fence," said Patrick.

"Shut the hell up!" said Ruth.

"Spare him thy ire; he hath the right of it," said Fence. He slid off the table, looking very tired. "And so hath Randolph also. Give you good day."

And he, too, went with a certain stateliness, his hands buried in his black, star-shimmered robe, to the door, and went out, and closed it quietly.

"Patrick," said Ruth. "Don't do that."

"All I did," said Patrick, "was make an observation. It was Fence who asked the wrong question."

"Don't argue," said Ted. "Things are bad enough without it."

Nobody contradicted him. Ruth put the glass of cordial to her mouth and drank its contents in three gulps. It tasted beautifully of blackberries; and enticingly, just a little, of alcohol; and even less, but unmistakably, of dust.

Chapter 11

On the day before they were to leave High Castle, they sat in their favorite spot on the wall above the moat, throwing biscuit to the swans, who ignored it. Some of it was snapped up by large, unidentified fish, and some of it sank soggily. The moat was flat and glassy, except where their exertions had disturbed it. Beyond the last wall, the huge plain had turned brown, but behind them in the garden late roses, limp, bright, and fragrant, spilled everywhere and climbed the wall and scratched Laura. Ted had given her his handkerchief to tie up the scratch, and she had dropped it into the water, where it, too, sank soggily.

"Ruth," said Ted. "What's it to Meredith if you and Randolph get married?"

Ruth let her breath out explosively and looked at him past Patrick and Ellen. "What's it to anybody?" she said. She sounded a great deal fiercer than was usual with her. "But when did *that* stop anybody in this abominable castle from having an opinion on the matter?"

"It's a political issue, Ruthie," said Patrick. "That's why they all have opinions."

"What I meant," said Ted, "was why should Meredith think she could make Randolph promise he'd marry you—her—before a year is out?"

"Presumably," said Ruth, "because, if he didn't mean to marry her, then he didn't have any business taking her away from Meredith. So Meredith made him promise, to test his sincerity."

"And," said Ellen, "if Meredith taught Claudia, maybe she knew Randolph was dangling after Claudia—"

"Or Claudia was dangling after Randolph," said Ruth.

Ellen shrugged. "So Meredith suspected Randolph didn't mean to marry Lady Ruth."

"*Did* he mean to?" asked Laura.

"God knows," said Ruth, in a tone of complete disapprobation.

Ted thought of asking her what the matter was, and decided not to. She probably felt that Randolph had treated Lady Ruth shabbily; and he had. Except that the hints they had received of unexpected, possibly unsavory, depths in Lady Ruth's character made it more difficult to feel defensive on her behalf. Then again, Lady Ruth was Ruth's other self. Ted felt protective of Edward, and hoped not to find out anything unpleasant about him.

He said suddenly, "I wish we didn't have to split up."

"I wish," said Ruth, "that the three younger ones weren't going off on their own with nobody to keep them in line."

"Celia's going with us," said Patrick, interrupting an indignant exclamation by Ellen.

"She doesn't know you," said Ruth, darkly.

"She knows her own kids," said Ellen, "and they're much worse."

"They're worse than you and Laura," said Ruth. "But nobody and nothing could prepare her for Patrick."

"What the hell do you expect me to do?" demanded Patrick.

"I don't know, but I'm sure you'll think of something."

"That wasn't what I meant," said Ted. "I really do fear some consequence yet hanging in the stars."

"For whom?" asked Ruth, leaning around her sister and brother again and looking distinctly alarmed.

"I don't know!" said Ted, irritably. "I just feel uneasy."

"Did Edward have visions?" asked Laura.

"I doubt it," said Ruth. "We could ask Fence at supper."

"I'll see you then," said Ted, who knew from experience that they would all go on arguing about what Fence might say. He climbed down from the wall and trudged along the winding, mossy path that would take him back to his part of High Castle.

In the little courtyard where the fountain was, he stopped to look at it, thinking of the play that had been performed here the night of his coronation. Randolph had taken the part of Shan, and, in a gesture Ted both hoped and feared was merely symbolic, Ted had given Randolph long life, whether Randolph chose it or not. Ted realized that, in all the tapestries that told the story of Shan's animals, there was a unicorn. But there had been no unicorn in the play.

Ted sat uncomfortably on the narrow, rounded edge of the fountain. A crisp yellow elm leaf eddied by on the rolling surface of the water. Ted scooped it out. Ellen came around the bend of the path, skidded to a stop in front of him, and said, "Whose untimely death do you fear?"

"Nobody's," said Ted. "Just something bad."

"Well, who do you think it will happen to?"

"Laura, I suppose. It's always Laura."

"I'll take care of her," said Ellen, quite seriously.

Ted looked at her. She meant it, and she was not offering the way she usually offered to do things, because she thought they would be easy.

"Can you?" said Ted. "Because that *is* part of my misgiving. She can't ride all that way; she'll pitch on her head at the first rough terrain. And none of them will watch out for her."

"I can tell Fence and Matthew *and* Celia," said Ellen. "Mark's always falling down; she'll understand."

"Mark's only six," said Ted, gloomily. "You expect it when they're six."

"What else do you want me to do?"

"Make her tell you those visions. Any time she clams up on you, she's had one. And tell them to Fence."

"Okay," said Ellen. She shoved both hands through her hair and made a face. "You like her a lot better than Patrick likes me," she said.

"Well, you and Ruth gang up on him."

"We *have* to," said Ellen.

"Yes, I know, but you can't expect him to like it."

"Well, you don't *like* it when Laura breaks things," said Ellen. "But you like Laura."

"Patrick likes you," said Ted; it seemed the only thing to say, although he had no idea if it was true. He had never known Ellen cared about such things. He added, thoughtlessly, "If he likes anybody."

"Maybe that's the problem," said Ellen.

Fence was not at supper; neither was Randolph, or Matthew. The five Carrolls ate with Celia at one of the smaller tables off in a corner. Celia, when Ted asked her, said that she doubted Edward had had visions, because if he had shown any sign of magical talent he would not have chosen to be a warrior.

"I thought he never took his nose out of a book," said Ted.

"That's true," said Celia, removing a mug of ale from the path of Laura's elbow. "But the books our Edward had's nose in were all of war and weaponry, strategies and histories, the most dry and lucid accounts of any battle he could hear tell of."

"Randolph said he was good with the sword," said Patrick.

"So he wasn't a milksop?" said Ted.

"No," said Celia. "But a was gentle in's heart; and a scholar. The art of war, the fine points of a sword fight, liked him well. He had not, look you, fought any battle; and Matthew thought it had liked him but ill, had he come to't."

"*Would* he have killed—" began Ted, thinking aloud with his mouth full of apple tart, and then he clamped his mouth shut abruptly. He had been about to ask if Edward would have killed Randolph in the rose garden. It was such a relief to talk to somebody who knew he was a fraud, he had forgotten she did not know quite everything.

"Well?" said Celia.

Ted ostentatiously finished chewing his mouthful, and then said, "Would he have killed somebody in a battle, or in a private duel, when the time came?"

"Very like he would. The wonder of so lovely a fight had held him, until the end, and that end duty had forced him to. He had a great regard for duty, which Randolph taught him."

That was ironic, thought Ted. He remembered Edward, in that shadowy realm of forgetful ghosts, saying to him, "Avenge our foul and most unnatural murder." As the game predicted, he would want vengeance for his father's too. In the kindly warmth of the Dragon Hall, Ted shivered, and Laura looked at him.

"Since you speak of duty," said Celia, "have you fulfilled your own, and read on what I did give you?"

"Yes," said everybody, overlapping.

"How sorteth it with your imagining?"

"Pretty well," said Patrick. "Ellie's the history expert."

"Well?" said Celia, looking across the table at Ellen.

Ellen stopped making little pillars of the carrot slices she had picked out of her beef pie, and said, "There was a lot more to the story of Shan. We didn't know about his animals, and we didn't know he lived for hundreds of years, or about his killing the unicorn. We didn't know Melanie lived for hundreds of years, either. And we knew that Melanie lived at High Castle when she was little; but we certainly didn't know that *she* got long life from a unicorn her brothers killed by treachery."

"We didn't want to know it, either," said Laura, feelingly.

"How so?" said Celia. "Melanie is no friend of thine?"

"No, she's been dead too long; nobody ever played her.

But," said Laura, "it's a much *nastier* story than ours." This remark gave Ted some obscure comfort.

"And that," said Celia, standing up, "no doubt explaineth how it hath prevailed, for all thy sorcery."

"We don't have any sorcery," said Ruth; she had said it so often recently that she had ceased to say it with any heat.

"You know none," said Celia, picking up the skirts of her blue gown and stepping neatly over the bench. "You may have't nonetheless."

"It is the little rift within the lute," said Patrick, catching Celia's eye across the cluttered table with a look that made Ted nervous, "that by and by will make the music mute."

Celia's hands tightened on the folds of her skirt. She said, " 'And ever widening slowly silence all.' "

"Who said that?" Patrick asked her.

"Melanie," said Celia.

"Tennyson," said Ruth to Patrick.

Celia opened her hands and made a violent gesture, like somebody telling a rambunctious class of third-graders to sit down *now.* "*Another* play-maker?" she said. "With how many of this pestilent breed is your country cursed?"

"Thousands," said Ruth, "but we don't count it a curse. And I don't think Tennyson wrote plays; just poetry." Her gaze shifted over Ted's shoulder, and fixed. She looked appalled.

"Give you good even," said a sharp, clear voice behind Ted.

Ted dropped his spoon in his lap and felt it slide to the floor. He turned his head slowly. Yes, it was Andrew, tidy and amused. What the hell did he want?

"You also," said Celia, in a pleasant tone that was nevertheless not normal. She might speak just so to a child who was trying to lie by omission. She sat down again where she had been, between Ruth and Ellen.

"Hello," said Ellen, alertly.

Patrick and Laura mumbled something at about the same moment.

"Good den," said Ruth, in the flat voice of despair.

"Won't you join us?" said Ted, crazily.

Andrew smiled and sat on the empty stool between Ted and Laura. Laura leaned away from him, and almost fell off her stool. Luckily, Andrew was looking at Ted.

"By your gracious leave," Andrew said. Ted suddenly felt as if he had invited a fairy over his threshold, and was about to be visited with untold disasters. Andrew said to Celia, "What dost thou with this motley brood?"

He had said something similar about them once, to Fence and Randolph. He had said, "Strange company," to which Randolph had replied, "'Tis strange to thee," leaving the honors, Ted supposed, about even. It had been clear, by the way Andrew spoke, that he disliked both Fence and Randolph. It was not at all clear that he disliked Celia; he sounded more as if he were commiserating with her for having to put up with their company. Did Andrew ever do anything except bait people?

Celia said, "Their other mentors are engaged, save Agatha. For that she'll have the care of mine own brood when I am gone, I'd thought to give them some days in one another's company. Thereby they may discover their grossest points of grievance while I am by to mend them."

Ted saw that Andrew was not interested in this account, and that Celia knew he was not. He hoped she was enjoying herself. Her neat-boned face with its scarred forehead and uninformative eyes was as bland as custard.

"Yours do stay, then?" said Andrew.

"Of a certainty," said Celia. "Wherefore should they go?"

"Wherefore should these?" said Andrew.

Celia looked at Ted in mild inquiry, as if Andrew had asked her what the flowers were in the jug in the middle of the table, and she thought Ted ought to know.

"I," said Ted, clearing his throat, "am the King, and it's my duty to go. Not much of a King, you may say," he added as Andrew opened his mouth, "but the best you're going to get."

This last remark seemed to him, on reflection, to be ill-advised; but it appeared to take Andrew aback. "A King with teeth," Andrew said, without any sarcasm that Ted could detect. "Mean you, my prince, to close them upon me?"

Ted had no idea what he meant. "Not," he said, more or less at random, "if you stay outwith my range."

"I am within it," said Andrew, still as if he spoke to an adult whom he took seriously, "by blood, by circumstance, and by appointment."

Ted felt outmaneuvered, and thought before he spoke again. "Therefore," he said, "the range wherein I'll snap at you is lessened. It is your deeds, my lord, and not your coign of vantage, that will determine if I snap at you."

"I am well warned," said Andrew. He stood up. "Celia," he said, "have a care. Being children yet, they shall do damage though they will it not. Farewell." He looked thoughtfully into Celia's steady eyes, bowed generally to all of them, and left.

"Ted!" said Ellen. "What did he mean?"

"I don't know," said Ted. "I don't even know what I meant."

"No, about doing damage."

Laura said, "He knows the Crystal of Earth got broken. I saw him looking at the pieces, on our way home from the battle."

"But does he know we did it?" said Ted.

"What *did* you mean, Ted?" said Laura.

Ted took a deep breath, leaned an elbow on the crumby table, and looked at his sister. She had lost her left-hand hair ribbon; the right-hand one, a yellow silk with black and scarlet flowers embroidered on it, had been retied by somebody with great vigor and little grace; probably Ellen. She had pastry crumbs on her forehead. She looked intent and a little worried, as she would when she made a mistake in a coloring book.

"Okay," said Ted. "When I told Andrew I was the best King he was going to get, I think he took it as a threat. So I tried to tell him how much of a threat I was."

"Or how little?" said Celia.

"Do you think," said Ruth, "that he knows you know he's a spy of the Dragon King?"

"I want a word with Fence, touching these matters," said Celia. "Can you refrain from mischief these few hours?"

"Don't you think," said Patrick, looking up from his plate, "that you'd better let us make mischief now so we can be good when we're traveling with you?"

"No," said Celia, standing up again. "Meseemeth rather, an thou practiseth not thy goodness now, thou'lt have no skill at it when most thou needst it. Good even." She went out briskly in a billow of blue.

"Touché, Patrick," said Ruth.

"Listen, all of you," said Ted, very quietly. "Andrew thought it was a threat because he thinks I helped Randolph kill the King. If anybody finds out for sure Randolph did it, they'll have to deal with him; and we need Randolph. And Edward will need him, if we restore Edward."

"Do you think we will?" said Patrick.

"I don't know," said Ted.

"We *have* to," said Ellen.

"Have to's harrow no fields," said Patrick, in excellent imitation of Benjamin.

"Don't they?" said Ruth.

CHAPTER 12

LAURA knew she was dreaming. She had been here before. She trudged through knee-deep waves of crackling leaves, throwing up the scents of cinnamon and dust and dampness. It smelled like Halloween. The trees were huge, the light the color of clouds. She was looking for something. The last time she had dreamt so, she had spoken aloud to herself and woken up. She tried to do this again, but she could not make her voice work.

She was going uphill, and the path under all these leaves was rocky. As she gained the top of the rise, a little sunlight sifted down between the great smooth trunks. Not far ahead of her the wood grew up against tall gray rocks spotted with moss and lichen, the lichen delicate as lace, the moss as green as beryls in the dull air. There was a cleft in the rocks. Laura walked forward among the wet leaves and looked through it. It was wide enough for three or four people to walk abreast, and not very long. A bar of sunlight sharp and vivid as a piece of yellow silk fell halfway along its stone floor from the opening at the other end.

Laura went quickly through the cleft and out the other side, onto a little lawn of short grass and goldenrod. Beyond this, the slope dropped very swiftly, and through ribbons of mist she saw a winding water laid out before her like a sleeping snake, striped with water-weed and bordered by tall, frondy plants with long purple flowers and whole clouds of goldenrod.

There was a house on the other side of the water. Tile for

red roof tile, window for leaded window, graceful front and awkward wing and gray stone and white and yellow, it was a copy of the house at One Trumpet Street, Claudia's house, the house that Laura and Ted had done their best to burn to the ground.

"We know who the copyist was, all right," said Laura. And as she had both hoped and half feared, her own voice woke her.

Laura sat up. Agatha had lit a lamp in the corner. Ellen, in her long white ruffled nightgown that could have passed for a fancy dress at home, was folding clothes and handing them to Agatha. The black cat sat at the end of the bed, upright like an Egyptian statue. It was chilly. A thin light came through the window, and a clean, wet smell, and the sound of rain.

They were going to leave today. It *would* rain.

"Hi," said Ellen over her shoulder.

"It's raining," said Laura.

"Do you think Claudia did it?"

Laura made shushing gestures. Agatha turned around, plucked the half-folded shirt from Ellen's hands, and said, "Faugh!"

"Why shouldn't it be Claudia?" said Ellen. "Nobody knows where she is."

Laura thought of her dream. But where was the twisty lake set about with goldenrod? She looked blankly at Ellen, who added, "And Fence agrees she made it cold and rainy last summer."

"Those were unnatural rains," said Agatha. "That she called them I doubt not. But this is a September storm after a spell of fine weather, as we see more years than not." She put the pile of folded clothes into a leather bag that looked like a suitcase, except that you had to strap it up with strips of leather. "Drink your chocolate," said Agatha, beginning this strapping. "And dress yourselves. Fence will not stay for you."

When they were packed and dressed to Agatha's satisfaction, the three of them went down to the Dragon Hall, where they found gathered all the members of both expeditions, eating voraciously and complaining about the weather. Benjamin was standing by the fireplace with Fence and Celia. Agatha made for them at once. Laura and Ellen slipped quietly along the wall to the sideboard furthest from Benjamin. They had not had to talk to him yet. Perhaps they could leave without having to, and when they returned everything would be fixed, and they would be heroes, not villains.

They served themselves haphazardly and went to sit with Ted, Ruth, and Celia at their out-of-the-way table. Ted was dressed much as usual, but with a thick vest-like garment of dark blue wool over everything else. Celia was dressed like Ted; the men's clothing made her look taller and much thinner. Ruth was actually wearing something other than a white dress. She had put on several of her large shirts, and over them a black serape-like thing and a black wool skirt of generous dimensions. Lady Ruth must have been fatter than her counterpart.

"You think Claudia made it rain?" said Ellen, sitting down next to Ruth.

"I know where she is," said Laura, "but it doesn't help." She told them about it. Then she told them about her first dream. They found that more intriguing.

"Be sure and tell Fence," said Ted. He thumped his mug down on the table. "Hell! I wish we knew what all this meant."

"Well," said Ruth, "there are mountains in the south, where we're going. And there are evergreen forests in the north, where the rest of them are going. And I wouldn't advise anybody to sing 'James James Morrison Morrison,' unless you've lost your flint and tinder."

"I think," said Laura, "that it was the flute."

"Well, don't play it on the flute, then. You're supposed to use that flute to communicate with, not to fool around." Both this speech and the tone in which it was uttered were abnormally cross for Ruth. Laura's feelings were hurt. It seemed unfair to be taken to task for something you had done in a dream. She applied herself to her oatmeal.

"The flute's to be played," said Celia, mildly.

"Sorry," said Ruth. "I am *not* looking forward to this trip. Sorry, Laura."

Laura felt better, but by the time she had swallowed her oatmeal and could say so, Patrick sat himself down at the end of the table and attacked his pile of food. He was dressed exactly as he had been when they first saw him in Australia, including the green pack, and the stocking-cap falling out of his jacket pocket. Now that, thought Laura, was stupid. They were supposed to be playing their parts, and Prince Patrick would never have worn any such garments.

"Wilt thou find that warm enough?" said Celia.

"I've got a cloak too," said Patrick. He grinned at his older sister. "Any last-minute lectures?"

Ruth sat up straight and glowered at him; Celia looked ready to intervene to prevent violence; and Ted said, "Yes."

Patrick looked at him with interest, and with neither fear nor affront that Laura could see. Ted went on. "Patrick, you are pushing things right to the edge. Fence is going to hate that outfit. You can get what you deserve, as far as I'm concerned. But I bid you remember that you are the oldest of us in your party. I make you responsible for the well-being of your little sister and my little sister. And you'll answer to the King of the Hidden Land, not to your cousin, if anything happens to either of them that you could have prevented."

This speech aroused more indignation in Ellen than in Patrick. Laura, when Ellen caught her eye with an exasperated face, shook her head hard and pointed her spoon at Patrick.

Ellen should realize that Ted's purpose was to prevent Patrick's doing what Patrick did best. Asking Patrick to take care of Laura and Ellen was not an insult to them.

Patrick seemed less than pleased, and then he grinned. "You've really got it down pat, haven't you?" he said. "Your Majesty." He said that with an inclination of his head just short of sarcastic.

"It's easy when you know how," said Ted, peaceably. This line had been a joke between the two of them for an entire summer. Laura had never figured it out, but it could still make Patrick laugh. He did laugh. Laura stopped worrying about what trouble he might get into, and began wondering what it would be like to be under his merciless supervision. Well, at least she wouldn't drown. She might not even fall off her horse.

Celia got up abruptly. "Say your farewells," she said. "We'll leave anon."

The five of them sat and looked at one another. Laura was no longer worried, but she felt depressed. They had always been together in the Secret Country. The Hidden Land was separating them.

"Laura," said Ted, "don't kill yourself, and don't forget to tell Fence all your visions. Ellen, don't you get yourself killed pretending you can do anything."

"Ruth," said Ellen, "don't forget to practice your flute."

"And don't get all mushy," said Patrick to Ruth. "No misadventured piteous overthrows."

"Fear me not," said Ruth, with the utmost seriousness. "I had rather hear my dog bark at a crow." Patrick stared at her, and she grinned. "It'll come to you," she said.

Laura gave them a moment to explain themselves, and then said to Ted, "Don't kill Lord Randolph."

"I don't intend to," said Ted. He stood up. "Have we delivered our instructions all around? Let's go, then."

Andrew's party, the embassy to the Dragon King, was leaving from the main door of High Castle. Fence's party, which was smaller and burdened with less baggage, would be departing from a little postern that gave onto Stillman's Wood. High Castle was fond of ceremonies of leave-taking, and of conducting matters in their proper order; the greater embassy was seen off first. Everybody in Andrew's party, everybody in Fence's, and a great many who were staying home, jostled through High Castle's three sets of gates: across the paved yard shining with rain; through the gardens, with their drooping roses and their bare, muddy patches where the beans had been pulled up; over the moat all pocked and dimpled with raindrops; across the drenched grass, where Andrew's party stopped to collect its horses; through the roofless, pink-paved tunnel to the last gate, and outside.

It was pouring. Ted came up to Laura where she crouched against the wall with Ellen. "Stand under the archway of the gate," he said, rather irritably. He pulled Ellen's hair, gave Laura a very hard hug that almost undid her, and disappeared into the surging crowd.

Laura swallowed with great force and pretended it was the rain making her eyes hurt. She and Ellen moved back under the archway, where one was subjected to large, discrete drips instead of a steady sheet of water. They almost collided with Ruth.

"Oh, good," Ruth said. Her fuzzy black hair was misted with damp and stood out in all directions except straight up. "Ellen, behave, and don't kill Patrick, we'd never be able to explain it to Mom and Daddy. Laura, don't you kill him either. Your father likes him." She knelt in the soaking grass, hugged each of them with one arm, stood up with mud on Lady Ruth's black skirt, and said, "Don't you dare cry. All may yet be very well." And she, too, made for the center of the confusion.

"Make way!" called a voice from inside.

Laura and Ellen looked around and saw several wagons rumbling over the drawbridge. With one accord they darted back through the tunnel, ran along the inner side of the pink wall, and took shelter in the overhang of the nearest tower. The wagons went ponderously by them, mud clogging the red and yellow paint of their wheels, the rain sheeting off the leather covers tied lumpily over their contents. Laura and Ellen, shivering, stayed where they were, and thus missed whatever ceremony Andrew departed from High Castle with, and did not say good-bye to Randolph. Laura didn't care. Her hair was dripping down the back of her neck, inside all the layers of good dry clothes, and they had not even begun their own journey.

She looked at Ellen, whose pale face was beaded with water and whose hair was so wet that it was almost flat. "The rain it raineth every day," said Princess Laura.

CHAPTER 13

TED belatedly pulled his hood over his dripping head and pushed through the crowd. On the way he passed the blue-clad trumpeters with their horns as long as a yard-stick. He must have missed whatever leave-taking ceremony there had been. Andrew and Randolph were already mounted. Benjamin was holding the reins of Andrew's horse and talking to him intently. Fence was holding the reins of the unoccupied horse, an inoffensive-looking white one that was not Prince Edward's stallion and should suit Ted much better than that cantankerous beast. Randolph was holding his own reins. Fence was looking at Randolph, and neither of them was saying anything.

"Does it always do this in September?" said Ted, coming up behind Fence.

Fence turned, a little twitchily. He had put a black cloak of thick felt on over his wizard's robe, and its hood hid his face. His voice was as usual. "Not so early as this," he said. He nodded at the horse. "This one's fast but biddable."

"Thank you," said Ted. It—she, he ascertained—might be biddable, but she was still extremely large, and Benjamin was here. He thought of Edward and mounted competently.

"I wish you were coming with us," Ted said to the top of Fence's hood. It had a little tassel on it, like the ones on the seniors' graduation caps.

Fence tilted his head; the hood fell back, and Fence produced a rather unconvincing grin. "I'm better with the young ones," he said. "And with yon Patrick's meddlings. You'll be well enough. Randolph hath promised it."

That word was a dangerous one just now. Ted looked over at Randolph, who wiped the rain out of his eyes and said, "Fence, no more."

Fence looked startled and then rueful. "Nay, I cry you mercy," he said. "That was ill done, in Ruth's chamber."

"It was as well done as may be," said Randolph, with extreme grimness. "Wherefore I say to you, lean not on me."

"There's no one else," said Fence.

Randolph smiled at him, with a perfect naturalness that made Ted feel cold. "And that was ever the doom upon us," he said.

Fence held his gaze and said nothing. Randolph gradually stopped smiling, until he looked very sober indeed, but neither chagrined nor angry. Ted, his burning eyes braced wide open, felt something hotter than the beating rain slide down his face, but could not look away.

"Rest you merry," said Randolph.

"Not until thou art," said Fence. He reached up a hand. Randolph gathered the reins in his left hand, leaned down, and closed his right hand over Fence's wrist. Ted blinked, since no one was regarding him, and looked down at the mare's ears.

"So, then," said Fence; his voice trembled a little, and if Ted could have escaped without being noticed, he would have been gone. As it was, he sat still, and the mare was quiet under him, and the rain slid down the coarse, pale hair of her mane like beads on a broken string. Randolph was silent, and Fence said, "As well cut off mine own hand. As well have done the deed. An thou but keep safe, we shall yet read this riddle."

"I can read it," said Randolph; his tone had sharpened, and Ted looked up involuntarily. "It means death," said Randolph.

"That is a faulty reading," said Fence, quite steadily this

time. "Edward being dead, this is a matter to settle between us. Not in solitude. Dost thou understand me?"

"Oh, aye," said Randolph.

"And wilt obey?"

"How not?" said Randolph, and let go of Fence's hand.

Fence came back to Ted. "Be not o'er-hasty," he said. "We'll meet again." And he pulled the hood over his head again and went away through the crowd, back into High Castle.

Ted would not have looked at Randolph for anything. He carefully pulled the mare around until his back was to Randolph and he was looking at Andrew's profile. Andrew was staring down his straight nose at Benjamin, and Benjamin was glaring back. Ted did not want to know what they had been saying; but he might need to. He started to speak, and stopped. He had managed to avoid an encounter with Benjamin so far; what was the point in saying good-bye when you had not yet said hello? He tried to back the horse, but either she felt stubborn or he hadn't given her the right signals. She moved neatly three steps to the left, bringing her head level with Benjamin's, and Benjamin put his hand on her nose and looked up at Ted.

Benjamin couldn't say anything much in front of Andrew, of course; and, to Ted's relief, he managed to school his face as well. "I wish you were coming with us," Ted said, and immediately regretted it. In the first place it wasn't true, and in the second it probably constituted an insult to Andrew.

Benjamin rubbed the mare's head; then he rummaged inside his cloak and came out with two pieces of carrot, and fed one to each horse. Over the sound of crunching he said, "My prince, I wish so also. But consider High Castle in the grip of Celia's children, and none to say them nay."

Ted could not help grinning. "We couldn't have that, could we?" He thought, and ventured, "Prosper well, then."

"And you," said Benjamin. He looked at Andrew. "Fare well, my lord," he said, and left them.

Andrew gazed after him with a less than pleased expression. It occurred to Ted that he and Andrew were going to have to endure one another's company for several weeks. He said, "Was Benjamin haranguing you?"

Andrew whipped his head around so fast that a strand of wet hair fell over his forehead. Ted could not tell if he was angry, or just startled. "Not above the usual," said Andrew, in his pleasant, neutral voice.

So much for that, thought Ted. He looked over his shoulder for Randolph, but Randolph wasn't there. Ted scanned the crowd, which had diminished greatly, probably because of the rain. Randolph was over by the wagons, talking to the little cluster of soldiers that Andrew had chosen to accompany the embassy. One of them rode off a little way and then waited; the wagons followed, each with a soldier riding beside it. Andrew moved his horse off after the wagons, and so did Randolph.

Ted and Ruth followed them. The white horse had a nice gait; Ted blessed whoever had thought to give her to him, and spared some attention for the rain-sodden plain. Nothing moved in the brown grass. The road was covered with a thin layer of water, but there was no mud, and the horses' hooves sounded on it as sharply as on concrete. Patrick would have wondered what technology had produced such a surface on what looked like a dirt road. Ted was merely grateful for it. He sat up straighter and wiped the rain off his face.

Ruth called across to him, "With an host of furious fancies Whereof I am commander, / With a burning spear—"

"And a horse of air," Ted answered her, out of his own memory, "To the wilderness I wander—"

"By a knight of ghosts and shadows," said Andrew's clear, carrying voice, to Ted's immense discomfiture, "I summoned am to tourney / Ten leagues beyond the wide world's end. / Methinks it is no journey."

There was a brief silence, and it began to rain harder.

"Well," said Andrew, who had fallen back and was now riding on the other side of Ruth, "we go not even half so far as that."

"Thank God," said Ruth, in the dry voice she had never used to use, "for small favors."

Andrew looked vaguely puzzled. Ted said nothing. This was the long, straight road that led to the Well of the White Witch, and Claudia's house, to the mountains of the border and through them, south and west to the lands of the Dragon King. And to the Gray Lake. There, in some sense, Ted thought suddenly, was the wide world's end. Or at least Edward thought so. Ted wished that Edward would either come in or go out; this hanging around with the door open was disconcerting. Edward promptly faded out. Ted put his hood back on.

Laura and Ellen waited until they saw Fence come back through the pink tunnel. His face was not encouraging; they fell in a few feet behind him and were quiet. He led them to the little postern in the southeast corner from which the five of them had escaped their first day in this country. There was a great clutter of horses and baggage and milling people. Patrick was there, leaning on the damp pink wall and watching the chaos as if it were a movie for which he was considering requesting the return of his money.

Matthew was putting saddlebags on the horses and doing, Laura thought, a very good job of pretending that his youngest son, Mark, was helping. John really was helping Margaret with the same task. Benjamin moved from horse to horse, talking to them. They were remarkably quiet for horses in such a turmoil.

Fence went up to Benjamin and began walking around with him, talking also, but not, from his tone, to the horses. Laura made sure that the two bags Agatha had packed for her and Ellen were there. She wondered if only the six of them were going, or if there would be men-at-arms. She knew nothing of the lands east and north of the Hidden Land, and very little about what dangers might lurk in the Hidden Land itself. The Hidden Land had not seemed, on their journey south for the battle, to be very heavily populated; but neither had there been bears or wolves or even any deer. Maybe there would be deer in the north, and, if they traveled quietly, they would see some.

It began to rain harder. Matthew came over to them, his fair skin flushed and the red hair sticking to his brow.

"Is anybody else coming with us?" asked Laura. She realized that this was not what her fifth-grade teacher would have called a clearly phrased remark, but Matthew seemed to understand.

"No," he said. "We must go swiftly; and the librarians of Heathwill frown on parties o'er-large."

"Aren't there bandits?" said Ellen.

Matthew laughed. "In Fence's Country?" he said.

"Well, but before we get there?"

Matthew laughed again, a little more exasperatedly. "None," he said. "There are farmers and traveling merchants."

"Why?" said Ellen; she was disappointed.

"Because," said Matthew, kneeling in a puddle without seeming to notice it, and looking first Ellen and then Laura soberly in the face, "that is the country of the unicorns, where even the innocent may come to grief. The guilty have no more joy there than a lump of butter in a hot pan."

"Matthew!" said Ellen, and Laura saw on her face a look of unholy glee, like the one she had had the day she let all Ted and Patrick's frogs loose. "Are we going to travel through the Enchanted Forest?"

"Thy geography is without fault," said Matthew. "Now mind thy face."

He stood up and returned to the packing. Everything was loaded, including the people, and Celia still had not arrived. Mark, John, and Margaret hung around looking glum. Benjamin stood behind them looking glummer. Matthew dismounted twice to tell them good-bye. Laura sat behind Patrick on a black horse with one white leg. Patrick's pack was going to bump her under the chin once they started, but it was still better than riding a horse by herself. The rain had settled into a steady drizzle that seemed capable of going on all day and got you much wetter than it looked as if it could.

Celia finally came trudging over the pink paving, lugging a bulging, misshapen pack. She hugged her three offspring, and said something to them that Laura couldn't hear. They nodded, resignedly, and opened the little door of the postern. Celia patted Benjamin on the shoulder and swung briskly onto her horse.

They rode out the postern one by one, Celia, Patrick and Laura, Ellen, and Matthew, who was leading the pony with the luggage. Laura turned and waved, and the three yellow-haired children whose parents she was stealing waved dutifully back. Laura had thought, the first time she saw them, that they looked just as children in a fairy tale ought to look; and they still did, even wet and gloomy-faced. Behind them, Benjamin raised his hand and waved too; Laura felt absurdly better. The three children disappeared behind the door and slammed it. Laura heard the bolt snick shut, and felt desolate. She turned around, and hit her nose on Patrick's pack.

They rode down a long, shallow slope toward the edge of Stillman's Wood. It bordered on the Enchanted Forest, but did not itself look enchanted, or at least not in any appealing way. Its oaks were a dark, grim green that the wet only made worse. The beeches had been a pleasant coppery color all week in the sunlight, but now looked like dried blood. They rode along the edge of the woods until Celia found the path. It was narrow and clogged with ragged brown leaves, which, stirred up by the horses's hooves, smelled musty.

The dull spaces of the woods were misty with rain. Laura remembered her dreams with longing. Either of them had been better than this. They rode on further. Laura began to think she recognized this stretch of path. They had come this way for the King's funeral. It had rained then too.

Behind them, Matthew began to whistle, and the words slid upward from the bottom of Laura's mind. O *Westron wind, when wilt thou blow, the small rain down can rain?*

But that was for spring, thought Laura; and this was autumn.

CHAPTER 14

WHEN the army of the Hidden Land had come south in August, it had stopped at the Well of the White Witch for a ceremony. Ted assumed, without thinking about it, that his party would do likewise. But the horses and wagons ahead of him went on by the Well, which sat squatly in the sad, wet grasses, its lid tightly in place, its pink stone darkened with rain, and glowed not at all. Ted looked to his right, through the trees, to where Claudia's house loomed. Its gray stone walls were muted by the rain, and its red tile roofs showed sharply against the dark forest and the pale sky.

There was a light in the window of the smaller tower. Ted reined his horse abruptly, and she responded with a very good grace. "Ruth!" said Ted. Ruth pulled her horse to a stop; Andrew stopped too. They sat there in a row, all looking sideways. Randolph rode up beside Ted. "Look," said Ted, and looked, himself, at Randolph.

Randolph stared past Ted and Ruth and Andrew, and his eyes opened wide, in an expression of startlement very unlike him. "Shan's mercy," he said. "What sorcery is this?"

"I've never seen a light in that house," said Ted. "Hadn't we better take a look?"

Randolph, his astonished gaze still on that vivid yellow line high up in the dark of the woods, said, "Thou art the King. If thou shouldst choose to delay thy embassy in searching out this riddle, who shall gainsay thee?"

"Well, you'd better stop the rest of them before they

disappear," said Ted, not entirely pleased to have had his question answered with another. Randolph rode off.

"Good grief," said Ruth, in a voice where Ted heard exasperation warring with nerves, "didn't anybody think to search here, after Claudia disappeared?"

"Oh, aye," said Andrew. "Fence did order the lords Jerome and Julian to do so; but they found nothing."

Randolph came back, followed by the wagons and the little clump of men-at-arms. The latter began dismounting.

"I have given orders, my prince," said Randolph to Ted, "that food be prepared. Who shall accompany thee?"

"You," said Ted. "And Ruth and Andrew." He hesitated. "Do you think men-at-arms would do us any good?"

"No," said Randolph, "but thou mightst do them good to ask them."

"Okay, find two, could you please?"

Randolph dismounted; so, after a pause, did Ted and Ruth and Andrew. Some of the soldiers came up and took their horses. Two of them bowed to Ted and intimated that they were at his service. One of them had a mallow embroidered on his sash; he had been in the battle. His name was Stephen, that was it; it was he who had told Ted that Conrad was sore hurt. He was tall, thin, fair, and amiable-looking. The other was a young woman with a peony on her sash. She was a stocky person with sleek brown hair who seemed nothing like a peony.

They all stood expectantly and looked at Ted. He felt like Captain Kirk at the outset of some hazardous mission, which did not help in the least. "This is a sorcerer we call upon," he said, "but, should she prove troublesome, remember that a goodly anger can break a spell of stillness, and that, do you move quickly enough, she can be surprised with simple force." That was all he knew that might prove useful, and magic probably didn't make these people half as nervous as it made him. "Let's go," said Ted, and started up the hill. They followed him.

As he stopped at the little wooden bridge, Ruth caught him up. "Just how goodly an anger?" she said, quietly.

"Very goodly," said Ted. "Remember the time Ophelia had kittens on your green velvet dress."

"You're on the wrong track," said Ruth. "That was profound sorrow, tempered by an awful desire to laugh."

"You could've fooled me," said Ted, only half attending. He was discovering in himself a craven desire not to go one step nearer that house. He and Laura had burned it down, in Illinois. He wondered if he would have to burn it down here, and on the shores of the twisty lake Laura had seen in her dream; he wondered how many such houses there were, and if Claudia would await him in each one, with her husky voice and her matter-of-fact recital of the things she had done and her offer to allow him to help her go on doing them. He had not been tempted, but he might be next time; and, quite apart from anything she might be able to do to him, he was afraid of her.

The rest of his party came up behind them. Ted turned around and gestured at Randolph, who came forward. "I might feel happier with a few drawn swords," said Ted.

"As you will," said Randolph, and drew his.

The Peony and the Mallow looked at each other, and drew theirs also. Ted's was in his baggage. He started abruptly across the bridge, the rest of them clattering hollowly behind. Having crossed, they were obliged to go single-file along the narrow space between the edge of the stream and the beginning of the brush. The haphazard undergrowth gave way to the hedge, and Ted found with no trouble the gap one could crawl under.

"I wonder," he said, "if it would be better to use the gate."

"It'd be more dignified, certainly," said Ruth. "But the gate's been locked whenever we looked."

"I keep the key of it," said Andrew's precise voice, from somewhere behind Randolph and the Peony.

Ted looked up at Ruth, whose face was as surprised as he felt. Ted leaned around Ruth to examine Randolph's reaction. Randolph was astonished, so it was probably safe to ask questions. "By whose leave?" said Ted.

"By King William's," said Andrew.

That surprised Randolph too. There was something in Andrew's voice that warned Ted to be careful. "Do you keep it for me also," he said. "But now, of your gracious will, lend the use of it to me." That last sentence he got from Edward; it was the way in which the King asked for things nobody had the right to deny him.

The key was on a silver chain that looked too fragile to hold it. The chain was warm; Andrew had probably been wearing it around his neck. The key was wrought iron with a tree-and-leaf pattern, like the gate, and as cold as clay. Ted walked along the hedge to the brick arch with the gate in it and fitted the key into the lock. It turned silently, and the gate, as heavy as it looked, moved inward before he began to lean on it. Ted hastily pulled the key out of the lock, and the gate went on swinging until it bumped gently into the hedge. The blue-gray flagstones of the walk, swept clean of their maple seeds, were slick with rain.

"How about somebody with a sword up here?" called Ted.

Randolph, Ruth, and Ted walked together up the flagstone path to the steps of the porch, followed by the others. Ted did not remember very clearly the porch of the Illinois house: he and Laura had walked up to it not because they wanted to but because Claudia's spell had made them. But this porch seemed tidier than that one. It was newly painted, in a pleasant red that matched the roof.

He climbed the steps and went across the porch. The double doors were carved around their edges with the same old story. The right-hand one had an iron knocker in the shape of a cat's head. The ring in its teeth with which you hit the door was, Ted discovered as he dropped it against the wood, actually a very long, thin, iron rat with its tail in its mouth.

"Cute," he said to Ruth.

"Verily," said Ruth.

Nobody answered the knock. Ted looked up at Randolph and said, "I'm not sure why I think we ought to be polite. Shall we just go in?"

"You've given fair warning," said Randolph.

Ted put both hands on the damp wood of the doors, and pushed. They opened as easily as the gate had, and a warm gust of cinnamon-scented air swept out onto the dripping porch. Claudia's other house smelled like this too. Ted said to Randolph, "Should we leave somebody to guard the front door?"

Randolph, maddeningly, did not answer him. Ted looked at the Peony and the Mallow. Stephen, the Mallow, looked hopeful, as if he were curious about the house. On the other hand, Ted didn't know the Peony's name.

"Stephen," he said, "will you forego this exploration and guard the door?"

Stephen bowed, smiling, and went to stand on the steps. Ted walked into Claudia's front hall, and Ruth and Randolph and Andrew and the Peony came with him. There was a perfectly standard Oriental rug on the polished floor. Before them on the left was a narrow flight of steps, carpeted in red, and on the right the long hall hung with odd dark pictures down which Claudia had led Ted and Laura, in another house.

"I think," said Ted, in response to a kind of stirring at the back of his mind, "that to get to the smaller tower we go up the stairway as far as we may, bearing always to the left." He looked at Randolph. "You're my general; why don't you make the dispositions?"

"As you will," said Randolph; he did not, to Ted's relief, sound displeased. Nor did Andrew or the Peony look as if Ted had said anything out of the way.

Andrew, on second glance, did not look as if he had heard anything since he stepped inside. He seemed to be listening for something behind the voices and the drip of rain and the profound stillness of the house; and he looked as if all the hair on the back of his neck were standing on end. Ted wondered how much Andrew knew about his own sister, and whether he was fond of her. He wasn't sure he could imagine anybody at all being fond of Claudia. Even Randolph had implied that he was not so much fond of as bewitched by her.

They had to go up the narrow stairs one at a time. They passed three landings, all with little square windows having a border in red stained glass alternating with clear, with an occasional clump of grapes or stylized flowers. On the fourth floor the stairs let them into a wide hallway lined with open doors. It was dusty up here; Ruth sneezed, Ted said, "Bless you," and Randolph looked at him sharply before going through the nearest door on the left. This room was empty, and had another door at the far end of its left-hand wall, which proved to lead to an even steeper and narrower flight of steps. The steps ended in a trapdoor.

Randolph heaved the trapdoor open, maneuvering his sword into such a position that he had some chance of slicing anybody who might try to come down. The flat slap of the door on the floor above died in its echoes, and the echoes dwindled, and they could hear the rain hitting the roof of the tower. There was no other sound, except for everybody's breathing. The light falling through the square in the floor was a very rich yellow, mellower than sunlight and stronger than lamplight. It fell on Ruth's upturned, intent face and made minute, sparkling globes out of every raindrop in her hair. It was cold up here at the top of the house.

"Oh, *no*," said Ted. "Ruth. The color of the light."

"Oh, good grief," said Ruth. "It can't be."

"Randolph," said Ted. "Can we come up?"

Randolph, without answering or looking around, heaved

himself through the opening. There was a clattering thump, presumably his sword being dropped on the floor. Just as Ted began to worry, Randolph's head reappeared, outlined in gold, and he reached a hand back through the trapdoor to help Ruth, who stared at it dumbly.

"Go *on,*" said Ted under his breath.

Ruth took Randolph's hand, which she probably didn't need, and disappeared into the room above. Ted clambered up the last ten steps, pulled himself onto the floor, stood up, took two steps sideways to leave space for the rest of the party, and looked at the contents of the room. There were two wooden benches with arms carved like dragons' heads, a purple rug worked with blue and green dragons, and a round oak table that supported an enormous globe sparkling with motes of color and shot through with miniature lightnings. The globe was much bigger than the one in High Castle.

"Jesus!" said Ted.

"Don't swear," said Ruth, "you're getting as bad as Patrick."

"Shan's mercy!" said the Peony, scrambling to her feet behind Andrew. In that light the polished blade of her sword was the color of honey. She looked horrified. "My lords! How came this here?"

"That," said Randolph, "is the question."

"No, it isn't," said Ted, without in the least meaning to. "That isn't the Crystal of Earth."

"How do you know?" said Ruth.

"Look at it," said Ted, and when instead she went on looking at him with every evidence of exasperation, he mouthed "Edward" at her. Ruth turned obediently and stared at the shining globe.

"It's larger than the one in High Castle," she admitted.

"But of the same fashion otherwise," said Andrew.

"No, not quite," said Ted, having consulted the back of

his mind. "Isn't the light yellower? And the other one wasn't so—so active, was it? I don't remember all that lightning."

"Still," said the Peony, without lowering her sword, "what manner of thing is this?"

"Break it, and find out," said Andrew.

Ruth turned on him, pushing her hair out of her eyes with one hand and flourishing the other at him as if he were a dog that was about to jump up on her. "You sound *just* like Patrick!" she said.

"It's not a completely crazy idea," said Ted. "If the one in High Castle is the real thing, then breaking this one won't destroy the Hidden Land. And this is in Claudia's house, and it's the second of something there's supposed to be only one of."

"*If* the one in High Castle is the real thing," said Ruth.

"My Lord Randolph?" said Ted, again without meaning to. Edward, damn his eyes, must have been accustomed to getting sorcerous advice from Randolph when Fence wasn't available.

Randolph was silent for so long that Ted wanted to repeat the question, but he was afraid to. Finally Randolph said, "There are five signs whereby one may know the Crystal of Earth. These are the color of it, the shape of it, its texture, its place of abiding, and that which showeth in its depths when the full moon shines upon it."

"Lovely," said Ruth.

"What's the color of it supposed to be?" said Ted.

"As the apples of Feren," said Randolph.

Ruth fished in the pocket of her skirt and pulled out one of the little hard yellow apples that had come into season just as the five of them tried to leave the Hidden Land. "Like this?"

"That is an apple of Feren," said Randolph.

Ruth gave Ted a look compounded of relief and resignation, and held the apple up. "Well?" said she.

"How can you tell?" said Ted. "That light colors everything."

"This is profoundly silly," said Ruth.

"The method may be so," said Randolph. "The results are far other." He looked around at them. "An it please you, my lady, give Andrew the apple. My lord, you have a fine eye for color. Will you look on this globe, and descending view the apple in some other light, and return to us with your verdict?"

"Well, if none of you will play at chess the nonce," said Andrew, smiling, "this game likes me as well as another." He took the little apple from Ruth's unresisting hand, crossed the room with his graceful walk, so like his sister's, and disappeared down the steps.

"What next?" said Ted. "The shape of it? It's round. So's the other one. What about texture?"

"The Crystal of Earth," said Randolph, "though it appeareth as glass or crystal to the eye, and is called so, is yet to the hand like unto a piece of fine velvet."

Ruth caught Ted's attention and rolled her eyes heavenward. Ted did not respond; he had suddenly remembered how the panes of Claudia's window had given before his avenging hand like cloth, not glass. He walked forward to the round table, and cautiously put out his hand. The globe did not seem to have an edge at all; but about two feet in from the spot where the yellow glow faded into the weird sparkling air of the room, his hand encountered a surface that was indeed like cloth. It was nothing like velvet, but had rather the sleek, soft feel of silk. Ted looked over his shoulder at Randolph, and Randolph came forward and laid his own hand on the globe.

"Silk," said he.

"That's what I thought. Well, what's the next thing? The place of its abiding?"

"That is the North Tower of High Castle."

Ted called up a view of the house to his mind's eye, and groaned. "This is a north tower," he said, "but this isn't High Castle. Well, what's next?"

"The full moon," said Ruth, in tones of disgust.

"There is a full moon tonight," said the Peony.

"If the rain stoppeth," said Randolph, looking thoughtful.

"I thought this embassy had a certain urgency about it," said Ruth. "Do we have time to hang around testing dubious magical artifacts by methods that are, to say the least, extremely subjective?"

"Now *you* sound like Patrick," said Ted.

"Patrick may be a jerk, but his principles are not invariably wrong," said Ruth.

"This artifact," said Randolph, saying the word as if he rather liked it, "is a matter, on account of what its action on the world may be, far more urgent than this our embassy."

Ruth's face took on the most obstinate expression of which it was capable. Ted had seen it only once or twice. He had opened his mouth to forestall whatever she might be going to say, when the sound of Andrew returning distracted all of them. Andrew put his head over the edge of the trapdoor. "The light that this globe giveth," he said, "hath a more warm and golden nature than the tint of the apple."

"Our thanks to you," said Randolph. "Now, my lady, do but consider."

"What should I consider? At least two of your signs don't match this object, so why should we hang around on the off chance that the sky will clear?"

"If this be not the Crystal of Earth," said Randolph, "it is yet something like, and therefore, it may be, a most potent force for good or ill. If to damage it ruineth not the Hidden Land, it may yet ruin some land other."

"He means, Ruthie," said Ted, "that it's a dangerous thing to leave lying about."

"And suppose Claudia left it here just to delay us?"

Randolph, looking suddenly very tired, opened his mouth; and Ted realized that they did not have to argue. He was the King. "We'd better stay," he said.

Ruth gave him a betrayed and furious look. He met it, with some difficulty, while he said, "Randolph, could you go get the rest of them and tell them to stop whatever they're doing? We might as well use the kitchen, and be in out of the wet."

"As Your Majesty wills it," said Randolph.

Randolph shepherded Andrew and the Peony back down the steps. The sounds of their feet grew faint and stopped, and Ted and Ruth went on staring at each other. She looked unnervingly like Randolph. The yellow light of the globe showed little gleams of red in her hair and made her eyes the color of new leaves. It did not soften her expression.

"Come on," said Ted.

"Suppose Claudia left it here just to—"

"Okay, she might have. But it doesn't exist just to delay us. It's too like the real thing. I think it has powers."

"Well, leave somebody to guard it, or send back to High Castle for Meredith to deal with it."

"Ruth, it's just one night. The Dragon King expects us anytime before winter."

"It makes me extremely nervous," said Ruth.

"Not investigating would make me extremely nervous."

"And you're the King."

"Well," said Ted, "I'm afraid I am."

Ruth heaved a deep sigh. She no longer looked angry, or obstinate, but her face was very sober. "Thou wouldst not think," she said, "how ill all's here about my heart."

Ted decided to take a risk. "But it is no matter?"

Ruth made an angry gesture, and then suddenly smiled at him. "It is but foolery," she said. "But it is such a kind of gaingiving as would perhaps trouble a woman."

Ted said, and meant it, "If your mind dislik

obey it."

"No," said Ruth. "My mind doesn't dislike anything that much. Let's stay, and consider this thing with such a scientific detachment and precision as would make thy brother proud of us, did he know of 't."

"I'll give you the pleasure of telling him," said Ted.

Ruth did him a courtesy, very gravely; and they went downstairs to join the others.

Somebody in this party—probably, thought Ruth, either Randolph or Andrew—was efficient. By the time she and Ted had finished their discussion, matters downstairs were well advanced. The unfortunates who had been preparing food outside had descended upon Claudia's kitchen; the horses had been snugly incarcerated in one of Claudia's outbuildings; a fire had been built in Claudia's parlor and everybody's wet outer garments hung about the room to dry; and Ruth found herself in Claudia's vegetable garden with Lord Andrew, foraging for late tomatoes and the fall crop of beans.

The rain had slackened to a mild drizzle. The water-laden plants and ankle-deep mud of the garden were troublesome, but Ruth had always liked getting muddy, so long as there was a clear prospect of a hot bath afterward. There was a fire in the parlor and a huge copper tub in Claudia's kitchen; so Ruth, with a basket over her arm, was enjoying herself.

Andrew seemed to know his way around a garden; he was finding twice as many tomatoes as she was. Ruth would have ventured some pleasant remark, except that she was ignorant of his previous relations with Lady Ruth, and no longer trusted Lady Ruth to have behaved in a manner that would not embarrass somebody taking her place. Andrew did not seem disposed to conversation; he looked, in fact, sulky, and so consistently kept his eyes from Ruth that by the time they had moved on to the beans, she felt safe in staring at him.

He did look like Claudia. He didn't have her coloring; she

had hair so black you could see neither blue nor red in it, and big brown eyes, and her eyebrows, without looking in the least as though she plucked or shaped them, were arched like the ears of a cat. Andrew had ordinary brown hair and eyes of an indeterminate color between brown and green. But the shape of them was the same, and the arch of the light brows, and an extremely stubborn chin. He didn't look like a villain. But then, thought Ruth, straightening her back and hurling a bunch of blackened beans over the tomatoes to land squelchily in the patch of broccoli, he wasn't really a villain. He was there to divert suspicion from Randolph, and to subvert the King with his vile philosophies. But he believed the philosophies, and they were inaccurate rather than evil.

There was, of course, the matter of his spying for the Dragon King. If he had. It was maddening; even when the game was over, its mystifying effect lingered. Was Andrew a spy or wasn't he? Fence and Randolph thought that so being would suit Andrew's character. But to Ruth it seemed very odd that a man who did not believe in magic should serve a seven-hundred-year-old shape-changer who generally chose to appear as a dragon. She wondered how the Dragon King appeared to Andrew.

Andrew straightened his own back, and caught her looking at him. Ruth felt herself turning red, but managed not to look away. "Shall we try for some eggplant now?" she said.

"A light thought," said Andrew, "to accompany so deep a gaze." There was an accusing tone in his voice that she was at a loss to account for. He acted as if she owed him an apology.

"I was thinking about dragons," she said.

Andrew began walking toward the corner occupied by the eggplant, and she went with him. Claudia had a very good drystone wall around her garden, three feet high and solid. It was mostly gray and white stones, mixed here and there with slabs of the familiar pink. Andrew leaned against one of these and looked at Ruth. "Dragons. Those whose whim may destroy us," said Andrew, with a kind of exasperated sarcasm.

"Just one, I thought," said Ruth.

"Ah," said Andrew, "sith we know not which, we must guard ourselves 'gainst all. A monstrous dissipation of strength."

"I don't see what's the point of doing any guarding," said Ruth. She detached three fat, bloomy-purple eggplants from their stems, and decided that the others were too small to pick. "The whole nature of a whim is that it's irrational."

"Imbue thy kingly cousin with that thought," said Andrew, in what sounded like complete earnest, "and this land will prosper under him."

Ruth nodded soberly. They made a brief foray into the broccoli and then took their harvest back to the house.

Ensconced at the kitchen table, cutting up onions, were Stephen and a lithe young man with blond hair and a cheerful face. Julian, one of the King's Counselors. Ruth gave him her basket of vegetables and felt, all of a sudden, extremely cold. She had had an argument with Ted, about three years ago, concerning who, exactly, should be killed in the battle with the Dragon King. She had wanted Julian to be among the slain. She tried to remember why; oh, yes. He was a friend of Matthew's, and she wanted Matthew to be so distracted with grief that he would fail to discover that Randolph had killed the King. If she had insisted, Julian would not be sitting at Claudia's scrubbed wooden table, slicing onions; his body would be in that mass grave at the desert's edge and his ghost drifting foggy and forgetful in the land of the dead.

Ruth was shivering. She went and stood by the fire. Her cloak began to steam, which was very interesting. Andrew, appearing next to her on the hearth, held out his hands to the fire and said, "You were best to keep your eye from Julian, my lady. He honoreth Randolph exceedingly."

Whatever that meant, it was nasty. Ruth cursed Lady Ruth and settled for saying, "And so do I also, my lord."

Andrew said, "He did murder the King."

Hell! thought Ruth. They were standing close together; the fire made a lot of noise, and so did whatever was bubbling in the iron pot hanging over the flames. Stephen and Julian were the room's width away. Ruth stared Andrew in the eye and said, furiously, "That is a vile slander; I won't hear it; if you bandy it about you'll be sorry." She was so angry she stopped shivering. She stalked over to Stephen and said, "Shall I wash the beans? They're all over mud."

Stephen nodded, and Ruth bundled the beans, mud and all, into the front of her skirt and hauled them over to the sink. Though made of slate, this was recognizable as a sink, and even had running water; but there was some sort of pump arrangement, not a faucet. Ruth was good at figuring out how things worked, but she found when she tried to use the pump that her fingers were shaking and she couldn't think.

Andrew said, "If you will allow me," and she got out of his way. He filled a large red bowl half up with water and put the beans into it. He said, "Hath your heart truly changed?"

Jesus Christ! thought Ruth, staring at him. Had that prize idiot Lady Ruth been secretly engaged to Andrew as well as to Edward? Or had she just told him her troubles, whatever they were? "I honor Lord Randolph," she said, taking refuge in repetition, and also incidentally in the truth, "and I won't hear slanders about him."

Andrew drained the beans and rinsed the bowl. "Having spoke so many of them, thou hast perhaps a surfeit?" he said, still pleasantly.

Oh, hell, thought Ruth, again. God help us all. She didn't want to marry Randolph and she told Andrew all about it.

"I've come to see," said Ruth, as steadily as she could, "that speaking slander doth naught but harm."

Andrew stared at her for a good fifteen seconds. "Do I then have thy help no longer in my enterprise?" he said.

Shit, thought Ruth, for the first time in her life. She did not know what to say. If she told Andrew she would still help him, she might find out what his enterprise was. Or she might just give herself away. She shook her head. She had just realized that this gesture was ambiguous when Stephen requested the beans. Ruth snatched the bowl from the sink and carried it over to him; and she stayed in the kitchen, close to either Stephen or Julian, cutting up vegetables and, later, stirring the pots and helping Stephen decide on the seasonings. Andrew hung around for ten minutes or so, looking neither angry nor puzzled, but not looking easy, either. Julian finally sent him to set the table.

At dinner, which they ate in a hollow, chilly room with a field of goldenrod painted on the ceiling and no other decoration at all, she contrived to sit between Ted and the Peony. This gave her a sense of security, and she was able to tell Ted quietly that she had to speak to him later. Then she was able to attend to the vegetable stew and the fresh bread, which were both good. She hoped there wasn't anything unwholesome in Claudia's cloves, or her flour, or her butter, or her vegetable garden.

The conversation was all of practical matters: when the moon would rise, how few rooms they could get away with lighting fires in, who should sleep right after dinner and who later, who was to go sit with the second Crystal of Earth, who was to stand guard outside the house, and who should wash the dishes. This last problem, thought Ruth, was never easily resolved in any world, real or imaginary. She grinned at Randolph's suggestion that they scrape the dishes and leave them for Claudia, and set herself to putting names to the less-familiar faces.

The Peony was called Dittany. The Mallow was Stephen. Ted, Randolph, Andrew, Julian, she knew. That left the large, blond, gloomy man sitting next to Julian. Except for the size and the attitude, they bore a strong resemblance to each other. Of course, they were brothers. The large one was Jerome, another of Ted's counselors. He had had charge of Claudia after she tried to kill Fence; and from his charge Claudia had escaped. It was impossible to tell if this meant that there was something sinister about Jerome.

As people began folding their napkins (and who's going to wash and iron those? thought Ruth), Ted whispered, "Come upstairs. They can't expect a King to help with the dishes."

"Not just us," breathed Ruth, who had doubts about his last assertion but did not think this the time to argue about it. "We can't sneak off together."

"Randolph doesn't care now; he knows who we are."

"I'm afraid Andrew might care."

Ted raised both eyebrows; she shrugged. "Okay," said Ted, softly, "you go on up, and I'll bring Randolph."

All the adults were still arguing, amiably, about the dishes. Ruth slipped out of the room, snagging a candle in a brass holder from the sideboard as she went, and climbed quickly up the steps. She went as far as the fourth floor, to the dusty hall lined with open doors. She went clockwise around it, peering into all the rooms. Most of them were empty, but the last one on the left held a rag rug in red and gold, and six carved chairs with gold cushions. Ruth put the candle on the floor and sat down in the nearest chair. It was not dusty here. Even the windows sparkled in the small light of the candle. Outside it was still raining.

After ten minutes or so, Ruth grew uneasy with her thoughts, which were turning on Andrew's remarks and the probable character of Lady Ruth. She got up and went to one of the windows. It looked east, over a great many wet trees that faded into the misty sky. Ruth tried the other window. There were the garden and the outbuildings and a lumpy, thinly forested land through which wound dimly the rough road they had taken when they rode to fight the

Dragon King. Ruth could pick out two minute white cottages. Nothing moved in the whole drenched landscape. It couldn't be more than two in the afternoon, but it looked like twilight. Ruth leaned her forehead on the glass. Three crows flew in slow circles over the stubble fields around the cottages. Faintly, the back of her mind said, *Your future, your future I'll tell to you, / Your future you often have asked me. / Your true love will die by your own right hand, / And crazy man Michael will cursed be.*

Ruth jerked her head back from the glass, which was not cool as glass ought to be, and spoke aloud to the six chairs and the innocent rag rug. "You're a fine sort of morbid person to have in the back of one's mind. Why couldn't you die decently? A fine murderer Claudia must be."

Murder, said the remote voice, tinged this time with a slight and indefinable accent, *though it have no tongue, will speak / With most miraculous organ.*

"Oh, *thank* you!" said Ruth, more or less automatically; in the central part of her she was extremely frightened, but this was a source of information that, unlike Andrew, could not betray her true nature. "I've always wanted to be a miraculous organ."

The playing of the merry organ, / Sweet singing all in the choir.

"You're wandering," said Ruth, severely; and Ted and Randolph came into the room.

Ted had another candle, and Randolph had an iron lantern, which he hung from a hook on the wall. Ted put his candle next to Ruth's and looked at her. "You're talking to yourself."

"I am not. I'm talking to Lady Ruth."

"Is she answering?" said Ted, eagerly. "Edward doesn't pay any attention to me."

"Well, she doesn't pay much; or at least, she's easily distracted. Randolph, did Lady Ruth speak with an accent?"

"Oh, aye," said Randolph, "through having been brought

up her first five years in the Dubious Hills. We thought she had outgrown it this past summer." He closed his mouth abruptly.

"Why don't we all sit down?" said Ruth, doing so under the lantern. "Why was she brought up there?"

Randolph took the chair across from her, and Ted dragged another between them. Randolph said, "For that her lady mother loved her not."

Ruth was disgusted. You couldn't even enjoy a pure, just anger against Lady Ruth; she had had a warped childhood.

"Why did you ask?" said Ted.

"Well, I think there are *two* people in the back of my head; Lady Ruth, who speaks with an accent, and somebody else, who doesn't."

"What saith the other?" said Randolph.

"Lots of things," said Ruth. "Most recently, it said, 'The playing of the merry organ, / Sweet singing all in the choir.'"

"Well," said Randolph, dubiously, "bear it in mind. Now. Wherefore calledst thou this conference?"

Ruth, who had practiced on her way up the stairs, repeated to him the conversation she had had with Andrew.

"Oh, Ruthie!" said Ted when she had finished. "Why didn't you say you'd still help him?"

"Because," said Ruth, "I thought I'd just give myself away. His 'enterprise' doesn't have to be spying for the Dragon King. And even if it is, I don't know what that entailed. Ellen remembers, for all the good that does us."

"We do have a means of communication," said Ted.

"I didn't get the impression," retorted Ruth, "that it operated as if it were a telephone. Lord Randolph? Can one talk back and forth as if the person receiving the message were in the same room?"

"No," said Randolph, looking intrigued. "Thou sayest this telephone performeth so?"

"Yes," said Ruth, "but you can't have one here. God knows what it'd turn into. Anyway, Ted, I didn't exactly tell

Andrew I wouldn't help him. But I refuse to talk to him again without some idea of what's going on here."

"Oh, come on," said Ted. "You've been playacting with *Meredith* for three months and didn't give yourself away. Andrew should be child's play."

Ruth was exasperated. Being King was making Ted entirely too autocratic. "Look," she said. "I have the feeling that Lady Ruth's relations with Andrew were not such that I would like to take them up. Okay?"

"What?"

"She was a baggage!" said Ruth, furiously. "No better than she should be! Getting engaged to people right and left!"

"Ruth, watch it!"

Ruth was consumed with confusion and remorse. She made herself look at Randolph, who had raised his eyebrows again but did not seem notably disturbed. "Forgive me," said Ruth. "It was just a feeling I had. Maybe it was all Andrew." She was sure it had not been all Andrew, but there was no point in harrowing Randolph's feelings. If Ted would drop his insistence that she conspire with Andrew, she wouldn't have to harrow them.

"It's no matter," said Randolph.

It occurred to Ruth that neither of Randolph's women had been what he thought her. She wondered if he were stupid in that regard, or just unlucky. Either way, it seemed unwise to say more.

Ted said, "Did you want to marry Lady Ruth?"

Randolph's head came up in a gesture of such affront that Ruth wished herself at the other end of the universe. Then his face cleared, as if he had remembered that allowances must be made for them. "No," he said.

Ruth thought they should leave it at that. Ted said, "Then why—?"

"For the uniting of the two schools of sorcery," said Randolph.

Well, thought Ruth, that explained a lot. She decided to risk it. "And why did the others want Lady Ruth to marry Edward?"

"To unite rival branches of the family," said Randolph. "Look you; I believe that Edward loved her."

"Ah; but did she love him?" said Ruth.

Randolph shrugged.

"I hate this," said Ruth. Nobody having any reply to this, she went on. "We should keep an eye on Andrew."

"We should anyway," said Ted, "on account of the spying."

They were quiet; Ruth supposed there was no point in going downstairs until the dishes were done. She tried to imagine Lady Ruth's being in love with Edward. She could not conceive of being in love with Ted, though there was nothing wrong with him that a few years and a few inches wouldn't cure. She supposed she had known him too long. But then, Lady Ruth had known Edward for the same length of time. It seemed far more likely that she had loved Randolph, regardless of what other slimy intrigues she might have been plotting. Ruth looked thoughtfully at Randolph's bent head, and looked away.

CHAPTER 15

At ten o'clock, as calculated by Dittany's astrolabe, when the moon would shine through the window of Claudia's north tower and hit the golden globe, they all sat on the floor of the tower room. It had stopped raining while they slept, and a vigorous east wind had snatched the clouds over the horizon.

Ted squinted up at the globe and wished for Laura. It looked like a good thing to see visions in, if you had the knack. All he saw were minute, shifting scenes, as if somebody had made a kaleidoscope with its openings in the shapes of houses and trees and faces. Every time he had something in focus, a little stab of lightning would obliterate it.

"Get ready," said Randolph, from his post by the window. He stood up.

"Get read-y!" whispered Ruth to Ted, "the world is coming to an end!"

What had gotten into *her*? Well, maybe this *was* a Thurberesque situation. "This cold night," Ted whispered back, "will turn us all to fools and madmen."

With a dramatic suddenness that you do not expect from a world in which you have lived for three months, and which has rained all day on the road you have to ride tonight, the dark arch of Claudia's tower window lit up with silver. The roiling depths of the golden globe stilled; the rich light dimmed to gray; and from a little spark of red in the globe's center there grew the stately form of a dragon. It grew to the size of the globe, to the outermost diameter of its glow; and stopped, before Ted had to decide whether he was going to leave the room, possibly dragging Ruth with him.

The wind rattled the windows. Ted could feel his heart thumping in his ears. He had a good side view of the dragon, which floated with its tail to the trapdoor and its head toward Randolph, at the window. The dragon was bright red with touches of black. It was a very twisty, decorated dragon, with seven claws on each foot and a great many tendrils and spikes and whiskers.

Ruth leaned over so close that Ted could feel her breath in his ears, and said very softly, "Speak to it; thou art a scholar."

Ted forebore to shush her; he didn't want that huge, tapering head to look in his direction. It had black eyes with red pupils and could have looked at him, if it had wanted to, without turning its head. But its gaze was bent on Randolph. Randolph went down on one knee and bowed his forehead onto the other. It was the most extravagant gesture of respect that Ted had ever seen anybody in the Secret Country make. Randolph could not have heard Ruth; but he did speak, and in the very words with which the scholar Horatio once addressed a ghost. " 'If thou hast any sound, or use of voice, / Speak to me: / If there be any good thing to be done,/That may to thee do ease and grace to me, / Speak to me: / If thou art privy to thy country's fate, / Which, happily, foreknowing may avoid, / O, speak!' "

The dragon's long mouth opened. Ted thought that he wouldn't be at all surprised if, having been sown in the ground, those teeth came up armed men. The dragon's voice crackled and fizzed like a badly tuned radio. It said, "Knowest me not?"

And Randolph, his face stark white in the mix of gray light and moonlight, and his eyes like saucers, said, "Belaparthalion."

"Welcome," said the dragon. There was something in its voice that Ted had heard before.

Randolph said, "Art thou imprisoned?"

"A part of me," said the dragon, and Ted had it. The remote amusement of the unicorns, the dry glee, the sense of some joke beyond one's ken.

"What may we do?" said Randolph.

"For me, naught," said Belaparthalion. "For thyself, walk warily."

"What part is so imprisoned?" said Randolph. "And by whom?"

"This shape thou seest," said Belaparthalion, with a shade of sharpness, "and the speech whereby to make my captor known."

"That smells of Claudia," said Ruth.

"Most strongly," said the dragon. It did not turn its head to address her. Ted wondered if it could. It was very unpleasant to think of so large and powerful and humorous a creature held captive; not least because of what this said about Claudia.

"What may we do?" repeated Randolph.

"Thy present enterprise will serve thee well enough." There was a long pause. The dragon said, "Ask for me in the land of the dead."

"I will so," said Randolph, and bowed in the usual Secret Country fashion.

"All may yet be very well," said Belaparthalion, in a tone of resignation mixed with very little humor. It tucked its long head under its long belly and folded its spiky, fragile wings and attenuated limbs, shrank steadily to a spark of red, and vanished. The globe stayed dull gray, swallowing the moonlight.

"For the love of heaven," said Randolph, "let's find some warmer place."

"Is it the Crystal of Earth?" asked Ted.

"No," said Randolph, lighting a candle. "By no means." And he disappeared through the trapdoor before Ted could ask him anything else.

"Julian?" said Ted, irritated with his Regent. "Could you stay and guard this thing?"

"As you will, my lord," said Julian, and sat down again in the corner.

They reassembled in the kitchen; Dittany fetched Jerome from his watch outside. Stephen was asleep, and they left him alone. Andrew hung the kettle over the fire and made a large pot of very strong tea. The pot was red. The mugs, also red, were styled like those of High Castle, but each of them had a little white plaque of a unicorn's head in unglazed clay on it, and the eye of each unicorn was picked out in yellow. Ted found them unnerving, but the tea, if you put enough honey in it, was very welcome.

"Well," said Ted, when he was tired of watching people slurp tea and avoid one another's eyes. "What meaneth this apparition?"

"Yon globe," said Randolph to his empty mug, "is not the Crystal of Earth. Yet it is like unto that Crystal. Now that Crystal contains the Hidden Land in little, and whoso breaketh it breaketh also the Hidden Land. Yon globe containeth the dragon Belaparthalion, also in little." He stopped.

"Wherefore," said Ruth, impatiently, "whoso breaketh it breaketh also the dragon?"

"No," said Randolph. "Breaketh, most like, the dragon-shape merely. Dragons walk abroad in many forms. But look you, the dragon-shape is native to them, and in it alone do they possess their full powers. This is truth. 'Tis said, and may be truth also, that outwith that shape they may run mad. Wherefore, with the whim of the dragon among those things that may destroy the Hidden Land, we may not so provoke that whim."

"May it not, so imprisoned," said Andrew, "equally run mad and destroy us?" There was humor in his voice also, but it was neither remote nor dry.

"Not yet," said Randolph.

"Besides," said Ruth, "it told us not to mess with it."

"Most clearly," said Jerome, in a dissatisfied tone.

"'Twill abide 'til we come to the land of the dead," said Randolph.

"All right," said Ted. "What does this tell us about Claudia? Who can imprison a dragon? What are they vulnerable to?"

"Jests," said Randolph, "games of chance; and the promise of gold."

"These things are poison to them?" said Ruth. "Or they have a weakness for them?"

"A weakness only," said Randolph. "Unicorn's blood is poison to a dragon; naught else."

"What a very unpleasant thought," said Ruth.

"All right," said Ted again. "What do we need to do?"

"Ride posthaste to the Gray Lake," said Randolph, "where we may ask after Belaparthalion in the land of the dead. But first I think we must send word to Fence. It may be that the Council of Nine at Heathwill Library can read this riddle."

"I'll get the flute," said Ruth. "You compose your message."

Randolph got up and went into Claudia's front hall, whence he returned with a huge sheet of paper, a glass pen, and a bottle of ink. Ted observed the pen with fascination. Its nib was the usual sharpened goose-quill, but this had been attached to a hollow cylinder of red glass. You dipped the pen and filled the cylinder, and could write whole paragraphs before having to dip the pen again. Ted had struggled with ordinary dipping pens at High Castle, and hoped Randolph was taking proper notice of this improvement.

Randolph seemed to be engaged in some sort of parlor

game with Dittany, Jerome, and Andrew. Dittany took it very seriously, but gloomy Jerome warmed and brightened as it went on. Randolph kept asking them for rhymes and laughing at their suggestions. Andrew affected to be bored and skeptical, but the three most difficult rhymes were all provided by him; not to mention the abominable part-rhyme "crystal / mizzle," which, after much argument, was pronounced acceptable on the ground that the message was about a dragon.

Ted, who was tired and who had not been present at Celia's instruction of Ruth, finally figured out that they were putting the news about Belaparthalion into verse. It sounded like any anonymous fifteenth-century ballad by the time they were finished. Ruth meanwhile could be heard in the hallway, squeaking on the flute and finally producing an even and euphonious version of "Puff the Magic Dragon." Ted thought this was both silly and risky, but nothing seemed to come of it.

Ruth returned with the flute, and Randolph handed her the ink-smudged paper. Ruth scowled over it. "Maybe 'Matty Groves,'" she said. "No, I don't think so; that's awfully ill-omened. Oh, I know! We'll use 'The Minstrel Boy.' How odd; I never thought of those tunes as interchangeable." She grinned at Ted, who frowned repressively at her; she put the flute to her lips and played briskly through six repetitions of "The Minstrel Boy."

It was not until Ted, feeling bored at the fourth repetition and thinking that one would have to wrench the words to make them fit that tune, peered at the paper again, that he realized what was happening. The first three blotched verses had vanished from the paper, and the fourth was evaporating as Ruth played. There was nothing special about the pen and paper; she was doing it all with the flute. When she stopped, Randolph had a clean, empty sheet of paper and a pen full of ink. How thrifty, thought Ted. But it seemed uncanny to him. Nobody looked at all tired, and they hadn't even used up any ink. Maybe the work was all done by the receiving end. He hoped it wouldn't be too much for Laura.

"Well, good," said Ruth. She began to unscrew the mouthpiece of the flute. "I suppose now we ride away and make however many miles we were supposed to have made by now?"

"Alas, yes," said Randolph.

"At least it's stopped raining," said Ted.

"I've stopped its raining," said Randolph; "'twill begin again within the hour."

He got up and went out, followed by Dittany and Jerome, leaving Ted and Ruth to stare at each other. Andrew tipped his heavy wooden chair back like an insolent student awaiting his turn to be spoken to by the principal, smiling faintly.

Ted reflected that Edward knew little about magic, and took a risk. "When'd he do't? He didn't make a production of it."

"The Blue School doesn't," said Ruth. "It's the Green Caves that like ceremonies and drama."

"We should let Ellen join them, then," said Ted, thoughtlessly, "and give you to the Blue School."

This suggestion produced a harrowing silence. Ted looked from Ruth, who was very red, to Andrew, who had restored the chair to its upright position and was upright in it, staring at Ruth with an expression of disbelieving discovery.

"Don't look like that," said Ted to him. "I'm not going to marry her."

He plunged out of the kitchen, followed by Ruth, who grabbed the sleeve of his shirt and shook his arm violently. "Why did you say that? It would have been better to keep him guessing. Now he'll think I'm going to marry Randolph."

"Well, he'd better think so," said Ted. "If he bothers you too much, why don't you tell him about the bargain with Meredith? Blame it all on her."

"I am not telling him anything," said Ruth. She had relaxed her grip on his sleeve, but she made a sudden surprised noise like that of somebody who has been poked in the ribs, and clutched Ted's arm in a grasp that hurt. "Oh, *Lord*! What if it's nothing to do with the Dragon King? What if I said I'd help him keep Randolph from murdering William?" She giggled hysterically. "'Murder, though it have no tongue, will speak / With most miraculous organ.'"

"Shhh!" said Ted. They were out of earshot of Andrew, but not of Stephen, if he should wake up. "Stop quoting Shakespeare. Haven't we got enough of that?"

"Lady Ruth said it," said Ruth. She had stopped laughing, but she was still holding on to his arm. Her hand quivered. "I thought she meant her own murder, Ted. What if we meet the King in the land of the dead?"

"The ghosts don't remember who they are."

"But if Andrew asks the King's ghost—"

"'Don't borrow trouble,'" said Ted, quoting Agatha. Ruth seeming unconvinced, he added something of his own. "We can burn that bridge when we come to it."

Ruth laughed, as if in spite of herself. "The readiness is all," she said.

They left from behind Claudia's house, following a narrow path through a meadow and up a little rise, on the other side of which they found the road they wanted. The moon shone clear, and made sparkles on the wet leaves and stones. Ted looked over his shoulder once, and saw the dead gray light pouring out of Claudia's tower. He wondered where the golden light had gone, and half wished they had left things alone. The back of his mind said, *And, for thou wast a spirit too delicate / To act her earthy and abhorred commands, / Refusing her grand hests, she did confine thee.*

Ted thought of the intricate, muscular shape of the dragon, and the remote humor of its crackling voice. A spirit too delicate? "Somehow," he said aloud, "I can't see it."

Chapter 16

Laura had always been so petrified by the dangers of horseback riding that its discomforts had not occurred to her. By the time they stopped for lunch she was extremely stiff; by the time they stopped for the night, she hurt all over.

The Enchanted Forest did not act enchanted. It did not even keep off the rain. Laura realized that both its appearance before the Unicorn Hunt, when it had been wild and tangled, and its appearance afterward, when it had been park-like, were forms of holiday attire. Now they were seeing it in its everyday dress. It had enormous beech and oak and rowan trees; clear paths; a plenitude of yellow, white, or orange flowers like stunted chrysanthemums; a dearth of undergrowth, aside from the little bushes that look as if they ought to be growing seventy feet tall in a prehistoric forest, and turn bright red in the early fall; and convenient logs and rocks in clearings perfectly suited for building a fire and spending the night.

Laura stood under a beech tree and watched Celia and Fence build a fire. They had erected a little awning of oiled leather over it, to keep off the rain the trees let through. Fence thought this precaution unnecessary, but had given in, smiling, when Celia insisted. Ellen had gone to get water, and Patrick to find more wood. Matthew was unburdening the horses and covering them up with blankets.

Ellen trudged into the clearing, lugging a skin of water. "There's more unicorn footprints by the stream," she said.

Laura was grateful that Patrick was absent. Unicorns left flowering plants and trees behind them the way cats leave hair; Ellen had decided this morning to call these manifestations unicorn footprints, and Patrick, being Patrick, promptly began calling them fewmets. Laura suspected that he would have called them something considerably more vulgar if Celia had not had her eye on him. Laura hadn't figured out why Patrick respected Celia when he scorned everybody else in High Castle, but it was a great blessing.

"What kinds of flowers?" Laura asked, rather tardily. Ellen had dumped her water into their camp kettle and was rummaging in the heap of saddlebags.

"White violets," said Ellen, pulling out six little yellow apples and lining them up on a flat stone. "Forget-me-nots. Crocuses. And just in case you might think it's spring, a huge great clump of Michaelmas daisies."

"What's a Michaelmas daisy?"

Ellen blinked up at her. "That's weird," she said. "They're asters; kind of a dusty blue. But Princess Ellen calls them Michaelmas daisies. *Michael*-mass," she added. "Not *micklemus*, which is how we say it."

"What's Michaelmas?"

"The feast of the archangel Michael," said Ellen.

"Do they have archangels here?"

Celia came over to fetch the kettle, and Ellen said to her, "What's Michaelmas?"

"September twenty-ninth," said Celia, "is Michaelmas's Day. 'Tis a feast of Heathwill Library; something to do with the end of the wizards' wars."

"Who's Michaelmas, then?" said Laura.

"Prospero's apprentice," said Celia, simply.

"I can't stand it," said Ellen. "Michaelmas is a *person*?"

Celia smiled. "Some might dispute," she said. "A walketh very like one. Of your courtesy, find me the jars of stew i'th'other pack." She carried the kettle away to the fire.

Laura followed her. "What does Michaelmas's name mean?"

"That Michael who hath been dismissed," said Celia, straightening. "There were three named Michael on the Council of Nine when Heathwill Library was planned, wherefore they found other names for two of them."

"Who dismissed the Michael who was dismissed?"

"Prospero. Ellen, the stew?"

Ellen leapt up with a start and began searching through the other bag. Laura, with several questions begging for resolution, chose at random, and said, "Who was Prospero?"

"Say not was," said Celia. "He's of the Council of nine that found Heathwill Library; a most formidable sorcerer once, and now the most terrifying of scholars."

"Why'd he stop being a sorcerer?"

"A was of the Red School," said Celia, accepting the earthenware pot Ellen handed her and beginning to pry off its wax seal. "And their tenets did lead him on to most dreadful acts; which, when he saw their issue, he did regret."

"What acts?"

"A was Melanie's eldest brother," said Celia, rather shortly.

"Oh!" said Laura. He was one of the family that had killed a unicorn by treachery. Which was, of course, why he was alive still; the blood of a unicorn killed by treachery conferred immortality. Laura had always thought this a supremely stupid setup; it was one of the remnants of earlier games that Ted and Ruth had played before the rest of them were old enough, and they had insisted on retaining it. She wasn't at all sure that she wanted to meet Prospero, no matter how regretful he was.

People having finished their various tasks, they sat around the fire and ate their stew. Laura recognized it from dinner at High Castle the night before. She also knew, having helped Celia unpack for lunch, that there was not much of it in their baggage. She had seen quantities of dried fruit, little square cakes with oatmeal and raisins in them, dried meat, and a few long-keeping vegetables like onions and potatoes. They would not eat this well for most of the trip, unless somebody shot a rabbit or something. Laura didn't care for this notion.

And shot it with what, anyway? Nobody had a bow. Archery did not seem to be much practiced at High Castle. But there were arrow slits all over the castle. Laura looked sideways at Patrick, planning to ask him to read this riddle for her, and then she figured it out herself. The arrow slits must have been put in before the Border Magic, when it was still possible that an enemy army might besiege High Castle.

Laura came out of her reverie with a jerk as Ellen passed her a squashed apple tart. There wouldn't be more of those, either. Laura savored it while she could, and listened to the others.

"How long do you think it's likely to rain?" said Patrick.

"I'd thought it had cleared sooner," said Matthew.

"Claudia?" said Patrick.

Celia said, "'Twould be a petty persecution."

"Maybe it's just a warm-up act," said Patrick.

Nobody chose to take up this remark. Celia made tea out of half the hot water and passed the mugs around. In the wider spaces of the woods, the rain fell steadily, a background murmur very like the fire's. In their clump of beech trees, an occasional huge drop hit somebody on the head.

Celia prepared to wash the mugs and the knives and spoons in the remaining hot water, and sent Laura and Ellen to the stream to wash the plates, exhorting them to be certain to scrub them well with sand.

"There's sand by the unicorn footprints," said Ellen, when they were safely out of Patrick's hearing.

She led the way along a narrow path. On their left a vast, tumbled slope of round rocks and vivid green moss fell, nastily steep, into a misty valley of young trees. Laura was glad the plates were tin and wouldn't break. She could hear water running at the bottom of the valley. She followed Ellen, and the path turned and dragged them slipping and stumbling down the rocky slope and disgorged them suddenly onto a flat grassy place overflowing with flowers. The stream hissed whitely over a little falls and widened into a pool whose glossy surface was perfectly still and unmoving. It had stopped raining. Or, thought Laura—picking her way among dusty blue and purple and dark red daisy-like flowers the size of the plates she carried; and clumps of white violets whose leaves were the size of her hand and their flowers as big as an ordinary daisy; and forget-me-nots of the proper size but of a blue almost luminous; and crocuses, gold and purple and white, the size of tulips—it just wasn't raining *here*.

They knelt at the stream's edge, and scrubbed the plates. The remnants of the stew were remarkably clingy; Laura supposed they shouldn't all have sat there brooding and let it get cold.

"I'd like to call a unicorn," said Ellen, stacking her last plate with the others and rinsing her hands in the water.

Laura, who had two plates left, scrubbed harder. The water was cold but very silky to the touch. "Do you think we could have a drink?" she said.

"That won't call a unicorn. What did you do to make the one you saw show up?"

"I didn't make it show up," said Laura. "I whistled 'The Minstrel Boy.' Then I whistled like a cardinal; and a cardinal came. I said to it, 'Please, I'm looking for a unicorn.' And it flew away, and made a fuss when I tried to follow it. So I waited, and it came back with Claudia. Claudia and I had a stupid conversation, and she told me that the unicorns had gone south for the winter, and she left. And I looked down and there was a unicorn standing in the water."

Ellen stood up and shook water off her hands. She wore an expression unnervingly like Patrick's when he was clicking through in his mind the possibilities of a given situation. "It was the cardinal," she said. "I bet it was. Let's whistle."

"No!" said Laura, standing up in a hurry and dropping all her plates. "We don't want them to know we're here."

"No; we don't want them to know where we're going."

"Well, once they know we're here they could follow us."

"They could have been following us all along," said Ellen.

Laura knew the sinking feeling of somebody who is going to lose an argument, because it isn't really an argument at all. She said, "There's no point in asking for trouble."

"We don't know it will be trouble," said Ellen. She tipped her head back, and a little breeze stirred her crazy black hair. She whistled, clearly and accurately, the song of the cardinal. And a red bird dropped from the empty spaces of the forest and landed on her shoulder. It was the biggest cardinal Laura had ever seen. It was as large as a crow.

"Please," said Ellen, standing very still, "we're trying to find a unicorn."

The cardinal rose off her shoulder and flew downstream. Before it had disappeared, they heard a regular sloshing, and a unicorn came wading through the water, unconcernedly, as if it were walking in a field of grass. Laura wondered if they really liked water so much, or just liked getting other people wet. Both the unicorns she had talked to had appeared in the water.

This one strode into the middle of the little pool and wheeled to face them. Laura looked at it carefully; its eyes were not gold, but violet. It was not Chryse, the one she had just told Ellen about. It might be the one she had talked to in the lake. She wondered if she and Ellen looked alike to the unicorns. Somehow she doubted it. She wished Ellen would say something; she had summoned the unicorn, after all.

The unicorn stood there with its head cocked as if it heard

something in the distance. Laura became aware of stirrings and rustlings in the woods around them, as every animal that could tell a unicorn was here came out of its burrow or down from the sky. At least in this forest, the unicorn was the king of beasts.

It was extremely beautiful without seeming in the least unreal. Laura could feel its warmth from three feet away; it had whiskers on the sides of its nose; its eye, however purple, was properly liquid. The tuft of hair on the end of its tail was wet and draggled. But it looked so *clean.* No white animal looked truly white; white cows or horses had dingy yellow or gray casts to their coats, and sheep were just hopeless. Laura had seen white cats that were almost as clean as the unicorn. She wondered if unicorns groomed themselves like cats. She doubted that they would have the tongue for it. She watched the orange fish flash around the unicorn's legs in the shallow water of the little pool, and thought of cats, dozens of cats, washing the unicorn until its coat gleamed. They would get hairballs you wouldn't believe.

"The hair is not so coarse as that," said the unicorn, in the clear and piercing voice of its kind. "Thou thinkst of horses."

"No," said Laura, startled into the truth; "goats."

"What?" said Ellen.

"I should rather ask thee that, youngling," said the unicorn. "Wherefore stoppest thou me?"

Laura distinctly heard Ellen gulp. "I hope we didn't disturb you," said Ellen.

The unicorn said, "Hoping not to disturb, wherefore didst thou send my messenger?"

"Because," said Ellen, more boldly, "we weren't sure he was your messenger. Can you tell us about the cardinals?"

The unicorn said, "'I can' must wait upon 'I will.'"

"Do you know who we are?" said Ellen.

"I know who you do seem." The unicorn took two steps

toward them in the water and nuzzled the top of Laura's head. The unicorn smelled like very clean, dry, crispy autumn leaves; which was to say, it smelled like Fence. Laura shivered just the same. The unicorn blew vigorously into Ellen's hair, altering it very little, and backed up again. "You carry your seemings within," it said, "but you are other. Read me your riddle and I will read you mine."

"Don't you mean that the other way around?" said Ellen.

The unicorn made a very odd noise, like somebody unpracticed trying to play a trumpet. "As courtesy to the visitor, no doubt," it said. "No matter that the visitor be uninvited and a most pert intruder. Well. The cardinals serve whom they will and also whom they must. They must serve Belaparthalion; they do serve the Outside Powers, none knoweth by choice or upon compulsion; and they will serve us. Now, what of thy oddness?"

"That's a very long story," said Ellen.

Laura gave her a reproachful look. It was nevertheless true that the gray light was heavier than it had been, that it was getting very chilly, and that from every part of the stream except the pool in which the unicorn stood, wisps of mist were rising off the water. It was also true that telling their story to a unicorn might not be the wisest thing to do. Unicorns were odd; they could be malicious. The only one Laura knew to be well disposed toward the Secret Country was Chryse, and this was not she.

"I think we're out of our depth," she said.

"Thou standest not in the water," said the unicorn, in a tone of mild pleasure.

"Contrariwise," said Laura, startling herself, "I and my kinsmen stand in water so deep that every seventh wave doth choke us. An thou shouldst be that seventh wave, what then?" Whew, she thought, where'd that come from?

"I?" said the unicorn, rather sharply. "I made not this bargain."

Both the unicorn and Laura looked at Ellen, who cleared

her throat and said, "I'll keep it; but may I ask counsel of those wiser than I am?"

"Ask," said the unicorn, with a great deal of humor.

Ellen stared at it, and then stared at Laura. Laura looked back at her, shrugged helplessly, and then grinned. "Ask what harm will be done," she suggested. Maybe the unicorns liked ironic situations even when the irony was against them.

Ellen said slowly, "We know thee not. How if to tell us our tale does us harm, or harm to those we love?"

"Bring on thy counselors," said the unicorn; "this counsel is beyond my ken."

"I'll be right back," said Ellen, and before Laura could move she had scrambled up the slope and disappeared, leaving Laura on the stream's edge with a unicorn and a motley collection of birds, squirrels, fish, foxes, and badgers. On the other side of the water they lined the bank like a shelf of stuffed animals, they held so still. On her side, Laura could hear them rustling up on the hill, but the only creatures she could see were well up in the trees.

Laura decided that she might as well sit down. She did so very carefully, both because of her horse-battered muscles and because of the animals. As soon as she was quiet again, three squirrels ran down the nearest tree and sat a foot away from her on the sand. She hoped the badgers and the foxes would stay farther back. *But keep the wolf far thence, that's foe to men*, said a distant voice in her mind. It wasn't Princess Laura. She wondered if it were the unicorn. She didn't want to ask. It would only end in another awkward bargain that nobody could see the consequences of. Ellen was brave, but sometimes she seemed to have no sense.

Ellen sprinted up the rocky path at a reckless pace, panting, and scattering before her dozens of startled small animals. The squirrels swarmed up the trees and scolded her, and farther overhead than that she heard the harsh, laughing voice of a crow. She could also hear her traveling companions before she was halfway back to the camp. They were singing rounds.

Ellen burst into the clearing. "Come quickly!"

Celia and Patrick stood up, and Patrick said, "*Where's Laura?*"

He was taking his commission from Ted seriously. Ellen felt a twinge of doubt; but in what safer company could she have left Laura? The unicorns might confuse her, but they would never hurt her. Patrick was starting to look murderous, and Celia's and Fence's expressions to change from exasperation to concern. Ellen squashed the temptation to make them all squirm, in compensation for not trusting her, and said, "She's fine. There's a unicorn, and it wants us to tell it everything!"

"I doubt that," said Fence, dryly.

"I'm afraid I made a mess of things," said Ellen, "but you can tell me about it later. Just come on."

While the grown-ups were exchanging a variety of glances and mutterings, Patrick came over and said, "What's going on, Ellie?"

"It's your fault," said Ellen. "I was testing a hypothesis. But it was right, and then I had a unicorn to deal with. You can't just say, 'Thank you so much, go away now' to a unicorn, the way you can with atomic particles."

"You can't say that to them, either," said Patrick. "The trouble with *you* is that you are treating a problem in sociology, or diplomacy, as if it were an exercise in physics. Have a little sense. Atomic particles aren't sentient."

"I think magic is *like* that," said Ellen. "It seems to have personalities in it." She explained what she had done, and Patrick snorted.

"That wasn't magic," he said. "You weren't testing a magical hypothesis. You were just—"

"Ellen," said Celia. "Fence and I had best bear thee company. Patrick, speak not so sharp to thy sister, but help Matthew in the rigging of the tents."

"Ha!" said Ellen.

"Gloat not," said Celia. "What's this but the very thing Patrick is forbidden to do?"

Ellen didn't know if she meant speaking sharp, or experimenting with the Secret Country. It was not the time to ask. She led Fence and Celia down the steep path to the stream. Laura had sat down; otherwise everything was as it had been. Laura looked around when she heard them, and her face was relieved.

"Give you good even," said Fence to the unicorn.

"My sister speaketh well of thee," said the unicorn. Ellen wondered if it meant Chryse.

"I joy to hear it," said Fence, very gravely.

"Lady Celia," said the unicorn, "when thou returnst, do thou sing more merry."

"As you will," said Celia.

"So, then," said the unicorn, "these are thy counselors?"

"They are," said Ellen.

"Ask their counsel, then," said the unicorn.

"Should we tell the unicorn who we are?" said Ellen.

"Mercy, child," said Celia, swiping a loosened strand of yellow hair off her scarred forehead and sitting down on a rock. A pigeon and two mice scuttered off behind her. The unicorn made a little whistling noise at them, and the mice came out of the clump of asters they had hidden in and sat by Celia's right boot. Celia didn't look at them. "How should I know?" she said to Ellen. "Thy story's odd, but not o'er-merry. How like the unicorns but half a loaf?"

"Fence," said Ellen, feeling impatient.

"How madest thou this tangle?" said Fence to Ellen.

"Out of curiosity and thoughtlessness," said the unicorn.

"Is such advantage to thy credit?" demanded Fence.

The unicorn considered him with a large, purple, dubious eye; but when it spoke, it sounded on the verge of laughter. "We'll take the cash," it said, "and let the credit go."

Nor heed the rumble of a distant drum, said some other voice, dimly. Ellen saw that Laura jumped and Celia rolled her eyes, and surmised that they had heard it too.

Fence said, "These two are strangers; they know thee not."

"They shall," said the unicorn. "Wherefore, first must I know them. Tell thy tale, black maiden; thy fair cousin's cold."

Tom's a-cold, came the distant voice, that was neither inside your head nor outside it. *Do poor Tom some charity, whom the foul fiend vexes.*

Ellen felt rather cold herself. "Couldn't Fence tell it?" she said. "He'll take less time than I would."

Love's not Time's fool, remarked the voice.

"Hold your tongues," said the unicorn, mildly.

Everybody was quiet, including the voice. The unicorn said, "Very well, then Fence shall tell't."

Celia sat down by Laura; Ellen, feeling disgraced without knowing what she would have wanted to do differently, stayed lurking in the background with the bolder squirrels; and Fence came to what would have been front stage, center, if the unicorn had been a theatre audience, and began to speak.

He did in fact deliver an admirably abbreviated account of their story; its flaw was that it stated as facts a number of things Ellen thought were just conjecture. He described their game briefly, and said that the power of their thoughts had been so great that Claudia had become aware of them, and knitted them unawares into her schemes. He said that she had killed the real royal children in order to allow the five who had played them into the Secret Country. Everything else he told scrupulously.

The unicorn stood perfectly still during this recitation, with its eye bent on Fence in a way Ellen thought should unnerve him. It looked skeptical, but as if it were willing to put up with much for the sake of a good story. When Fence had finished, it said, "This is none of our doing. What name did the red man give himself?"

Fence looked at Laura, who said, "Apsinthion."

"Wormwood," said the unicorn. "My lord Fence, knowest thou not that name?"

Fence stood very still, in the way he had; then he smacked his hand into his forehead. "The Judge of the Dead," he said. "Oh, this likes me not. Wormwood indeed! That's the unchanciest power I know."

Let the galled jade wince. The worm is your only emperor for diet, said the distant voice. Others joined it. *Men have died from time to time, and worms have eaten them, but not for love. Then worms shall try this—*

"Hold your tongues!" said the unicorn in the water, in a way that chilled Ellen's skin like an ice cube going down her back. "Be of good cheer, thou wizard. Anyone may put on a name, as one may put on a red robe and an aspect somewhat like thine and somewhat like thy student's. Where's he?"

It asked this question reflectively, but Ellen saw Fence jump. "He goeth south, with an embassy to the Dragon King, whom lately we bested in battle."

"Bid him have a care," said the unicorn.

There was a long pause; Ellen saw that Fence was quite simply frozen where he stood, and that Celia was appalled. It meant something, then, if a unicorn told someone to have a care. Whom were they talking about? Fence's student; was that Ted, or Randolph? Probably Randolph. Fence gave himself a little shake, and bent his knee. "More thanks than I can say," he said.

"Thou shalt say it in time," said the unicorn.

Ellen didn't like the sound of this. She said, "Excuse me. Was your answer about the cardinals or your reading of our riddle, or can you tell us more? I mean," she amended hastily, "will you?"

"Ask," said the unicorn, pleasantly enough.

"*Several* cardinals have done mysterious things," said Ellen, and we'd like to know on whose orders they did them."

"Say on."

"First of all," said Ellen, "in our world, a cardinal showed Ted and Laura the Secret House."

"Spare those stories," said the unicorn. "All events in your own world you must lay on the doorstep of the Outside Powers. We have no kingdom there."

"Drat!" said Ellen. "Sorry. Okay. The first day we came here, Benjamin cross-examined Ted about why he was acting so oddly. And a cardinal whistled, and Benjamin stopped."

"Nay," said the unicorn. "None of ours."

"Were *any* of the ones that rescued us from betraying ourselves yours?"

"How so, when we knew naught you might betray?"

The unicorn's words were impatient, but its tone was not. It sounded like somebody musing over his letters in a friendly game of Scrabble. Ellen decided that she could go on. "All right, then. The strange place, where the air is like a sheet of glass and the sky is the wrong color and you feel too small, the place Lady Ruth stood in to bargain with the Guardian of the River of King Edward's life. She was there another time—"

"Playing the fool with Shan's Ring. We know."

"There was a cardinal singing in the yard."

"The burden of that song," said the unicorn, rather grimly, "was 'get thee gone.'"

"Thank you," said Ellen. "She did." She fought down the desire to question the unicorn in detail about the strange place Ruth had visited. That wasn't in the bargain. She would have to consider carefully just how much any information was worth to her, before she asked the unicorns for more of it. She had known what they were like; she had made much of it up. But, perhaps because she still felt them to be her own creations, even though she knew better, she had not really taken them seriously until now. She hoped her frivolity would not cost somebody else dear. "Just a few more," she said. "What about the cardinal that brought Claudia to Laura, after the Unicorn Hunt?"

"That cardinal did bring Chryse," said the unicorn. "Did Claudia choose to come, blame not the cardinal."

"I'll tell you something, then," said Laura. Ellen had almost forgotten she was there. "Either Claudia or the cardinal wanted to make me think the cardinal brought her."

"The cardinal deceiveth not," said the unicorn. "But Claudia is a tale-weaver."

It sounded definitely, thoroughly, unmistakably amused. Ellen was seized with irritation. "It's nothing to snort at," she said. "We are all tale-weavers too, and look what we've done. And we didn't even know. Claudia knows. What if she weaves a tale about *you*?"

"She hath," said the unicorn, with a sort of rippling chuckle like somebody running a hand along the keys of an out-of-tune piano. "She did tell thy fair cousin that all our kind run south for the winter, as if we were the robin or the cuckoo. Yet here am I to jest with thee."

"No, no!" said Ellen, exasperated beyond bearing. "She only *said* that, off the top of her head. What if she wove a real tale about you, with all her mirrors and her little diamond windows, nudging you around the way she nudged Lord Randolph?"

There was a very long silence. The forest about them was dark. Their clearing had still a thin gray light like that of a rainy afternoon. It was not coming from the unicorn precisely; if you looked at the shadows, it appeared to be coming from directly overhead; but up there were only the dark branches of the shadowy trees. Ellen could see Celia's intent, somber profile, and the back of Fence's untidy head, and Laura's hunched figure with the braids unraveling down her back. Finally Fence stirred.

"Forgive us," he said, "but I fear me you must think on this."

"No," said the unicorn. "Thou thinkst we must fear't."

"'Twould serve," said Celia, in the brisk tone of somebody telling you to take out the garbage, "if thou didst but answer the question."

"What if?" said the unicorn. "What then? Why, then we should see infinite jest and most excellent fancy." It looked from one to the other of them, Celia, Fence, Laura, then Ellen, with its great purple eyes; and then back, very thoughtfully, at Fence. It bowed its head so low that the fringe of its mane trailed in the water. "Fare you well," it said. "This meeting shall cost some dear." It flung its head back and plunged down the stream, showering Fence and Laura with water, sprinkling Celia, and hitting Ellen with exactly three drops, one in each eye and the third smack on top of her head.

"Smart-ass!" she muttered, and walked forward to join the others. The unicorn's last statement was profoundly upsetting. "Fence? What did that mean?"

"I know not," said Fence, shaking water out of his hood.

The gray light lingered behind the unicorn, enclosing them in a cheerless sphere of illumination that made everybody look unhealthy, as fluorescent lights do. Fence's round face was hollow with sheer worry. Ellen didn't like to see him looking that way. She put her hand on his shoulder, which she could do easily, she had grown so much this summer. Fence patted the hand and said, "I'm yet revolving on an earlier wheel: if the man in red that sent you back in truth is the Judge of the Dead, wherefore should he send you but to ensure Randolph's death? This Judge did give up Ted, for which Randolph is his payment; maybe he groweth impatient."

Ellen asked a question she had learned to ask. "Have I caused a lot of trouble?"

"That's the question," said Celia. "Didst thou cause it, or didst thou but discover it?"

Laura said, "It *was* a trap? I made Ted go; he didn't want to follow the cardinal."

"Remember what the unicorn said," said Fence, smiling at her. "Anyone may put on a name. But we shall warn Randolph, and walk warily."

"And tell Matthew," said Celia.

Go and tell Lord Grenville, said the distant voice, *that the tide is on the turn.*

"Hold your tongue!" said Ellen; and for a wonder, it did.

CHAPTER 17

LAURA was very sleepy when they got back to camp. While she was gone, Matthew and Patrick had put up two tents whose shadows danced crazily in the firelight, like jigsaw puzzles falling and falling, on all the trunks of the trees. They were singing.

"Lord Rameses of Egypt sighed / Because a summer evening passed, / And little Ariadne cried / That summer fancy fell—"

"Matthew, for the love of heaven!" said Celia, coming forward. "The unicorn hath bid us sing more merry."

Matthew stood up to greet her. "If that's the worst—no," he said. "I see 'tis not."

Celia smiled at him. "Let's sing more merry, and then we'll tell you," she said.

"More merry?" said Fence, in tones of disgust. "We'll give them more merry. An they'll rant, we'll mouthe as well as they."

Celia sat down next to Laura, Fence on the other side of the fire.

"It isn't funny," said Ellen, in a stifled voice.

"I know," said Fence. "Matthew, wilt thou sing Terence?"

Matthew sat down again, between Celia and Fence, and grinned. "Gladly," he said. "Celia?"

"I trust you know what you're about," said Celia, very dryly. "Let's sing and be done with it."

Matthew said, not altogether seriously, "Spite the unicorn and drown thyself."

"That saying," said Fence, "was made by a unicorn for the jest of watching folk obey it. Sing."

And all the grown-ups did.

"Terence, this is stupid stuff:
You eat your victuals fast enough;
There can't be much amiss, 'tis clear,
To see the rate you drink your beer.
But oh, good Lord, the verse you make,
It gives a chap the belly-ache."

It was a long song and not, except for the rollicking tune, what Laura would have called merry. It had Milton in it, which was disconcerting. The whole song was disconnected. First they sang about drinking, which was where Milton came in, for some odd reason; then they sang about how the world had far more ill in it than good, so that making verse that gives a chap a belly-ache constituted "friending" said chap "in the dark and cloudy day"; and then they sang a creepy story about a king who ate poison and thus immunized himself against the plots of his enemies.

"They put arsenic in his meat
And stared aghast to watch him eat;
They poured strychnine in his cup
And shook to see him drink it up."

Thank goodness, thought Laura, that Randolph's not here. She heard Fence's light voice falter, when it was he who had proposed the song; he should have remembered what was in it.

"They shook, they stared, as white's their shirt:
Them it was their poison hurt."

Laura remembered Ted's account of how Randolph had looked after the poisoning. The trouble was, it wasn't only

Randolph his poison had hurt; the King was dead. Too bad Fence hadn't sung him this song. But nobody expected Randolph to do such a thing. The Hidden Land was not the East where kings get their fill, before they think, of poisoned meat and poisoned drink.

"—I tell the tale I heard told.
Mithridates, he died old."

"What a gruesome song!" said Ellen.

"'Twill like the unicorns well," said Fence.

Matthew said, "Now, Celia, thy tale?"

"Fence's, I think," said Celia.

"Nay, I did tell the last tale needed telling," said Fence; "my purse is empty."

"As empty as the ocean when three little boats have brought home a good catch," said Celia, rather sharply, "but as you will."

As Celia spoke, Laura watched Matthew's face, with its sardonic bones and deep eyes. He was utterly impassive until Celia came to the part where the unicorn said that Randolph should have a care. Then he put a hand over his eyes.

"Shan's mercy!" said Matthew. "What hath Randolph done?"

"He hath made an unwise bargain with the Judge of the Dead," said Fence, with a perfect tranquility that made Laura's eyes prick with tears. Celia looked up with a stricken face.

"The bargain for Edward's life," said Matthew, in a throttled voice. "No; for Ted's?"

"'Twas for Edward's life," said Fence.

"And Randolph did agree?" said Matthew.

"Randolph," said Fence, bitterly, "did suggest it."

"And Edward did agree?"

"No," said Fence. "Nor Ted neither."

"How then call this a bargain?"

Patrick made a restless movement; Ellen thrust an elbow into his side; he turned his head and gave her a steady, opaque look. Underlit by the fire, his face was much older.

"Ted's alive," said Fence.

"But Randolph did promise for Edward's life?"

"Now look," said Ellen.

"Hush," said Matthew. "They err but seldom. Cannot we turn this to some good account?"

"Randolph may do so, at the Gray Lake," said Fence.

"But the unicorn saith, he must have a care?"

Somewhere nearby, muffled, two notes sounded, as if someone had begun to play a flute and given up. Celia jumped up and ran for the pile of baggage, from which she returned carrying the flute of Cedric and a large, flat leather pouch. The flute played two more notes as she sat down, and two more. Laura recognized, with resignation, that it was playing "The Minstrel Boy." "The minstrel boy to the war" was as far as it had gotten.

Celia took a sheet of thick paper from the pouch and flattened it out on the rock she had been sitting on. Then she removed, to Laura's astonishment, a little jar of ink and a pen. She filled the pen, held it ready over the paper, and with her other hand held out the flute. "Come, Laura," she said.

Laura got up, walked slowly around the fire, and took the flute. It was as cold as if it had been carved out of ice. She said, "Do I play 'The Minstrel Boy'?"

"Aye," said Celia. "As many times over as thou art moved."

This turned out to be six, by which time Laura's fingers were numb and her lips burned.

"There!" said Celia, laying down the pen and shaking her hand.

Laura followed this example. There was a constriction in her chest like the feeling a bout of bronchitis had once given her. She wondered if they had antibiotics here.

Celia waved the paper in the air gently, and laid it down on the rock again. Fence and Patrick joined her. Matthew pressed gently on Laura's shoulder until she sat down, and then handed her a tin cup of tea.

"Something's amiss," said Celia.

"Read it," said Matthew; he was watching to see if Laura would drink the tea, so she drank some hastily.

Celia read it.

"Belaparthalion lived alone.
The wind blows the sand about.
Belaparthalion cracked dry bones.
The waves on the shore run in and out.
Belaparthalion cracked dry jests.
The unicorns rhyme in Griseous Lake.
Three wizards came at his behest.
The dry bones in the desert bake."

"That doesn't fit the tune!" said Laura.

"Not well, no," said Celia. "Sometimes that can't be helped. But look you, all the message is but those verses, writ thrice o'er."

"Belaparthalion," said Matthew, thoughtfully. "Think you it likes him not that we flute his name hither and yon?"

"Why *should* they flute his name in the first place?" demanded Patrick. "I thought they were going to the Gray Lake and then to the Dragon King."

"Griseous Lake!" said Ellen.

"Aye; 'tis the same," said Celia. "They will not arrive there for some several days."

"But Belaparthalion?" said Patrick.

"What makes you think the real message was about Belaparthalion?" said Ellen.

"The very alteration of such a message," said Matthew, "doth feed on its original. None may alter it into utter falsehood."

"Could we send them a message back asking what the hell they think they're doing?" said Ellen.

Celia looked around and grinned at her. "Not this night," she said. "Laura and I are weary. We must send the warning to Randolph, that's more urgent. Laura, canst thou play 'Heat o' the Sun'? One verse only; that one begins, 'No exorciser harm thee.' Randolph will know what's meant by't."

"I think so," said Laura, reluctantly.

"No!" said Fence. "Not that. 'Twill be misconstrued."

"What, then?" said Celia; she was clearly puzzled, but willing to let Fence have his way since he spoke so vehemently.

Fence pressed his fingers to his eyes, the way Laura's mother would do when she had a headache. "Laura, canst thou play 'What if a Day'?"

Laura thought about it, and the fingerings rose from the bottom of her mind like fish coming up in clear water when you drop the breadcrumbs in. "Yes," she said. She was very tired.

"The second chorus," said Fence. "As slowly as liketh thee."

Laura picked up the flute and almost dropped it, it was so cold and her fingers so sore. But once she had gotten them placed for the first note, they played of themselves. The words ran along in her mind. *All is hazard that we have, / There is nothing biding; / Days of pleasure are like streams / Through fair meadows gliding. / Weal and woe, time doth go, / Time is never turning; / Secret fates guide our states, / Both in mirth and mourning.*

"Many thanks," said Fence, and he picked up the hand from which the flute was drooping and kissed it, with a flourish. Laura would have enjoyed this more if he had not also deftly taken the flute from her and given it to Celia.

"Fence," said Celia. "This bargain for Ted's life."

"It's done," said Fence.

Matthew looked at him. "Let's consider this false message," he said.

Patrick suggested that it was in fact the true beginning of the message Randolph had sent; Celia said Claudia was too canny for that. There was an argument concerning whether it was Claudia who had interfered. The only conclusion Matthew, Fence, and Celia could agree on was that Belaparthalion had had some jest with Randolph and that Belaparthalion had not been at his best when he had it. Their reasoning was obscure, and their attempts to explain it worse.

"Explain something else to me," said Patrick, who had been pestering them the most, and who usually knew when it would be best to stop.

"Ask it," said Fence.

"How could you forget the Judge of the Dead's name?"

Fence's face cleared; Laura wondered what he had thought Patrick would ask. "The Judge of the Dead hath a hundred names," he said. "I learned them when I was ten years old, and have had little enough use for them since. Also, Apsinthion is a jesting name, by which you would not address or invoke that power; and so 'tis of little matter."

"He *would* use it outside, to the children," said Celia, in the tone Ruth would use to say, "That's *just* like Patrick."

"Is the Judge of the Dead a unicorn?" asked Ellen.

"Nay, naught so solid," said Fence.

"He seems to have the same sort of sense of humor."

"The unicorns did choose the name," said Fence.

"Why'd he let them?" said Ellen.

"Ask him when thou meetest him," said Fence. "I did undertake to answer one question, and that from thy brother." He spoke lightly; but Laura shivered.

Ellen returned to the previous subject. "Can't we just send a quick message asking what they meant to tell us?"

"You," said Celia, rounding on her, "are in no case to ask for favors. Do you consider yourself under the same stricture as your brother touching experimentation." She rolled the word around in her mouth as if it tasted sour.

That tone of voice and the use of the rebuking "you" would have shrivelled Laura up like a raisin. Ellen said, "But—"

"Do you so consider yourself."

"Yes! I won't meddle anymore. But can't we just—"

"Tomorrow," said Celia.

"Grown-ups everywhere," said Ellen. "You're all alike."

"To bed," said Celia, whereupon both Ellen and Laura burst out laughing.

"Aren't we going to set a watch?" asked Patrick.

"Against what?" said Fence. "Canst thou prevent a pouring of poetry into the porches of our dreaming ears, by all means make thy dispositions."

"I'll think about it," said Patrick.

Fence only chuckled. They all went to bed, the children in one tent and the grown-ups in the other; and if anybody poured poetry into Laura's dreaming ears, she did not notice. She dreamt that she was back in school and had forgotten her homework. She woke up in a cold sweat to Ellen's snoring, and Patrick's light breathing, and a dapple of moonlight on the blackened remnants of the fire. The weather had cleared, and nobody cared that she had not looked up twenty-five botanical terms in the dictionary and copied down their major definitions in a clear hand with no mistakes in the spelling. Nobody was bothering her at all; but everybody else was bothered. Laura stared at the dark and tried to decide which was worse, and fell asleep again.

CHAPTER 18

WHEN the song that summoned her came next, it was not from a dream. Claudia walked down the hall to her back room, and laid a hand upon the yielding glass, and smiled. The summons was stronger than the spell that kept her here. It might be that she had a choice of where to go, that the summons, being played not by intention but in ignorance, might unlock all her windows. She called the cats, quickly; three of them came. She moved her hand on the glass a little, and said, "Krupton Chorion."

She stepped through, the three cats winding about her ankles like some benign variation of the Nightmare Grass. She stood in the back room of her whole, clean, true house in the Hidden Land, and knew that someone had been here. *Someone*, said the voices, fading, *has been sitting in my chair.*

The cats, pleased to be home, purred thunderously. She could still feel the summons. It had no physical power, but it called monotonously, like a cat in a locked room. It came to Claudia that it might benefit her to know where her summoner, however unconscious, was. She moved in the direction of the calling voice, and peered into the little diamond pane toward which it guided her. The stuff of the pane wavered like water. She saw the false Laura just putting the flute away beneath the huge trees of the Enchanted Forest. But she saw also, fading in and out like an agitated water-beast, the counterfeit Lady Ruth in the parlor of this very house, under the ceiling painted with goldenrod, playing a mundane flute. Andrew was tardy; or disobedient; or likeliest of all, cautious. She snatched at the poem as it ran between the shivering lines of the two scenes she saw, snapped it off short, and let the greater part of it fall back into the house.

It spoke tunefully out of the sunny air of her porch, in the mingled voices of Randolph and Andrew and others she did not know. She heard it through and laughed. Andrew had not been disobedient, nor very cautious. His abominable rhymes had let her catch the song and turn it aside.

She took her hand from the window, which settled into the scene of the Enchanted Forest. Claudia looked at it, and frowned. "Past," she said, "passing, or to come?"

She went quickly into the kitchen. The sink was full of scraped dishes, and a smell lingered of garlic and tomatoes.

"Past," said Claudia. "Belaparthalion."

She ran across her front hall and took the steps two at a time, not because she thought she could do anything but because she was too curious to go slowly. The cats bounded after her; this was a game they liked. One last lone voice said thoughtfully, *With help of her most potent ministers, / And in her most unmitigable rage.*

They had spoken to Belaparthalion, but they had not released him. She strode around to lean on the window, and addressed his remote, red, whiskered face. "Didst thou not fix them with thy glittering eye?" she said.

The englobed dragon was like a carved and enameled piece of jewelry. The light of the globe was as gray as the moon. She waited, and slowly the golden color flooded back, and the dragon closed its red-and-black striped lids, opened them again, and smiled. "Did thy sojourn like thee," he said, "in thy old house?"

"Liketh thine thee, in thy new house with my sputtering beasts?"

"We're well enough," he said.

"Is thy power so minished that thou couldst not bring thy minions to release thee?"

"My power is so well kept," said he, "that I did persuade them from that rescue. I know this prison cell, and I know you. I'll come forth in my true shape, or not at all."

"And shall Chryse come for thee?"

But he would not answer her.

CHAPTER 19

ON their second night, the embassy to the Dragon King camped on the enormous plain of waist-high grass from which, farther south, the mountains would rise with great abruptness.

The air was very still and crisp, and the huge stars of the Secret Country sprinkled the darkening sky. Ted looked at the circle around the fire, and grinned despite himself. They were arranged in such a way as to make everybody unhappy. He was sitting between Andrew and Randolph. Ruth was on Andrew's other side, but Andrew couldn't bother her because on Ruth's other side was Dittany, who had noticed that Ruth disliked Andrew, and seemed to take pleasure in getting in his way. Ted couldn't talk to Randolph about anything important because on Randolph's other side was Julian; Julian was made uncomfortable by having to sit next to Stephen, who had annoyed him the first day out with some theory of farming. Stephen had to put up with Julian's refusal to discuss his theory, and also with the presence of Dittany, who called him "Boggy"—presumably because mallows grow in marshes—and only laughed in genuine delight when Stephen snarlingly addressed her as "Dropsy"—presumably because peonies fall over in midsummer. But Dittany had to put up with Jerome, who didn't think there was any dignity in the entire exchange; while Jerome had to put up with the exchange on one side, and a lack of attention from Dittany on the other, because Dittany was keeping Andrew from bothering Ruth.

Ted laughed. Everybody instantly looked at him. He watched them formulating various ways of saying "What's so funny?" and decided to forestall them. "Look at us!" he said. "We ought to be hung on a wall to scare the crows. We were merrier than this when we rode to lose our lives."

"We've sent all the musicians north, that's it," said Ruth.

"You rate yourself too low, my lady," said Andrew.

"You've brought your flute, haven't you?" said Ted.

Ruth shot him a furious look. He wondered too late if it would be better, on principle, not to fall in with anything Andrew wanted, no matter how innocent.

"That flute's for messages," Ruth said, flatly, "and all my musical talent is for magic. You'd rather—you'd rather hear your dog bark at a crow," she finished, somewhat hysterically, "than me play a song that's not a spell."

"What of 'King Conrad's Last Journey'?" said Andrew. His voice was pleasant, his tone helpful. But there was something in it more than friendly; Ted's mother would sometimes say mundane things to his father in a tone like that. He had the awful feeling that Ruth had been right about Lady Ruth; certainly she was right about Andrew's attitude toward that enigmatic person.

Ruth sat absolutely still, staring at Andrew. Ted could see her face quite well in the firelight; she had no expression at all. Then, slowly, the corner of her mouth curved up, in a smile Ted had never seen in all the years of their acquaintance.

"That's true, my lord," she said, lightly. "I had forgot. I'll play that tune, an all do will it."

There was a chorus of assent, half-polite and half-eager. Ruth started to get up to fetch the flute and was forestalled by Andrew. Andrew was then beaten to the baggage by Stephen, who either was developing a crush on Ruth himself or had heard that tone in Andrew's voice and decided, like Dittany, that Ruth didn't care for it. Ted groaned inwardly. Why, oh, why, had they ever wanted to put any romantic complications in the blasted game? And what the hell did Ruth think she was going to play on that flute? He didn't know any song called "King Conrad's Last Journey," and he would bet that Ruth didn't either. Ted put his face in his hands suddenly; he was going to laugh or shriek, he wasn't sure which. Ruth might not know that song; but Lady Ruth would. Had that smile been hers? Were these dribs and drabs of knowledge broadening into some insidious possession?

Randolph laid a hand on Ted's knee, and Ted almost jumped out of his skin. "What's amiss?" said Randolph, very quietly. Andrew had not sat back down, but was looking thoughtfully after Stephen.

"Didn't you see her look at him?" breathed Ted. "Ruthie never looked like that in her life; that was Lady Ruth in the back of her head."

Randolph raised both eyebrows, but was prevented from saying anything else. Stephen had come back with the flute, which returned Andrew's attention to Ted's immediate vicinity.

Ruth unwrapped the flute, put it together, warmed it briefly, and, without any other preliminary, began to play "Good King Wenceslas." Ted, confounded, looked around the circle. Nobody seemed surprised. Eventually they all began to sing.

"Conrad lived in yonder wood,
Conrad spurned his kingdom;
Conrad thought on Chryse's blood;
Messengers did fear him.

Softly shone the moon that night,
Though the frost was cruel;
Seven came by candlelight,
Gathering winter fuel."

Oh, fine, thought Ted. It's even got some lines from the real song. What the hell is going on here? Claudia didn't explain the half of it. Maybe she didn't even do the half of it. I'm going to go crazy if we can't figure this out.

The song went on forever. If Andrew had really wanted to cheer people up, he had chosen a good way to do it. They were all singing; and though the song didn't have a chorus, it used three repeating verses, which came not at regular intervals, but rather on some cue Ted could not figure out. The singers themselves were always guessing wrong or coming in late, and they seemed to be enjoying themselves hugely. Even Randolph was smiling, although he sang only when nobody else could remember the words.

Ted couldn't decide what the song was about. It was a rambling tale of various adventures, but the main point of it seemed to be that, once King Conrad became enraged about whatever it was that had made him spurn his kingdom, it was impossible for anybody he knew to talk to him. He was followed in all his doings by pages and messengers from his court, asking advice on how to run the country; but he wouldn't answer them, or they were plagued by interruptions whenever they seemed to have worn him down, or they couldn't find him at all. And as soon as the people he met became friends instead of strangers, they would decide that he really ought to go back and run his kingdom, whereupon he would refuse to speak to them and they too would fall prey to the misfortunes that dogged his messengers. The crowd of people trying to follow him became larger and larger, and they began to quarrel among themselves. It was an amusing song, but there was something disquieting about it.

He looked at Randolph, who was sitting with his arms around his knees. His hood hid his face, but the moment Ted moved he leaned over and said, "What's the matter now?" He was not exasperated; he sounded as if things being the matter was the way of the world and it was to Ted's credit to have noticed.

"This song bothers me," said Ted, speaking softly.

"Which of your play-makers now?"

"None of them. I know the tune, and some of the lines, but not the story. Is this a normal kind of song for the Hidden Land?"

"No," said Randolph; "but Conrad was no normal kind of king."

Somebody touched Ted on the shoulder; he looked around wildly, and Andrew let go of him and laid one finger across his own mouth in a gesture that any parent might have used.

"Sorry," whispered Ted. He turned back to Randolph and said, "Our talk's a trial to Lord Andrew; will you walk apart with me?"

Randolph grinned at him, the grin that made you feel pleased and clever and as if the world were not in such bad shape after all. "Gladly," said Randolph, and got up, and gave his hand to Ted. Ted needed the help; one of his feet had fallen asleep, and he felt, of a sudden, shaky inside, as if Andrew had given him an ominous look instead of a mildly rebuking one.

They walked away from the fire, following a little path in the grass that the army had made when it camped here, and that animals, or perhaps other human wanderers, had kept clear until now. Ted trudged all the way to the quarry, Randolph behind him. Their breath steamed in the starlight. A few late insects creaked industriously. The quarry was a circle of quivering silver surrounded by ghostly white rocks. Ted sat down on one of these, and Randolph sat down beside him.

"What was the matter with Conrad?" said Ted. He added, "Which Conrad was this? The one who wouldn't mend the Great South Door?"

"Nay; his grandson," said Randolph. "The fourth of that name. He was King when Melanie and her brothers did murder the unicorn."

"Did he think it was his fault?"

Randolph nodded inside his hood. "Some had warned him; but he so trusted the brothers of Melanie that he did summon and ask them if this were truth. And they said it was not; and so the Hunt was held as always, and the unicorn killed."

"So," said Ted, "he decided he would never listen to anybody he knew? That's *just* like somebody in a fairy tale."

"Knowing he had given his trust amiss," said Randolph, rather sharply, "how could he bestow it again?"

So that was what was the matter with him. "That's foolish," said Ted. "Did he expect never to make any mistakes?"

"Some must not be made," said Randolph, with finality.

Ted did not have the courage to argue further. "Why did Andrew want Ruth to play the song?"

"He trusted the Lady Ruth, and thinketh now that she doth betray him," said Randolph, slowly. "Also, very like, to sting me. He knows the King did trust me and I did betray him."

Ted reflected that a great many kings seemed to have been betrayed in the Hidden Land, one way or another. He said, "Ruth's afraid we'll meet the King in the land of the dead."

"Her fear is my hope."

"Are you mad?"

"Not now," said Randolph.

"Fence told you—" began Ted, and stopped.

"Oh, I may do nothing; I have promised," said Randolph. "Wherefore my hope lieth in thy mischance."

"Thanks a lot."

Randolph did not trouble to answer this, which was probably just as well. Ted looked at him, but there was nothing to see. He sat still, as he had sat beside the fire, his hands laced around his knees and his hood half over his face.

If Ted had still been Edward—if Randolph had thought he was, he amended quickly—he would have had no qualms about telling Randolph that he was on no account to so much as wish for death. As Ted, he felt he had no rights one way or the other. And it was painful to speak of Edward, who might come back and might not. And who, if he did, might very well kill Randolph. Ted stared gloomily across the shining surface of the water to the high white cliffs opposite, muffled in starlight and a little mist. It looked like the land of the dead here and now. If he closed his eyes halfway, he would see the shapes of the rocks waver and grow familiar, and would meet himself and the counterparts of his four relations.

"Jesus Christ!" said Ted, and grabbed Randolph's arm. "We can't take Andrew down there! He may or may not see the dead King and ask him awkward questions; but he's bound to see the dead children; we need to talk to them. Oh, criminy, what a dull pupil you've got yourself. When do you suppose I'll bethink myself what to do about it?"

"They're singing still," said Randolph.

Ted took a deep breath. "All right," he said, trying to think like Patrick. "Either we come up with a good reason to keep him out, or—or we tell him the truth. Why is it, Randolph, that in the Hidden Land one is always faced with such wonderful choices?"

"Is it otherwise in your country?"

"Well, probably not. But it was for *me*, except in the game." Ted shoved his hood back. "Except in the damn game," he repeated, bitterly.

"An this were yet thy game, what wouldst thou choose?"

"Oh, if it were the game, it would be easy. We'd think of an ingenious excuse to keep Andrew outside, but something would happen that would oblige him to disobey, and he'd come and figure everything out and be mad as hell."

"Truly?"

"Truly, my lord. Because that would be more interesting."

"And now?"

"And now," said Ted, "I think we'd better tell Andrew the truth."

"There's no interest in that course, then?" Randolph sounded as if he were about to laugh.

"Less, anyway. He'll want to come to the land of the dead just so he can sneer at it. He'd hate making the discovery down there and being made to look like a fool. And he's already suspicious; if we tell him now, and let him think this is what everybody is nervous about, maybe he'll let his suspicions about the King's death lie quiet a little longer."

"That he discover my crime is a greater evil than that he discover thy nature?"

"Damn right," said Ted.

Randolph was silent.

"Well, isn't it? What would he do?"

"Refuse thy orders."

"Fine. He has to take yours, doesn't he?"

"So long as he proveth not my crime."

"Well, he can't prove it, can he?"

"I know not. He hath with him on this journey, by his own request, Julian and Jerome, who do not love me."

"Well, if he won't take my orders and he won't take yours, whose would he have to take?"

Randolph pushed his own hood back and shoved both hands through his hair, exactly as Ellen would do. "His own."

"Which is all right, or not, depending on whether he is in fact spying for the Dragon King."

"Aye. We might do better to let him discover the truth by seeing those children below the earth."

"Well, if they tell him his sister killed them, maybe he'll think again about whatever plots he has with her."

Randolph looked thoughtful. "Aye. Our word would not suffice. He and Claudia are very fond."

"How the hell can they be very fond when she's the most powerful sorcerer in the entire place and he doesn't even believe—oh, never mind," said Ted. "I don't want to know. All right, let him find out the hard way."

"What troubleth thee else?"

"Ruth," said Ted. "Why did she smile like that? Did Lady Ruth ever smile like that?"

"I never saw her so," said Randolph.

"Do you know anything about this contriving of Melanie's, this stuff in the back of the head?"

"How should I?" said Randolph. "When in all our history have we had strangers that are the doubles of our dead to walk among us?"

"I'll talk to Ruth, then; I want to know what she thinks happened."

There was a meditative and uncomfortable pause.

"Well," said Ted, "now you know what all I'm worrying about. What are you worrying about?"

"We've heard naught from Fence," said Randolph, at once.

"Could our message have gone astray? Should we send it again?"

"There's little harm in the trying," said Randolph.

They sat on amid the cold rocks. The nearby singing broke up in laughter. Somewhere in the distances of Ted's mind, Edward said, *I will friend you, if I may, in the dark and cloudy day.* The singing began again.

"Don't call us," said Ted, a little wildly, "we'll call you."

"What's that?" said Randolph.

"Edward just offered to friend me in the dark and cloudy day."

"I knew not he spoke to thee as well as in thee."

"Well, that's a recent development. And, having watched Ruthie's face this evening, I don't think I like it."

Randolph pushed his hood back and looked at Ted for a moment. His pale face was all angles in the moonlight, and the curling black hair stuck to his forehead as it would stick to Ruth's or Ellen's. His eyes were shadowed. He said, "Spoke Edward thus? 'I will friend you, if I may, in the dark and cloudy day'?"

"Yes, exactly," said Ted, rather unsettled.

"That's from a song," said Randolph. "Canst tell Edward from the other voices in thy mind?"

"I never *had* any voices in my mind until I came to this mad country!" said Ted.

"Thou canst not, then?"

"No," said Ted, ashamed of his irritation. "I thought it was all Edward. What else could it be?"

"When we come to Gray Lake," said Randolph, "I will know."

"And when thou knowest, oh counselor, wilt thou tell me?"

"Of a certainty," said Randolph; and in his voice was something Ted found very comforting, and something he found fearful. Neither of them said anything more.

CHAPTER 20

ON the northern party's third day of travel, they descended into Fence's Country. Laura squinted at the trees, the smooth, sharp green of the pines, the violent red of the fire-maples, the deeper red and sullen brown of the oaks, the paleness of birch branches from which the yellow leaves hung like coins. Princess Laura had been here once. They went down and up and down again, for three hours, leading the horses, and then struck a road. It was narrow, its cracked slabs of stone wedged in lopsidedly between the hills and the river. They were able to ride again, which was a mixed blessing. In another hour the road brought them to a town.

Laura was astonished. She had never in all the Secret Country seen a town. This one had a grim-looking wall around it on three sides; on the fourth was the river. The hills above the wall were striped with stubble fields and tidy rows of grotesque apple trees. The wall had a gatehouse with a tower. The town was three streets wide and four long, with two wooden piers and small boats moored to them. Its houses were of stone, some with thatched roofs, some with slate. Laura could see a man working in a bed of dark red flowers; and two children throwing a stick for a dog; and a cat sitting atop one of the crenellations of the gatehouse, washing its foot.

"What's that?" said Ellen.

"Feren," said Fence.

They rode up the road toward the gate. Fence stopped them about ten feet away from it, rummaging in his belt-pouch. While they waited, the heavy door of the gatehouse creaked its way up, and a man ran out. He wore a brown tunic and breeches and a red cape. He had brown hair, and a brown beard, and very large blue eyes. To Laura's relief, he did not remind her of anyone.

"Milord Fence!" he called. "What's amiss? Hath—" He stopped, staring not at any of the party, but at their horses. "Who are you?"

"Your lord Fence," said Fence, and held out the ring he had taken from his pouch. It was of twisted silver, with a blue stone that, just at the moment, glowed faintly. The sun had disappeared behind the trees, and the ring in Fence's grimy hand looked like the first star of evening wandered from its appointed rounds.

The man in the road must have thought it looked like something else. His face was sick. "We have your horses within," he said. "You took the boats and rowed upriver two hours since."

"And had I this ring then?" said Fence.

"Milord, you did not. Your—their answers came so pat; they knew my name, they knew of your letters."

"And," said Celia, "there was a kind of glamour on them that so pleased you, you considered not, but obeyed them."

The man's face relaxed, as if he recognized in Celia somebody who could put matters right. "You know our weakness," he said.

Celia smiled. "Everyone born in this country were well advised to spend a century outside it. Exile sharpeneth the eyes."

"And the wits," said the man in the road, as if he were capping a quotation. He looked back at Fence. "Milord, I am sorry for our carelessness. I think your foes are very great. Will you take their horses?"

"I'll take my boats," said Fence.

"You'll take your money, an it please you," said the man; "but the boats are taken already."

Fence pressed one palm to his forehead and let his breath out. "Matthew?" he said. "Celia?"

"I think we must ride," said Matthew.

"The road's good," said the man. "'Twill take you halfway to the house of Belaparthalion."

"Have you lodging for the night," said Fence, "or is that taken also?"

"That we have," said the man.

"Deliver it, then," said Fence.

"Is there time for this?" said Matthew.

"The horses need rest, if we do not," said Fence.

Matthew smiled. "Take the horses of those that removed our boats."

"Take them by all means," said the man in the road. "We have little enough fodder for our own beasts; and though we're well paid to house these, neither we nor they can eat silver."

"Celia?" said Fence.

"I don't advise it," said Celia. "They're too like to turn to sticks and land us in the river; or worse, drown all our victuals there."

"We could send our message, if we're somewhere Laura's fingers can thaw out," said Ellen.

Laura's fingers were not so much cold as sore and swollen, but she supposed they would perform better in a heated room.

Matthew looked at his wife; she raised her eyebrows; Matthew sighed heavily and turned to Fence. "Know you this man?" he said, gesturing at the man in the road, who stood comfortably with the air of somebody watching a medium-good magic show.

"As well as he knoweth me."

"Which is to say, not well enough?"

If anybody had spoken about Laura in that tone of voice,

she would have been indignant, whether she understood what was being said or not. The man in the road looked resigned. Fence said to him, "Will you, of your courtesy, bring the horses to us here?"

"An you take them away, aye."

"Until I see them, I know not or I shall or I shall not take them."

"Why are you so eager to get rid of them?" said Patrick to the man in the road.

Laura thought this was a shrewd question. The man in the road said, "As I did say, we have not their maintenance."

"Why'd you take them, then?" said Patrick.

"For that they did, we thought, belong to your party, toward whom we have some obligation."

Fence said, "An we take them not, I'll leave you a letter wherewith you may have from High Castle the fodder to maintain those beasts the winter."

The man moved his thoughtful blue gaze from Matthew's irate countenance to Celia's judicious face, past Patrick's considering expression and Ellen's delighted grin. He glanced briefly at Laura, who tried to look alert but feared it had come out startled. Finally, last of all, he looked at Fence. Fence quirked the corner of his mouth.

"I'll bring them," said the man, turned smartly, and went back through the gate.

"All right, *quickly*," said Patrick. "What is going on here?"

"I sent letters," said Fence, "asking for the hire of three boats. A party in our likeness hath come before us and taken the boats, leaving behind their horses, which belike are no horses at all."

"And do you think you know who this party was?"

"I know what they were," said Fence.

"Shape-changers," said Ellen. "Since they came in our likeness, you know," she added to Laura.

"Does that mean the Dragon King sent them?" said Patrick.

Laura didn't want to think about it. Apparently Fence didn't either; he got down off his horse and handed his reins to Celia. Matthew did the same. Laura wondered what Celia could be expected to do if one of the four horses she was suddenly in charge of took fright or felt perverse. But the horses just nosed about the road and bit off the grass in its cracks, seeming far more disposed to go to sleep than to cause trouble. Perhaps Celia had been taking lessons from Benjamin.

The man in brown and two children in yellow came back out of the gate, leading three nondescript brown horses. One had a white blotch on its nose and another had three white stockings. They looked as bored as the Secret Country horses. But the Secret Country horses suddenly flared their nostrils and put their ears back and showed the whites of their eyes. Laura felt the one she and Patrick were sitting on jump and tremble. Celia said something in some language Laura didn't recognize, and the horses stood still; but they kept their ears back and looked distinctly uneasy.

"No closer," said Fence.

The three leading the strange horses stopped where they were. Fence and Matthew came forward, cautiously. Fence said, in an extremely prosaic voice, "They'll shape me in your arms, Janet, / A dove, and but a swan: / And last they'll shape me in your arms / A mother-naked man. Cast your green mantle over me, / I'll be mysel' again. Wherefore," said Fence, much more vigorously, "thy mantle, Ellen."

Ellen stood up in her stirrups, pulled off her green woolen cloak, and flung it at Fence, who caught it neatly and in his turn hurled it at the three horses. It billowed hugely, like a queen-sized bedsheet being snapped open, and settled over all three horses and one of the little girls. There was a tremendous commotion from under the green folds, and a certain amount of heaving and stamping. The man in brown backed hastily off the road, climbed the slope until he came to an evergreen with branches like the rungs of a ladder, climbed that too, and appeared to settle in to watch the fun. Laura wanted to emulate him, but Patrick was holding the miserable horse firmly where it was, and she would attract attention if she got off.

The heaving mantle slumped suddenly to the road, to the accompaniment of a huge blast of hot air and a pelting of dust. Laura and Patrick both sneezed; Ellen coughed; the grown-ups just put their hands over their eyes.

When the dust had settled, Ellen's half-sized green cloak lay meekly in the middle of the road. The man in brown sat in the tree and laughed. One child crouched in the ditch, gaping.

"Wow," said Patrick. Laura couldn't remember ever having heard him say that. Patrick did not like to appear impressed.

"Wherefore laugh you?" shouted Matthew to the man in the tree.

"I feared they were monsters," gasped the man; Laura realized that he was not so much amused as hysterical. "I thought them poisonous, direful, dangerous; and what were they but a puff of air and a screeching as of cats?"

"What were they but concerned elsewhere?" said Fence, grimly. He walked forward, picked up Ellen's cloak, and shook it briefly. The child in the ditch sneezed. "So, thou'rt real enough," said Fence. Laura deduced from this that shape-shifters didn't sneeze, and that Ellen's mantle had known which creatures were shape-shifters.

Fence helped her back onto the road. She backed away from him and ran, which Laura thought ungrateful.

"What about the other kid?" said Ellen.

"An she's gone, she's one of them," said Fence. He surveyed his party. "Celia," he said, "I do commend thy stubbornness. I think we must stay the night."

In the little town, they were given a square room, about ten feet by ten, with a stone floor and a fireplace, and tapestries on the walls. The tapestries had largely to do with quarrying rock and building castles. Nobody seeming inclined to trust the food offered by the denizens of the town, they ate their usual rations, except that Celia crumbled up the oatcake in boiling water and made porridge. It was hot, and as far as Laura was concerned, that was all you could say for it.

After this vexing meal, Laura and Ellen sat on a pile of all their bedclothes, looking dismally through one of Patrick's physics books and trying to find something to laugh at. Ellen rather liked "mean acceleration," but Laura was not finding anything very funny. Mean acceleration just sounded like what a horse did when it wanted you to fall off. They had a branch of candles to read by; its light was bright but rather wavery. Patrick had the fire, and was, infuriatingly, reading the only piece of fiction he had brought along.

Matthew and Celia were sitting on two more wooden stools, holding hands, their heads leaning against one of the quarry tapestries and their eyes shut. Fence had spread a battered map the size of a game of Twister out on the floor, and was kneeling in the middle of it, scowling.

"Fence," said Matthew, "Heathwill will furnish us a newer map."

"The man of Feren," said Fence, "did say the road ran halfway to the House of Belaparthalion."

Laura looked up from an uninspiring picture of two wooden carts with roller-skate wheels being smashed together to demonstrate the conservation of momentum, straight into the firelit swirls of Fence's robe. She saw Claudia and three black cats standing in tree-dappled sunshine on the bank of a stream. The cats were fishing; Claudia appeared to be making sarcastic remarks, which they ignored. She was still wearing the red checked dress in which she had greeted Ted and Laura on their return to Illinois. It was limp. Claudia looked different. She was still elegant, as she leaned against a rowan tree and laughed at her cats. She was one of those people of whom Laura's mother said that they had elegant bones. But the conscious grace she had displayed even walking in the damp woods gathering herbs was missing. She was somehow more likeable and less alarming than Laura had seen her. She cocked an eye at the wet-footed cats, shook her head, sat down on a convenient rock, and picked a white crocus the size of a tulip.

Laura leaned forward to see better, and found herself staring at a mud-smeared nebula on Fence's gown. She rubbed her eyes. Claudia was where they had been the night before. Why should she be following them on foot, with three cats?

"Laura Kimberly Carroll," said Ellen, glancing up from the physics book and fixing her with a look as stern as any of Agatha's, "what is the matter with you?"

Laura shrugged.

"Fence," said Ellen. "She's seen something."

"Seen what?" said Fence, to Laura.

It was no trouble to tell her visions once she was cornered. She obliged. This one was not very dramatic, except for Claudia's location. Her attempt to describe in what way Claudia seemed likeable was not a success. Ellen and Patrick stared at her, and Celia made a very sharp remark, for Celia, about people who killed children but cherished cats.

"You never should have called that cardinal, Ellie," said Patrick, laying his pen down. "I bet that's how she found out where we were."

"But how could she get there so fast?" said Ellen. "I think she was following us all along."

"With three cats?" said Laura. "Cats that fish?"

"Well," said Matthew, who still had not opened his eyes, "if travel one must with cats in the wilderness, let them by all means be cats that fish."

"I wish we knew more about her powers," said Patrick.

"Her greatest deeds meseemeth are performed with the aid of the windows in her house," said Fence. "She hath none now."

"She can escape the spell of Shan's Ring," said Ellen.

"Or," said Patrick, rather smugly, "the spell of Shan's Ring has a limit to it."

"She knows what I taught her, and what Meredith taught her," said Fence. "That sufficeth to follow us, but not to catch us."

"Let's go in the morning early, all the same," said Matthew.

"Wherefore," said Celia, "let us to bed now."

"Celia," said Laura, with a silent apology to her sore hands, "shouldn't we try to send the message about Belaparthalion?"

Celia got up, came across the room less briskly than usual, and examined Laura's hands. "Well," she said, "an it be short, and we have the horse-salve for it after."

"That stuff smells awful," said Ellen. "I have to sleep with her."

"Canst thou play the flute?"

"You know I can't."

"Well, then," said Celia.

Laura dug the flute's case out of her bedding and took out the mouthpiece. It hurt her hands with a cold throb, not so much on the surface as in the bones. She dropped it onto the physics book. Celia touched it with the tip of her finger, let her breath out softly, and, picking up the mouthpiece in one hand and the next piece in the other, began fitting the flute together.

"No use, I'll warrant, in warming this?" she said.

"No," said Laura.

"Well," said Celia, "may there be much music, excellent voice, in this little organ."

She handed it back to Laura. Laura put it to her lips hurriedly. It played "Good King Wenceslas." Always before, she had played the flute. She had not always known how she played it, or what, before she started, she would be playing; but it was she who had played. This was the flute. Ellen stared at her, and then at Patrick, who had closed his book and was looking exasperated. But Matthew leapt from his resting place with a face full of consternation, and Fence stood up in the middle of his map, both exclaiming disjointedly.

Laura stopped after one round of the tune, laid the flute down on the physics book again, and shook her hand hard.

"May heaven confound them!" said Celia.

"What's the matter?" said Patrick.

"That's a pestilent song," said Matthew; "it's a spell that turneth messages from their ways, delivering them amiss."

"Who hath set it?" said Fence.

"Worse, who in th' other party shall know of't?" said Celia. "Will Lady Ruth warn her other, or be silent?"

"I wouldn't count on anything," said Patrick. "The help we get from our others is erratic."

"Can Andrew play the flute?" said Celia.

"Not to my knowledge," said Fence, with an astonishing bitterness; "but then, what is that?"

He flung this last remark at Matthew, but Matthew only pressed his hand over his high forehead and back into his flaming hair, and shook his head, and walking across the room, stooped for the flute and picked it up.

"I'll tell you this," he said, hefting the flute with one hand and patting Celia's arm with the other. "This showeth either an unpracticed hand, or a confident. There are spells little harder that do merely twist a message into some plausible semblance, whereby those receiving it may keep unsuspecting. This spell saith most loud that one desireth our silence."

"Claudia's confident, I imagine," said Patrick.

"And in some matters, it may be, unpracticed also," said Fence, more calmly.

Ellen said, "Does this mean Randolph got the earlier message telling him to watch out?"

"It should," said Fence, frowning. "Celia?"

"It should," said Celia, not very confidently.

"You people are so vague," said Patrick. "Why is that?"

"Because magic is an art, not a science, smart-ass," said Ellen.

"And none of us is master of this art in special," said Celia. "Matthew is a scholar, who knoweth but may not perform; I but dabble; in his own field Fence knoweth much but in this he must be cautious. Content you until we are come to Heathwill Library. Its council may be more sharp than thou desirest."

Laura rubbed her stinging hands together. It was infuriating not to be able to send a message. It was enough to make you wish for a telephone.

"Frown not so earnest," said Celia; Laura jumped. "Come to bed; we must be up betimes."

Laura dreamed about home again. She had lost her third bus ticket in two months, and was afraid to tell her parents. She had been using her allowance as bus money, but Ted caught her at it. She was having a furious argument with him, in which he promised to help her talk their parents out of cutting her hair if she would confess to the loss of the bus ticket. When she wouldn't agree to this, Ted threatened to tell Fence. Even in the dream this seemed odd to Laura. She had a powerful feeling, though, that telling Fence would be disastrous. She was trying to explain this to Ted when Celia shook her awake. She got up extremely indignant, with no one to vent her outrage on.

They left when the sun had barely cleared the eastward hills and the mist from the river hung blurrily in all the valleys. Laura went on feeling cross. She also felt shy of Fence, as if she were in fact keeping some secret from him because it would hurt her to have him know of it.

"If this is a good road," she said to Patrick, "I'd hate to see a bad one."

"It's a road," said Patrick. "The point is not that it is done well, but that it is done at all."

Ted had once said something similar about a batch of cookies from which Laura had omitted the salt and baking soda. She bared her teeth at Patrick's sleek head, so like her brother's; and leaned her forehead into the slick nylon of his purple pack, trying to think of something soothing. Somewhere very far away, a voice remarked, *Can honor's voice provoke the silent dust, / Or flattery soothe the dull cold ear of death?*

Laura jerked her head up and looked wildly around. The countryside revealed itself in layer after layer of tree-furred hills, all red and yellow and orange, as the mist dwindled. The sky was a murky blue that set off the brilliant trees better than a cleaner color would. Three crows swooped by on the left, lower than the road but high above the bottom of the valley whose upper rim they rode along. Another voice, closer, said, *Where shall we gang and dine the day-O?*

"Fence!" said Laura, and the caution of her dream caught her by the throat. She heard herself say, "When's lunch?"

"When we arrive at Heathwill Library," said Fence. He was riding next to them, and he frowned a little, as if he knew that was not really the question she wanted to ask.

"Are we that close?" said Patrick.

"We'll be there by sunset."

Not marble, said the distant voice, in a tone that clutched Laura's heart and made her tighten her grip on Patrick, *nor the gilded monuments / Of princes shall outlive this powerful rhyme; / But you shall shine more bright in these contents / Than unswept stone besmeared with sluttish time.*

"Hey!" said Patrick. "Laura, you're breaking my ribs. What's the problem?"

"It seems a long way down," said Laura.

Fence was silent, but Laura could feel his troubled look. She shut her eyes and tried to think of nothing. *Give to airy nothing a local habitation and a name,* said somebody. Laura held very still, and the voice said nothing more.

It *was* a long way down to the valley; they descended the slope very slowly in a series of switchbacks. The road got better; Laura wondered if, among their other crimes, the people of Feren had neglected the roads around their town. Then she wondered where this thought had come from. Princess Laura, perhaps. They descended into the valley and rode between the rows of towering hills. The day grew warm, and cool again. There was a great noise of birds, and the sun disappeared behind the hills on their left.

"Are we *there* yet?" said Ellen, in a pseudo-whine.

"Just fifteen minutes," called Patrick; and they both laughed.

Then Ellen said in a heartfelt tone, "I'm starving."

"Good grief, if you're starving, Laura must have died of hunger an hour ago," said Patrick.

Laura felt that this remark did not deserve the dignity of an answer. She was surprised not to be hungry. Maybe Princess Laura was above such things as food. *Dost thou think,* said the distant voice, *that because thou art virtuous there shall be no more cakes and ale?*

"They'll feed us well in Heathwill Castle," said Fence.

"Oh, yeah?" said Patrick. "What's to keep the shape-changers from taking our dinner the way they took our horses?"

"Shape-changers," said Matthew, from behind them, "eat the air, promise-cramm'd."

The distant voice said, *You cannot feed capons so.*

"They knew me not at Feren," said Fence, "but at the Library they will; their arts are very great."

"Heh," said Patrick.

They rode on up the valley. Eventually it broadened out before them, and in the blue twilight they saw a tower on a hill. It looked grim, with its thick walls and dry moat, its stingy arrow-slits and toothy crenellations. But there was something wrong with the crenellations. Laura saw as they drew nearer that each one was topped with a large earthenware pot full of flowers. She supposed one could tip them off onto the heads of enemies.

"What!" said Ellen. "Somebody's yelling poetry."

"Saying what?" said Matthew.

" 'When wasteful war shall statues overturn,' " said Ellen, rather wildly, " 'and broils root out the work of masonry, nor Mars his sword nor war's quick fire shall burn the living record of your memory.' "

"That's a building spell," said Fence. "It is no matter—but I knew not thou hadst the ear for sorcery."

He broke off abruptly; remembering, Laura supposed, that Princess Ellen might not have had such an ear but there was no telling what Ellen Carroll had. *Lord,* said her own private voice, *we know what we are, but know not what we may be.*

Nobody challenged them from the tower. The road bent eastward; a stream crossed its path, and they clattered over a wide stone bridge. Laura heard water running, louder than the stream, and saw a river on their right. Soon there loomed ahead of them in the growing dusk the glimmer of a very high circular wall. As they rode closer Laura saw that within that wall, on its riverward side, was another higher one, and within that, in the middle of the river itself, a higher still; and within that, one last wall, highest of all. Laura thought that the question "Are we there yet?" might have a variety of answers.

"Which gate?" said Fence.

"The market, since we come so late," said Celia.

They rode up to the first wall, and were admitted by a couple of guards who merely looked them over without comment and then stood aside. They rode into the second town Laura had seen here. Everything seemed to be made of stone: little stone huts with thatched roofs, high stone houses with roofs of slate and red tile, stone walls enclosing gardens and fountains, stone benches, stone statues, stone pillars standing about with no visible purpose, stone pillars with stone lanterns on them. People were coming with torches and lighting these as they passed. They rode slowly past one cross-street and five or six houses, and into a wide square. Suddenly the air smelled of overripe fruit, and spoiled vegetables, and frying, and spices. Laura had a vague impression of striped awnings rolled up, and shuttered windows.

They rode on through the empty square, past more houses, and took the first right turn that offered itself. And there was the second wall. It belonged to what looked like a miniature castle, with a gatehouse and corner towers. Light shone through all the arrow-slits, and there were no flowers on the crenellations. A woman in shirt of mail came out to them, holding a torch. She looked surprisedly at Celia.

"My lady, I thought I saw you yesternight," she said.

"You were the more deceived," said Celia.

"Saw you me also?" said Fence.

"Oh, aye, and all thy crew," the guard said, gesturing at the rest of the party.

"Did they swear aright?" said Fence.

"Oh, aye."

"They might mean harm to us, Fence, and none to Heathwill Library," said Celia.

"Well," said the woman, "can you swear aright?"

"I do swear by the mercy granted to Shan and the three precepts of Belaparthalion," said Fence, "that neither I nor any of my train come with the will or the power to do harm to Heathwill Library, its members, or those whom it doth protect."

"That's more than they could do," she said; "I had to speak it to 'em." She looked again at Celia. "You did say that you'd forgot all civil discourse, being so long in a barbarous land."

"An you stop now, I can forgive," said Fence, rather sharply. "May we go our ways?"

"Heartily," she said.

They were challenged, as they came out the other side of the gatehouse, by two more guards, who accepted their account of themselves amiably enough, but took issue with Fence's desire to ride the horses further. There was plenty of room, they said, here in the Refuge Close; and Heathwill Castle's stables were crowded.

"Who's here?" said Fence.

"I couldn't say," said one guard, in a sour tone that Laura thought was directed not at Fence, but at those about whom he couldn't say.

Fence seemed disposed to argue, but Matthew touched his arm and he was silent. They dismounted, and handed over the horses to the guards, and were given a handcart for their luggage. Somebody came out of the darkness to pull it for them. Laura was too stiff and sleepy to pay much heed. They had to wait while a great deal of grinding and clattering went on: the drawbridge being let down. They walked across it, over the dark-sliding, fresh-smelling river, and came to the next wall. This one was so high it disappeared into the darkness. Another gate, four guards, their voices cautious and Fence's patient.

"I thought as much!" exclaimed one of the guards.

"But they did take the oath," said Fence.

"Well, in that case the quarrel's yours," said the guard, "but I take it ill that we should be so trifled with you. Do you send for us an they confound you."

They were allowed into a torchlit, oddly shaped courtyard inside which loomed the highest wall of all, a great blocky building just like an apartment complex, dotted with squares of yellow light. They went along its length to a far door, and up a narrow stair, and into a large, square room, blessedly warm, with a table, and chairs, and a bewildering clutter of objects on every available flat surface. A fair-haired man in yellow sat writing at the far side of the table. His moving elbow was going to knock a stack of books into his inkwell any moment, thought Laura, and she woke up a little.

The man who had pulled their handcart and guided them up the stairs tapped on the frame of the door, and cleared his throat, and finally shouted, "My lord!"

The man at the desk looked up, and smiled, and stopped smiling to lay down his pen. "Fence?" he said.

"This time for sure," said Patrick.

"So I believe," said Fence.

The fair man stood up. "Well, we must sift these matters. But for the moment, welcome," he said, "to Heathwill Library."

As they filed into the room, Ellen caught Laura by the sleeve. "That's him!" she said. "That's Michaelmas!"

The voice, very close now, so close that for a moment Laura thought it belonged to the fair man, spoke pleasantly. It said, *Up, lass: when the journey's over / There'll be time enough to sleep*. And then it said, *Welcome indeed, to Heathwill Library.*

CHAPTER 21

IT was the fourth day of the journey south. Ted was tired. He had not had enough rest since they started, what with setting up camps, and tearing them down; and Randolph's being in a hurry without saying why; and the toll taken by perplexing conversations. It was a good thing the setting sun was shining in his eyes, or he would be asleep where he sat and the perspicacious horse would be plotting its revenge.

Ted sat up with a start, and the perspicacious horse twitched and stretched its neck hopefully. West. Why were they riding west? The road went south. The domains of the Dragon King were south of the Hidden Land—weren't they? The army of the Hidden Land had traveled south to fight the Dragon King, but its aim had been to get out of its own territory, not necessarily to get into the Dragon King's. Maybe the Dragon King's domains were west, and he had missed a crossroads, being so sleepy.

"Ruth?" he called.

Ruth, a little ahead of him, looked inquiringly over her shoulder and then slowed her horse until they were riding abreast. She looked tired and pale herself. This morning, when she could have been helping them strike camp, she had wrestled her crazy hair into a knot at the back of her head and crammed somebody's straw hat over it. It made her look older and a little silly. Nor could Ted see the point of the arrangement; the weather was cooler than it had been the day before. He tried to remember how Lady Ruth had looked in the land of the dead. He thought she had worn her hair down, but couldn't be sure.

"What do you want?" said Ruth, patiently. Well, at least that wasn't a reaction of Lady Ruth.

"Why are we riding west?" said Ted.

Ruth smiled faintly. "Andrew says it's misdirection disguised as sorcery."

"I suppose that means it really is sorcery."

"Probably. He says Randolph is doing it, though; I wasn't sure Randolph was allowed to do sorcery anymore."

"This does seem more serious than making the rain stop."

Behind them, Stephen and Dittany were involved in some discussion that created a great deal of laughter. Ahead of them, Randolph rode alone, his hood up and his shoulders tired; ahead of him, Andrew and Julian were talking earnestly, while the breeze blew their hair about; and ahead of them, Jerome rode by himself, and rather faster. Ted realized that the character of the plain had changed. The grasses were shorter, and the land went up and down like a sine wave. It was all scattered with clumps of trees and gleams of water. And on the far edge, below the reddening sun, where yesterday the flat land had met the flat sky, there was a tiny, irregular line of purple.

"Ruth. Mountains."

"I saw them yesterday," said Ruth.

"This may be the way to the Gray Lake, but isn't it taking us the long way around for the Dragon King?"

"They said the Gray Lake was on the way."

"Well," said Ted, dubiously, "I guess what sorcery is getting us into, sorcery can get us out of."

"Do not meddle in the affairs of wizards," said Ruth, sepulchrally.

"Cut it out. We *are* the affairs of wizards."

"What a very uncomfortable thought," said Ruth.

"You ought to be used to it by now."

"Well, there are affairs and affairs."

Oh, thought Ted. "Andrew," he said, firmly, "is not a wizard."

"I wish," said Ruth, suddenly sounding furious, "that I could get blasted Lady Ruth to come into the front of my mind. She knows what Andrew is."

"Randolph and I wanted to ask you about that," said Ted. "Come on." He asked the mare to catch up with Randolph's horse, which pleased her, and then held her to Randolph's slow pace, which she didn't like at all.

Ruth rode up between them. "Since I'm to be interrogated," she said.

Randolph shook his hood back, and Ted saw Ruth smile at him. Randolph didn't smile back. He was getting a tan from all this traveling in the sun, so he no longer looked so white and strained; but he still had hollows under his eyes. *Oh heavy burden!* cooed the voice in Ted's mind, unkind and ironic. *Oh my offense is rank, it smells to heaven.*

"Shut *up*!" said Ruth.

Ted and Randolph stared at her, Randolph in simple bewilderment and Ted with uncomfortable surmise.

"I'm sorry," said Ruth. "The one who isn't Lady Ruth is acting up. Smells to heaven indeed!"

"You're hearing *my* back-of-the-head voice," said Ted.

"Leave the voices," said Randolph, patiently. "You did but look upon me and have a like thought. Your blood, your training, your—" He stopped.

"Exactly," said Ted. "Wrong blood, no training. So why?"

"The whispers of your others confound me," said Randolph. "But those neutral voices that take a chance word in your thoughts and expound on it as sorcerer to his apprentice—those our proximity to the Gray Lake doth explain."

"But why can we hear them, without the blood or the training?" said Ted.

"You have the ear for sorcery," said Randolph. "Anyone can have it, though few untrained could hear those voices at this distance from their abiding."

"Did Edward and Lady Ruth have it?" said Ted.

"Aye, both."

"Yes, that's an idea!" said Ruth to Ted. "Maybe we're just hearing what they hear."

"Not if what you hear correspondeth to your inmost thoughts," said Randolph.

"But if Edward and Lady Ruth hear our inmost thoughts—"

"That," said Ted, ruthlessly interrupting this theoretical discussion, "is what we wanted to talk about. What happened to you last night, when Andrew asked you to play that song?"

"She sang the tune under her breath, and I recognized it."

"Ruthie, you got such a look on your face. Why did you?"

"Because I—" Ruth stopped. "It's all muddled," she said. "She knew that Andrew thought she couldn't play that song; but she could, because it's necessary for some rituals of the Green Caves. And I could, and I could play it better than she did. So he was trying to embarrass her and it backfired on him; and it backfired doubly because I'm not Lady Ruth."

"That song's a spell?" said Randolph, seeming to wake up.

"I'm not sure. Conrad did go to the Green Caves, so it might just be a piece of history."

"Do you think she took over your actions?" said Ted.

"No," said Ruth. "We both wanted the same thing, to discomfort Andrew."

"But would you have wanted to discomfort Andrew if she hadn't been angry that he was trying to embarrass her?"

"Yes! He scares the living daylights out of me."

"Or out of Lady Ruth?"

"No," said Ruth. "As far as I can tell, *nothing* scares Lady Ruth. If she wants to help me keep Andrew at bay, why should I kick?"

"Because for all we know, she could take you over."

"I'll be careful," said Ruth, patiently. "It would help to know what she was up to with Andrew."

"When we get to the Gray Lake," said Ted, "you can ask her."

He thought Randolph had stopped listening some time ago, but now that lord remarked, "She may refuse thee."

Edward said, *I thrice presented him a kingly crown, which he did thrice refuse: was this ambition?*

"Did you hear that?" said Ted, sharply.

"Hear what?" said Ruth.

"Nay, I heard nothing," said Randolph.

Ted looked at him, but he seemed perfectly tranquil. Ted rode on silently, trying to compare the cooing voice they had all heard with the one he thought of as Edward's.

Before the sun set, the land had begun to change when Ted looked down at his horse, or closed his eyes for a moment, or put his gloves on. Before the twilight became darkness, the land changed while he looked at it. He would see that the plain he was riding across ended in a steep, forested slope; and the next moment he would be halfway up the slope; and the moment after that, across a brook he hadn't even seen yet, on the slope's far side. And yet he and his horse had crossed the brook; the horse's legs were dripping. It made Ted feel sick, but it didn't seem to bother the horse at all.

"Some misdirection!" he shouted at Ruth.

Ruth shook her head without looking around; and in front of her, Andrew turned and glared at him. Ted grinned back, and hoped Andrew felt sick too.

It was almost dark when they rode to the top of a hill, and saw the road running down its other side to yet another little stream. Across the stream there was no road, only a vast gray shadow on the far bank. Ted looked behind him. The hill showed clear against the darkening sky, and one small tree was faintly red in the lingering light. So that gray shadow before them was not darkness only. Ted looked around at his companions. Everybody seemed blank, except for Andrew, who had the dour expression of somebody who has been trifled with long enough, and Ruth, who smiled at Randolph and said, "Well done."

"Fence had done it swiftlier," said Randolph.

Ruth caught Ted's glance and rolled her eyes.

Jerome said, "What now, my lord?"

"I think some of us must make a camp and wait," said Randolph. He looked at Ted. "Whom will you have to accompany you, my prince?"

Oh, wonderful, thought Ted. *And after that,* said Edward, *out of all whooping.* Ted ignored him and considered the question. "How many know the way to the Gray Lake?"

"I alone," said Randolph.

"You, then," said Ted to Randolph. "And Lady Ruth. Do any of the rest of you earnestly desire this journey?"

Stephen looked hopeful, but Andrew spoke first. "As my next lesson in the sensibility of magic," he said, "I dare not omit it." His tone was ironic.

Ted looked at Randolph. Randolph ran both hands through his hair and said with perfect seriousness, "He hath the right of it, my prince. I would not impede such a progress as this."

This made no sense to Ted, but he understood that Randolph either wanted Andrew or despaired of keeping him from coming.

"Okay," he said. "Four to go and four to stay. Ought we to camp here also, my lord, and ford the stream in daylight?"

"No," said Randolph, "time presseth."

There was some complicated trading around of baggage; about halfway through it Ted realized that Randolph meant them to leave their horses with the camp. He put on the pack he was given. It was no heavier than his typical load of schoolbooks for a weekend. He watched Ruth settle hers on her shoulders. She bounced it experimentally and said to Randolph, "How far is it to the Gray Lake?"

"We can't get there by candlelight," said Randolph.

"Nay," said Ruth, disgustedly, "nor back again."

Randolph, rummaging through his fourth saddlebag in search of something he couldn't find, looked up with a startled face. "Whence cometh that?"

"It's a *nursery* rhyme," said Ruth. "But—"

"Only in so strange a nursery as thine," said Andrew.

Ruth gave him a freezing look of a sort Ted had seen on her face exactly once, when the boy who drove the ice-cream truck past the farm had implied that her father was crazy. Ellen had thrown an unpaid-for ice-cream sandwich at him and followed it up with a handful of gravel; but Ted thought it was the look on Ruth's face that made the boy drive his truck away without even swearing at them, let alone running them over.

Andrew was less impressionable than the ice-cream vendor. He smiled, and Ruth looked away.

"Ah!" said Randolph, and pulled from the fifth saddlebag a dull gray globe about the size of an orange. "Now are we well victualled."

Ted hoped he was being metaphorical. The gray globe was less than appetizing. *Your worm is your only emperor for diet,* said Edward, with a nasty chuckle. *We fat all creatures else to fat us, and we fat ourselves for maggots.*

Ruth shivered suddenly, and Ted caught her hand and pulled her away from the others, onto the gravelly edge of the stream. "What'd Lady Ruth say just now?" he said.

"It was the other one. It said, 'Your worm is your only—' "

" 'Emperor for diet.' "

"And so on. Edward said it too?"

"Maybe it isn't Edward in the back of my mind after all?"

"How would you know?" said Ruth. "I can only tell mine apart because Lady Ruth has an accent."

"Lucky you," said Ted, gloomily.

They looked back at the others. Andrew was talking to Jerome; Randolph was addressing the rest of them. It was cold down here by the stream. Ted started to move back toward the others, but then Randolph came down the slope, Andrew behind him.

"Now," Randolph said. "This is the Owlswater. 'Tis neither deep nor strong, but 'tis otherwise treacherous. Do we hold to one another." He held out a hand to Ruth, who hesitated, then took it and quickly gave her other hand to Ted. Ted was therefore obliged to offer his hand to Andrew; Andrew didn't seem to mind. Everybody was wearing gloves or mittens anyway. Ruth was too picky.

"Come on," said Randolph, and stepped into the stream, followed by Ruth.

Ted held tightly to Ruth's hand and went after them. The water was less than knee-deep and as cold as snow. The bed of the stream was rocky and uneven, but none of the rocks shifted as he stepped on them. The mist slid around him; he could no longer see Ruth, or even hear her splashing, though her hand still pulled him on. *The water is wide,* said Edward, if it was Edward. *I cannot get o'er.* "You've *been* o'er," muttered Ted. *That undiscovered country from whose bourn / No traveller returns,* said Edward, in the tone of one answering an argument.

Ted bumped suddenly into Ruth, who dropped his hand and said, "Watch it!" The mist cleared ahead of them. Ted moved to one side quickly, and let go of Andrew as Andrew came out of the water. They stood on a wide beach of round, smooth pebbles, beside a wider stretch of running water whose far side was veiled in gray mist. It was quite dark; the sky on this side of the stream was overcast. *How is it,* said Edward, *that the clouds still hang on thee?*

"Ruth?" said Ted.

"Time, like an ever-rolling stream, / Bears all its sons away," she said.

"No. How is it that the clouds still hang on thee?"

"Oh, no, my lord," said Ruth, her voice all lit up with mischief, "I am too much i'th'sun."

"Don't *you* start!"

"Order, if you please," said Randolph, mildly. "We must walk yet awhile tonight."

They walked beside the stream, sliding a little on the round stones. The stream grew wider and noisier, and wound about so much that Ted wondered why they bothered to follow it. Maybe there was no straighter way. On their right a profound darkness topped with pale points stood up against the dim sky: mountains. One wouldn't want to climb among those in the dark.

Ted was lagging behind. His legs ached. He made an effort to catch up, and saw Ruth stumble. Andrew caught her. Ted came panting up in time to see her thank him politely, and remove her arm from his grasp after a decent interval.

"Randolph, we seem to be getting tired," said Ted.

"I am not," said Ruth, a little raggedly. "I just can't see."

"That can we remedy," said Randolph. He pulled something out of the front of his cloak, held it up in both hands, and said thoughtfully, "The morn in russet mantle clad walks o'er the dew of yon high eastward hill."

A dim red light filled his hands, and warmed and lightened and spread until he held a glowing golden globe the size of a grapefruit. Ted recognized the color, and repressed sternly a desire to ask Andrew what misdirection he thought had produced such an effect.

"That's better," said Ruth.

"Do you carry't, then, and lead the way," said Randolph.

Ruth took it promptly in her mittened hands. "It isn't warm," she said.

"That's a second spell," said Randolph, reaching for the globe.

"No, don't bother," said Ruth.

Edward said, *The air bites shrewdly; it is very cold.*

"Maybe where you are," said Ted, under his breath.

They followed Ruth along the stony shore. It was a very quiet night; or maybe, thought Ted, everything in that circle of golden light had fallen silent. The little globe lit up the landscape for an amazing distance all around. Ted could see on his right where the tumbled rock gave way to grassy slopes, and on his left how the river widened and widened, while the mist slowly dispersed from its far shore, which was revealed as a narrow, stony beach overhung by crumbling dirt banks with the grass hanging over them like uncut hair.

They went on. The dark, irregular shape of a clump of trees loomed up against the left-hand banks. Randolph, who had been walking next to Ruth, turned around and held up his hands to the rest of them.

"We must cross the water again," he said. "Here 'tis no sorcerous boundary, but a shallow water merely."

He turned around and splashed into the river. They followed him. This water was not so cold, and under it was firm sand. Ted trudged along next to Ruth. The dazzling globe turned the rippled water and the air itself to gold, and shone in her hair and eyes like the shining from shook foil.

Edward said, *Ask me no more where Jove bestows, / When June is past, the fading rose; / For in thy beauty's orient deep / These flowers, as in their causes, sleep.*

Ted went on walking through the water, and even scrambled up the opposite shore without mishap; but he did it all staring at Ruth. At the way her hair sprang from a peak in the middle of her high forehead, and wound in hundreds of curling tendrils around her pale face; at her thick black eyebrows arched like the ears of a cat over her huge, black-bristled green eyes; at the severity of her nose and the delicacy of her mouth; at the scar on the back of her thin hand where he had dropped a candle on it, unintentionally, when she tickled him.

"*Ruth*," said Ted.

"What?"

"Edward's in love with you."

"Shhh," said Ruth. "Lord Randolph, of your courtesy, would you carry this globe awhile? My wrists ache."

"I'll take it," said Andrew, doing so.

"Thanks," said Ruth, and fell back with Ted to the end of the procession. They were in among the trees now, on a broad, smooth path. Ruth said, "Now what's all this?"

"Edward's in love with Lady Ruth."

"Poor fool," said Ruth, bitterly.

"Where'd you get that scar on the back of your hand?"

"Bumped up against a baby-sitter's cigarette," said Ruth. "That was the last we saw of *him*. Patrick was furious; the guy was reading him *Gödel, Escher, Bach*. Not that Patrick was old enough to under—" She seemed to shake herself, and said, "Why do you ask?"

"Lady Ruth's got one too. Edward spilled candle-wax on it. Edward," added Ted, on reflection, "is getting to be a nuisance."

"He's got to be better than Lady Ruth."

Edward said, *Comparisons are odious*, and Ted shut his mouth on what he had thought of saying.

They walked in the woods a long time. Finally they found a huddle of rocks, wrapped themselves up in their bedding, and slept without setting a watch or even consulting about it. Ted hoped that if anything came to kill him it wouldn't wake him up first.

Chapter 22

TED dreamt that he was at a school concert with his parents; Laura was playing the flute of Cedric. She was playing "Good King Wenceslas," with more flourishes than Ted had thought it possible to wring out of a flute; but the music teacher, who was sitting next to his mother, was extremely angry because Laura had been supposed to play "What if a Day," whatever that was. The music teacher was explaining all this to Ted's mother in an angry whisper; Ted's mother kept trying to shut the music teacher up so she could hear Laura. Then the sixth-grade choir filed onto the stage. Ted suddenly realized that Laura was wearing one of her Secret Country dresses; and he was jolted out of his pleasant dream-state, wherein everything was as it had been before their cousins moved to Australia.

Then the sixth-grade choir sang not "Good King Wenceslas," but something that jarred uncomfortably with it. Ted caught snatches of the words. "Cannot a chance of a night or an hour cross thy desires?" Laura's playing faltered, and then steadied. The choir sang, "All our joys are but toys, Idle thoughts deceiving." Laura stopped playing and stood looking thoughtful. "None have power of an hour in their lives' bereaving," sang the sixth-graders.

Laura grinned and lifted the flute again. She played a song Ted had never heard; but the words to it rose out of the back of his mind, and covered the sounds of his mother arguing with the music teacher and of the choir still singing. *And from the Dragon's mouth that would / You all in sunder shiver / And from the horns of Unicorns / Lord safely you deliver.*

Edward's voice rose triumphantly, with the piercing sound of the flute. Light flashed off the silver thing, and hurt Ted's eyes. He blinked, and opened them again on a dazzling shaft of sunlight. One little ray had found its way into their clutter of rocks, and it had to hit him in the eye. Around him the blanketed forms of his traveling companions breathed gently. Ruth had her head on his knees. Her face was dirty, and her hair was wilting into a semblance of what other people's hair looked like. Ted remembered vividly the time Ruth had decided that not washing it for a month would make it straight and flat, and the reaction of his aunt Kim to this proposal.

He was afraid that if he looked at Ruth any longer, Edward would wake up and behave badly. He raised his eyes and considered the rest of them. Andrew lay beyond Ruth, on his stomach, with his face in his folded arms, lank brown hair leaking out from under the blanket pulled over his head. Randolph was sitting up against a rock near the opening of this rocky hollow, his arms around his knees and his head tipped over at an uncomfortable angle, as if he had not intended to sleep at all. His face was scratched and his hair looked like Ruth's.

Ted poked Ruth in the shoulder. She twitched once, opened her eyes, and made a horrible face at him. "Oh, God!" she said. "*This* is what I hate about traveling in the Hidden Land. Waking up like this and knowing I can't have a hot shower."

"What did you dream about last night?" said Ted.

He kept his voice low, and Ruth's when she answered was lower also. "Hot water," she said. "Are your legs asleep, or can I lie here and enter gradually into the true horrors of my state?"

"Did you dream about anything else?"

"You ought to have helped out in the Spanish Inquisition,"

grumbled Ruth. She shut her eyes. "Let me think. Yes," she said, and opening them again, she gave him an upside-down frown. "I dreamed of home. Not Australia, but the first farm. That's odd. I haven't dreamed of home since we've been here."

"What happened?"

"I was playing the flute," said Ruth, slowly.

Ted's heart jerked within him. "Well?"

"It was Christmas Eve," said Ruth. "You guys were there. It was nice. Except we were arguing over the music. Mom wanted 'Good King Wenceslas,' but Ellen and Laura insisted on this weird prayer. I didn't know the music, but they insisted anyway. Then Laura actually took the flute away from me; and I saw it was the flute of Cedric and got very upset; but I didn't think yet that this might be just a dream. Laura started playing a song I didn't recognize, and Patrick started singing, and Ellie; and then I saw that Celia and Matthew and Fence were all there too, and they sang. And then you poked me."

"What was the prayer?"

"'And from the sword (Lord) save your heart, / By my might and power, / And keep your heart, your darling dear, / From Dogs that would devour. / And from the Dragon's mouth that would—'"

"'You all in sunder shiver,'" said Ted, "'And from the horns of Unicorns / Lord safely you deliver.'"

"You too?"

"Different setting," said Ted. "Same song."

"Your mumbling," said Andrew, sitting up and flinging off his hood, "waketh not the dead, but waketh me most rudely."

"Sorry," said Ted. "Shouldn't we be going, to wake the dead in earnest?"

"Give you good morrow," said Andrew.

"What's good about it?" said Randolph, without moving.

"My sentiments exactly," said Ruth. She sat up. "How far to the Gray Lake?"

"A short walk only," said Randolph. He opened his eyes. "There is a house there wherein we may find refreshment."

"Let's go and find it, then," said Ruth, standing up.

Randolph and Andrew got up stiffly and went outside. Ruth shook out her skirts and held a hand down to Ted. "Your legs *are* asleep."

"Not as much as my brain," said Ted. "Those dreams must mean something. I just can't think what."

"Neither can I," said Ruth. "Maybe the refreshment will revive our failing wits."

They came out blinking into the glittering sunshine. The trees around them were mostly oaks, and clutched still their dry brown leaves. The wind hissed in them. Their trunks were greened over with moss. A little ahead the wood grew up against tall gray rocks spotted with moss and lichen, the lichen delicate as lace, the moss as green as beryls. There was a cleft in those rocks.

The floor of the forest was crisp oak leaves, with damp ones underneath. The path Randolph found and led them along was rocky and rather narrow. Randolph stopped at the cleft in the rocks, and everybody crowded behind him and looked through it. It was wide enough for three or four people to walk abreast. A bar of sunlight sharp and vivid as a piece of yellow silk fell halfway along the stone floor from the opening at the other end.

Randolph, without saying anything, walked quickly through the cleft and out the other side, and they followed him, Ruth and Ted together and Andrew behind them. They came onto a little lawn of short grass and goldenrod. Beyond this, the slope dropped very swiftly, and through ribbons of mist Ted saw a winding water laid out like a sleeping snake, striped with water-weed and bordered by purple loosestrife and whole clouds of goldenrod.

There was a house on the other side of the water. Tile for red roof tile, window for leaded window, graceful front and awkward wing and gray stone and white and faint yellow, it was a copy of the house at One Trumpet Street, Claudia's house, that Ted and Laura had done their best to burn to the ground.

"*That's* where we may have refreshment?" said Ruth.

"How not?" said Randolph, without turning. "Thou didst have't in th'other house."

"Yes, but if Claudia wasn't in that one, won't she be here? I don't want to be entertained by Claudia, thank you very much."

"'Tis not her house," said Randolph.

He started down the hill; and again, they followed him. Ted cast a quick look at Andrew. Claudia's brother looked as he had looked in her other house: as if he felt creepy. It didn't make him walk any slower, thought Ted. All these people appeared to be of the type that takes the earliest dentist's appointment that offers itself, just to get it over with.

They reached the shore of the lake, and turned right to walk around its near end. The flowering plants were pleasant to look at, and the little slosh of the waves on the shore was pleasant also; but Ted did not like the look of the lake. It was flat and shining, but it was not clear. The morning sun laid no glittering path across it. It looked like a Midwestern sky before a very bad thunderstorm.

They walked up a narrow dirt path to the house. It had no lawn; goldenrod grew up to its foundations and covered half the steps to the porch. These had once been painted blue, but were weathered gray with only thin streaks of color remaining. The windows of the house were filmed with dirt, and drifts of leaves and dead grass lay in the corners of the porch.

Edward said mellifluously, *Egypt's might is tumbled down / Down a down the deeps of thought.* Oh, go to sleep, can't you, thought Ted; and a whole concourse of voices rose up and answered him. *Macbeth shall sleep no more; / To die: to sleep; / No more; and, by a sleep to say we end / The heartache and the thousand natural shocks / That flesh is heir to. We have come, last and best, to that still center where the spinning world sleeps on its axis, to the heart of rest. Lay on thy whips, O love, that me upright, poised on the perilous point, in no lax bed May sleep. Knit up the ravelled sleeve of care, and scatter thy silver dew on every flower that shuts its sweet eyes in timely sleep. Life death does end and each day dies with sleep.*

"Randolph!" shouted Ted over the din.

"Though you bind it with the blowing wind," said Ruth, "and buckle it with the moon, the night will slip away like sorrow or a tune."

"That is most certain," said Randolph, turning from a gloomy perusal of the house.

He took Ted and Ruth each by a shoulder, and said, "Now heed me. A little firmness shall set them packing. But fix your eyes on some common object and consider not its name, nor any word. Thereafter, but guard your thoughts and speak not to them, and you shall do very well."

Ted obediently looked at the black woolen hem of Ruth's cloak, snagged in five places and spotted with mud. The voices quieted and vanished.

"That's better," he said, and no chorus commented.

"Yes, it is," said Ruth.

"Good; you have the knack of it," said Randolph.

"What is this yammering?" demanded Andrew. He had gone up the porch steps already, and nobody had paid much attention to him. He was quite pale, and his forehead was damp. "Why is the air full of voices?"

"*Oh*," said Ruth.

Ted looked at her quickly, but she was frowning at the ground, so he turned back to Andrew. "What foul trick is this?" cried Andrew.

"Peace, break thee off," said Randolph.

"Look, where it comes again!" said Andrew, wildly. "In the same figure like the king that's dead!" He checked as if somebody had hit him, and then ran down the peeling steps and seized Randolph by the shoulders.

"Read me this riddle," he said between his teeth, and shook Randolph.

"A little firmness," said Randolph, rather jerkily, but with no evident surprise or anger, "sets them packing. Do you smooth out your mind, my lord, but while one with moderate haste might tell a dozen, and they'll quit you."

"Smooth out my mind," said Andrew, as if Randolph had suggested something both impossible and repellent. "Drink up eisel; eat a crocodile." He stopped shaking Randolph, but Ted saw his fingers close hard on the stained wool of Randolph's cloak and on the flesh under it. "What foul place is this, that but requires we do divide ourselves from our fair judgment, without the which we are pictures or mere beasts?"

"For the merest jot of time," said Randolph. If Andrew was hurting him, he showed no sign of it. He put a hand over one of Andrew's and said mildly, "What fear you? Are you so splenitive and rash that in so short a time reason shall flee you? How do you sleep? Think, man; you're muddy-mettled with this yammering."

"Answer me again," said Andrew.

"I cannot," said Randolph, still mildly. He wrenched himself out of Andrew's grasp and took the porch steps two at a time. He strode hollowly across the porch, grasped the knocker of the door, and slammed it down with a violence Ted suspected he wanted to use on Andrew. The sound echoed inside the house.

Randolph turned and said, "Andrew, there's no answer that can please you. Shall I say, these are the grazing-grounds of the unicorns, whose meat is words and their drink music?"

"Pah!" said Andrew.

"Andrew," said Ruth, to Ted's surprise, "if you won't think of nothing, try thinking of something nobody would ever write poetry about."

"Go to," said Andrew.

"Then will you let me try a superstition?"

Andrew shrugged. Ted saw that he was hardly listening to her; even that "go to" might have been spoken to the clamoring voices.

"Come up on the porch, then," said Ruth. "I want to get everybody. Ted, you might have to help."

Ted followed her up onto the porch. It creaked alarmingly under all their weight. The door was gray and weathered, its carvings threaded with fine cracks. The knocker must originally have been brass; it was now green. This one was not the dead rat; it was a long, whiskery dragon holding in its formidable teeth the drooping and very dead-looking body of a unicorn.

"That's disgusting," said Ruth.

It made Ted very uneasy, but it also made him want to grin. He said, "If it is the unicorns yammering, I can see how somebody might get tired of them. And think of all their nasty jokes."

"It's still disgusting."

"None answereth," said Randolph, and put his hand on the door.

"No, wait," said Ruth. "Please, may I employ a superstition first? My mind mislikes me."

"Superstition mislikes me," said Randolph, frowning.

"I dreamt a prayer last night," said Ruth, "and I want to say it, that's all."

"What manner of prayer?" said Randolph.

Ruth grinned at Ted and said, "'And from the sword (Lord) save your heart, / By my might and power, / And keep your heart, your darling dear, / From Dogs that would devour.'"

Ted said, "'And from the Dragon's mouth that would /

You all in sunder shiver, / And from the horns of Unicorns / Lord safely you deliver.'"

"Thou didst dream this?" said Randolph. Ted could not tell what he thought of it.

"I dreamed it too," said Ted.

"They're quiet," said Andrew. His face cleared and settled into his usual calm. He bowed to Ruth and said, with no sarcasm that Ted could detect, "Lady, I do thank you."

"Think nothing of it," said Ruth.

Randolph looked from her to Ted to Andrew, with the face of somebody who is trying to remember a poem and has it all except for the first line. Ted felt the same way, but dared not indulge the wish to compare speculations with Randolph; not when Andrew was listening. He made a helpless face at Randolph.

Randolph scowled at him. Then he shrugged, and said, "Let us go in."

Ted put both hands on the dry, rough wood of the doors, and pushed. They swung open, grating, and a cold gust of dusty air swept out onto the porch and clouded the clear smell of the morning. Randolph walked into the front hall with Ted on his heels. Before them on the left was a narrow flight of steps from which the faded remnants of red carpet hung dismally, and on the right a long hall whose walls were studded with picture hooks. There was no rug on the floor, only the thick gray dust.

"Some have been here," said Randolph.

Ted looked more closely at the dust, and saw a line of footprints that looked as if they had come from ballet slippers, several lines of prints from cats or other small animals, and a number of odd impressions that looked more like craters on the moon than anything else. These all led down the long hall.

Ted looked at Randolph, and they went down the hall also, with the other two behind them. It led to a sun porch running the whole width of the house at the back, whose three outside walls were all windows. From the windows of the right-hand wall they could see the fields of goldenrod staggering uphill to meet the brilliant sky. But the windows of the left-hand wall looked out on a view from High Castle: the glassy lake, the slopes of forest, the insubstantial mountains. And every little diamond-shaped pane in the back wall held a different picture.

Ted took hold of Randolph's wrist before he realized what he was doing. "Here," he said. "Here's where she does it."

Randolph wore a very Patrick-like expression, alert and interested. He moved closer to the back wall, towing Ted with him. He laid his other hand over Ted's clutching one and said, without looking at him, "How may we govern what we see?"

"I don't know," said Ted. "If you try to concentrate on a particular piece of a scene that's there, you'll be able to see it as if you were quite close to it. But I don't know how you determine what scene is there in the first place."

They all peered at the wall; then Randolph put his hand on a pane right before Ted's nose. Ted moved back a little and then, reluctantly, looked at the view it offered. He saw the topmost room of Apsinthion's house, the one full of mirrors. A black night sky with three stars in it pressed against the skylight. The room was lit with the peculiar harsh glare of fluorescents. The man himself stood in the middle of the room, surrounded by bubbling pools of purple. He was laughing. They sounded angry, like tomato sauce that is boiling too fast. Ted recognized them. They were the water-beasts you could find around High Castle.

The voice of the man in red came faintly out of the window.

"I'm fire," he said to the sputtering creatures, "and you are but the semblance of water melded with the actuality of earth. Wherefore shall you damage me? Who hath served you so discourteously as to send you to this comfortless house wherein no wish of yours may be gratified save that to be instantly gone again? May I make amends, I shall do so." The water-beasts began a prolonged and confused sploshing and smacking; they sounded like a mudball fight on a very wet day.

"That's him, Randolph!" said Ted. "The man who sent us back."

"That," said Randolph, "is no shape that I know."

Ruth said behind them, "Can he hear us?"

Randolph said promptly, "My lord Apsinthion!"

The man in the window did not look up.

"Who might say he was fire?" asked Ruth.

"Any one might say so," said Randolph. His jaw dropped slightly; his hand fell away from Ted's, and he turned and leaned heedlessly on the glass wall and looked at Ted and Ruth, and over their heads at Andrew lingering in the doorway. "Any one might say so," said Randolph, with a startling exuberance, "but one only so saith truthfully."

Ted felt bewildered, and Ruth looked it.

Andrew said resignedly from the doorway, "Belaparthalion," in about the way an eight-year-old who has just discovered where his parents are hiding the Christmas presents might say, to a younger sibling, "Santa Claus."

Randolph turned around and addressed the wall again. "Belaparthalion," he said.

The man in red swung a mirror parallel with the floor, apparently to show the water-beasts themselves in it, and took no notice.

"If Claudia put him in there," said Ted, "probably only Claudia can get him out."

"He doesn't look very upset," observed Ruth.

"That's for the dragon-shape," said Randolph.

Ted backed up until he was standing next to Ruth, and looked the whole wall over. It seemed to have some method in its arrangement. The scenes from the front door's carvings, from the tapestries in High Castle, were all there, two in each corner and the last one in the middle of the wall. Ted concentrated on that. All the animals fled from the center of the little diamond pane, where there was a ragged hole like a nail-tear in a shirt. Ted went quickly forward, but the pane was above his line of sight. "Randolph," he said, "of your courtesy, look on this pane here and consider carefully the hole in the middle."

Randolph looked away from some window in the lower right corner, blinking a little. "Gladly, an thou wilt look on this one," he said.

Ted changed places with him, but watched him rather than the window. Randolph leaned his forehead against the glass and then jerked back. "It's warm," he said.

"I know," said Ted. "What do you see?"

"Profound darkness," said Randolph. "And a golden glow in its midst, like unto an apple of Feren in its color, but unto the sun drawn by an artist in its shape."

"And in the midst of the golden glow?"

"A sword that shineth blue, and in its hilt three blue stones."

"Like Shan's sword. Is there anything in the sword?"

Randolph was still for a long time. Ted looked at the pane Randolph had assigned him. It showed a moonlit clearing in an evergreen forest. Somebody stooped and lit a fire; the red light washed up cheerily and Ted saw that it was Claudia. She sat down on a stump, and three black cats climbed into her lap, complaining. She laughed and said to them in the throaty voice Ted remembered, "There shall be fish tomorrow."

Ted looked at the wedge of the black sky visible in the upper part of the pane, and stared at it until it widened and filled the whole diamond. It was full of stars.

"Naught within the sword," said Randolph.

"See if you can identify these constellations," said Ted.

Randolph knelt beside him and stared obediently. "Those are northern stars," he said. "As you might see at the furthest tip of Fence's Country, in the realm of Belaparthalion."

"So Claudia and her cats are right where the rest of them are going?"

"Or have been; or will be. Saidst thou not that, in that other house, were scenes both past and present and to come?"

"We'd better warn them just in case," said Ruth.

"What we need's a ladder, or a stool," said Ted. "Somebody ought to peruse every one of these panes."

"Do you begin on the lowermost," said Randolph, "and one shall relieve you."

"I'll bring you some tea," said Ruth, "if there's any to be had."

Ted thanked her. The rest of them trooped out, and he settled down to his task. It was worse than looking something up in *The Oxford English Dictionary*. There were distractions everywhere. Any pane on which he fixed his attention would stir to life and begin its slow progression; but most of them held nothing that he recognized. Many showed only empty landscapes. He went back to the pane that held Claudia and her campfire, but she just sat there petting her cats while the fire died. She might do something in five hours, or five minutes, but how could you tell? Ted went on watching her anyway. The voice he thought of as Edward's, and which was beginning to distinguish itself from those other voices, said, *For God's sake, let us sit upon the ground / And tell sad stories of the death of kings.*

"That," said Ted, "is what got us into this mess."

Nor are we out of it.

"Is that really you?" said Ted. "Edward Fairchild, heir to the throne of the Hidden Land?"

To err is human, said Edward dimly; and Ted felt his shadowy presence dim also and go out. He shook his head and went back to staring at the windows.

CHAPTER 23

MICHAELMAS'S room had a large table that he was using as a desk, an even larger round table with chairs set about it, several extraneous chairs, a wardrobe, and a collection of chests and cabinets. On the chairs were papers, books, very small sundials and astrolabes, crumby plates, mold-scummed teacups, and sleeping cats. These last didn't want to be sat on, but were amenable to being scooped up and put on one's lap. Laura and Matthew and Patrick each got a cat, gray, orange, and orange-striped, respectively. Celia might have had a large and scruffy black one, but she looked at it and sat on the table instead.

The man in the yellow robe, who Ellen said was Michaelmas, had picked up his pen again while they shuffled through his belongings to find the chairs, and wrote placidly until they were all seated. Laura noticed that none of the grown-ups tried to recall his attention, and that he looked up and spoke just as Patrick evidenced an intention of saying something.

The man in yellow said, "Wherefore do you grace us with your presence?" He did not say this ironically, nor as if he meant it, but, Laura thought, like the "May I help you?" salespeople use. He looked from Celia to Fence and back again, as if the rest of them didn't matter.

"We seek the answers to three riddles," said Fence.

"The other party," said Michaelmas, hunting among the piled scrolls on his desk and knocking a mug to the floor, "seeketh knowledge of Shan's Ring, and of the swords of Shan and Melanie."

Patrick, who had been slumped as far down in his chair as he could get without falling out of it, sat up abruptly. Laura and Ellen looked at each other. Fence had Shan's Ring; Ruth had left it for him when they made their unsuccessful attempt to leave this place behind them. Celia had the swords of Shan and Melanie in her baggage; but Fence had plans for them. They also happened to be the only sure way the five children had to get home again.

There was a less-than-friendly silence. Fence stood up. "Did they bring these objects for your examination?" he said.

Michaelmas gave him his full attention. "No," he said.

Fence said, "Give me some light."

Michaelmas, seeming not in the least put out at being spoken to so peremptorily, gazed the room for a moment and said, "Light breaks where no sun shines."

Warm golden light sprang out at them from ceiling, from floor, from every corner. It was not dazzling, but it did startle. Laura saw, when she had recovered, that there was a large number of things rather like grapefruit, strung or just lying around the room. They all glowed. Disordered though the room might be, there were no cobwebs in it and no dust.

"Thanks," said Fence, and fished in his pouch. He walked up to the man in yellow's table and laid two objects on it. "This is my ring of sorcery," he said, "and this is the Ring of Shan. Had the other party any such tokens?"

"They are not required," said Michaelmas. But he looked intently at the two rings, one of shining silver with a luminous blue stone in it; the other, clouded brass with a black rock of the sort anybody might pick up out of a flowerbed. Then he held out his hand. "May I look at them?"

Fence scooped them up and dropped them into his palm. There was less inimical silence while Michaelmas looked them over, held them up to the light, and finally took a lens out of the drawer of his table and examined them through that. The silence was broken by impatient-sounding footsteps in the hall, heralding the appearance of a middle-sized woman in a blue robe, with a bunch of keys at her wrist and a wool cap on her head.

"Michaelmas!" she said. She had a vigorous voice, a sharp face, and brown hair in braids. "You've lit up every mage-light in the library. Use the morn in russet mantle clad; it doesn't reach so far." Then she looked around the room and seemed about to make some apology; and then she said, "Celia!"

"Chalcedony," said Celia, with quieter but very real pleasure; and she got off the table and hugged the woman.

"What strange names they have here," said Ellen to Laura.

"Madam," said Fence, "sawst thou the party that did arrive yesternight?"

"You *are* that party," said Chalcedony, perplexed. She let go of Celia and considered the rest of them. "All except Celia. What makest thou from High Castle one day late?"

"Michaelmas," said Fence; the man in yellow looked up. "Who made up the other party?"

"All save thou," said Michaelmas.

He and Chalcedony stared at each other.

"There!" said Fence. "That's better than tokens."

There was a meditative silence. Celia and Chalcedony moved into a far corner and began talking in low voices. Fence and Matthew shook their heads at each other. Michaelmas began rummaging again in the mess on his desk.

"You know," said Patrick, cheerily, and Laura jumped. "It's all very well sitting here making deductions; but why don't we just find these characters and ask them what the hell they think they're doing?"

"I'd sooner go without seeing them," said Fence, not to Patrick but to Matthew. Matthew nodded. Fence said to Michaelmas, "Where have you quartered them?"

"Atop the westernmost block," said Michaelmas, still rummaging.

"You've got to be kidding," said Patrick.

"Can we resolve our riddles and be gone by morning, we shall do so," said Fence.

"You never did say if you thought the Dragon King sent them."

"I trust he hath," said Fence. "If they answer to him, at least they do answer."

"Fence, where's your spirit of adventure?" said Ellen, entering the fray with such suddenness that Laura jumped again.

Michaelmas looked up from his search and said to Fence, "Speak your riddles."

Fence said, "What beast is it the unicorns pursue each summer? Before what beast doth winter flee? What beast maketh that which putteth the words to the flute's song?"

Michaelmas sat back in his high, cushioned chair and whistled. "And you think to be gone by morning," he said.

"You know them not?"

"I know one only, the second."

"But," said Laura, seized with irritation, "they're a matched set. They all have the same answer. What's the answer to the second one?"

"The dragon," said Michaelmas. "But look you, this is clean impossible. The unicorns pursue not the dragon; nor maketh the dragon that which putteth words to the flute's song."

"Are you sure?" said Laura. "Because the one who gave us the riddles said that when we knew these things, then what manner of thing he was we would know also. And he talked as if he could fly; and he had a red light in his eyes."

"Where met you this man?" said Michaelmas.

He had found what he was looking for: a large brass bell. He rang vigorously, and Chalcedony came across the room and took it out of his hand.

"The cook's asleep," she said. "It's late. I've tea in my room."

She went out, and came back with a tray, giving Laura time to wonder if she had said too much to Michaelmas about the man in red. Fence didn't seem disturbed.

The tea was extremely strong, and unsweetened, but it was hot. Laura decided that, if she really couldn't stand to drink it, she would leave it sitting on the floor to get moldy, and nobody would know the difference.

"Where she met this man," said Fence, when they were all settled, "is all entangled with the matter of Shan's Ring. Now, I'd meant to tell you of that; 'tis knowledge you can sift better than we, and of a sort that does belong in this Library. But I'd as lief th'other party had it not."

"Had it never, or not for this present time?" said Michaelmas.

"Not for this present time."

Michaelmas looked over Laura's head to where Chalcedony sat on the table with Celia. Laura craned over her shoulder in time to see Chalcedony looking whimsical. Chalcedony said, "How long must this present time endure?"

"A year and a day," said Fence.

Both Michaelmas and Chalcedony fell upon this proposal with scorn, and there followed about twenty minutes of wrangling. Laura, comfortably ensconced with a purring cat in a cushioned chair so big that she could pull her legs up into it, a chair that moreover was not jogging her anywhere at a pace too fast for comfort, did not pay them much attention. Both members of the Library staff appeared to view with horror the notion of hiding knowledge from anybody, even an unknown group of shape-shifters that had impersonated the party from the Hidden Land and made off with their boats. Patrick tried to enter the fray and was abjured to shut up, unsuccessfully by Ellen and successfully by Fence. Laura dozed, hearing dimly the four of them snapping "Nine months!" "A fortnight!" "Six months!" at one another like people bargaining in a market.

Laura shot to wakefulness as her relaxing hand tipped the mug and spilled warm tea all over her knees. It wouldn't show on the dark green of her hose. Michaelmas's cushions, however, were of yellow silk with a fetching border of running squirrels. She mopped surreptitiously at them with the hem of her cloak.

Fence said, "Until spring, then," and Michaelmas nodded.

Laura decided to drink the rest of her tea. It would be safer inside her; and she might need to stay awake.

Fence explained what Ruth had discovered about Shan's Ring, and what, he kindly said, Patrick and Laura had discovered about the swords of Shan and Melanie. Laura, listening to him, was stricken with a combination of admiration and horror. He wasn't lying. You couldn't say he was lying. But he conveyed the impression that Laura's own world was a third version of the Secret Country, as the glassy place Ruth had gotten into was a second version of it. This concept was apparently a pet theory of Michaelmas's; he thought that, if there were a second version devoted to bargaining with unicorns, there must be a third one devoted to bargaining with dragons. Chalcedony pointed out, in the tone of one who has said this before and knows she will have to say it again, that never in the history of the world had anybody bargained with a dragon or any dragon evidenced the slightest desire to bargain with anybody. Michaelmas agreed with her but seemed not to think it mattered.

Laura was interested to see that Fence agreed with him and Celia did not. Matthew, if he had an opinion, did not vouchsafe it. He said, "Forget not the man in the stark house."

Fence gave him a look half-grateful and half-impatient,

and told Michaelmas about the man in the stark house, who, in addition to the characteristics mentioned by Laura earlier, wore red, and used cardinals as messengers, and knew three riddles about the unicorns, and used mirrors as if they were windows, and called himself Apsinthion.

"I would I could see his face," said Michaelmas.

Laura had to clear her throat, it was so long since she had spoken. "My lord, he looks like Fence and Randolph," she said.

She felt silly as soon as she had said it, but Michaelmas looked suddenly alert. "In what particulars?" he said.

Laura rallied her courage, gave herself time to think even though Patrick was bumping his foot impatiently against the leg of his chair, and spoke. "He had black hair, but it was straight like Fence's," she said. "He was sh—as tall as Fence. He had Randolph's hands and nose, and his chin, but his eyes were round like Fence's. His voice wasn't like either of theirs, but I recognized something about it."

"High or low?" said Michaelmas.

"Low," said Laura, "and rather crackly." She heard him in her mind's ear, saying, *Oho. Sits the wind in that quarter? "Oh,"* she said. "It wasn't his voice, it was the *way* he said things." She stared at Michaelmas. That dry voice, talking as if everything it said were a joke you weren't getting. "In the way of unicorns," said Laura.

"Would their fancy take them so far?" said Michaelmas to Fence.

"To wear red?" said Fence. "To come under a roof in that place wherein dragons may bargain?"

Laura didn't see why not, but Michaelmas seemed to find this a cogent argument. "The other, then," he said, slowly. "Well, Fence, what are thou and Randolph, commingled?"

"An ill fighter and a worse wizard," said Fence, dryly.

"What's amiss with Randolph, then?" said Chalcedony. "He was your excellent good student when I saw him last."

"I jested," said Fence, very shortly indeed.

Laura looked quickly at Chalcedony. She seemed doubtful, but said no more. Fence was getting careless; things must be weighing on him.

"Well," said Fence, and stood up. "You have your knowledge, the which you may impart to any visitors you will, in the spring. We have the answer to one riddle, and with that, I think, we must content ourselves and depart. I had rather have these meddlers behind me than ahead of me. Can you direct their researches into some byway of detail, Michaelmas, until we're a day gone?"

"You can't go unsatisfied," said Michaelmas. "Stay but an hour; Prospero's your man for riddles; I'll wake him."

"You'll—" began Chalcedony, and looked at Celia, and shut her lips.

"There's no need, i'truth," said Fence.

"I'truth, there is," said Michaelmas, standing up also. He was as tall as Benjamin, but half as broad. "We've sent no one hence so soon since Shan came to us; and that once will serve us a mort of years. Sit down. Those who shadow you are long abed, awaiting report from some three of our apprentices. And that," said Michaelmas, coming around his desk and frowning, "might have been a sign to me, had I been quicker. When did the scholars of High Castle send apprentices to do their reading for them? Well," he said again, and putting a hand on Fence's shoulder bore him back into his chair. "Rest, and I'll bring Prospero." He left.

"Rest," said Fence; he sounded as if he were going to follow it up with "Ha!" but in fact he said, "Celia? Thou mayst take this chance to hobnob with thy schoolfellow."

"If she can spare the odd hour," said Celia.

"Gladly," said Chalcedony.

They went out together, Celia bestowing on Fence as she went by a very curious look, compounded of wryness, reproach, and irritation. Their footsteps sounded on the stone floor outside, and a door opened and closed again. The two rings on the desk winked in the golden light, and burst suddenly on Laura's eyes like a display of fireworks. Huge shapes of fire blossomed against a starry sky. They illuminated, falling, the massive bulk of a square castle set in the middle of a sheet of water. Blue and green and red and yellow shot streaming across the sky and rippled blurrily on the surface of the water. Very faintly, she heard Ted's voice cry, "Have at you now!"

She blinked, breathing hard, and the two rings winked tranquilly at her.

"What's the matter?" said Ellen.

"Fence," said Laura, "don't you think you should take those rings back?"

"No doubt," said Fence, and coming forward he picked them up and dropped them into his pouch. His mild gaze lingered on Laura, but he said nothing. Ellen glared at her, but she didn't say anything either. Laura expected to be tackled later. She ought to tell them about this vision, right now. Some reluctance she could not define nor defeat closed her throat. The dread of her dreams was with her still, the baseless feeling that Fence was not a safe repository of confidences.

"Now," said Matthew, leaning forward. "What in truth, Fence, do thou and Randolph make, commingled?"

"A fool and his twin," said Fence, turning around and leaning on Michaelmas's desk. His face was not encouraging.

Patrick said, "I wondered when you'd think of that."

"Thou wert not o'er-hasty wi'thy advice," said Fence; his voice wasn't encouraging either.

"Why let him know we'd caught on, if there's anything to catch on to; if there's not, why offend him?"

"I am of two minds, to go or stay," said Fence to Matthew. "How well acquainted is Celia with Chalcedony?"

"Very well, once," said Matthew.

"She'd know a deception?"

"Very like," said Matthew; and got up suddenly. "Wherefore—" he said.

“She’s seasoned,” said Fence, irritably. “What’s thy acquaintance with Michaelmas?”

“It is but slight,” said Matthew. “Prospero, however, I do know well.”

“Mayhap thou shouldst wake him,” said Fence.

“Fence, if we’re contemplating leaving soon, should we disperse all over the castle?” said Patrick.

“If Michaelmas is not himself,” said Fence, “it is too late. Matthew, go.”

Matthew went. Laura would have obeyed that tone too, no matter how unwelcome the task it assigned her. She was beginning to feel cold, although this was the warmest room she had been in since they came back. She looked at Ellen. Ellen wore a half-smile and an air of deep interest. Laura gave up on her.

“Now,” said Fence. “Heed this lesson. The hair meaneth appearance, the hands deeds, the eyes intention, the height potential, and the dress desire.”

Ellen and Patrick and Laura all looked at him blankly.

“Well,” said Ellen, after a moment, “that might make sense if somebody were drawing a picture.”

“If the man in the stark house is the Judge of the Dead, or a unicorn gone mad, or some other great power,” said Fence, “then he is but a picture; a weareth that shape but as a garment.”

“Why should the garment tell us anything?” said Patrick.

“Any shape-changer is constrained by his nature,” said Fence.

“Of course,” said Patrick, rolling his eyes.

“Any artist is named by his work,” said Fence, rather sharply. “Think on’t in that light, an it please thee better.”

“I’m sorry,” said Patrick, to Laura’s shock. “I don’t mean to fault your explanations. But it’s all so *subjective*.”

They embarked on a discussion that Laura didn’t listen to. She was remembering what Fence had said. When there was a pause in the conversation, Laura marshalled her list carefully and leaped into the gap. "So," she said, "he's got your *and* Randolph's appearance—"

"Which is obvious anyway," said Patrick, with such alacrity that she knew Fence had been getting the better of the argument.

"It meaneth, the outward seeming where that differeth from the inward form," said Fence.

"—Randolph's deeds, both your intentions, and a desire for redness."

"And a limited potential," said Fence, grinning at her. "An my middle name be not tact, I know whose is."

"What's a desire for redness?" said Ellen.

Fence shrugged. "The knowledge of the Red Sorcerers," he said. "Fire. Iron. Blood. The carnation."

"Wisdom," said Ellen, suddenly. "Don't you remember? Black for death, yellow for sickness, white for health, gold for faith, violet for purity, silver for treachery. And the major schools of sorcery: red for wisdom, blue for sorrow, green for novelty."

"That was the game," said Patrick, scornfully.

"It's true just the same," said Fence. He was beginning to look tired. "So. What have we, then? A man whose intentions are whatever few Randolph and I yet have in common, whose desire is for wisdom, whose deeds are murderous, and whose power is small."

"That doesn't seem to get us anywhere," said Ellen.

"Have patience," said Fence. He sat down again and propped his forehead on his hands. The thick, ill-cut hair tumbled over his scraped knuckles; he always forgot to put his gloves on until he had bumped his hands on something. He had a birch leaf caught in his collar. Laura looked at him worriedly. She herself might be stupid, and just now figuring out what they were talking about; but indeed Fence ought to have thought sooner that, if there were shape-shifters loose in Heathwill Library who could look like the party from the Hidden Land, they might just as well appear as members of the Library staff.

Nobody said anything. Patrick got up restlessly and began examining the room, poking into corners and lifting piles of papers. Ellen looked at Fence, as if expecting a remonstrance; when none came, she got up and began an exploration of her own. Laura's cat jumped out of her lap, climbed into Ellen's abandoned chair, and went to sleep again. The cats Patrick and Ellen had disturbed followed them around the room.

Laura left them to it, and watched Fence, and thought about shape-shifters. There must be several kinds. There were the ones they had fought in the battle with the Dragon King, which Matthew said were held to seven shapes only. Then there were the ones that could look like other people; and then there were the ones that could look like whatever they chose, except that it would reveal their nature one way or another.

"Fence?" she said.

Fence looked up, with his usual accommodating expression.

Laura said, "Were the horses you threw Ellen's cloak over the kind of shape-shifter that is held to only seven shapes?"

"Five," said Fence. "Horse, cat, dog, eagle, unicorn."

Those were the animals in all the tapestries about Shan. Laura decided to ask about that later. She said, resignedly, "What other kinds are there?"

"Those held to three shapes, to five, to seven, and to nine. All these are animal shapes only. Those that have a shape of their own and can but mimic other forms of't, as a young white hart may make itself a mighty buck or a helpless fawn; or a child form itself as an old woman. Those that have no shape of their own but may form themselves as they will, by memory or by imagination."

Well, she hadn't been completely wrong. "So the ones

looking like us could be either of the last two kinds? Because if they were people to begin with, they could look like other people? Or if they could form themselves as they would, they could also look like other people?"

"Well done," said Fence, and smiled at her.

Then he stopped smiling, at the sound of footsteps.

Celia and Chalcedony came back into the room. Chalcedony looked sober and Celia irate. Celia sat down next to Fence, in the chair vacated by Ellen.

"This lady's herself," she said. "She saith that were Michaelmas other, she'd know't."

"Wherefore we must look to Prospero," said Chalcedony.

"Both Michaelmas and Matthew have gone to fetch him," said Fence. "Chalcedony, how well doth Michaelmas know Prospero?"

"As well as a knoweth anyone," said Chalcedony. "Which is to say, did a expect to see Prospero, a child waving a rag on a broom-handle and talking with a raspy voice might persuade him."

"Great," said Patrick, from the opposite end of the room.

"But Matthew would note a deception," said Fence.

"The matter," said Celia, between her teeth, "is, what may not Michaelmas tell a seeming Prospero atween Prospero's room and this?"

"That's the matter," said Fence.

More footsteps in the hall averted what would certainly have been an argument. Michaelmas came back into the room, followed by a remarkable figure. Prospero wore a black, starry robe like Fence's, except that all the stars were embroidered in some metallic thread in every possible color, and they had the obligingness to stay still when you looked at them. He had white hair rather like Einstein's, and a magnificent white beard tucked into his belt. He looked so very much like a wizard that Laura wondered about him.

"Welcome to Heathwill Library," he said. He had a deep voice, and a slight accent; he said his L's oddly, as if he were on the verge of trilling them into R's but could never quite make up his mind to it. His R's he said as Laura and her relations did; people in the Hidden Land trilled theirs a little, especially when they were excited.

"Thank you," said Fence.

He stood up and bowed, and then looked at Chalcedony. She bit her lip. "Prospero," she said, "where are my ten pennies?"

"I gave you them a month since," said a voice in the doorway. It was a deep voice, and rather raspy. Its owner was a tall man in an embroidered black robe who looked exactly like a wizard.

"Will the real Prospero please stand up," said Patrick, in a tone of considerable enjoyment.

The first Prospero turned and looked at the second. On their identical faces were identical expressions of amusement; they looked like Patrick and Ted in the middle of a contest of puns. They looked so exactly alike that Laura doubted both of them. She was glad they were enjoying themselves; an angry shape-shifter was not something she cared to think about; nor was an angry wizard.

Ellen said, "Where's Matthew?"

CHAPTER 24

TED wasn't accomplishing anything with the windows. He found Claudia again. Her fire had burned low and the cats were asleep. She was not; the small red light glimmered in her open eyes. She was staring straight out of the window at him, but her gaze was unfocused. Her mouth drooped a little. She looked as if she were waiting for something unpleasant, without either fear or resignation. Ted thought this might be the first really natural expression he had ever seen on her face; even the several flashes of anger he had witnessed seemed now, next to this calm distaste, contrived for someone else's benefit.

Andrew's clear, unimpassioned voice said behind him, "Canst thou catch my sister in the net of her own contrivances?"

Ted's stomach clenched, both at the question and at the uncanny echo of his thoughts; but he managed not to start. He turned around. Andrew knelt on the floor next to him, looking not unfriendly.

"I suppose it might not be her own contrivance," said Ted, laying his hand on the window. It was warmer than his skin, and repellent in some indefinable way; not exactly greasy, not exactly sticky, not exactly rough. He removed his hand. "Somebody might have made it for her; or she might have taken it over. But she did use it. I saw her."

He was talking too much. Andrew might be about to learn everything; but he might not. Andrew, looking over Ted's shoulder at the pane in which Claudia sat, did not question him further. And Ted, looking at Andrew's face, a little lined with tiredness, did not want to be the one to shatter Andrew's illusions about his sister.

"Where's everybody else?" he said.

Andrew shook his head, and turned away from his sister and her fire. "Contriving baths, and a meal," he said. "We must look our best when we seek to parley with the dead."

His tone showed that he thought this a silly notion; Ted thought he probably considered it silly quite apart from his disbelief in the possibility of talking to the dead.

"It is possible to talk to the dead, you know," said Ted. "I've been there."

"Truly, do you believe this?" said Andrew.

"Truly, I do," said Ted.

There was a protracted pause. Andrew sat back on his heels and rubbed a soiled finger over his moustache. "Forgive me," he said. "This thought will not be father to any action. But hearing you speak so, my liege, I do find in me for the first time some small, weak understanding of Randolph's reasoning, when he did murder thy father."

"I've been speaking so," said Ted, recoiling hurriedly upon the safer area of this supremely unsafe speech, "all along. What did you think, that I was lying? That I was part of some conspiracy of wizards to deceive the populace? I take that badly, my lord," said Ted, looking Andrew straight in his troubled brown eyes. "I take that very badly." And he did, on behalf of Edward, who might have been stuffy but had certainly been honorable and had probably never told a lie in his short life.

"If you're not a deceiver, then you are one of the deceived," said Andrew, unruffled. "Take you that in better part?"

"Better a fool than a knave," said Ted, bitterly.

"Oh, aye," said Andrew, growing rather heated, "a fool to be cozened by such a knave as Randolph. This conspiracy thou deniest did slay thy father."

"Randolph didn't do it," said Ted. And that was almost true. Claudia had done it; Laura and Ruth and Ellen and Patrick had done it; Ted had done it, literally, when he knocked from Randolph's hand the poisoned bottle into which Andrew had already slipped an antidote.

"Give me strength!" cried Andrew, jumping to his feet and glaring down at Ted.

"And I'll tell you something else," said Ted, tipping his head and glaring back. "Nobody is a fool in every part. I might be deceived in Randolph, and still have the right of it concerning magic. Or I might be deceived by this pack of rogue magicians, and still know Randolph's heart better than my own. Do you think on that, my lord."

"If you did think Randolph harmless and kindly," said Andrew, breathlessly, "why knocked you that bottle from his hand the day the King died?"

Ted was beyond caution. "Because it did pass by you, my lord, ere it came to him."

"Is that the story you hope will fadge?" said Andrew.

"You did put somewhat in that bottle," said Ted.

"What I put in that bottle, sweet prince," said Andrew, whitely, "was an antidote."

"And who told you you'd need one?"

"My sister."

Ted no longer felt so tender of Andrew's illusions. "Your sister killed the King," said Ted.

"She knew not you'd knock Randolph's arm."

"She could *make* me knock Randolph's arm if she had to," said Ted, "and she did know I'd do it, because—oh, hell, it's too complicated. She did it, Andrew. I'm sorry, but she did."

"And that's what this mummery of visiting among the dead is to accomplish," said Andrew, very quietly. He leaned on the left-hand wall. Behind his sleek brown head the ghostly mountains of the Secret Country floated like clouds, and a little wind rippled the water of the lake. Ted saw with compunction that Andrew was shaking. But Andrew's voice, when he went on, was perfectly steady. "You'll show us by your vile illusionist's arts the piteous figure of the murdered King, all pale and wan, distraction in's aspect, pointing a shaky finger crying, 'She, 'twas she, thy sister, Andrew!'"

"What the hell good would that do?" said Ted. "How should the King know who did it?"

That remark, he was pleased to see, stopped Andrew. "I'd thought the dead knew all things."

"Why should they?" said Ted. He grinned suddenly. "Yes, I know; they should in order that they may serve the conspiracy of wizards. But really, Andrew, I don't see why they should know any more than they did while they were alive." He felt much better, for a moment. Then he stopped grinning. Edward had certainly known who killed *him*. Ted did not know if Edward had found this out before or after he died. What did go on down there? "Well," said Ted, "we'll have to wait and see, won't we?"

They had their baths, and Ted began to understand Ruth's views on the subject of hot water. They dressed in clean, if creased, clothing. They foraged in the garden behind the house, which reassuringly was not laid out like the garden of the house near High Castle. They found an orchard behind the garden. They ate their limited meal. They sat on the dusty floor of the dining room in a litter of apple cores and dirty bowls, and looked at one another.

"'Never put off,'" said Ruth, quoting Agatha. "Randolph, how do we get where we're going?"

"Through the cellar," said Randolph.

"Oh, great," said Ted. "I suppose it's full of cobwebs and spiders and all the doors creak?"

"In Claudia's house," said Randolph, dryly, "I doubt the doors creak not." He stood up, brushing crumbs of oatcake from his shirt. "Ted?" he said.

Ted, startled at being addressed by his ordinary name, stared at him. Randolph said, "Is it cold below?"

"Haven't you ever been there?" said Ted, without thinking.

Randolph didn't answer him. Ted said, "I was dead. It didn't feel like anything. It looked cold. There's a river and a lot of mist. Let's not go dancing down there in our shirt-sleeves, if that's what you mean. We'll be cold with nerves, if nothing else." Nerves was right; he was talking too much. Ruth, sitting on the floor across from him in a welter of blue wool and pink legwarmers, smiled and shook her head.

They all stood up and put on some or all of their outer garments. Randolph took something rather like a hurricane lamp from a carved shelf. It was made of a rough, greeny metal like the door knocker, and consisted of three cats wound lovingly around the central glass chimney, their tails encircling it at the top and their bodies at the bottom. Randolph made a small motion in the air with his free hand, and a little flame bloomed obediently from the candle in the middle of the lamp. Without a word, he walked through the hall into the kitchen, and they followed him.

The door to the cellar was undersized, but otherwise normal. Randolph pushed it open and ducked through it. He went down the steep flight of steps, set the lamp on a short stone pillar, and beckoned to Ted. Ted came cautiously down the steps, and the others followed.

The cellar was a little damp and completely empty. Its floor was made of great blocks of stone, like the floors of High Castle. Two of these had been propped up. Darkness gaped below them. Randolph held the lantern down near the opening, and Ted bent over next to him and looked. A clean smell of rock and water rose from the depths. A shaft walled with stone blocks dropped maybe twenty feet to a stone-block floor. Down at the bottom of the shaft were six square dark doorways. Thick metal bars were fastened into two of the walls of the shaft, to make ladders. They shone as bright as a well-kept sword, with no sign of rust.

"This lamp casts a lot of light," said Ted.

"'Twill cast less below," said Randolph. "Only honest light's allowed below, and this flame's someways tainted with sorcery."

Ted wondered at his choice of words; was he baiting Andrew?

Randolph went down the ladder one-handed, carrying the lamp. Then he stood at the bottom, out of the way, and held the light for the rest of them. The metal bars were so cold that Ted expected his hands to stick to them. It was colder at the bottom of the shaft than in the cellar.

Ted began to fasten, absently, the brooch of his cloak, watching Ruth's nimble progress down the ladder and worrying a little about Andrew's intent eyes on her downbent head. Then some warmth, some slight tingling, in his cold hands made him look at the brooch. It was of twisted silver, set with a blue stone. He had taken it from Shan's robe of state, in the West Tower, on that day in August when he and Randolph chose their costumes for the feast at which the King died. He tried to remember, of all the times he had fastened and unfastened this cloak in the course of their journey, one in which he had noticed the brooch. He couldn't. He finished fastening it, and said nothing.

"What passage?" said Andrew, arriving last.

Lo! said Edward, richly and pleasurably. *Death hath reared himself a throne / In a strange city, lying alone / Far down among the dim West, / Where the good and the bad and the worst and the best / Have gone to their eternal rest.*

And, "West," said Randolph, "but westward, look, the land is bright."

The western passage was perhaps seven feet high, and seven feet wide, clean, cold, and empty. The wavering light of the cat-lantern made and then spurned behind it twisty shadows that proved, when walked through, to hold only air. Little echoes ran away from their footsteps. Ted felt no urge to yell something and hear its echo come back to him.

There was nothing here to dislike, and yet he did not like it here. After fifteen minutes or so, Ruth, who had been ranging among the company like somebody looking for a dropped pin, fell into step with him and put a cold hand in his.

"This place mislikes me," she said.

"You too? I thought I felt so creepy because I've been there before."

"Don't turn around," said Ruth, "but Andrew's got a look on his face as if he's being followed by a hoofed fiend."

This seemed to wake up Edward. "'He can sleep while the commonwealth crumbles,'" repeated Ted, hazily, "'but a strange sound in the pantry at three in the morning will strike terror into his stomach.'"

Ruth exploded into giggles, then stopped suddenly and said, "Why are you quoting Thurber?"

Ted said, "Edward was."

"I don't know why that should be any more mysterious than Edward quoting Shakespeare," said Ruth, "but it seems so."

"I know," said Ted.

"Ted? Was it really bad down there?"

"It's a fine place to visit," said Ted, seized by a desire to laugh, "but I wouldn't want to live there."

Ruth squeezed his hand. "You must have a pulse of a hundred and fifty," she said. "Your hand's all sweaty."

"You can go hold Randolph's hand if you'd rather," said Ted, irritated. "What does *he* look like he thinks is following him?"

Ruth didn't let go; nor did she seem angry. "He doesn't look like he thinks anything is following him," she said. "He looks as pleased as punch."

"I was afraid of that," said Ted.

"And I wouldn't hold Randolph's hand for a wager," said Ruth.

Something in her tone made Ted wary of questioning her.

They walked on. The passageway sloped downward. After a while a breeze began blowing up it. The lantern Randolph carried dimmed and wavered. The passage turned a sharp corner, and another, and another. Then a square of dim gray light made itself known ahead of them. They stepped through it, out onto a glimmering, featureless plain, under a dull, gray, misty sky.

It was subtly different from the place in which Ted had found himself after he was killed in the battle. After a little thought, he realized why. He had not been, really, in the land of the dead. He had been on its borders. They had refused to let him cross the river, because he was neither dead nor alive, but being bargained for. Why he and his companions, who were unequivocally alive, had been allowed this time into the very midst of this realm, he had no idea. But they were in it, and probably in for it, now.

"Well," said Andrew, "call your ghosts."

Ted stared at him. They had forgotten the blood. The ghosts would talk to you if you gave them blood to drink. "Living man," they had said to him, "hast thou brought blood?" Edward had talked to him without it, but Edward had recognized himself. Shan and whoever else Randolph might want to talk to would probably not be so accommodating.

The lantern went out. Randolph set it on the ground and put a hand on his belt. Ted, in the wake of a horrible suspicion, leapt wildly at Randolph and grabbed his arm with both hands. "Oh, no, you don't," he said.

Randolph looked at him without surprise. "It needs but a little," he said. "Do it thyself, if thou wilt." And as Ted's nerveless hands fell from his arm, he pulled the dagger out of his belt and offered it.

Everybody else was staring. Ted felt profoundly stupid, but he did not quite regret his action. Randolph wanted to die, and his moods had been erratic. Ted took the dagger. Its hilt was silver, with blue stones in it. Ted wondered if Randolph was still allowed to use it. Fence had not required it of him when he took Randolph's ring of sorcery away; and it did not make Ted's hand prickle as an enchanted weapon would.

Randolph was holding out his hand to Ted. Ted took a firm hold of his chilly wrist, drew a deep breath, and made a small cut on the side of Randolph's hand, where it should give the least trouble. A thin black line of blood sprang up. Randolph took the knife back, squeezed the blood onto its blade, knelt, and drove the knife up to its hilt in the gray stuff of the ground.

"We call," he said, "by Chryse's blood and the mercy granted to Shan, the smilers with the knife under the cloak, the gracious presences of the Lords of the Dead."

Then he stood and waited. Nothing happened.

"This entertainment's someways lacking," said Andrew, after perhaps fifteen minutes. He grinned at Ted. "I'm for a jig, or a tale of bawdry, or I sleep. I'll go sit on the wholesome stone; do you call me when your prompt arriveth." And he turned his back on them, walked over to the little square stone house they had emerged from, and disappeared inside.

Something in the air of the place, thought Ted, squelched the desire for action. Just standing and waiting was a wearisome task. He went on doing it. Nobody spoke. Then the character of the plain they stood on changed. It might have been a field of white flowers under the moon. Somebody was walking toward them, a short, slight figure. He came closer, a young man with dark hair and decided eyebrows, with a cat on his shoulder. He wore a robe like those worn in High Castle, like Apsinthion's. It might have been red.

The young man came to within two feet of Randolph, and said, "Who calleth Shan?" He had a light, very pleasant voice, a voice you would like to hear reading to you at bedtime when you were very young. *But now we are six*, said Edward.

"Randolph," said Randolph, "King's Counselor of the Hidden Land."

"You are welcome," said Shan, gravely. "Take back my greetings to the world of light. How may I serve you?"

"Act as our ambassador to the Lords of the Dead," said Randolph. "They answer not, and our errand is most urgent."

"I will essay it," said Shan. He cocked his head, and his inquisitive eyes moved from one to another of them, and finally returned to Randolph, at whom he looked steadily for a very long time. Randolph returned the look, with no particular expression; but Ted, behind him, saw how his hands clenched in the folds of his cloak.

"What's amiss?" said Shan at last, in the friendly and resigned tones of a parent or a cousin.

"Naught that death can't mend," said Randolph, tranquilly.

"Randolph," said Ted, stepping forward.

Shan looked at him; and stared; and put out a hand. Ted felt it on his arm, very lightly, like the brushing by one's legs of a cat that has other business. "Edward Fairchild," said Shan. "How art thou translated?"

"Edward Fairchild's dead," said Ted. "I come from elsewhere; and I came," he added, "by your sword."

Shan's whole face lit up in a flash of delight so intense that Ted found himself smiling back. "That," said Shan, "is news I have waited long to hear. Soft you now," he said, apparently to himself, and stopped smiling. "How came Edward Fairchild dead?"

Faith, e'en with losing his life, said Edward.

Shan's head jerked upward and his hand fell from Ted's arm. The cat jumped from his shoulder and stalked away into the misty distance. "Leave thy unicornish games and speak to me," Shan said.

Then he stood waiting. His face was remote and a little worried. Ted considered his flesh-and-blood companions.

Randolph was looking at Shan as if he were the answer to a prayer. Ruth was looking at Randolph as if he were crazy.

After some indeterminate time, the shape of the cat returned across the flowery field, followed not by one figure but by five. Edward Fairchild, in an unlaced white shirt and hose and soft boots, a velvet cap on his head and on his face a kind of eager scorn, walked up to Shan, swept off the hat, and bowed. He was taller than Shan, and taller still than Ted. Behind him the dimmer forms of Lady Ruth, of Prince Patrick and the Princesses Laura and Ellen, stood silent, the sourceless light gleaming in their eyes. Ted heard Ruth draw her breath in.

Shan did not return Edward's bow. He said, "How came you here?"

"Ask thy lady," said Edward.

"Oh, Lord," said Ruth.

Lady Ruth said, "What distorting mirror is this?"

"Be quiet," said Shan, without heat. "Edward: what power hath the Hidden Land over the Lords of Death?"

"That the mercy granted to Shan did leave that land at the mercy of Melanie," said Edward, with an astonishing bitterness. He sounded as if he were reciting a rote answer that had suddenly taken on meaning, and that meaning was not a welcome revelation but a disaster.

"And what mercy did she show to thee?"

"As much as she did show to you," said Edward, more calmly.

"What wouldst thou have then from the Lords of Death?"

"That they bestow the same mercy upon Melanie as she did bestow upon us," Edward rattled off, and flung his cap to the ground. "My lord, this is folly. Death is no mercy, nor is the death of our murderer a boon to us. We died almost before we lived. What will it avail us to bring Melanie to cheer our exile? The boon I beg from the Lords of Death is our lives again, in their full measure."

"Edward," said Ted, "you told me to avenge your foul and most unnatural murder."

Edward wheeled on him. This was not the diffident, stuffy prince Ted remembered from their last meeting. Edward said, "I was but half awake when I told thee that; and what else hadst thou power to do?" He turned back to Shan. "The Lords of Death are very great in power; and by their debt to all my country, Shan the Red, I do demand this recompense. Let them sate their greed on Melanie; she's lived more years than I and all my cousins can come close to. But send us home again."

"Wait," said Ted. He pressed both hands to his head, where the blood was pounding like drumbeats. "Wait. You told me Claudia killed you."

"Verily, in that guise were we slain."

Ted was speechless. Ruth came up beside him and said carefully, "*The* Melanie? Who helped kill the unicorn?"

"She is that."

"Angels and ministers of grace defend us," said Ruth.

Ted looked at her. Claudia's being Melanie would explain a lot; but the explanations would be worse than the mysteries. "Amen," said Ted.

"How?" said Randolph to Edward. He had no expression at all, and there was very little breath behind his voice.

"She's of the blood of the unicorn," said Edward, rather impatiently.

Shan said, "She hath a blithe spirit, when she doth choose to set it free. And in her time she's learned every trick, great or trifling."

Ted remembered that Shan had loved Melanie too. He was answering the question Randolph had really asked. Ted watched this realization come more tardily to Randolph, who looked blankly at Shan and then nodded.

"Thou canst not flee her beneath the earth," said Shan.

Around them rose a thin murmuring, like the wind in a grove of willows. Ted looked up. The whole gray plain, which had seemed like a field of white flowers when Shan walked across it, was thronged with ghosts. Looking at them, he realized how solid by comparison Shan and Edward had become. Very distantly, a voice that was not Edward's said, *and what i want to know is / how do you like your blueeyed boy / Mister Death?*

"Melanie, the architect of all our woes," said Randolph, as if Shan had said nothing at all. "Well, 'tis tidier so. But heavens, what a web of deception must we now unravel."

"Andrew thinks she's his sister," said Ruth, suddenly. She flung her cloak about her with a determined motion and marched off to the little stone house. She returned very shortly with Andrew, talking vigorously and keeping a wary eye on him, like somebody shut in a room with a bat. Andrew wore a weary, resigned look under which some wilder emotion was struggling to make itself known. Ted felt rather like that himself.

"Shan," said Ted, "where *are* the Lords of Death?"

"They came not," said Shan, perplexed.

"Call them louder, then," said Andrew, in a cracked voice.

Shan turned and looked at him with an expression that froze Ted where he stood, although it was not aimed at him. Andrew stared back as if he were looking at a very badly painted picture. Shan's face cleared suddenly, and he said, "What's amiss here?"

"Leave thy damnable doctorings and call thy masters," said Edward. Shan swung on him as if he would have liked to knock him down; but Edward had forgotten him. He was gaping at Andrew; and then his anger seemed to clear away and he said, "My Lord Andrew of the limpid thoughts. What do you in this cloudy place? Edward Carroll, this is very ill done."

"Very ill done indeed," said Andrew, "if you must be your own commentary." He looked shaken just the same, and stood staring from Ted to Edward and back again.

"Shan," said Ted, "*please* call your masters."

"Those are not my masters," said Shan, his face shadowed again by a lighter version of the look he had turned on Edward.

"All right, I'm sorry. I'm a stranger. We have got to speak to the Lords of the Dead. This is getting out of hand."

"Your presence alone should draw them," said Shan. "Forgive me; I'll return." He disappeared into the crowd of ghosts.

Ted's gaze, following him and trying to distinguish his wake through the crowd, stuck suddenly on a very tall figure moving purposefully toward them, out of the drifting mass of figures. It was King William.

Ted took two steps and closed his hand hard around Randolph's arm. "Brace yourself," he said, and pointed.

Randolph looked along his extended arm, and Ted felt him shiver. Then he smiled, which was even worse.

"Don't do anything stupid!" said Ted.

"That advice cometh too late," said Randolph; but he neither shook off Ted's hand nor advanced to meet the King.

He did not need to. The King was coming to him. In his lined face were purpose and knowledge and recognition; but no anger, and no accusation. Maybe he didn't know.

The ghosts of the royal children sank suddenly to their knees. Andrew, his face like a mask, knelt too. Randolph stood where he was; Ted, feeling obscurely that while he had hold of Randolph he had some small control over the situation, stayed standing too. Ruth came up on Ted's other side and said, very softly, "Why is Andrew kneeling for a bad play?"

King William stopped a foot away from Randolph and said in his firm, carrying voice, "How fared the battle with the Dragon King?"

"My lord, we have won it," said Randolph. His voice was steady, but not very strong.

"Using what strategies?" said the King.

"My lord, those in King John's Book."

"Thou hast done well, then," said the King; and he put his ringed hands on Randolph's shoulders and kissed him.

Randolph's arm under Ted's was like wood. Ted was the one who was shivering. The King was within six inches of him; the trailing sleeve of the King's gown brushed Ted's hair. And yet Ted had no feeling of any living presence; no warmth, no breath, hardly even the differences in the feel of the air that one has from a chair or a wardrobe. But the figure of the King filled his vision and the King's voice lingered in his hearing.

The King stood back from Randolph, still holding him by the shoulders, and said, much more quietly, "By the oath you swore me, dear friend, I do abjure you now—hold your tongue."

"I thought all for the best," said Randolph, as if he were in the middle of some other conversation altogether.

"I know it," said the King. "I tell thee again, Randolph, hold thy tongue. Take thy doom from the mouth of thy victim: guide my son, and confess not this deed." He said in his original tones, "Where's Fence?"

"Gone north, my lord, to beg with Chryse and Belaparthalion that they will impose some order on the Dragon King."

"Edward," said the King, turning his hollow eyes on Ted.

"Here, Father," said Edward from behind the King.

The King turned; Ted saw his straight, broad back grow rigid. When he spoke he woke echoes, in this place that should be capable of none, and stilled the murmuring dead. "What makest thou here below the earth?"

"Oh, God," said Ruth.

Randolph leaned suddenly on Ted's shoulder and began to shiver. After a moment he sat down on the ground and put his face in his hands. Ted sat down with him, keeping hold of his arm.

"Don't listen," said Ruth. "Randolph. Don't listen. If you don't concentrate, the voices fade away."

Randolph did not answer her; Ted, unable not to listen while actually looking at the tight cluster of King and children, turned around.

"Andrew?" said Ted. "How is it?"

Andrew's strained gaze, stretched wide over Ted's shoulder, jerked to Ted's face. Andrew said, in a stronger voice than Ted had been able to muster, "'Tis a pretty show, my prince; you must show me the strings and the mirrors one day."

"I hope," said Ted, judging that concern was not what Andrew wanted from him, "that you note the absence of the piteous figure and the shaky finger and the distraction in the aspect?"

"The distraction's all in Randolph's," said Andrew.

This was inaccurate, since nobody could see Randolph's aspect. But Randolph instantly dropped his hands and tossed his hair out of his eyes. Ted let go of his arm, and Randolph laid a hand on Ted's knee. Ted suspected that it meant, "Keep your mouth shut."

"'Tis in your aspect also," Randolph said.

"He spoke you very lovingly for one so estranged in his philosophy," said Andrew.

"He'll speak you twice as fair do you but pluck his sleeve," said Randolph.

"He loved you ever," said Andrew. "I made him doubt you, but to hate you I could not move him one whit."

"Nor could your attempts move him to hate you," said Randolph. "Go speak to him; you'll have no peace else."

Andrew looked over Ted's shoulder again, and shock wiped his face clear of all expression. "*With whom doth he speak so close?*" he said. He snatched his horrified gaze back to Ted. "Lady Ruth, in her habit as she lived," he said. "*What are you?*" He half rose, telling over one by one the dim figures grouped around the King. Then he sat down hard and awkwardly, and looked for a very long time at Ruth.

"Edward," he said to her at last, "I cannot tell one from t'other; but thee, my lady bright, I know for a false jade. My lady's with her father; and what art thou?"

"Hold your tongue," said Ted, creakily.

"Wert puzzled?" said Andrew to Ruth, in rising tones. "Wert much afeared? Didst wreck thy thoughts on the tangle of my most—" He let out a wavering breath very like a sob, and set himself, visibly, to regaining his control. "How came matters to this pass?" he said at last; and he said it to Randolph.

"Later," said Randolph. "Speak to the King."

Andrew got up unsteadily and walked past Ruth and Ted and Randolph. None of them watched him go. Randolph put one hand over his eyes for a moment, and said, "Ruth, take not on so."

Ted looked quickly at Ruth, who was choking into the crook of her elbow. Ruth never cried.

"Sorry," said Ruth, thickly, from behind her arm and a cloud of hair. "What a fiasco." She sniffed hard and shook herself as if she were about to emerge; then she said, "Oh, hell," and choked again.

Randolph fished in his sleeve, and in his belt pouch, and then patted himself vaguely, like a man in a three-piece suit looking for his parking ticket. He finally pulled a handkerchief from the sleeve of his cloak and tucked it into Ruth's hand. Ruth blew her nose and tidied her hair back from her face.

"There's Shan," said Randolph, and stood up hurriedly. "I pray you pardon me."

He strode past the clump of King, children, and Andrew, and walked into the clustering ghosts. They parted for him like a curtain of beads. Once Ted was alone with Ruth, he was able to pull her hair and say, "'I have a speech of fire that fain would blaze, but that this folly douts it.'"

"Don't quote Edward to me." Ruth blew her nose again.

There was some commotion among the ghosts. Ted looked over Ruth's shoulder and said, "Randolph *did* see Shan."

Ruth stood up; so did Ted. Randolph and Shan were coming slowly toward them; Shan kept stopping to talk to the ghosts, who then grew noisy. It seemed that, after he had spoken to a group of them, its members grew more solid and distinguishable, and their voices less shrill.

Shan and Randolph came out of the crowd and crossed the open gray ground toward Ted and Ruth. Something in their walk, their disparate heights, the absorption on their faces, was familiar to Ted. As they arrived before him, and Shan bowed, Ted realized what it was. Just so were Fence and Randolph accustomed to pace around together, arguing.

"What news?" said Ruth, in a not altogether natural tone.

"Good for these folk," said Shan, "but bad, I fear, for all your party."

"Don't tell me," said Ruth. "They heard we were coming and they've fled the country."

"I know not what they've heard, my lady, but in truth, they are not here."

"They're *all* gone?" said Ruth.

"All nine," said Randolph.

"What about the Judge of the Dead?" said Ted.

"You may speak to him, my lord, an you will," said Shan. Ted surmised that Randolph had told him that Ted was the King of the Hidden Land. Shan went on, "But he cannot act; he can but bring suasion to bear upon the Nine Lords, when they do return."

"I want to ask him some riddles," said Ted.

"Why bother with him?" said Ruth. "You've got Shan right in front of you."

"Ask, by all means," said Shan. "Most I meet here do ask me riddles, and cry aloud when I do answer them, for 'tis too late. For you the answers may prove more timely. Say on."

"What beast," said Ted, obediently, "is it the unicorns pursue each summer?"

"The dragon," said Shan, in a curious voice.

"Before what beast doth winter flee?"

"The dragon."

"And what beast maketh that which putteth words to the flute's song?"

"Not the dragon," said Shan. "The third question is rightly—"

"But what's the answer to our third question; please?" said Ruth.

And Shan said, "The Outside Power."

The three living people looked at one another.

"Outside power is unfurled," said Randolph.

Shan caught hold of his cloak, altering its hang only by a little; and said excitedly, "You did use the Ring?"

"Why don't you tell us," said Ruth, in a flat voice, "about the Ring."

"Why don't we sit down?" said Ted.

They did. Watching Shan sit down was rather disturbing; where he and the ground met it was hard to tell which was which. The ground was soft, dry, and cold, and gave no reassurance by any of its characteristics that it would still be there the next minute.

Shan told them, with a loving attention to detail that reminded Ted of Patrick, about Shan's Ring. The unicorns had given it to him in reparation for some injury, which he did not elaborate. They had told him it would bring him his heart's desire. Shan's heart's desire, it appeared, was death. Randolph raised his head at this point, and he and Shan exchanged a very long look, which Shan ended by saying, "Take better heed than I was able of dear, beauteous death, the jewel of the just."

Randolph said nothing, and Shan went on. He had thought, he said, that this remark of the unicorns was one of their cruel jests, because they themselves had deprived him of his death. He thought of his next dearest desire, and whether Shan's Ring might aid him to achieve it. This was some means whereby the mere people of the Secret Country and its surrounding lands might receive justice from the magical creatures they lived with. There was no meeting ground between them, no appeal. The dragons and unicorns took offense, or took a fancy, and did what they would without consulting the people involved.

Now the Red Sorcerers, of whom Shan was one, had been accustomed to use enchanted mirrors to see things far away.

"That's a device of the Red Sorcerers?" broke in Randolph. Ted remembered the hand mirror in Fence's room, that they had used to scan the two hundred and eight steps for signs of Claudia. He thought of the innumerable mirrors in the stark house of Apsinthion.

Shan grinned at Randolph. "Aye, Blue Mage, that it is." He went on. He had found that if one looked in such a mirror while wearing Shan's Ring, one saw many and diverse places, some pleasant and some dangerous. In one of these places, which looked like the Hidden Land and yet unlike, he had seen unicorns. After a great deal of thought and what he called "blundering," he had made a sword to take him there. And on that ground he had proposed to the unicorns that they consent to bargain with anyone they had wronged who had the courage and the means to take himself there. The unicorns had been amused, and had consented; but there was a catch, as always. Anyone who found them on their bargaining ground might indeed bargain; but if he lost, worse would befall him than he had already suffered. If he won he would truly be better off; but it would be hard to win.

"What about 'Time awry is blown'?" said Ruth.

"That," said Shan, soberly, "is an incidental kindness of the unicorns the backlash whereof I do still await. They do nothing that profits them not, but this attribute of the ring seemeth to profit only their petitioners. For look you, time in this place of the unicorns runneth quicklier; an Shan's Ring did not yoke it to the time of the human lands, for the duration of a human visit, even a man who won his petition might return to find his family dust and his grandchildren old as he."

Ted began to laugh. "Wouldn't you know it!" he said. "In our world, time runs the same as it does in the Hidden Land. But that didn't suit us; so we used Shan's Ring for just the opposite effect, to slow down time at home so we could return a bare instant after we left."

"Why so?" said Shan.

"To keep the grown-ups off our backs," said Ruth.

"Art so young, then?"

"Not anymore," said Ruth, with unexpected grimness.

"Well," said Ted, "the bargaining ground of the dragons?"

"I found it not," said Shan. "Nor, they tell me, did any Red Sorcerer ever lay eyes on't."

There was a brief silence. Ted, looking around, saw that most of the crowding ghosts had dispersed. Andrew still stood with the King and the five royal children, but their voices were subdued. Ted was cold, and very tired. He pulled his cloak more tightly around him, and his hand brushed Shan's brooch. He unpinned it hurriedly and held it out. It blazed like the ocean under a noonday sun.

"Is this yours?" he said.

"It was," said Shan. In the rich blue light his face was thoughtful.

"Then take it back again," said Ted.

"I'd not thought," said Shan, not taking it, "that it would prove so potent below the earth."

"You could use some power around here," said Ruth.

Shan said to Ted, "These things do not fall out by chance."

"Well, maybe I found it so I could give it to you. You take it."

"An I may hold it," said Shan. He took it from Ted's

fingers, and it lay on his small, wavery hand and did not fall to the ground.

"My thanks to you," said Shan. "May it be long ere I see you again. Or thou," he added, to Randolph.

Ted looked at Randolph, but Randolph only smiled. He looked back at Shan, and for a moment saw through him Randolph's hand and arm.

"My lord, you look tired," said Ted to Shan.

"The blood runneth dry," said Randolph.

"Where's your dagger?" said Ted.

"No," said Shan. "You'll need a whole skin and all the blood that's in you. Quickly, have you any questions more?"

"How did Melanie get hold of your sword?"

"Melanie!" said Shan, scrambling to his knees and staring.

"She left it for us to stumble on," said Ted. He added, "And she left her own for some friends of ours. Did you know she had one that would do similar work?"

"Of what color?"

"Green," said Randolph.

Shan slapped his hands down on his knees, a violent motion that made hardly a whisper of sound. "Oh, I'm justly served," he said. "I should have stayed. I am sorry, that I left this menace to ravage you. My lords and ladies, beware that sword of green. It will show you your own hearts in such a guise you'll cut them out."

He stood up, an agitated, wavering figure fading rapidly into the gray land and the gray sky.

"Where's the dagger?" shouted Ted, leaping up himself.

"No," said Shan; he was gone.

CHAPTER 25

LAURA could tell from Fence's face that he wished Ellen had not asked where Matthew was. Patrick seemed to see it too; and as Patrick terrifyingly sometimes did, he took his own advice.

"What the hell," said Patrick, walking up to the two tall men and looking from one to the other, "do you think you're doing?"

There was a petrifying silence. Laura considered her cousin, in his stained jeans and filthy tennis shoes and his dusty black cloak, and was stricken with admiration and jealousy. She looked at the two identical faces. One of them was grinning; the other wore an expression as of patience come abruptly to an end, like Laura's teacher just before he sent somebody to the principal.

The grinning Prospero spoke over Patrick's head to Fence. "You come carefully upon your hour," he said.

"I do not," said Fence. "I come abominably late."

"Not so late as we'd have made you," said the tall man, smiling still. There was something about the smile that oppressed Laura.

Michaelmas had been leaning in the doorway between the two Prosperos and preserving a perfectly blank expression. This latest remark, however, or perhaps that smile, appeared to stir him to wrath. "If that's a threat, my lords," he said, "go make it otherwhere."

The smiling Prospero and the frowning one both swung on him.

"Doubt you our word?" said the smiling one.

"No," said Michaelmas. "But I do doubt your manners. Having sworn to do no harm in Heathwill Library, it will behoove you not to threaten none. And concerning harm—what have you done with my colleague Prospero?"

"Why, nothing, save to look upon him in admiration," said the frowning man.

Michaelmas made an impatient motion with his hand. "Go in," he said; "sit down; and answer the boy's question."

The two men came in. Every cat in the room leapt up, sniffed the air, and curved across the floor to purr at the Prosperos. Michaelmas rolled his eyes at them, and sat down behind his desk.

The two Prosperos sat where Patrick and Ellen had been. Patrick and Ellen sat on the table. Celia and Chalcedony stood in the doorway.

"And for the love of mercy," said Michaelmas in a tone of profoundest irritation, "do you, one of you, or both of you, take some form other. And do you not," he added sharply, as the two men turned and smiled at each other, "assume some other, horrible form which might deprive our sovereignty of reason, and then say in innocence, I did bid you do't. Take you," said Michaelmas, breathing hard through his nose, "some harmless and inoffensive form that can speak with us, and leave your frivolings for but five minutes."

"You've dealt with us before," said the austere Prospero.

"And to my sorrow," said Michaelmas.

"Wizard, have a care," said the smiling one, and stopped smiling.

"Oh, go to," said Michaelmas. "You're as slippery as a mess of eels, but you do not break your sworn word."

"No," said the once-smiling Prospero, "but our memories are as long as time."

"Peace; make thy change," said the austere one.

The once-smiling one looked at him, and shrugged; and by what means Laura could not see, by the time his shoulders had leaned back on the cushion again, he was a little dark woman dressed in an infinity of layers of pink gauze. In a voice melodious as a flute, she said, "Will this serve?"

Behind Laura, Chalcedony made a muffled exclamation. Michaelmas, who appeared to be of a ruddy complexion and who had been growing ruddier in his exasperation, turned stark white, leaned forward, leaned back again with great deliberation, and swallowed hard. "It will serve," he said. "But I say to you now, my memory is long also."

"So," said Patrick, insouciantly but with a strained look on his sharp Carroll face, "is anybody going to answer my question?"

"We are come," said the dark woman, "to ask it of you, or of some minion of the Hidden Land. Something is amiss there."

"Took you long enough to notice," said Patrick.

"Patrick," said Fence, mildly but definitely. He turned his head and addressed the two shape-shifters. "Well, great ones, what amiss is this, and how may we mend it?"

"We look to you to tell us of the first," said the one who still looked like Prospero. "Michaelmas hath given us some clue. Is it true that you have dabbled with Shan's Ring?"

"It is," said Fence.

"That did awake us from our dreaming," said the dark woman. "But ere our start was o'er, before we could settle again, we did hear something other."

"A great shearing and clashing of swords," said the man.

"There was a battle in the south," said Fence.

The dark woman laughed. "We who slept through the ten years' agony of Owlswater, the twenty-five years' tossing of Feren atween Fence's Country and thine, to wake at that?"

Fence was silent. Laura knew what these two had heard. They had heard Ted and Patrick, practicing with Shan's and Melanie's swords in the rose garden.

"There are few sorceries," said the dark woman at last, "so potent as Shan's Ring."

"No doubt," said Fence. "Seek you the list of th'others in this admirable library, and come to me again when you have a more particular question. I'd tire the moon with talking, to tell you all our petty deeds since first we wielded Shan's Ring."

The tall man said, "Have you the swords of Shan and Melanie?"

"What is their fashion?" said Fence.

"Little one," said the man, in a clam voice infinitely worse than any angry tone could have been, "my patience hath an end."

"The swords are small," said the dark woman, laying her hand on the man's arm. He went on looking at her, as if the sight of Fence would be too much for him, all the time she was talking. She said, "Small, as for a Dwarf, or a child. Their hilts are black, and set with stones, Shan's with blue, Melanie's with green. Their blades from time to time do glow, with the colors of their several stones. They send a kind of tingling into the hand that toucheth them. Now, Fence, give us answer."

"I have a milliard such," said Fence. "How shall I tell the sword of Melanie from any that gloweth green?"

"Have you," said the tall man, still looking at his companion, "the swords of Shan and Melanie?"

"It may be so," said Fence. "You have not told me sufficient that I may mark them."

"They'll take you, an you carry them aright," said the dark woman, "almost as far as I'd send you, an I could."

"Have you," said the tall man, turning his cold yellow eyes on Fence again, and speaking in a deadly monotone, "the swords of Shan and Melanie?"

And Fence said, "Yes."

"Third time pays for all," said Patrick.

"We do require," said the tall man, "that you deliver them to us."

"By what right?" said Fence.

"None," said the dark woman, crisply. The tall man turned and glared at her. She said to Fence, "'Twill serve if you but promise to employ them no more."

"I do so promise," said Fence, without hesitation. He did not even glance at Ellen or Patrick or Laura, whom he had just condemned to the vagaries of Apsinthion.

"For your little lifetime," said the tall man. "A catnap; the space of a snore. What's that to us?"

"All you may have from so paltry a creature as I am," said Fence, looking right back at him. His hands were gripped hard on the carved arms of the chair and his jaw was rigid, but he sustained the look of the tall man, and it was the tall man who suddenly jerked his head around and said to Michaelmas, "Choose thy guests better."

Whereupon he and the dark woman got up and went out, closing the door behind them with a solid and unfriendly thud.

"Could I choose my guests at all, I know whom I'd unchoose first," said Michaelmas. He wiped his sleeve over his forehead. "Fence, you harrow me with fear and wonder."

"They are not in agreement," said Fence. "Had they been so, I do assure you, I had trod far softlier." He stood up, carefully. Laura suspected him of having shaky legs, but he spoke steadily enough. "Now," he said. "Let's find Matthew, and the true Prospero, and ask our riddles, and get us gone."

"You're better here," said Michaelmas. "Outwith these precincts they are bound by no oath."

"Can we but travel quickly, they'll have Chryse and Belaparthalion to deal with," said Fence. "'Twere a very great pleasure, Michaelmas, but no profit at all, to bide here."

"No pleasure, either, with the pair of them huggermuggering about," said Michaelmas.

Fence, who had turned for the door, looked around. "Which of them were those?" he said.

"Nay, I know not. Chalcedony?"

"They're strange to me," said Chalcedony. "Do you think, Michaelmas, that they may be some species other than the usual? There was something in their eyes; and the cruelty that took your daughter's form is of a different brand than what we're used to."

Laura wondered who Michaelmas's daughter was, and what had happened to her.

Michaelmas rubbed his forehead again, scowling at the drifts of paper on his desk. "I'd thought we had seen them all."

"I know," said Chalcedony. "But this troubleth me."

"Well," said Fence, "let's to Prospero's chamber, an you will."

Chalcedony and Michaelmas both came, leading the rest of them down the bright-lit hall and the narrow, winding stair and along yet another hall to a closed door. Michaelmas knocked at it. Nobody answered. Michaelmas rattled the handle, and then stood aside for Chalcedony, who took a key from her bunch and unlocked the door.

Prospero's room was the same size as Michaelmas's, but sparser in its furnishings. He had a bed, a table, a chair, a wardrobe, and many shelves crammed, but neatly, with books. If there was a bed in Michaelmas's room, thought Laura, it was well buried. Prospero's room was empty, though all its lights blazed and on the table were a half-written sheet and an uncapped bottle of ink. From the smooth bed a white cat blinked at them.

"Where would Matthew seek him next?" said Fence to Michaelmas.

Michaelmas looked helpless; Chalcedony said, "The Index Room; and then in the Special Collection. I'll go seek them; you stay here should they return."

She jingled off down the hallway. Michaelmas walked into the room, and after a moment of hesitation the rest of them followed him. There wasn't really anywhere to sit, and none of them, it appeared, felt comfortable wandering around looking at the books and other possessions of someone who had not invited them. Laura looked at the cat; that was not an invasion of privacy. The cat was large and clean, like the room, and well brushed. It wore a green collar with gems in it. Laura walked across the room, and the cat lifted its head.

Gold light flashed off the stones in the collar, and ran like water over rock, and dimmed and dulled until she saw a small bare room lit with cloudy light from one round window. A young man in a red robe sat on the floor, leaning forward over his crossed legs to write on a large sheet of waxy paper. He looked uncomfortable, but his voice when he spoke was pleased. He said, "Never go down to the end of town if you don't go down with me." Something tapped at the window; Laura looked at it, and saw a flash of red.

Ellen shook her arm. "Wake up, Laura, here's Matthew and Prospero."

The real Prospero looked just as the false one had. Laura received her introduction to him rather absently, and only just remembered to do him a courtesy.

Ellen shook her arm again, and she gave up. Michaelmas was delivering an admiring account of Fence's dealings with the two false Prosperos, for the benefit of the real one and Matthew. They greeted it with blank silence during which Laura sat down on the bed, careful to miss the cat. Prospero's embroidered black robe swam giddily before her eyes, behind a gloss of gray light and redness.

"What's the matter?" said Michaelmas, sharply.

"Fence, I'd credited thee with more sense," said Matthew, in a tone so unlike him that Laura forgot her vision completely.

"What do we need those characters for?" said Patrick.

"Matthew?" said Fence. "I see we do need them. What's the matter? Sit down, man, thou'rt like suet."

"Yon shape-shifters you all so blithely did offend," said

Matthew, "are the Lords of the Dead, come forth from their dominion for the first time since it was laid down. A fine welcome you gave to them."

"You didn't hear them," said Ellen. "They had terrible manners and they didn't care beans about us. They were miffed because we'd woken them up."

"We require a boon of them," said Matthew.

He looked at Fence until Fence sat forward and opened his mouth; then Matthew said suddenly, "I cry you mercy; I had done the same had I been here."

"No doubt," said Fence. "Do you do otherwise when you come to ask our boon."

Matthew looked as if he were going to object; Patrick said, "How do you know they're the Lords of the Dead?"

"I came upon two of them in the kitchen," said Prospero.

"You've seen them before, then?"

"How does seeing them before help?" demanded Ellen. "They're shape-shifters; they can look like anybody."

"There's a little fire in the eyes," said Prospero.

This kept getting worse. "The man in the stark house had a little fire in his eyes," Laura said.

"Of what nature?" said Prospero.

"Red," said Laura.

"Triangular, or i'the'shape of a diamond?"

"I don't know," said Laura, regretfully.

"For future reference," said Patrick, "which is which?"

"The triangular flame defineth the Lords of Death."

"Prospero," said Fence. "Is the Judge of the Dead among them?"

"I know not," said Prospero. "I got no speech of them."

"Wiser than I," said Fence. "Well, we'd best get it now. Matthew?"

Matthew looked around at all of them. "Said the rest of you aught to discomfit them?"

"I asked them what the hell they thought they were doing," said Patrick.

"Aught else?"

The rest of them shook their heads.

"Well, then," said Celia from the doorway, "Patrick and Fence shall stay here and beguile Master Prospero with the tale of our adventures; for our poor part, we'll seek out these lords and beg their favor."

"I think not," said Matthew. "Fence, they'll not hear me. I am neither a wizard nor a king."

"I begin to think I'm neither also," said Fence.

"They will tell you otherwise," said Matthew.

They looked at each other for some time; and then Fence nodded. "Come, then," he said.

Ellen, Chalcedony, and Celia moved from the door, with an alacrity that Laura found disturbing. She herself went on sitting on the bed, hoping to be forgotten. But Fence looked back at her quite kindly and said, "Come, lady; this concerneth thee closely."

Laura got up and went out the door in the others' wake.

"Well, Mistress Chalcedony," said Fence, as they reached the juncture of the two halls and headed for the staircase again, "what ground wilt thou choose for this battle?"

"The Reading Room," said Chalcedony. "Any such company will think thrice, e'en on the verge of breaking all its oaths, afore 'twill do damage there."

"What if somebody's studying there?" said Ellen.

"Then he'll garner a spectacle," said Fence.

Ellen caught Laura's eye and grinned at her. Laura shook her head and looked away. Celia and Matthew were holding hands again, and carrying on a complex and wordless conversation with their eyes. Laura and Ellen were accustomed to referring to such behavior, in their parents or in the older kids at school, as "making goo-goo eyes." But there was nothing gooey about this exchange of glances. Laura wished she knew what they were worried about; or perhaps she didn't.

They went back the way they had come, and turned into

the room across the corridor from Michaelmas's chamber. It was furnished with three large tables in the middle and a series of carrels, exactly as you could find in a modern library, along the walls. The furniture was heavy and beautiful, and perhaps half the material on the shelves was in the form of scrolls rather than bound books. The polished floor was scattered with intricately worked rugs; the light was warm and golden, not the harsh glow of fluorescents. But in its essentials, it looked like a library. Laura felt better immediately.

In a far corner of the room, somebody in a green robe and a black hat was scribbling furiously. Michaelmas went over and spoke to her quietly. She laughed, and appeared to thank him, and went back to scribbling.

"Well," said Ellen, sitting down sideways at one of the tables. "We're here. Who's going to round them up?"

"We who know the Library," said Chalcedony; and without further ado, she and Michaelmas made for the door. Ellen's voice arrested them halfway through it.

"Wait! Can we look at the books?"

"Wash your hands first," said Chalcedony. "Celia can show you." And they were gone.

The five remaining looked soberly at one another. Ellen did not clamor to be shown where to wash her hands. Matthew said, "I would we knew how th'other party fareth."

"They'll have been to the land of the dead for nothing," said Ellen. "Unless the Lords of the Dead can be two places at once."

Matthew smiled a little. "Not to my knowledge," he said.

Laura sat down next to Ellen and leaned back in the chair. The ceiling of the room was beamed and plastered. The wood was carved, the plaster molded; both were painted. The wood showed hunting scenes, and people building castles and making brooms and kneading bread and mending a wagon wheel. The plaster was formed into a series of medallions. Laura found the running fox of High Castle on its blue background; there were also an owl perched in a thornbush, and a mountain hare sitting up on the bank of a stream, and three brindled hounds with their tongues hanging out, each scene stylized and cleverly fitted into the confines of its circle. And there was also a scarlet curve of dragon with, horribly, a unicorn drooping from its toothy mouth. The dead unicorn looked like pictures Laura had seen of antelope being dragged away by the lions that had killed them. Its open eyes were picked out in gold paint.

Laura couldn't look away from them; and suddenly the glitter strengthened and spread. Good, thought Laura, maybe she could figure out what she was supposed to see in the young man's bare room. But what she saw was Claudia, in the back room of her house, leaning on the diamond-paned glass. She still wore the checked dress. Now she raised her hand to the glass, grimaced, and dropped it again. Then she smiled. She looked like somebody who has decided to eat a piece of chocolate cake despite a New Year's resolution to lose ten pounds. She went on watching her windows. Laura tried to see what she saw. A stone wall, a shelf of books, a golden globe for a lamp. Meredith's domain in High Castle? Heathwill Library? Some place other?

Laura blinked her way back to the Reading Room to find everybody except Fence staring at her. Fence had leaned his head against the high back of his chair and closed his eyes.

"I thought you were seeing things again," said Ellen. "What were you seeing back in Michaelmas's room?"

Laura told her instead of what she had seen in Prospero's room. Urged to tell what she had just seen, she told what she had seen in Michaelmas's room. She did not want to tell Fence about Claudia, even if he didn't seem to be paying any attention. Nobody had any comment. The woman at the far end of the room rustled her papers. It grew so quiet that they could hear the scratching of her pen. Laura was sleepy. It must be almost morning.

"Matthew?" said Ellen. "Do you want us to say anything to the Lords of Death?"

"Heaven love you, not a word," said Matthew. "Indeed, I'll say naught myself. Celia and Fence have the lighter touch."

"Oh, much thanks," said Celia.

There was a commotion in the hall outside. Five people came in, all scowling. It was hard to tell what they looked like; they were like sketches, or cartoon drawings, or the artistic efforts of a five-year-old. They made Laura's eyes hurt.

Matthew jumped to his feet and bowed; so Laura and Ellen scrambled out of their chairs and made the best courtesies they could manage, given their clothing and the inadequate warning. Celia stood up more naturally and bowed from the waist.

"The rest come by and by," said one of the newcomers, in a rich contralto Laura would have known again, she thought, in ten years, or fifty.

"Sit you down, then, and wait in comfort," said Celia.

The newcomers settled themselves at the end of the table, displacing the party from the Hidden Land. The dim voice in Laura's head said, *Move down; I want a clean plate.*

The newcomers began talking among themselves, in some language Laura did not understand, but recognized. It was that maddening tongue, used in the Secret Country's ceremonies, that one felt always just on the edge of understanding. It was less vexing this time because all of the speakers had such breathtakingly beautiful voices. Well, thought Laura, that made sense. They had come here to talk, so they had expended their arts on their voices and kept the appearance to a minimum.

She looked at Matthew and Celia, who were standing stiffly at about the middle point of the long table. They, it was clear, could understand the maddening language perfectly, and the lovely tones in which it was spoken were not mitigating in the least their reaction to what was being said.

Fence had opened his eyes and appeared to be listening, but not to be disturbed by what he heard.

The voice in her head said, more clearly, *Is't not possible to understand in another tongue? You will to't, sir, really.*

There was a burst of unintelligible speech in the corridor, and four more indeterminate shapes spilled into the room, followed by Michaelmas. The four sat down next to the first five; Fence got up and marched down to the head of the table; and Celia, Ellen, Laura, and Michaelmas sat at the foot, separated from the nine strangers by an empty chair or two, and from Fence by an appalling stretch of polished table.

All nine went on talking. Fence did not call them to order. It took them about ten minutes to calm down, during which Ellen amused herself by drawing cats with a stick of charcoal and some scraps of paper that she found in a drawer of the table, and the voice in Laura's head said, *The sun was shining on the sea, / Shining with all his might: / He did his very best to make / The billows smooth and bright.*

Finally the hubbub died and the shape with the rich contralto voice turned to Fence. "You have a grievance?"

"That's for you to determine," said Fence.

"Tell your tale," said a clear, lilting voice.

Fence told it, without adornment, and without explaining who the extra royal children were or where they came from.

"Five at one swoop," said the rich voice, consideringly. "This Claudia is bold."

Fence grew red; Laura could see that, all the way at the other end of the enormous table. He said nothing. The lilting voice said, "But we are cautious. Five at one swoop, back to the world of light? For what consideration?"

"For Shan's Ring," said Fence.

A babble of almost-sense broke out. Fence sat with his hands folded, his round face blank but rather light. The yellow light shone on the table, and on the almost-present shapes of the Lords of the Dead. A new voice, deep and resonant, said, "The River's Guardian hath been offered this token already, and hath refused it, on the ground that it was too eagerly given."

"I," said Fence, with considerable force, "give it not eagerly. We have but this year discovered its purpose and its power; a century of study might, an we were fortunate, show us its uses; a millennium of study might show us to avoid its dangers. It is my dear desire to have this thing."

There was another babble.

The lilting voice said, "Yet how will it profit us?"

"If you possess it, then none other doth so," said Fence. "Wherefore you will have peace from its thunderings."

"What bargain," said the rich voice, apparently not to Fence, "made we with Shan concerning this thing?"

"Oh, hell, oh, damnation, oh *perdition*!" breathed Ellen.

"Hush," whispered Celia.

"What did you make up?" hissed Laura.

Fence looked down the table at them, and they all shut up.

The lilting voice said, "That it be left as an heirloom of his house, and a weapon against Melanie, whom he could not vanquish."

"Offer us some thing other," said the rich voice.

"Will you take," said Fence, "the swords of Shan and Melanie?"

Matthew shot bolt upright in his chair, his shocked face flaming. Celia slammed her arm across his chest, and whatever he had been about to say turned into a huffing kind of choke. The mass of light and shadow that was the shapeshifters seemed to drift in his direction.

"We cry you mercy," said Celia, breathlessly; and they all turned back to Fence and broke out in their maddening speech.

"What's he thinking!" whispered Matthew.

"I know not," said Celia. "Don't cross him. Our division is their opportunity."

"So is his madness," said Matthew; but then he was silent.

The rich voice said, "That is our dear desire. For each sword, you may retrieve one child."

"Oh, *God*!" breathed Ellen.

Laura's throat hurt her.

"My lords," said Fence, in a grating voice. "Do consider one thing other. Edward Fairchild died in June. Edward Carroll was slain in battle in August. Lady Ruth and Lord Randolph and I did bargain with the Guardian of the River for the life of Edward Fairchild; but we did receive back Edward Carroll."

"That's easily mended," said the lilting voice. "Do you give us Edward Carroll, and we shall give you Edward Fairchild. Do you give us the swords, and we shall give you two other children of your choosing. That is three of the five. Are we agreed?"

Laura cast a stricken glance at Celia and Matthew. They sat like snow statues, as pale as their shirts, their enormous eyes on Fence as if daring him to say a word. Laura looked at him too, in time to see him drop his face into his hands. He sat that way for what seemed like forever. None of the Lords of the Dead moved or spoke.

When Fence took his hands away, they revealed a face with nothing in it at all. "Nay," he said. "We are not agreed. Edward Carroll is out of this reckoning. All five children do we require of you, my lords, or swords you shall have none."

"All five is too great a boon," said the rich voice.

"Fewer is too small," said Fence.

"Well, then," said the rich voice, "we have come to the end of our speech together."

"Mind you," said a voice that had not spoken in this room before, but that Laura had heard last from the mouth of a false Prospero, "should you at any time wish to change Edward Carroll for Edward Fairchild, that offer stands. All others we withdraw; should your mind alter, this must be all done again."

"Hold," said the lilting voice. "Speak not so hasty. The payment for Edward Carroll hath not been made."

"Tell Randolph," said Ellen, very softly, "to walk warily."

"Truly?" said Prospero's voice. "You may make change and payment at once, an you will."

"I thank your gracious presences," said Fence, dryly.

Their gracious presences, quiet for once, did something very like standing up and walking out of the room. The door shut behind them. Nobody looked at anybody else.

Laura's hands hurt. She unclenched them and looked blankly at the red creases in the palms. They were cold and wet. Her heart was trying to hammer its way out of her throat. She could not settle to any feeling: not relief, because of Fence's sorrow, and not sorrow, because of her own relief. They were all safe; and she hated being safe at such a cost.

Finally, she made herself look at Fence. He was staring at the space of polished table between his clasped hands. In the bright, warm silence of the Reading Room, the scholar's pen scratched busily. Laura wondered if she had even heard.

CHAPTER 26

MICHAELMAS got up and went after the shape-shifters, saying something about setting some guard over them.

"Fence," said Celia, in a wrung-out voice, "we should be gone from this place."

Laura had been listening to this suggestion all evening. But as Fence stood up without word and held the door open for the rest of them, she realized what it meant. No food; no rest; an uneasy seat on the jouncing horse, riding through the dark and cold—with, quite possibly, a host of practical, humorous, inhuman enemies at their backs. This time Ellen didn't smile.

They went without speaking back to Prospero's room. The door stood open. Patrick was asleep on Prospero's bed, with the cat on his stomach. All their luggage was piled in a corner, a blot on the room's tidiness. Prospero sat at the desk with three leather-bound volumes the size of pattern catalogues at a fabric store laid out before him. He glanced up as they came in, took one look at Fence, and sat back in the chair, his austere, bearded face very grave.

"No profit," said Fence.

"Fence, it's not thy fault," said Matthew.

Fence walked over to the desk, and recited to Prospero the course of the bargaining for the lives of the royal children.

"Indeed, Fence, I see no fault therein," said Prospero. "Their offers were impossible to be taken up, but those are the most liberal terms I've heard from these lords in a century."

"Oh, aye, but look you," said Fence, calmly. "An I angered them not, either they had been more liberal yet, did that liberality spring from a lessening of their habit and not from malice; or else they had been so ungenerous, did that liberality spring indeed from malice, that we were teased with no possibilities. Those terms they gave us will prick our dreams in years to come, so near were they to be accepted."

Laura's burden of guilt, having this speech laden on top of it, gave way suddenly to an exasperation so pure there was no space for caution in it. "Oh, for heaven's sake!" she burst out. "You're as bad as Randolph! You think everything has to be your fault."

"That were a pity," Fence said. "One snick-snatching conscience is aplenty for Ted's court, thinkst thou not so?"

"Fence, leave it be for an hour!" said Celia. "Sort out the blame at leisure, do you have any again; but now let us be gone."

"No, peace a moment," said Fence. He laid one hand on Prospero's open book. "What work have you done here?"

Prospero sat forward. "I have been nibbling at the shell of that hard nut, Apsinthion," he said. "Look you on this page."

Fence sat down in the other chair and began to read. Laura tried to read the page upside down, but it looked as if even right way up it would be very difficult. It resembled the homework she dreamed of not doing, a handwritten list of words and definitions. Ellen walked around behind Fence, peered over his shoulder, said, "What hideous spelling," and wandered away.

After a moment Fence said, "There's one new to me."

"Aye," said Prospero. "Wormwood: the abode of a dragon."

"Well!" said Ellen.

"But are dragons shape-shifters?" said Laura.

"No; there's the rub," said Fence.

"Well," said Laura, "Apsinthion could have been the name of the house. But we didn't see a dragon."

"The answer to the third riddle I have also," said Prospero. "The Outside Powers."

"Well," said Ellen, "it'd take an Outside Power to keep a dragon."

"What about the first question?" said Laura.

Prospero shook his splendid wizard's head. "Even the riddle is new to me," he said. "If you will but sleep here for the waning of the night, I'll search this matter for you."

"Matthew?" said Fence.

Matthew, who had been moving restlessly in and out of the doorway, slowly shook his head. "Better we were gone," he said. "If they reach an accord, they will be after us straight."

"They cannot be after you herein," said Prospero.

"We cannot linger herein; we have an errand in the north," said Matthew.

Prospero sighed. "Do you return this way, then," he said, "and I shall have news for you. Eat something before you go."

After a brief discussion Matthew agreed that they could eat something. Prospero went off to arrange for it. Matthew took his place and he and Fence read in the large books. Patrick woke up and demanded an account of the bargaining. All he said to Ellen's recitation was, "They sound crazy to me. You can't bargain with crazy people."

"They aren't people," said Ellen, "so maybe they aren't crazy."

"They might as well be," said Patrick.

The three of them sat on Prospero's bed in a gloomy silence. Laura looked from the gems on the white cat's collar to the golden globes of the lamps to the glowing caves of the coals in the fireplace. These last melted and brightened instantly. She saw a vast formal garden under a hot, bright sky. Around it reared high white walls, not the grayish white of High Castle, but brilliant, smooth, and blinding as snow in the sunshine. Two figures in the garden's center crossed swords. One of them was tall and angular, with a wild mop of black hair, and moved with a reckless abandon all too familiar. Laura clenched her hands together. The other was tow-headed, yes, and moved more cautiously. But he was almost as tall as Randolph, and he had a moustache.

Randolph and *Andrew,* fighting in a rose garden; but not the one at High Castle. This was not what she had hoped to see; she was looking for the young man in the bare room who quoted "James James Morrison Morrison." This one she might have to do something about.

"Fence?" she said. "Would they know some way here to counteract the pestilent spell-song?"

"Oh, I know the way," said Matthew. "One must but catch it in a fistful of fire. What we know not is the tune that maketh the fire-letters."

Laura sat very still. She remembered the tree in her dream, burning at the tune she played; and the young man, writing on a large sheet of waxy paper, quoting the same song. "I bet I know," she said.

Matthew came and sat on the bed. "Tell me," he said.

He looked extremely thoughtful when Laura had explained her reasoning. Patrick, however, just rolled his eyes.

"What's the matter with you?" said Ellen. "Do you have a better idea?"

"No," said Patrick, "I haven't. She's probably right. But God damn it, she shouldn't be. It's shoddy reasoning. It's all intuitive. It's not logical. It's like poetry," said Patrick, as if that were the worst thing he could think of.

"It *transcends* logic, nitwit," said Ellen.

"It may," said Patrick, "but you two sure don't. You haven't even gotten that far."

"Let's try it," said Laura to Matthew.

They went over and rummaged in the pile of luggage.

Laura's pack was almost too cold to touch. She wrapped an extra shirt around her hand and cautiously lifted out the flute. Matthew said, "Prospero, may we have the use of paper?"

Prospero gave him one huge waxy sheet of it, and pen and ink. Celia had built the fire into a towering forest of flames. Matthew moved to sit on the hearth, and dipped the pen into the ink bottle. Laura trailed after him and sat on the floor. She couldn't play the flute through a shirt. She unwound the cloth and picked up the flute. It felt very heavy, but was no colder than the pack. Perhaps it would give her chilblains. She had always wondered what they were.

Fence and Prospero had abandoned their books to watch; but when Laura looked inquiringly at Fence, he only smiled.

"Now, Laura. If the whole of the song burned a tree," said Matthew, picking up the pen, "one line thereof shall serve us well. Play the tune of the line the young man did speak, until I cease to write."

Laura did. Matthew wrote, covering both sides of the large sheet densely in minute characters. Finally he lifted the pen and nodded; he, or something, had timed his last line to end with hers. Laura laid the flute across her knees and caught her breath.

Matthew flattened the paper and dropped it into the fire. It did not curl or discolor, but the lines of ink ran together, into the center, swirled like dirty water going down a drain, and then ran up, not down, and spun up the chimney. The fire sank back to a bed of orange. All the wood Celia had fed it was consumed already. Matthew fished out the paper and returned it to Prospero.

If they were lucky, they had caught "Good King Wenceslas" in a fistful of fire. "Should I play 'What if a Day'?" said Laura.

Celia and Matthew looked inquiringly at each other.

"Something stronger," said Celia. "'And From the Sword.'"

"Laura?" said Matthew.

"Say the words," said Laura, "and I'll see."

Matthew said precisely, " 'And from the sword, Lord, save thy heart by my might and power, and keep thy heart, my darling dear, from dogs that would devour. And from the Dragon's mouth that would thee all in sunder shiver, and from the horns of Unicorns, Lord, safely you deliver.' "

"Whose might and power?" said Celia. "If Laura playeth those words, Matthew, to whose might and power dost thou commend Randolph?"

"It needs must be someone's," said Fence.

"This is a message, of my wife," said Matthew; "not a prophecy nor an abjuration."

"I've got it," said Laura, listening to the back of her mind. She was both pleased and terrified that Randolph should be commended to her might and power; she knew, perhaps more clearly than anybody, what might happen to him. She would think very hard about the danger of Andrew and the warning of the unicorn, and perhaps these things would come to Randolph when he heard the message.

"Play, then," said Matthew.

Laura played it through, holding up carefully her thoughts of Andrew and the unicorn. She liked the tune. She wondered if she would remember it, or any of them, if she ever got an ordinary flute into her hands. This one grew colder and colder as she played, as it had not when she played the phrase from "James James Morrison Morrison" for Matthew. She could hardly hold it for the last few notes; and dropped it gratefully.

Prospero came back with their food, which was mugs of soup and an assortment of dumplings stuffed with everything from broccoli to raisins. They ate it; and thanked him; and packed up; and left Heathwill Library. At Prospero's suggestion, they left without their horses, through a tunnel intended to supply the library in case of siege. Patrick, who was offensively cheerful and observant after his nap, was delighted with this means of egress; but the adults were too tired or preoccupied to answer his questions, and Ellen and Laura were too tired to be interested.

Dawn found them in a very wild country, rocky and dusted with snow and full of evergreens. The sky was a piercing blue and there was no wind.

Just before midday, when Laura had determined that she was going to die, and it was only a matter of whether she announced this fact first or simply fell in a piteous heap, they came to a long, low stone building with a brick chimney and one window. Nobody asked what it was doing there; they simply went inside. Laura only realized that she had gone to sleep by waking up again. It was sunset. They went on their way again.

They walked all night, under a blazing of stars like sugar thickly sprinkled on a cake, and in the spaces between their sticky clusters a sky so black it looked to Laura like a pit she could fall into. The land they traveled over seemed to her a tiny, made thing, a clutter of gravel held together with ice and the little feathery sticks of the evergreens. She kept drowsing off and then jerking awake, because it was not sleep she would fall into, but the endless empty sky. After the third time this happened, she was seriously considering tickling Patrick as a diversion, when Ellen said from beside them, "Can't we sing?"

Celia laughed. "How please both a dragon and a unicorn?"

"I was thinking of pleasing myself," said Ellen. "Something long and rousing."

"Kipling," said Patrick.

"Oh, well thought!" said Ellen, and promptly began to sing.

"Now Tomlinson gave up the ghost at his house in Berkley Square,

And a Spirit came to his bedside and gripped him by the hair—
A Spirit gripped him by the hair and carried him far away,
Till he heard as the roar of a rain-fed ford the roar of the Milky Way."

Patrick had joined in before the end of the first line. Laura knew she couldn't sing, but in this cold wilderness she didn't care. She came in on the second line. Among the three of them they made a creditable chorus, she thought, for volume if not for sweetness; but they did not get much further. The clear and tuneful voices of Patrick and Ellen, and even Laura's fainter and more wavery pipe, struck echoes like slivers of ice from all the naked rocks, and those echoes struck more; every word they sang burst into a shower of others, not only in the freezing air but in the warm depths of her mind.

Now let us sport us while we may. I gave what other women gave that stepped out of their clothes. Alas, poor ghost, as a moat defensive to a house, against the envy of less happier lands, another damned, thick, square book. Be thou a spirit of health or goblin damned. Where griping griefs the heart would wound And doleful dumps the mind oppress, There music with her silver sound With speed is wont to send redress.

Those last few words, spoken honestly with flesh and breath, falling naturally on the real air that Laura moved in, left behind them a frozen silence. The wind had died; the party from the Hidden Land stood in a perfect stillness, their soundless breath congealing in the dark air, and looked at the speaker.

Laura recognized the unicorn, by its gold eyes and by something in the timbre of its voice. It was Chryse. She seemed much larger; and, as with the other unicorn they had spoken to, although she did not shine herself, there was light around her. But her breath, too, made clouds in the frosty air, and from the wicked horn with its spiral of violet there hung a dingy tendril of dead vine.

"That," said Chryse in her ringing voice, "is the oddest music that ever I was summoned—" She broke off. Laura had never heard a unicorn do such a thing. "Fence," said Chryse. "What dost thou here among the barren rocks?"

"Seeking your gracious presence, lady," said Fence. Laura, accustomed to the way in which he had spoken to the other unicorns and to the Lords of the Dead, with that threadbare courtesy just covering his wariness, his disdain, his distrust, actually looked away from the unicorn to stare at Fence. He meant it. This one he respected.

"My brothers sent me word thou wast at Heathwill Library," said Chryse.

"Heathwill Library," said Fence, "is an abode of monsters. The Lords of the Dead do take their ease behind its walls."

Chryse made an abrupt and discontinuous sound, like a cat walking on a keyboard. There was an uneasy silence. "The strangest summons," said Chryse at last, "and the strangest news. What are these others with thee? Will you come and take what ease I can afford you?"

"Lady," said Fence, "for this relief much thanks."

They followed Chryse on a winding path through ice and rocks, and down into a valley that held a little wood of pine trees. It was much warmer here. They trudged up to a thick hedge of some evergreen, and shrugged off their packs. Matthew stacked them under the hedge, and Laura said to Ellen, "What kind of hedge is that?"

"Yew," said Ellen.

Fence joined them and said quietly, "Be somewhat scanter of thy knowledge in converse with Chryse. Do not lie, but do not speak more than you must."

"I'm sure Chryse knows what kind of a hedge it is," said Ellen, rather testily.

"It will like her an thou answerest thus pertly," said

Fence, unruffled, "but beware. She'll lead thee on to those delights, and thou wilt speak more than thou shouldst. Thou mayst strew dangerous conjectures in ill-breeding minds."

"I thank you for your good counsel," said Ellen, and did him a courtesy.

"Oh, go your ways," said Fence.

Matthew and Celia joined them. Fence said, tilting his head and looking from her to Matthew and back again, "Look the two of you to my weaknesses."

He walked away, and they all followed him, to a wide clearing where a pale light as of the moon behind clouds told them Chryse was waiting. She invited them to sit down, and Laura at least was very glad to do so. The pine needles were thick on the ground and very soft. Laura thought belatedly that it was perhaps impolite to sit while Chryse stood, and also that they would all have stiff necks from looking up at her. But once they were all seated in a half-circle—Matthew, Celia, Fence, Laura, Ellen, and Patrick—Chryse lay down neatly, as the unicorn they had hunted last summer had done, her forelegs stretched out before her like a cat's and her plumy tail spread fanlike on the scattered needles. She did not look smug; she looked expectant.

"You are welcome," she said. "Make me known, Fence, to your companions."

"Lord Matthew," said Fence, "King's Counselor of the Hidden Land."

Chryse looked down her long white horse's nose at Matthew, and said, "They speak well of thee in Heathwill Library."

"Celia," said Fence, while Matthew seemed to be struggling with a reply, "Onetime Queen's Counselor, and the King's Counselor and musician."

"And Belaparthalion speaks well of thy music," said Chryse.

Celia smiled; Fence said, "Laura."

"Well met," said Chryse. If she noticed the sudden absence of title or designation, she didn't mention it. Laura was not sure she was relieved. Chryse said, "Thou hast played the flute of Cedric and found the unicorn in winter, bereft of the cardinal."

"But, lady," said Laura, startled into speech, "it's October."

"Is it?" said Chryse.

"Ellen," said Fence.

Chryse said, "Thy spirit liketh my sister."

"Hers liked me too," said Ellen.

"And Patrick," said Fence.

Chryse said, "Think on't."

Laura, bewildered, looked at Patrick, who was scowling, but not in the manner of somebody who has been presented with a senseless remark.

"Well met," said Chryse again. "Now. What meaneth this embassy?"

Fence cleared his throat, pushed his hood back from his face, and spoke of the action of the Dragon King that had led to the war in August. He told of the doubts Andrew had sown among the King's Council; he told of the death of the King, which he termed "doubtful" and managed to imply it might have been in some way engineered by the Dragon King. He described the battle. He told of the death of Conrad, the only experienced general the Hidden Land had. He told of the death of the new King, and the bargain made with the Judge of the Dead for his release. Chryse, who after all had been there, interrupted him at this point.

"That was ill done," she said. "For we did not receive Edward."

Fence looked as if he wondered how she knew. He said, "I myself, lady, am loath to lose Randolph. But that is by the way, save as an instance of the farflung trouble the meddlings of the Dragon King have caused us, who have troubled him nothing. There is no honor in him; no statecraft will bind him to be quiet. Wherefore we come to give you a gift, and to ask in return the gift of your intervention. Celia?"

Celia reached under her cloak and drew out a wrapped bundle. She spun the long windings of cloth from it as if she were unrolling a carpet, and the swords of Shan and Melanie tumbled to the ground and lay there shining in pale blue and ghostly green. The stones on their hilts winked like stars between clouds. They sparkled in green and blue; but it was gold and red that Laura saw in them, a huge glow of gold light and a red, sinuous form coiled in the middle of it like a worm in an apple. She blinked, and the sparkles steadied, and the glimpse was gone.

Chryse stood up. "Glory and trumpets," she said. "I will have these swords. For my part, an you give them up, I'll read the Dragon King a prohibition shall stay him to the shape of a polecat until all these deeds are but a song the minstrels cannot trace to's makers. But my part is not all. We'll find Belaparthalion by and by. Now, look you; I will have also more knowledge than thou, Fence, didst tell my sister, touching these swords and their history. Is there aught thou wouldst have of me in return for that tale?"

"Fence!" said Ellen. "The three riddles."

"What!" said Chryse, in alert and joyful tones. "Riddles all Heathwill cannot read?"

"Dangerous conjectures," said Patrick, leaning across Laura and addressing Ellen in a disgusted voice, "in ill-breeding minds."

"Thy tongue breeds iller," said Fence.

"Fence," said Chryse, in a voice that for the first time held no shadow of laughter. "Thy dealings with us were ever circumspect."

"How, lady," said Fence, in a pleading tone laced lightly with irritation, "should they be otherwise?"

"Dost thou know," said Chryse, still soberly, "what time's gone by since any trusted us?"

"That same that's passed," said Fence, as if he were

painstakingly explaining long division to a slow pupil, "since you did warrant it."

"An you try us not," said Chryse, with the humor back in her tuneful voice, "how may you know do we warrant it or do we not?"

"Is this not wonderful?" said Fence. He sounded rather desperate; but there was a touch of irony in his voice also. "You have pleased it so, to punish me with this, and this with me, that I must be your scourge and minister."

"Thou art a wizard," said Chryse.

Nobody moved or spoke; Laura's nose itched, and she would not have scratched it for anything. The two swords on the ground, like stained glass through which the sun is shining, cast little motes of blue and green in all directions, blemishing Chryse's white coat and making the clearing look like a scene under water. Laura squeezed her eyes shut briefly, and in the dazzle of red and yellow afterimages she saw again the golden glow and the red snaky thing within it. These things were in a tower room, but not any in High Castle. The golden glow was a great globe; the red snaky thing in it was a dragon, all whiskered and tendriled and shot with streaks of black. It was looking at her out of one black eye with a pupil as red as a garnet.

Nothing in any of her visions had looked at her before. *To lie in cold obstruction and to rot,* said a crackling voice, like no voice she had ever heard in the back of her head. The sight snapped out suddenly, as if the dragon and not she had ended it. Laura opened her mouth, remembered Fence's abjurations to Ellen, and shut it again.

The silence stretched on a little longer. Then Fence said, "Ellen. Ask thy riddles."

"What beast is it," said Ellen, "the unicorns pursue each summer?"

Well, thought Laura, Chryse should certainly know the answer to that one.

"The dragon," said Chryse.

"And before what beast doth winter flee?"

"The dragon," said Chryse.

"And what beast maketh that which putteth the words to the flute's song?"

There was another silence. "The dragon," said Chryse, and chuckled richly, like three low notes of a pipe organ.

"The dragon?" said Ellen. "Not—ow!"

Patrick had leaned over and hit her in the arm; but it was Fence who said, "Hold your tongue."

"Heathwill thinketh otherwise?" said Chryse.

"Send to them, lady, and ask," said Fence.

"Well," said Chryse. "Tell your tale."

Fence told it, appealing occasionally to Matthew or Celia or Laura, and once to Patrick, but never to Ellen, for details. The sun came up before he had finished. Chryse twitched her tail from time to time, somewhat as a cat might do and somewhat as a horse might. She made no comment when he had finished.

"That," said Patrick, with relish, "is a packet of news and no mistake."

Chryse made an obscure hooting sound. Laura wasn't sure what it meant. Chryse said, "Fear not this bargain, Fence. I'll call Belaparthalion." She stood up, with considerably more grace than any of the rest of them, scrambling hastily to their feet at Fence's urgent gesture, could manage. Then she put her long white head back, like a donkey about to bray, and made sounds far more melodious.

In Laura's mind the words marched along with the music. "Wake: the silver dusk returning / Up the beach of darkness brims, / And the ship of sunrise burning / Strands upon the eastern rims. / Wake: the vaulted shadow shatters, / Trampled to the floor it spanned, / And the tent of night in tatters / Straws the sky-pavilioned land."

Which was very impressive, but Belaparthalion did not come. Laura was afraid that she knew why. "When you know these things," the man in red had said, "then what manner of thing I am you will know also." He had not said, I am the thing that is the answer. If he was indeed a dragon-keeper, she had just seen the dragon he kept. That tower room had not looked as if it were in the bare, blocky, modern house she and Ted had visited; but it might be. She might have seen Belaparthalion; but she might have seen some other dragon, in the present or the future or the past.

The others were milling around, shaking the blood back into their feet, yawning, and scanning the sky. Laura looked up too, but there were only two crows. Chryse stood still, her head cocked as if she were listening for the beat of scaly wings.

Fence was watching Chryse. The irrational dread of Laura's dream clutched at her stomach. There was something that Fence must not find out; that was what that dream had told her. Fence had intimated to them all there were things Chryse ought not to find out, that they should say as little on any subject as they could get away with. Both these circumstances and all the natural inclinations of her character told Laura to keep her mouth shut. But she thought also of her talk with the unicorns, long ago it seemed now, when they had hinted to her in their cheerful way what might be the consequences of a failure to shout abroad every vision she had.

"Chryse," said Laura, not caring if it was rude. "What color is Belaparthalion?"

"Red, curdled with black," said Chryse, readily.

"Somebody's got him," said Laura. "I saw him. He's in a big, glowing golden globe." She paused to disentangle her tongue, thinking, with a saving lightness, say *that* five times fast. "In a high room somewhere; a house, I think, not a castle. At least, the walls aren't stone. And he says, 'To lie in cold obstruction and to rot.'"

"Does he so?" said Chryse, slowly, and with a very unpleasant intonation. "Melanie's elder brother said so also."

"Chryse," said Fence, very gently, "have a care."

He and Chryse looked at each other, and Celia and Matthew looked at the two of them.

"I know where to seek him," said Chryse, suddenly. She took four strides for the edge of the clearing, and paused. "I can carry one," she said.

"Laura?" said Fence. "'Twas thy vision."

It seemed impossible to refuse. Well, Laura thought, it hadn't killed her last time. She took a step toward Chryse, and considered again. The worst thing about being a coward was the risk that you would choose the wrong moment to stop being one.

"I'll go if you think I should," she said to Fence. "But Ellen would *like* to go; and you, or Matthew, or Celia, might be a lot more use."

"But not Patrick," said Patrick; his voice was unperturbed, but he had chosen to say something.

"Send Patrick!" said Ellen. "He's the one who *needs* it."

"Patrick is incorrigible," said Matthew. "I'll go, Fence."

"Lady?" said Fence.

And Chryse, the omnipresent glint of humor magnified and shining like the sun in every syllable, said, "Patrick likes me well. Let him come and be witness."

CHAPTER 27

"IF Claudia is Melanie," said Randolph, rubbing the thumb and finger of one hand under his eyes, until they met at the bridge of his nose, which he pinched vigorously. He dropped his hand, looking no better for the exercise.

Ruth had lost track of the number of times it had been said. She sat, with Randolph and Ted, back on the floor of Claudia's diamond-paned sun porch, because it was cleaner there, and warmer, and because they hoped the windows might still show them something useful. Andrew was ostensibly exploring the rest of the house, also in search of something useful. He had not ranted anymore; he had not even asked quietly for some explanation. Perhaps the King and the dead children had told him something. Ruth was glad to be out of his presence. She thought his docility in the face of such discoveries boded no good.

Randolph had not finished his sentence. Ruth decided to sum up for him. "She's about five hundred years old," she said, "infinitely accomplished in Sorcery, marvelous wise in the ways of the unicorns, and bears a grudge against the Hidden Land and everyone in it that you never have explained properly but that we will grant to be weighty. What else?"

"She's not Andrew's sister," said Randolph.

"Unless Andrew's not Andrew," said Ted.

"He might really have been the villain all along," said Ruth, cheered. Then she scowled. "But I doubt it. He rings true, if you know what I mean. There was always something sleek and odd about Claudia, but Andrew I believed in."

"Yes, so did I." Ted pushed the thick hair out of his eyes. "So Andrew's just one more victim."

"Well, he might still be a spy for the Dragon King."

"Okay, leave him on the suspected list. Back to Claudia. Randolph, if she's so old and has such great sorcerous knowledge, why'd she have to apprentice herself to Fence and Meredith?"

"Her knowledge is of the Red School, now dispersed," said Randolph. "Each school hath its secrets that the others know not. One of the dearest goals of Heathwill Library is to abolish this secrecy, but they have not achieved it yet. Also, there surfaceth from time to time new knowledge; easier to pry it from some teacher of the art than to seek it out laboriously oneself."

Ruth looked at him. There was an edge of malice and disillusion in his voice that you had to expect, but that disturbed her just the same. Randolph and Claudia had kept company for almost a year; he had presumably been fond of her, and he was no doubt thinking now of all she had pried out of him: not only the knowledge, but the trust, the time, the confidences which remembering would scald the heart once he knew to whom he had so blithely given them. Damn Claudia, thought Ruth.

"Why did she lock Belaparthalion up in a golden globe?" said Ted.

"He's a protector of the Hidden Land, with Chryse, against the Outside Powers, and what other capricious forces may measure a ladder 'gainst our bulwarks."

"But she didn't lock Chryse up somewhere?" said Ruth.

"Who can say?" said Randolph.

"Well, she hadn't, as of our bargaining for Ted's life."

"Melanie is an old enemy of the unicorns," said Randolph. "And the unicorn is cannier than the dragon."

"*That's* what's been bothering me!" exclaimed Ruth, smacking her hand down on Claudia's hardwood floor. "I thought Melanie was dead. I thought Belaparthalion killed her because she broke her word to Shan."

"Oh, he did burn her house and she inside," said Randolph. "So the story goeth in some quarters that he did kill her. But look you, Melanie's original crime was that she did conspire in the death of a unicorn, and that meaneth immortality. She'll die when she wills it, and the Lords of the Dead will have her."

"Oh, *splendid,*" said Ruth. "Why—"

Randolph held up a long hand, smiling. The smile did not reach his eyes with their dark circles underneath, nor his voice. "Ask not me," he said. "These answers will come only from Claudia."

"How do you propose to find her?" said Ruth.

"Why should you want to find her?" said Ted. "Why should she want to answer any questions from us, and how could we make her?"

"For the first," said Randolph, still smiling, and in a lighter voice, "these events tend all to a purpose; and when it is accomplished, she will find us. For the second, I give less than the scrapings of an indifferent banquet for what she wants; and for the third, th'event will show us."

"You're just giving in?" said Ted.

"She will not come out," said Randolph. "We must needs walk in where we may find her."

"If the purpose is to kill us all," said Ted, hollowly, "won't the opportunity for questions come too late?"

"If that is the purpose, aye. But I think 'tis not so. She'll want a fate that hath some relish in't."

He sounded as if he were talking about a recipe, not his own fate. "How can you sit there and say things like that?" said Ruth.

Randolph looked at her. She could not tell if he was trying

to frame his answer properly, or only to decide whether to answer at all. She remembered what Fence had said to Ted, in response to a similar question: "What is the matter with you? We will do our best in the battle, and live or die as it falls to us."

But Randolph, when he answered her, did not quite say that. "I do not hold my life," he said, "at a pin's fee. As for yours, my dear children, I hold them something higher. But that, see you not, shall serve very well."

Ruth had some trouble catching her breath. "Don't you dare sacrifice yourself for us," she said at last, in rising tones. "We're not your dear children! And what the hell good do you think our lives would be to us without—" She stopped, horrified. Ted was staring at her. Randolph merely looked resigned; he either had not understood or didn't care.

"Isn't this a little premature?" said Ted, also rather breathlessly. "Let's just wait 'til we get there."

"Get *where?*" snapped Ruth, venting her anxiety and all the hideousness of her new discovery on her cousin's innocent head, and feeling a fresh flood of irritation because she could not keep herself from doing it.

"We have an embassy to accomplish," said Ted.

"Andrew doesn't look in any case to accomplish anything," said Ruth. "Lady Ruth must have been a—" She stopped for the third time. "Boil my brains!" she said. "Boil them and mash them and serve them up for turnips, for it's damned well all they're good for!"

Randolph actually laughed, which was perhaps more alarming than everything else. "Don't trouble yourself," he said. "She's naught to me; but do you school yourself in Andrew's hearing."

"Was she ever anything to you?" asked Ruth; and wished she had stopped for a fourth time, before she ever started the question.

Randolph said, "What was she to me in thy game?"

Ruth was so relieved to be spared any direct consequences of her own question that she answered at once. "Not a *great* deal," she said. "We didn't pay much attention to that part of it. The romances were just flourishes that we put in because they're expected in stories."

"I thought," said Ted, "that Lord Randolph had a soft spot for Lady Ruth that he didn't indulge because he thought it would be better if she married Edward."

"As well he did not," said Randolph, apparently exclusively to Ted, "for she was not what she seemed."

That was an uncomfortable remark, thought Ruth, no matter how you interpreted it. "If this discussion isn't going to get us anywhere," she said, "why don't we go see how Andrew's doing?"

Ted and Randolph got up promptly. They all went upstairs, past the three landings and their little square windows, each having a border in red stained glass alternating with clear and with an occasional clump of grapes or wildflowers, to the wide hallway lined with open doors on the fourth floor.

In this house, those open doors led to rooms full of books. In the largest of these, they found Andrew, leaning on the window frame as if he would have liked to climb out and fall four stories. Randolph thumped the woodwork and Andrew turned around.

"What have you found?" said Ted. Andrew gestured at the table, which was covered with coarse paper densely written over. "Melanie's journals," he said.

Ruth noticed that he did not call her Claudia. Maybe he was good at facing facts, once you had put them where he would have to notice them or fall over them.

"Have you read anything useful?" said Ted.

He walked into the room; Ruth and Randolph followed. Randolph sat down on a red velvet sofa with its arms carved like dragon's heads. Ruth wished she could see a good honest lion, or even a griffin, for a change. She looked at the sofa again, and perched herself on a ladder probably intended for reaching the upper bookshelves. Andrew was still leaning in the window, which was convenient, thought Ruth, because it meant his face was in shadow.

Randolph pulled out the grapefruit-like object they had used to light their way to this house, and said to it, "Strike a light or light a lantern." It lit up, and the gray, neglected room was suddenly warm and pleasant, as if the writer had just stepped out for a cup of tea.

Ruth, startled into a burst of laughter, completed the quotation. "Something I have hold of has no head!"

"Oh, no," said Ted, laughing too. "I hope that hasn't happened here."

"It had a happy ending," said Ruth.

"More of your fictions?" said Andrew.

"How do you know about that?" said Ted.

"She hath writ much of them, and of you," said Andrew. "It seems that you are ignorant and presumptuous, but not evil."

"But the fictions?" said Ted.

"The idea did give Melanie some little trouble," said Andrew. "But she did gnaw at the nut till it did crack for her."

Ruth marveled at how dryly he spoke. He sounded like Patrick expounding materialism; except that Patrick loved materialism, and Andrew must hate what he was saying. But he had come to understand it in the few hours he had been in this room. And after that display in the land of the dead, you could not accuse him of having no feelings. You had to admire him.

He said, "This is the way of things. Both your fictions, and all our sorceries, have their origins in the same impulses: the desire to make things; the lie told not to scape consequences, but as its own art. Now in your country, these impulses do grow to fictions; but in ours, mark you, they do grow to sorcery." Andrew made a sound that was probably supposed to be a chuckle. "We know our wizards young, by the greatness of their falsehoods. Wherein we who call them liars only have our excuse."

"That seems very odd to me," said Ruth, taking refuge from her thoughts in this theoretical discussion. "Don't children play games of make-believe? And how do you ever *teach* them anything, if everything you make up has to come true?"

"It has not so," said Andrew. "The games of children trouble no one; they may have the strength, but they have not the skill. As indeed the five of you had not the skill, though Melanie saith, you had the strength of five Shans amongst you. You troubled her sleep for ten long years fore she did see that you were not within the boundaries of the world."

"And Melanie, I suppose, had the skill," said Ted.

"Wait a moment," said Ruth. "I still don't understand. Does everybody who pretends as a child grow up to be a wizard?"

"No," said Andrew. "Some cease to make believe; some make little tales; but all the great ones do turn to wizardry. All our great tales are true."

"Wizards made them happen by making them up?" said Ruth. A voice in her mind that was not Lady Ruth's said to her, *Poetry makes nothing happen.*

"Wizards do make them happen by living them," said Andrew. "And do write them down afterward. Also—" He hesitated, and said, "I do not well understand this. Melanie did believe that your play-makers, your poets, did make some events to happen, long ago; but that in the end the Outside Powers did appoint the unicorns guardians, that not every tale should burst in and jostle with every other. And she did believe that the unicorns do suggest the tales to the minds of wizards and plain folk here, who do then choose them, or not, as they will. And what Melanie did was to take from them their means of choosing."

"And how do we come into all this?" asked Ruth, with a sinking stomach.

"I do not well understand that either," said Andrew. He looked, furthermore, as if he didn't want to. But he went doggedly on. "Think on this. In the natural way of things, tales made by thy poets do present themselves herein; the unicorns do choose or banish them; any with an ear to hear may choose or banish them from's own life. But Melanie did turn all these matters upsodown; she did present the history of the Hidden Land to your several minds; and you did choose or banish, and add your own embellishment, which did in the ordinary way return to us, to choose or banish as we did wish, according to our several natures, our inclinations, and the keenness of our inward ears."

"Jesus!" said Ted.

"Don't swear," said Ruth. "All right, I guess I'll accept that for now. But why did she do it?"

"I have said before," said Randolph from the depths of the sofa. "We can but ask her."

"Can but ask is easily said," said Andrew.

"I'm glad somebody here has some sense," said Ruth, frowning at Randolph's long form sunk in the red cushions. With his coloring, and more especially with the spectacular lack of it that had afflicted him since the King died, he looked better in red than in blue.

"There's sense," said Randolph, without rancor, "and there's authority."

"Which, in this matter," said Andrew, pushing himself away from the window, "is still mine. We've tarried enough. The court of the Dragon King awaiteth us."

"It'll be dark in an hour," said Ruth. Randolph had closed his eyes, as if to show that, whoever's authority Andrew thought he was challenging, it wasn't his. His lashes were longer than hers, blast him. She turned quickly to Andrew, who didn't look very healthy either. "Why don't we get some rest and have an early start in the morning?"

There was a difficult silence. Then, "Practical as ever," said Andrew, with no particular expression; and walked out of the room.

Ruth waited for his footsteps on the bare boards to die away. Then she sat down on the floor. "Whew!" she said.

"That," said Randolph, "was the triumph of sense o'er pride. Do you give him the credit for't, an he chide in the morning."

"I will so," said Ruth. She leaned her head against the arm of the sofa and closed her eyes. "Is anybody hungry?"

"The first rule of erratic travel," said Randolph, drowsily, "is this: eat when you may."

Ruth stood up. "Well, come on, then," she said to his recumbent form. "Or shall we come and drop it into your mouth?"

"I thank you," said Randolph, sitting up hastily and looking as if he had managed to make himself dizzy, "not with our rations."

"We could find some nice worms," said Ruth, tartly.

Ted was staring at her. She said, "Let's to the oatcake, then," bolted precipitately out of the room, and dived into the first open door she saw. She heard the rest of them, a few moments later, clatter downstairs. This room was the double of the one she and Ted and Randolph had had their conference in, back in the Secret Country. Ruth sat down in one of the carved chairs, on a gold cushion, and pressed her fists to her eyes.

What was the matter with her? No; she knew that. But why did she have to act this way about it? Ruth the contained and careful, whose father called her Elinor after the character in *Sense and Sensibility* who embodied the first of those traits. Ruth thought she would like to die. "Oh, you would not," she said to herself. "Think of where you'd end up. Well, at least you couldn't make a fool of yourself down there. My God, I've got to travel with those people for another week. I can't stand it." *Men have died from time to time,* said the voice, *and worms have eaten them; but not for love.*

"Who asked you!" yelled Ruth.

She jumped to her feet and paced furiously around the red and gold rag rug, trying not to think, trying to think of something else. The odious voice said musically, *Sing we for love and idleness, / Naught else is worth the having. / Though I have been in many a land, / There is naught else in living.*

"Irresponsible hedonist," said Ruth, breathlessly.

The voice continued unperturbed. *And I would rather have my sweet, / Though rose-leaves die of grieving, / Than do high deeds in Hungary / To pass all men's believing.*

It had drowned the sound of footsteps on the bare wooden floor of the hall. Ruth heard only the first step in the room itself, before the newcomer trod on the carpet and stood still. She flung herself around. It was Ted. Ruth was enormously relieved, and even more enormously disappointed.

"Ruthie?" said Ted. "What's the matter?"

"I," said Ruth, between her teeth, "am a jerk and an idiot."

"What?"

"Everybody is a jerk and an idiot at sixteen," Ruth explained to him. "I expected it. I figured I could confine it to a diary, or writing bad poetry. My God, how does anybody survive to be twenty?"

"Slow down," said Ted, painstakingly. "Have you remembered something vital, or what?"

"No," said Ruth, wildly. "I've forgotten something basic. I'm too young for this. I don't want this to happen. My *God,*" said Ruth, taking Ted by his wool-clad shoulders and shaking him, "no wonder teenage girls are pregnant all over the place."

Ted's face arrested her. He put both his hands, which were exceedingly cold, over hers, and said, "Say it again. Slowly."

"No, it's okay," said Ruth. "Or at least, it isn't, but—forget all that. Never mind."

"Okay, fine," said Ted. "Come on down to dinner."

"Oh, no," said Ruth, retreating from him. "I'm not going down there."

"What in the hell is the matter?"

"If you tell anybody I'll kill you."

"On my honor," said Ted.

Ruth looked at him.

"As crowned King of the Hidden Land, may any pain you care to name come upon me sevenfold if ever I reveal this secret without your express permission *what the bloody hell is wrong, Ruth?*"

"I'm in love with Randolph."

Ted's jaw dropped. Then he looked as if he were going to laugh, and Ruth prepared to hit him. Then a reflective look came over his face; and then he looked at her as if he were really seeing her, and said, "That's bad. I'm sorry."

"How would you know?" snapped Ruth, ungratefully.

"Remember I told you Edward was in love with Lady Ruth?"

"It's *monstrous,*" said Ruth. "How can anybody stand it?"

"Well, it had its moments," said Ted; his straightforward blue gaze altered momentarily, and became disconcerting. Then he rubbed his eyes and said, "Or at least, it would have if I'd been Edward."

"It doesn't have any God damn moments at all," said Ruth.

Ted looked at her thoughtfully. "I know what's the matter with you," he said.

"Oh yeah? Well, please enlighten me."

"I didn't know love made people sarcastic."

"I'm sorry. What is it that's the matter with me?"

"Remember right after we got here, when we were trying to figure out what was happening, and Patrick came up with all his theories about mass telepathic hallucinations?"

"I try very hard to forget it," said Ruth, despite herself, "but go on."

"And you told Patrick he was crazy, and he said, all right, you could explain it, then. And you said you didn't want to explain it; you wanted to know what to do about it."

"Well?"

"Well, you want to know what to do about being in love with Randolph. And you don't know; and I don't know."

"I don't want to do anything about it," said Ruth. "First love is a mistake; you just have to get over it. Nobody as idiotic as I am could possibly make a decision like that and get it right. I refuse. I don't want to do anything about it. But I keep doing things about it. I keep saying stupid things. Did you *hear* me in there? That was *flirting*. That was *despicable*."

"Do you want not to be in love with him?"

"Of course I—shit," said Ruth, for the second time in her life; and said it again, three times. The voice said implacably, *Let me not to the marriage of true minds / Admit impediments*.

"I thought so," said Ted. "Now come on down to dinner."

"Are you crazy?"

"You can't stay up here. Ruthie, look. Randolph probably didn't even notice. He's falling asleep on his feet."

"This," said Ruth, after a pause to examine her feelings, "is abominable. Am I relieved that he didn't notice? No."

"He's going to notice, if you don't come downstairs," said Ted, "and that will be worse. Just keep your mouth shut. I'll kick you if I think you're going to say something stupid."

"That's a splendid idea," said Ruth. "I'll have two broken ankles before we get out of the house in the morning."

But she followed him downstairs.

Ruth did not have any broken ankles when they got out of the house in the morning. Ted had not had to kick her at all, because she had not said a word. He began to wish he'd promised to kick her for sulking too; but she wasn't really sulking: she just looked glazed. Andrew, on the other hand, appeared to be sulking. Randolph was so tired that nothing else showed. Ted thought he looked as if he had given a great deal more blood than the token three drops. Perhaps in some sense he had.

They had eaten their supper, such as it was, at teatime, and gone to bed at suppertime, so they were able to make such an early start that even Andrew didn't complain. There was a line of red on the western horizon; the morning star glared at them like the beacon of a lighthouse; the huddled mountains were dark. It was chilly.

Randolph took the lead, without consulting anybody. Ted was so sleepy that it was not until the sun had risen and transformed the fantastic landscape of dawn into something more ordinary that he realized how far they had come. The mountains were gone. They were in a hilly country pocked with little lakes, riding on a good road under a sky filled with birds. There was a tower on almost every hill, and the rolling country was crossed like a chessboard with the lumpy white lines of drystone walls. It was a much homier and pleasanter-looking place than the Hidden Land; but something about it made Ted nervous.

He persuaded the mare to move up next to Ruth's horse. "What's wrong with this place?" he said.

Ruth looked at him out of the corner of her eye, her wild hair blowing. "There's something paranoid about those towers."

"At least nobody's shooting arrows out of them," said Ted.

Not long after, they overtook another party traveling in the same direction, a party cumbered with wagons, whose outriders, their plain cloaks abandoned in the warm morning, could clearly be seen to be wearing tunics appliquéd with the running fox of High Castle.

Stephen, Dittany, Jerome, Julian; the four they had left

behind when they went to brave the Gray Lake. Ted had completely forgotten about them. What prior arrangements, what arcane communications, what good planning or timing had brought about this rendezvous, he neither knew nor cared. The remote voice that was not Edward's said, *Why, what a king is this!*

And that, of course, was fair. He ought to care. Ted smiled at the four of them and let the chatter of reunion divide around him and flow on behind. Not only did he not care, but nobody had consulted him. Randolph, of course, had known all along that he was not the true heir; although for the beginning of the journey he had treated him as a proper king-in-training. Andrew had never had a high opinion of Edward, and now knew that Ted had not even Edward's claim to authority. This was a bad precedent; as was the fact that Ted didn't want to think about it.

The reassembled embassy to the Dragon King rode on down the good, broad road. Ted made himself think about it. If the Lords of the Dead had been doing their jobs, instead of gallivanting about nobody knew where, Edward might even now be restored to his rightful place. Ted would be able to drop back and be a piece of baggage. He didn't like that thought as much as he would have expected.

Nor did he like at all the thought of, sometime today, or tomorrow, or when they arrived at the house of the Dragon King and began their work, asserting what authority he had. It had probably not occurred to Andrew yet, among all the shocks recently administered to him, that he had in sober fact sworn Edward Carroll an oath that must be honored. Ted did not relish reminding him of it; but Ted's oath too would have to be kept: to deal lightly in the exercise of his privileges and straitly in the fulfillment of his obligations; to reward valor with honor, service with service, oath-breaking with vengeance.

All right, thought Ted. All right. But not just yet.

They reached the dwelling of the Dragon King just before sunset. It sat in the middle of a flat sheet of water. The water was a blinding gold on the right-hand side where the departing sun laid a path of light across, and dark green on the other. The castle was not the gray-white of High Castle's alternating walls, but a smooth, pure, unnatural white. And it was enormous. It was probably, thought Ted, smaller than High Castle. But High Castle was a hodgepodge, and only its inmost structure had been seriously intended as a fortress. This castle had been built all of a piece. Where High Castle rambled, this one was perfectly symmetrical. It had an eight-sided curtain wall that bristled with towers, each matched by its fellow on the opposite side. There were four drum towers, each with its own small turret towers sprouting from it; two massive D-shaped towers; dusky blue slate roofs capping the outer towers and sunk behind the crenellations of the inner ones. Ted could not begin, from this distance and in the flat red light of sunset, to tell how big it was.

Edward said, *It is sixty feet to the top of the towers, and twenty-seven to the top of the outer wall, but forty to the top of the inner. A hundred archers could hold this place against any force thou shalt name for longer than thou or I have lived.*

Ted recognized the enthusiasm of a genuine obsession. Thanks, he said inwardly. For the first time, he respected the Dragon King, and feared him, instead of taking on trust Fence and Randolph's—and the game's—assessment. Then he said, Edward? Is that you? And Edward, for the first time, answered him and said, *Aye.*

How comes this communion of thought? asked Ted. *Ask Melanie, when you meet her,* said Edward.

Andrew's voice calling, "Edward!" startled Ted and sent Edward back to wherever he had come from.

Ted rode forward and joined Andrew.

"Here's a party to ask our business," said Andrew. "'Twere best I spoke with them, but you must be near at hand."

"As you will," said Ted.

As it turned out, he did not have to say anything, though he did sustain a number of alert and curious glances; not from the herald himself, who confined his attention to Andrew, but from both the soldiers and the horses that made up the herald's escort. The herald challenged them courteously enough, and on being informed that King Edward of the Hidden Land had ridden forth for the sole purpose of showering his brother monarch the Dragon King with diverse rich presents, and to consult with him touching the future of their several states, the herald of the Dragon King invited them to slake their weariness and hunger, and have audience of the Dragon King the following morning.

After an impressive progress through several layers of fortifications, past a number of very grim-looking guards, during all of which time Edward poured into Ted's ears a hundred details of the castle's structure and defenses, they were relieved of their horses and guided across the soft grass of the inner bailey to the left-hand D-shaped tower. They trailed, all eight of them, bedraggled, behind the gorgeously dressed herald, through a sort of storeroom smelling strongly of cheese and smoked meat, up a narrow winding stair, and into a large room lit by a good fire.

The herald said something gracious; Andrew answered him properly; the herald departed, closing behind him the heavy door to the staircase. Ted sat down on his bedroll. The dragging tiredness was still with him. Randolph looked beat too; he was leaning on the doorpost with his eyes closed. Ruth sat down on the four-poster bed. It was Andrew who found a taper, lit it from the fire, and walked from sconce to sconce, setting the fat red candles to burn.

It was a beautiful room. The walls were plastered and painted with deep, clear colors; hunting scenes, mostly, and landscapes. The arch of the window was filled with stone tracery. The floor was tiled in blue and rust. So was the fireplace. Ted began to feel that perhaps High Castle was a little rustic, a little haphazard, a little neglected.

"Now," said Andrew, blowing out his taper, replacing it, and sitting down in one of the chairs by the fire, "let's have it clear how we'll conduct this embassy."

Ruth stood up. Randolph pushed himself away from the door and walked to the center of the room. He looked down at Ted, and then at the empty chair.

"Yours," said Ted.

Randolph sat down across from Andrew and said, "We made all clear in council. What would you now?"

"In the light of all the knowledge I have gained, by your most gracious provision," said Andrew, "stands it not upon us to alter the terms of this embassy?"

"In what regard?" said Randolph. Ted saw that he was perturbed, but did not intend to waste his energy, or perhaps give Andrew any satisfaction, by raising his voice.

"In several," said Andrew. "First, neither the true King nor a suitable Regent of the Hidden Land is present in this party."

Ruth made an abrupt movement; Ted looked at her, and their crossed glances said to each other, here it comes. Andrew's eyes were bright on Randolph. Randolph only leaned his head back in the luxurious chair and said, "Neither imputation is fair."

"Look you," said Andrew, closing his hands on the arms of his chair. "I have promised King William to hold my tongue, and by that word will I abide. But I have not promised to sit idle while such as you do finish the wreck of my country."

"Ted," said Randolph, still quietly, "hath sworn the oath of kingship." Andrew let his breath out scornfully and brought his fists down on his knees. "And you," said Randolph, in a stronger voice, "did swear to him, in his own name that is in truth Edward, truth and faith would you bear unto him, against all manner of folk."

"What," said Andrew, and his voice was now quieter than Randolph's, "shall my word be more to me, my lord counselor, than was yours to you?"

Ruth jumped to her feet and plunged across the room; Ted reached up and grabbed hard at her skirt, and she came down on her knees beside him and was silent. Ted heard a dog barking in the courtyard, and a bucket being lowered down a well, and, faintly, the lapping of lake water against the outer walls.

"If it be not more to you than that," said Randolph, "by what right do you assume the power of this embassy?"

"What would you have altered, Andrew?" said Ruth, so placidly that Ted stared at her.

"I would alter the whole tune of this approach," said Andrew. "Let our note be not chastisement, but true alliance."

"Shan's mercy, against what?" said Randolph, furiously, jerking his head up and coming half out of his chair. "E'en granting we might trust this adder to bite some other breast than ours, what neighbor doth threaten us save this alone? Against what scatheless state doth Dragon King spout mischief, save ours? Hateth he the Outer Isles? Do the Cavernous Domains trouble his sleep? Doth he agitate him what danger awaiteth in the Dubious Hills? What double-directed malice is there, to unite us?"

"Melanie's," said Andrew.

Randolph fell back into the chair as if somebody had pushed him, clutched his head in both hands, and began to laugh. Andrew sat stony-faced, waiting for him to stop. Ted, since nobody else seemed likely to enlighten him, looked at Ruth and discovered that she, too, was laughing.

"Andrew," said Randolph, gasping. "My lord. That is excellently well reasoned, with every fact that lards it false as hemp nettle to the ropemaker. Melanie did serve the Dragon King in her youth; over the continuance of that service did she fall out so fatally with Shan. Why should she quit him now, or he believe her aught but his good friend?"

"Magic may be true," said Andrew, "and wizards yet be false."

Randolph pushed his hand back over his hair and said, "Andrew. You cannot unravel these matters in the space of a night, or of a year. Keep this embassy in its intended form. If later it seems good to you that we and the Dragon King make common cause 'gainst Melanie, then make your case with true tales, and it shall be heard by whate'er King we have."

"That's a pretty speech," said Andrew, "but how if there be no time? She hath her agents in every corner of our councils; she's killed our royal children and our King; within a year, shall not this canker swallow us?"

"This canker will swallow us tomorrow an you represent us to the Dragon King as Melanie's enemies."

"Or as her victims?" said Andrew.

"We're not her victims save we make us so," said Randolph.

"What!" said Andrew. "The blame so ready to hand, and you'll fling it not at her? Your deed was not her doing; you were not helpless in your own despite?"

"Andrew," said Ted, desperately, "by your oath I do abjure you, abide by the agreed terms of this embassy and admit no other matter to it."

"I hear you," said Andrew.

That was not an acquiescence. Ted took a deep breath, and the door opened. A fresh-faced girl in a black dress said, "My lords and ladies, you are bid to supper."

CHAPTER 28

THE unicorn was not made like a horse. The coat of the unicorn was not like the coat of a horse, or of a goat. The smell of the unicorn was not like the smell of a horse, or of a goat. So much for appearances, thought Patrick, his hands clenched in a mane hardly more substantial than a cobweb, and his knees trying to grip a body that slid aside from him as a cat does when it prefers not to be picked up.

Nor did a unicorn proceed, foot placed in front of foot, as a horse might go over the ground. He could not feel or hear its hooves hit anything. He felt a great wind in his face; he saw before him a gray mist and on either side a blurring of colors, as if somebody had made a chalk drawing of a forest in autumn and then swept the side of his hand carelessly across it.

The wind stopped; the unicorn stood still. Patrick had been straining his eyes for just this moment; but he learned no more from the motion's cessation than he had from its inception. One moment he saw blurred colors, and the next everything was sharp, crisp, and ordinary. They were by the Well of the White Witch, facing uphill to where the Secret House rose untidily out of the trees.

Patrick slid to the ground, saying, "What next?"

"I may not come under a roof," said Chryse.

Patrick looked at it. He might have known. "What part of the roof do you want me to come under," he said, "and what should I do when I get there?"

"Go up into the smaller tower," said Chryse, "the which

you may do by keeping always to the left. Consider the globe that you find there. If it be small, you may bring it out; if it be too large, you must speak to it, naming Belaparthalion."

"I always did think," said Patrick, "that the heroes in fairy tales must feel extremely stupid. I guess I'll get to find out." He bowed to the unicorn, because being rude to them got you nowhere, and walked up the hill to the house.

The globe in the tower room was much too large to bring out. Its unhealthy gray bulge filled the room; Patrick wondered if it would burst the walls when it grew larger still; or just expand into some other dimension; or just stop, the way things happened here. He leaned on the wall, because his legs were tired from the climb, and said, "Belaparthalion."

There was no reply. Patrick did not feel stupid. He felt apprehensive. It was clear to him, through what sense he could not have said, that there was somebody else in this room. He said again, "Belaparthalion," and then, since he appeared to be in a fairy tale and it was best to use what rules you could, he said it a third time.

"Who goes there?" said a raspy voice, with a background like static.

"Patrick Carroll," said Patrick, "temporary prince of the Hidden Land."

The middle point of the globe turned from gray to red; the point swelled to a circle; the circle turned slowly and became a sphere; the sphere grew larger, and suddenly reassembled itself into a curved, red, reptilian shape, whiskered and tendriled, with a long head like a collie's, and pointed ears, and a gaping mouth full of carnivorous teeth. There were too many incisors, thought Patrick. What did it eat that it had evolved so many of them; and how did it keep them from shredding its mouth? He thought of the saber-toothed tiger, and shrugged.

The creature said, "What do you here?"

"I'm just the errand-boy," said Patrick. "Chryse waits below, but will not come under a roof. She said that if your globe were small enough I should carry it out, and that otherwise I should speak to you. I don't suppose you could shrink it?"

"I am very well where I am," said the creature. It might or might not, he supposed, be a dragon; but it certainly thought it was called Belaparthalion.

"Chryse doesn't think you are," he said.

"What wisheth Chryse?"

"She wants you to come and help her seal a bargain for the good of the Hidden Land."

"What bargain?"

"That in return for the swords of Shan and Melanie, you two prevent the Dragon King from bothering the Hidden Land. They're tired of scurrying around to their borders to repel invaders."

"Oho," said Belaparthalion, in an altered voice. "Sits the wind in that quarter? The swords of Shan and Melanie? Both?"

"I wouldn't know, myself," said Patrick, "but Fence and Randolph think so, and Chryse seemed satisfied."

"I pray you," said Belaparthalion, "break me this crystal."

Patrick's stomach lurched. The last time he had broken a crystal had been very unpleasant. Besides, Chryse had not told him to break it, only to speak to its occupant. Between Chryse and Belaparthalion, Patrick did not know where he would put his money. Three things might destroy the Secret Country: the Border Magic, the Crystal of Earth, the Whim of the Dragon. This was probably a dragon; and with a dragon, how did you know what was whim and what was reasonable? If you did destroy the Secret Country, exactly what were you risking, whom were you hurting? How did you judge such a deed? Decision without data, thought Patrick. That's the curse of this place.

"With what should I break it, my lord?" he said.

"Your hand sufficeth, an you have no sword," said Belaparthalion.

Patrick looked doubtfully at his medium-sized, square-knuckled hand, with the writing-bump on the second finger, and the grime under the nails. "If my hand will suffice from the outside," he said, "why won't your teeth suffice from inside?"

"Because," said Belaparthalion, in a tone of enormous amusement, "the crystal was made to keep dragons in, and not the children of men out."

"Didn't the people who made it think that the children of men might come along at an inopportune moment?"

"Inopportune for whom?" said Belaparthalion. "Look you, the breaking of this crystal, from within or from without, doth destroy the image you see within it. How should the maker of the crystal think that any trapped within might choose such destruction?"

Oh, brother, thought Patrick. "Is this a whim of yours?" he said.

"No," said Belaparthalion. "A sacrifice, an you will, but not a whim."

Patrick chewed over this for a while, and gave up. "Well, look," he said. "If I destroy the image of you I see, what is going to be left?"

"Break the crystal," said Belaparthalion, in the precise tone of somebody initiating a knock-knock joke, "and find out."

Chryse had told him to talk to it. This was what happened when you talked to it.

Patrick lifted his hand and smashed it down hard into the gray light. It gave before him like cloth, not glass, but with a tremendous shattering sound. A crystalline wheel of bright spray spun through the air. There was a crack of thunder, a blast of hot air, and a tremendous flash of colorless light against which Patrick shut his eyes. When he opened them, every surface in the room sparkled with splinters. On the wooden table where the globe had rested sat a man. He was not very tall; he had black hair and green eyes; he looked like Fence and Randolph. He wore a red robe and red boots. There were no shards of glass on him.

"Greetings," said Patrick, brushing cautiously at his hair. The splinters, that looked so sharp, felt like threads and scraps of cloth, and drifted easily down from his combing hands. "Are you called Apsinthion?"

"Sometimes," said the man in red. His voice held still the faint echo of laughter, but his face was grim.

When they came out of the house and walked down the hill to where Chryse was placidly cropping the wildflowers around the Well, Patrick found out why. Chryse suddenly flung up her head, laid her ears back, and like a string quartet badly out of tune, said, "What judgment would step from that to this? Could you on that fair mountain leave to feed, and batten on this moor?"

This did not make a great deal of sense to Patrick, but the scorn and horror in Chryse's voice were plain to anybody.

"That fair mountain was a prison," said Belaparthalion, "wherefrom this moor, howsoever damp and displeasing to thee, hath been a refuge."

"A refuge," said Chryse, "that will come down on your head at the first breath of wind. Is this your duty? Is this the manner you preserve this fair small kingdom from the hawks of song?" It lowered its head, and the early sunlight flashed off that horn as if it had been a mirror.

"This fair small kingdom shall do well enough," said Belaparthalion, "when Shan's and Melanie's swords are raised in its defense." Patrick noticed that he did not come close to Chryse.

"Those swords," said Chryse, "are for safekeeping, not for use."

"Those swords, dear cousin," said Belaparthalion, "are for translation, not for battle. I am old in craft, Chryse, and what I have lost in the dragon-form will return to me a thousandfold in these two swords."

"Excuse me," said Patrick, keeping between him and them what would have been a safe distance if the only threat they could offer had been physical. "Shouldn't we be getting back?"

Chryse turned on him, its head still dangerously lowered. "Thou," it said, "hast much to answer for."

"I did," said Patrick, "what you told me."

"When did the children of men ever so?" said Chryse; but it lifted its head again. There was a long pause. The wind blew softly in the long grass. Patrick shook the rest of the shards of Belaparthalion's crystal from his clothing.

"Well," said Chryse; and that same note of laughter was in its voice now also. "Cousin: will you ride on my back?"

Belaparthalion did not look amused; but he nodded, and beckoned to Patrick. Patrick came forward, trying not to look as reluctant as he felt. Those two were still angry at each other; what Chryse thought was funny he didn't know, but he doubted that it boded well. Belaparthalion gave him a lift up onto Chryse's back. Patrick gasped. The man in red's hands were fever-hot and as dry as snakeskin. Belaparthalion got up behind him, and the brisk autumn air in their vicinity became balmy. Patrick wondered if Belaparthalion were sick. If he were, it seemed unlikely that he would live long. If he didn't, Patrick had killed him.

The trip back seemed slower to him, possibly because he was so hot. They stopped at last, and around them was the clearing in the pine woods where they had left the others. The others had built a fire. The air smelled of woodsmoke, and a little of tea. Matthew and Celia were sitting on the ground on the far side of the clearing. They had brushed away all the pine needles from a spot about three feet square, and were drawing diagrams in the dirt beneath. Fence and Ellen and Laura sat around the fire, looking glum.

Laura saw them first. Why her face should light up like

that at the sight of the man in red, Patrick couldn't fathom. He felt pleased with himself, just the same, until he remembered how angry Chryse had been. The red man slid to the ground, and Patrick followed. Laura stood up.

"Well met!" said Belaparthalion to Laura.

"Sir," said Laura. "Patrick, where'd you find him?"

"Let me introduce you," said Patrick, resignedly. "This is Laura, pro tem princess of the Hidden Land. Laura, this is Belaparthalion."

Laura stared. Then she did Belaparthalion a pretty good courtesy, considering her disarray and her basic clumsiness. Patrick grinned at her; and his sister Ellen came around the fire, so he introduced her too, and she provided her overdramatic bow. Fence was still sitting on the ground, and Patrick could not discern his thoughts in his round, solemn, deceptive face. Fence, thought Patrick, should have been his first lesson in appearances, if he had had the sense to learn it.

"Fence," said the man in red; and he pushed, smiling, between Laura and Ellen, and sat on the ground too, rather closer to the fire than Patrick thought advisable. Even if his flesh wouldn't burn, his clothing might.

"We saved you some tea," said Laura, "but it's mostly cold."

"That's fine," said Patrick. "I'm warm enough." He took the tin cup they gave him and drank the tea. Then he sat down and prepared to watch the fireworks.

Laura knew from his face that he expected something interesting to happen. What Patrick found interesting, she usually found appalling. She sat down next to him, a safe distance from Fence and the red man, who were looking at each other steadily. Chryse folded herself to the ground in a posture that looked relaxed almost to the point of abandonment, like a cat about to roll on its back; except that she had her ears flat to her head, which in either a cat or a horse meant no good. Laura wished somebody would say something. After a few minutes, she said something herself.

"Chryse answered your riddles," she said to Belaparthalion.

His head came around. He looked startled, and then amused. "In change for what?" he said.

"A tale thou knowest," said Chryse, in a precise plucking of sounds like somebody tinkering with a harp.

"I wonder," said Belaparthalion.

"Thou wert in't," retorted Chryse. Yes, she was very cross indeed. Laura wondered what about.

"That I was in't by no means requires that I know't."

"We'll tell it you also," said Fence, "do you tell us how you came in this shape."

"And how you came to be in a globe in the House by the Well of the White Witch," rattled Patrick, for Fence's benefit.

"Done," said Belaparthalion, briskly. "Every dragon hath a man-shape, but few do employ it; it doth weaken us. Now Melanie, who is an old enemy of mine, did discover how to fling a dragon into his man-shape, and she did so to me, and then did imprison the dragon-shape in that globe wherefrom Patrick did so graciously rescue me."

"Why now?" said Fence.

Belaparthalion shrugged.

"How long were you thus?"

"She did so divide me on the eighth day of June last."

Fence looked across the fire at Ellen and Laura. Laura said, "We showed up on the fourteenth."

"And we showed up a couple of days earlier," said Ellen.

"She did desire, then," said Belaparthalion, "that we not meet."

"And now that we have, what of it?" said Patrick.

"First," said Fence, "to the business of the Hidden Land. Lord, will you in exchange for the swords of Shan and

Melanie given to you and Chryse, conspire with Chryse for the good of the Hidden Land against the devices of the Dragon King?"

"I will so," said Belaparthalion.

Fence closed his eyes for a moment. Laura thought suddenly that, to him, this might be the most important of all the things they were doing. Claudia, anybody could see, was a worry; the deaths of the royal children were a grief; the connection between this strangers' game and Fence's own reality was a puzzle. And of course something would have to be done about all of it. But this one thing he had at least ensured, that the Dragon King would trouble the Hidden Land no longer.

"Having given this word," said Chryse, very coldly, "do you tell us how you will keep it, in so puny a form and with so dulled a perception."

"Sweet cousin," said Belaparthalion, in no very affectionate voice, "being neither man nor dragon, you do hold too low the powers of either. Fear me not."

"I am in this oath also," said Chryse, "and must supply your deficiencies, an your own strength be unequal."

"When thou seest my deficiencies," said Belaparthalion, "ask me again."

"I do see them now," said Chryse. "Some do approach, and yet you hear them not."

Fence, looking resigned, called Celia and Matthew. They stood up, brushed pine needles off themselves, and came over to the fire. "Here's Belaparthalion," Fence said to them, "and the Lords of the Dead are coming."

"Good morning!" said Matthew, with a kind of good-natured ruefulness, and smiled at the man in red.

"Is that one pro tem also?" said Belaparthalion to Patrick.

"No, he's permanent," said Patrick. "Lord Matthew, Scribe to the King and King's Counselor. Matthew, this is your very own guardian dragon; show some respect. And this, my lord dragon, is Lady Celia, King's Counselor and musician."

Celia did Belaparthalion a courtesy; Matthew said to Fence, "What's amiss?"

There was a certain amount of crashing, and a flurry of unicorns bolted into the clearing, shied briefly at the clump of people, and converged on Chryse, hooting and chiming.

"What, they?" said Celia.

"I think that's just the cavalry," said Ellen. "So to speak."

"How can you tell?" said Patrick.

"Because," said Ellen, "the Lords of the Dead are of the sort of shape-shifter that is held to one kind of form only. They can't turn themselves into unicorns. Right, Fence?"

"Right," said Fence, absently. He cast his gaze around the clearing. Laura, following it, saw suddenly where the swords of Shan and Melanie still lay as Celia had unwrapped them. Their glow had dimmed with the rising of the sun, but now they were blazing in unkind colors that pressed sparks under one's eyelids and obscured the plain shapes of the trees.

Oh, come on, thought Laura, not now. But she was caught. She looked unwillingly upon a cluttered room bright with lamplight. Claudia sat at a round table, dressed in blue velvet, her black hair falling down her back, working with tiny tools at a band of tarnished metal. As Laura watched, she picked up a dull black stone from off the table and fitted it into the socket of the band. She had just made Shan's Ring, or something very like it. Then she picked up a red-and-blue wooden top that lay on the table, and pulled toward her a little carved clock. She took blue and green stones and made a circle around the clock and the top. She set the pendulum of the clock swinging. She spun the top with an unthinking expertise behind which Laura saw, with a jolt, hours of playing; how strange to think that Claudia had ever been a child. Then she tossed the ring into the air and caught it again, grinning.

Somebody wiry who smelled like burning leaves took Laura under the arms and swung her off her feet, and the sight tattered and vanished. Fence had grabbed her and deposited her with the rest of the party at one edge of the clearing. The whole of the empty space was thronged with unicorns. She looked frantically for the swords. Matthew, a little farther back in the trees, was holding Shan's, swinging it casually in one hand as if it were a skipping-rope. Fence touched the top of Laura's head and, when she looked up at him, showed her the green glow of Melanie's sword, thrust through his belt under the muddy black cloak.

"Where," said Ellen, "are the Lords of the Dead going to stand, when they come?"

"Where's Belaparthalion?" said Patrick.

"He's standing with Chryse," said Fence. "Patrick. What's their quarrel?"

Patrick, keeping a wary eye on the unicorns, and raising his voice from time to time to be heard over a sudden blare of horn or organ, a trilling as of two hundred piccolos, a quivering barrage as of somebody dropping a harpsichord down a cement stairwell, answered this question with more detail than was usual with him. Laura was seized with equal parts of envy and of relief that she had not been faced with such a choice.

" 'Sblood!" said Ellen, when he had finished. "That was stupid, but it certainly wasn't cowardly."

"Why stupid?" said Fence. "If Belaparthalion said this was not his whim, then 'twas not. I do not know, however, what this translation meaneth, nor what benefit Belaparthalion hopeth to gain from Melanie's sword sufficient to salve him for the loss o'the dragon-shape."

"And that's Chryse's quarrel," said Patrick.

"But if that's our Apsinthion," said Laura, "and Apsinthion is the Judge of the Dead, then—"

"He answered to Belaparthalion," said Patrick, stubbornly.

"Fence?" said Laura. "Could he be both?"

"I trust not," said Fence.

Matthew stepped forward, grabbed Fence by the arm, and pointed southward. "Look there," he said.

A soberly dressed, harmless-looking crowd of people was coming through the trees. There were nine of them. They wore neither cloaks nor swords. A shiver went up Laura's spine. The unicorns melted away to the other side of the clearing, and the nine people walked to where the party from the Hidden Land stood. The light of the sun seemed flatter; Laura felt oppressed; and in several quick glances upward, she saw that a yellow flame stood in all their eyes. They nodded amiably at the party from the Hidden Land, and then turned their backs.

A lilting voice Laura knew addressed the unicorns, "Hail, blithe spirits!" it said. "We mean you no ill, but seek one of our own."

"None of your own is here," said Chryse's voice. A swelling chorus in the back of the mind added, *How shall I your true love know from another one?*

"Lady, he is. Apsinthion!" said the rich voice, imperatively.

The man in red made his way through the unicorns like a setter breasting a field of daisies, and halted in the small space left in the center of the clearing. "You're far from your wonted ways," he said to them.

"No further than thou," said the austere voice.

"I have been out before," said the man in red, "while you were sleeping. For I did think, how should I judge the dead who had not seen the living?"

"That's your affair," said the rich voice. "But we do hear that you hold in trust somewhat that we desire."

"You may not have't," said the man in red.

"We do not wish it," said the lilting voice. "We wish it silenced. Do you swear never to use it in any wise?"

"Peace, break thee off," said Chryse's voice, in precisely

the tone Laura's father would use to say, "Now just a God damn minute!" She, too, pushed through the mill of unicorns until she stood next to the man in red. The inward chorus said peacefully, *Break, break, break, / On thy cold gray stones, O Sea!* Laura saw one or two of the Lords of the Dead rub at their foreheads, and hoped that the poetry was giving them a headache.

"Belaparthalion," said Chryse, and there was very little music in her voice. "What art thou?" *There is no art,* said the chorus, *To find the mind's construction in the face.*

"I am the man-shape of a dragon," said the man in red. "I am the Judge of the Dead. And, though thou would it were not so, I am thy cousin."

"The Judge of the Dead," said Chryse, with less music yet, "is an Outside Power." The chorus was silent.

The man in red said, "That is so."

"I do not well understand this," said Chryse. "But I do understand well indeed that you and I are sworn to guard the Hidden Land 'gainst the depredations of the Outside Powers. I'll do my duty well, then, to guard it 'gainst thee."

The unicorns, still silent, foamed backward among the trees and quivered there, white in the shadows. Chryse backed away and lowered her silky head, with its golden eyes and its whiskered nose and its long, sharp, mortal horn.

Fence dragged Melanie's sword from his belt. "My lord!"

The man in red reached back a hand, and Fence slapped the hilt into it. The sword flashed like breaking glass as he touched it. He took it between his two palms and extended it toward Chryse. "I cry you mercy," he said. "This will do naught but ill."

Chryse said, with a full complement of melody ringing behind her words, "All may yet be very well."

Laura looked wildly at Fence. His fists were clenched and his eyes were enormous, but he seemed to feel that he had done all he could when he gave the sword to the red man. But all that did was even the odds. One of the guardians of the Hidden Land was going to kill the other. Some guardians. They were behaving irresponsibly in the extreme. But Laura's outrage was not enough to make her tell them so; nor were they likely to listen. Stealth would have to serve.

"Fence!" she whispered. "Give me Shan's Ring."

Fence had plunged his hand into his belt-pouch before the surprised look was off his face. He pressed the ring into her hand. Laura, plucking bad poetry out of her memory, breathed. "And Shan's sword." He wouldn't do it. A peculiar magical artifact, sure; but not a weapon. But Fence drifted backward, as if to give the combatants more room, and pulled Matthew with him.

Chryse and the man in red had begun to circle each other. Laura wondered if they would actually have a fencing match, with the horn serving as a sword, or if Chryse would charge and stab with that horn and the man in red fend for himself as best he could. If Chryse wanted to show him his weakness, she might succeed.

Fence edged up beside Laura and said, "It's beneath my cloak. What mean you to do?"

"Blow time awry," said Laura, "so everybody can think. Hand me the sword."

She still thought he would not do it. She could not explain her reasoning, if he should ask. Patrick would not call it reasoning at all. Chryse moved suddenly and drove the needle-sharp icicle of her violet-spiraled horn straight at the red man's breast. He skittered to one side; Celia, right in Chryse's path, did not move, and Chryse stopped in a shower of pine needles.

"Think, lady," said Celia, the scar standing out on her forehead.

Chryse backed without looking at her and lowered her horn again. And the hilt of Shan's sword, so perfectly sized for a ten-year-old's hand, tingled from Fence's hand into Laura's nervous grip. Laura took three steps forward, dropped Shan's sword onto the ground between the combatants, stepped back, hurled Shan's Ring into the air, and gabbled, "I am a trinket in the world, unvalued gold and sullen stone, but Outside Power is unfurled, when outside power I am hurled, and time awry is blown."

Chryse and Belaparthalion stood still, Chryse in a graceful pose that any sculptor would have been proud of, and the man in red with one foot in the air and the sword arrested between one useful position and another. Their eyes were alarming; so wide and empty that neither of them seemed to be there at all. Laura remembered Claudia, staring on the steps of Fence's tower with a knife in her fist.

"Nice work," said Patrick, a little hoarsely. "But they're going to be just as mad when they wake up."

"I thought," said Laura, "that if we got the unicorns to surround Chryse and took the sword away from Belaparthalion, we could calm them down enough to explain what's going on."

"Excellent," said Fence; there was congratulation in his voice, but also a definite irony. "Now we've only to find out that we must explain to them."

"I thought," said Laura, coming back to his comforting vicinity, "that the Lords of the Dead could tell us."

"The Lords of the Dead," said the piercing voice of a unicorn, from the froth among the trees, "have been sleeping."

"The Lords of the Dead," said the lilting voice, "wish only to go on sleeping. Give us these raucous swords and we'll trouble you no longer."

"And also that shrieking ring," said the rich voice.

The unicorns made a sound like an entire acre full of wind chimes. It came to Laura that they were laughing. She hoped the Lords of the Dead would not notice.

"Know you aught of the Judge of the Dead?" said Fence, to the soberly dressed party generally.

"He is of the Outside Powers," said the lilting voice.

"Are dragons also of the Outside Powers?" said Fence, patiently.

"Dragons," said the rich voice, "are not so much as of the immortals. We have seen dragons beneath the earth; Apsinthion hath judged them; do you ask him."

"By and by," said Fence.

"So Chryse's charges are true," said Celia.

"How came matters to this pass?" said Matthew.

"That would we know also," said the lilting voice.

"Well, Apsinthion aka Belaparthalion ought to know," said Ellen. "He's the one who's fish and flesh. So to speak."

"Why should he know?" said Patrick. "You might as well say, when we got into this country we should have known what was going on, just because it happened to us."

You might as well say, chorused the unicorns, *that "I sleep when I breathe" is the same thing as "I breathe when I sleep."* There was a pause, and as the white horde drifted and nodded just a little in the direction of the Lords of the Dead, they added, *It* is *the same thing with you.* Laura and Ellen burst out laughing. Patrick, who scorned Lewis Carroll, rolled his eyes at them.

"Well, we'd better figure out something," he said. "We don't know how long this spell lasts."

"Come to that," said Matthew, gently, "we know not how to remove it. Laura, why not have used 'From the horns of Unicorns'?"

"Because that wouldn't have done Chryse any good," said Laura. "He was mad at her by that time."

"True," said Fence. "And very well done."

Laura began to feel foolish just the same. There was no use in averting a crisis if all you achieved was a limbo. She looked at the two arrested figures, and at the sword of Shan where it lay among the dry brown needles. She unclenched her cramped hand from around Shan's Ring, and held it out to Fence. And she remembered something.

"Hey!" she cried. "You unicorns! Didn't I do it? Didn't I change time of my own power?"

"What hast thou seen and not told?" said one of them.

Laura felt herself turning red. She dropped the ring into Fence's palm and sent and stood on the far side of an immense pine tree. Stupid, stupid, stupid. She thought of Cedric's flute. No, this could not be called the end. This was a silly situation, but it was hardly the end. The stupid tears dazzled her vision.

She groped inside her cloak to find a piece of shirt clean enough to wipe her eyes on, and the blur of sun and saltwater sharpened suddenly into a scene that was not the green pine woods with their dusty shafts of sunlight. It was the massive castle she had seen once at night, garlanded with fireworks; and folded within one corner of its vast stretch of walls, between the low outer wall with its bristling of towers and the high, thick inner wall, lay the formal rose garden she had also seen before. Andrew and Randolph crossed swords; a clump of brightly dressed people watched. Then Ted flung himself out of the crowd, yelling something she could not hear, and with his own sword struck to the ground the crossed blades of Randolph and Andrew. A figure with flying black hair grabbed Andrew from behind. And Randolph lifted his sword again and lunged at Ted.

It was what they had come back here to avert. And she could tell, by the length of Ted's hair, by the clothes they wore, festive clothes she had helped Agatha pick out for the embassy to wear at the court of the Dragon King, that it was happening soon; or perhaps it was happening now.

"Fence!" shouted Laura, and bolted around the tree. "Listen. Ted is fighting Randolph in the Dragon King's rose garden. We've got a magic ring, a magic sword, and a magic flute; can't we do something?"

"This is a present vision?" said Fence.

"I don't know. It's not very future."

"Let's not take the risk, for God's sake," said Patrick. "You're a wizard; do something."

"I can't fly through the air!" snapped Fence. He drove both hands into his hair and strode between Chryse and Belaparthalion, ducking under the vicious horn as if it were a dangling vine. He plunged in among the unicorns, gesticulating. Laura could not hear clearly what he was saying in his light voice, but the replies of the unicorns were clear.

"We can take thee."

"Aye, we can take you all."

"But upon one condition; that thou releasest our sister."

Fence's reaction to that was louder. "An I release thy sister, will you stand surety for the safety of her enemy there?"

"That is her affair and thine, not ours."

"Shan's sweet mercy!" shouted Fence. "I am making it your affair. I will release her only on that condition."

"He can't release her anyway," said Patrick.

"Shut up," said Ellen.

"An you release her not, we carry you nowhere," said a unicorn.

"I'll give you Shan's Ring," said Fence, in less furious but carrying tones.

The little knot of the Lords of the Dead stirred. In very mellow tones, a unicorn said, "The bargain made touching that ring precludes our having it."

Something in the voice alerted Laura. It wanted to be argued with; it wanted to coax some particular statement out of them, so that it could take the ring. She pushed through the crowd of unicorns and caught Fence by the hand. His burning-leaf smell mingled with the spicy scent of the unicorns. "Listen," said Laura. "Shan's Ring was supposed to save the Hidden Land from the machinations of Melanie. But she made the sword that woke you up; she made Shan's Ring too." Fence's hand jerked in hers; he had not known that. "This is *all* a machination of Melanie," said Laura; and stopped. That was not true; and her intuition failed her suddenly. It had all been so clear in her head.

But the unicorn said, "Well enough. Now what of the second condition, that that ring become an heirloom of Shan's house?"

Once again, you could tell that it hoped for the point it made to be properly countered. Laura's invention had dried up.

"The children of Shan's house," said Fence, with a terrible grim triumph, "are below the earth. That condition's forfeit."

The unicorn was taken aback by this; but the rich voice of a Lord of the Dead said, "'Twere better you gave it to us."

"What will that profit me?" roared Fence, without turning.

"First, we will deliver all present to the court of the Dragon King. Second, we will deliver Shan's Ring to Edward Fairchild, that both conditions of the bargain be met."

There was a small silence.

"Well, fair ones?" said Fence. "White ones? Drinkers of verse? What say you to that?"

"Give it them," said the unicorns, in overlapping waves. "We'll have no peace else." Even in the midst of her anxiety, Laura thought how curious it was that magical creatures wanted sleep and peace more than they wanted anything else.

Fence said, "Stand you witness to this bargain?"

"We do."

Fence turned around. "Done," he said to the Lords of the Dead.

The Lords of the Dead did not believe in preliminaries. Being delivered by them was not like riding a unicorn. It was a great deal more, Laura thought, like being picked up by a tornado. Darkness stabbed about with red fire, howling voices, and a vast noise of distant water overtook her. Dwindling down the distances of her mind, the unicorns remarked, *I pray you pass with your best violence.*

Chapter 29

THE fresh-faced girl sat at the head of their table; saw to it that whatever she thought they needed arrived promptly; and conducted the conversation with the same absent-minded skill Ted's father exhibited when he played solitaire at four in the morning because he was too tired to go to bed. She had sorted them out so that it was impossible to continue the argument in any kind of privacy: on her right were Ted, Jerome, Ruth, and Julian; at the foot of the table, pale but smiling, was Andrew; and up the other side, from Andrew to the fresh-faced girl, sat Stephen, Dittany, and Randolph. Ted was sure she had seated them that way on purpose.

Sometime after the roast chicken and the potatoes cooked with cheese and radishes and the three kinds of bread and the sweet butter and the cucumbers and several dishes veiled in pastry that Ted couldn't identify had all come and gone, the conversational topics she had sown over the table actually took root down at its foot; something about a new kind of stone they were digging up in the Outer Isles. The five at that end were absorbed by it, while Dittany, Randolph, and Jerome got tired of shouting their comments into the intellectual morass at the table's far end and diverged into a discussion of the castle's architecture. Ruth sat stranded between these two conversations, a line between her black brows, biting her lip and eating when she remembered. She looked as if she were doing a stiff homework assignment.

That left the fresh-faced girl only Ted to deal with. She

smiled and commended him on his part in the battle just past, as if she were congratulating him on a good game of tennis. It would be rude to appear horrified, especially when he had no idea of the exact status of all the creatures he had killed. Ted said something deprecating and watched her peel a peach. He remembered Conrad at the Banquet of Midsummer Eve, eating a peach without bothering to peel it; and his cheerful acceptance of the fact that Ted, going for Andrew, had spilled his dinner all over Conrad. Conrad was dead; one of the creatures of dubious status had killed him. And the other people those creatures had killed, strangers to him, he knew their status also. Edward had known all of them.

The fresh-faced girl finished her peach and looked inquiringly at him; he had missed her last question. Wanting still to be polite, both because it would be disaster to be otherwise and because she was so pretty, he looked up at her, readying a change of subject that would not seem too abrupt; and saw the little blue flame standing in each of her eyes. Edward said remotely, *They will turn me in your arms into a lion bold.* And Ted saw her clear eyes and fresh skin and silky yellow hair and clever hands all as a garment she was wearing, the black dress but a cloak dragged carelessly over it.

They were clearing away dishes and bringing in the rosewater by then. Ted swallowed hard and asked her, completely at random, if she played any musical instrument. This got her off the subject of the war; but it also brought her, lute in hand, back to their rooms with them, for three acutely uncomfortable hours. She was a brilliant musician. Ruth got out her flute; Randolph took a turn at the lute; everybody sang. But there was no comfort in it and all the camaraderie was false.

When she trailed her black skirts out the door at last, thanking them all graciously and bidding them to have pleasant rest, it was after midnight. The Dragon King had granted them audience at nine in the morning.

Stephen, Dittany, Jerome, and Julian looked hopefully at Randolph, and then went upstairs. Ted lay on the bed and looked around. Ruth was sunk in the armchair Andrew had sat in earlier. Randolph sat on the hearth with his head in his hands. Andrew was sitting on a stool in a far corner. To reiterate his order to Andrew would be an insult. But Ted wanted to say something, after the constraint of the evening.

"Was that a strange dinner," he said, "or am I just uncivilized?"

Randolph gave a brief snort of laughter from under his hands. "I hope you never see one stranger," he said.

"Did you see that woman peel that peach?" said Ruth. "It would take me ten years to learn to do that."

"That wasn't a woman," said Ted. "Randolph, what does it mean that she has little blue flames in her eyes?"

"That she is of the shape-shifters that choose what form pleaseth them," said Randolph. "All present were but so."

"Why did that form please her?" said Ruth, sitting forward.

"A courtesy to us, who have been but the one form, perhaps," said Randolph.

"Well, that would be why she didn't turn up as a tree or a horse; but couldn't she have been a nice wholesome-looking boy?"

"She's the Dragon King's daughter," said Andrew, "and her eye's on Edward."

Randolph lifted his head and looked at Andrew. Ruth, too, turned and peered over the edge of her armchair at him; and both of them looked as if they wondered, not at the assertion itself, but at how Andrew knew it.

Ted said, as levelly as he could, "Is that part of your idea of an alliance rather than a chastisement?"

"You could do worse," said Andrew.

He did not look at Ruth; he clearly meant Ruth; and nobody in the room took him up on it. Ted rolled over and sat up on the bed. Randolph said, "What have you promised him?"

"I?" said Andrew. "How should I promise him aught?"

"Aye, how? Do tell us."

Andrew seemed unlikely to answer. He was the only relaxed person in the room; the rest of them were strung up like so many overwound crossbows. Then he made a little impatient motion of the head, and said, "An the servers call her Princess, is she not the Dragon King's daughter? An she make eyes at Edward, shall I not note it?"

Randolph swung around and caught Ted's eye. Ted stood up. "Andrew," he said, "I'm sorry, but I fear your tongue. I think you had better not come to our audience with the Dragon King."

"You should fear't," said Andrew. "Shall I call our four companions?"

Ted thought of them; one unknown quantity; one of the old King's men-at-arms; two of the old King's Counselors, whose opinion of his heir was not high, who had served on the board of inquiry into the old King's death. If there were factions in that odd body, the old King's Council, Jerome and Julian were not of Fence and Randolph's faction.

"You gave your word to King William," said Ted.

"Randolph, believing King William misguided," said Andrew, "did wish to do him a great injury. Wherefore should not I, believing Randolph misguided, do him a lesser?"

"Andrew," said Randolph, "do but consider the injury you do yourself. Your nature is not made for these convolvings; the leaning of your thought is to plain proceeding."

"And thine is better made for crooked ways?" said Andrew.

"No," said Randolph. "Wherefore I may so advise you."

"I will come to this audience," said Andrew.

"You know," said Ruth, reflectively, "I don't think you can stop him."

"For God's sake," said Ted, "let's go to bed."

There was a large alcove with a bed for Ruth, and a smaller one with a bed for Andrew. Ted and Randolph got the four-poster, which had a feather mattress into which you sank so far you hardly needed the blankets. Ted hoped he wouldn't have to leap out of it in a hurry. He was sleeping in his clothes, as was Randolph, precisely out of a fear that he might want to leave this room quickly. He lay enfolded in lavender-smelling linen and watched Randolph bank the fire, and move around the room, blowing out all the candles and bolting the door. Cold moonlight trickled in from the window to the inner courtyard, which nobody had bothered to shutter. Randolph came to Ted's side of the bed, holding a long, thin shape that glinted.

"Is that my sword?" said Ted.

Randolph bent briefly. "I've laid the hilt ready to thy hand," he said.

"Or my foot," said Ted.

"Hence the blade is under the bed," said Randolph. He walked to the other side, laid his own sword down, and got into bed.

"Give you quiet rest," he said.

"And nice, innocuous dreams," said Ted. "Randolph? What do you think Andrew will do?"

"Good night," said Randolph.

Ted didn't have one. He dreamed disjointedly of people with flames in their eyes, red or yellow or blue, who spoke him fair and hugged him warmly and turned in his arms to adders and asps, to flames that burned fast, to doves that beat their wings in his face and swans that pecked him. Last of all came the fresh-faced girl, who, when he smiled and kept his distance from her, turned appallingly into Margaret, Celia's daughter, and asked him in the most prosaic possible manner if he would play the part of the cat for her, for she had been overtaken with sickness. Ted refused politely, whereupon she smiled, Margaret's own bright mocking smile; and he saw in her eyes, where no flame stood, the little image of what she was looking at; and it was not his own familiar unprepossessing figure, but a cat.

Ted jerked upright. The whole bed was bathed in moonlight and he had gotten himself tangled in the blankets. He began to set them to rights softly, so as not to wake Randolph, and saw then that Randolph lay staring open-eyed at the dark ceiling. He turned his head and took the edge of the misplaced blanket Ted held out to him, but he did not speak.

The Dragon King held his audiences in the formal garden, before breakfast. The grass here was still green, and so were the dark, red-veined leaves of the little ornamental trees. The roses were everywhere, the smell of them heavy on air already warmer than a fall afternoon would be in the Hidden Land.

The Dragon King looked like his daughter; or at least, the guise he had chosen, rosy-skinned, yellow-haired, quick-handed, and young for what he was doing, resembled hers strongly. He had a very deep voice. He sat on a raised platform that looked as if it were made of teak and was carved in closely packed shapes of animals and trees. His chair was silver. The people awaiting audience had carved chairs with silk cushions. The embassy of the Hidden Land sat, tense and sleepy and hungry, not speaking to one another, for about fifteen minutes while the Dragon King dealt incomprehensibly with a delegation from the Outer Isles, come to sell stone, and with two people who had some business to do with lions. Then the fresh-faced girl beckoned to them. Ted, Randolph, and Andrew walked over the long strip of carpet laid on the grass to where the Dragon King awaited them.

Randolph, having received permission to speak for his King, who was young and but newly come to his eminence, was allowed to get all the way through his speech. Ted admired it. In the most flattering and mellifluous terms imaginable, it called the Dragon King an unprincipled meddler from no other motive than malice, and required him to desist or he would be sorry for it. It also required payment of damages for the waste of lives and property attendant on the late war.

The Dragon King heard it all, smiling. He did not deny the charges; he did not, either, cloak his answer in the same flowery terms so that he would sound, superficially, as if he were admitting nothing. "I offer you in compensation for your wrongs," he said, "the most precious thing in my power: the hand of my daughter in marriage."

Ted stared at Andrew; but Andrew had merely allowed mild interest to overtake the bland expression he had been wearing since he got up. It was impossible to tell if he had expected this, let alone engineered it.

Ted looked at Randolph, in case he was, God help him, supposed to answer this offer himself. Randolph only regarded the Dragon King thoughtfully, and let a good long silence develop before he answered. "That is a most generous offering," he said; and actually made his best bow in the direction of the fresh-faced girl, who did him a courtesy in return. "I do regret exceedingly that King Edward is betrothed already, and neither can nor will give offense in that quarter."

Ted was afraid to look at Andrew. The Dragon King allowed his own silence to develop. He said at last, mildly, "Might that quarter be otherwise satisfied? I have a son."

Ted felt his jaw dropping, and quickly clamped his mouth shut. Was this some kind of joke?

Andrew said, "The King's betrothed is here, your grace."

"Let her come forward," said the Dragon King, agreeably.

Ted jerked, and felt Randolph's hand on his arm, very lightly. Then Randolph turned and walked back along the red carpet, past the brightly dressed people in their carved chairs, to where Ruth sat petrified in the midst of her traveling companions, and held out his hand to her. Ruth had put on one of Lady Ruth's white dresses, a gauzy thing that didn't show creases. It was better suited to this weather than the layered silks and velvets everybody else was wearing. She was whiter than the dress; but when she took Randolph's hand and stood up, the red mounted in her face until she looked as she had three summers ago, when she won their influenza competition with a temperature of a hundred and four.

She and Randolph walked back up the strip of carpet, and Ted and Andrew fell aside for them.

"What say you, lady?" said the Dragon King.

"I cry you mercy," said Ruth in an admirably steady and carrying voice. "It grieves me to refuse your splendiferous offer. But my heart is given already."

Oh clever Ruth, thought Ted.

"Is it, lady?" said Andrew. "And to whom? Not to your King, to your betrothed, is that not so?"

"It is given," said Ruth, "what matter where? Why should I insult the son of the Dragon King with an empty betrothal?"

"There is no insult," said the Dragon King, equably. "A marriage of policy likes us well. He's richly dowered; and how in conscience could we make war on any country wherein he lived and was happy?"

Ruth stood dumb; she was out of her depth, and Ted couldn't blame her. He had the horrible feeling that the Dragon King was not playing a part; that his understanding of marriage and giving of hearts was extremely faulty, and that he truly thought, making this monstrous offer, that he was offering just, even liberal recompense.

"What saith the King of the Hidden Land?" said Andrew.

Ted looked at Randolph, who returned him a steady gaze of which Ted could make nothing, and who did not offer to answer for him. Ted assembled what courage he had, and addressed the young, benign face of the Dragon King. “I am sorry,” he said. “But I think it would be a greater wrong than that you so liberally seek to recompense, to break up these old agreements and shatter all the fabric of policy they uphold in our country. Nor could we be easy having wrested from you the fairest flower of your land. Some more modest payment, surely, would serve better, as is commonly given after war.”

The Dragon King still looked benign, but as if he were turning this speech over in his mind to see what it was made of.

Andrew said, “There is no fabric of policy. These are lies. Lord Randolph is—”

“Andrew,” said Randolph, softly, as if he were asking him, under the hum of dinner conversation, to pass the salt, “hold your tongue.”

“I will not so,” said Andrew. He addressed the Dragon King, on whose unclouded countenance a shadow of trouble was appearing. “My lord. It’s time for plain speaking. These men do fling your offer in your face because they are most—”

Randolph whipped the sword from its sheath at his side and slammed the flat of it across Andrew’s chest. “One of us,” he said, “will die ere the next words leave thy mouth.”

In fact, Andrew could probably have blurted out a few words before Randolph killed him; but Ted saw from the reaction around him that this was not an extemporaneous remark, but the beginning of a ritual challenge. He didn’t see why Andrew should choose to abide by it when he was willing to flout any other convention that hindered him; but Andrew stood still, his face flaming and his eyes burning into Randolph’s, while all around them people got out of their chairs and moved them back and created a wide open space, dotted with a few rose trees, for their arena.

“I cry you mercy, lord King,” said Randolph, without looking around, “that these our private woes should come to their conclusion in the realm of your pleasures.”

"All may yet be very well," said the Dragon King, placidly.

Ted turned slowly and stared at him; Ruth was doing the same. Randolph, however, disengaged his look from Andrew's and turned it on Ted. "Do you remember those words," he said.

"Now wait," said Ted, "just a—"

But the daughter of the Dragon King touched Andrew on the shoulder, and both Andrew and Randolph followed her to the center of the open space. All the brightly dressed people crowded around in a circle, like the audience at some open-air juggling act. Ted saw the alarmed faces of Stephen and Julian, with Dittany shaking her head behind them and Jerome looking furious; but none of them, it was clear, proposed to do anything except watch. The Dragon King joined the crowd. Whether from respect, scorn, or suspicion, nobody stood closer than a few feet to Ted and Ruth.

Andrew drew his own sword. He and Randolph saluted first the Dragon King and then each other. The fresh-faced girl held out a short sword of her own, over which they crossed theirs. She removed her sword with a hiss of metal, and Andrew and Randolph began to fight.

Andrew was amazingly good. Ted doubted that he was as good as Randolph; but of course, Randolph was not going to do his best. He was going to give them a good show to save Andrew's face, and then he was going to let Andrew kill him. William had told him to hold his tongue, so he would hold his tongue; but both his natural inclinations and his bargain with the Lords of the Dead had determined him to die. Ted could see it in his face.

"Ruth, we've got to do something," he said, very quietly.

"He wouldn't," said Ruth, who had clearly come to the same conclusion Ted had and was now rejecting it. "He wouldn't leave us in a mess like this."

"I'm not prepared to take the risk. This has got to stop. Besides, I don't want him killing Andrew either, just to keep our secret. Or for any other reason. I'll introduce some due process into this place if I—*Die for it,*" finished Edward. Ted let his breath out.

"Good point," said Ruth. "Which of them do you want to tackle? If we stop Andrew, Randolph will stop."

"You can't just stop him," said Ted, "you've got to shut him up long enough for Randolph to retrieve the situation."

"All right," said Ruth, "I'll go for Andrew; he's not very big."

This is crazy, thought Ted. "I," he said firmly, "will distract Andrew so you can get near him, and then grab Randolph."

To a point, this worked. Ted pushed his way through the intent crowd, awaited his moment, ran out into the open space, and smashed his own sword, the one he had found in the armory of High Castle, which fit into his hand as one piece of a jigsaw puzzle fits into its neighbor, down on the momentarily crossed swords of Randolph and Andrew. Andrew disengaged at once, and turned on him. A pair of gauze-clad arms wrenched Andrew's arms behind. Ruth wasn't strong enough to stop his mouth too, but he didn't shout anything distinguishable while he struggled. She twisted at his wrist in a way Ted thought she must have gotten from Lady Ruth, and Andrew's sword bounced on the grass.

None of the Dragon King's people seemed likely to interfere. Ted, breathing hard, looked at Randolph; and Randolph struck Ted's drooping sword upward with his own and lunged at him.

Ted's sword, the sword he had dreamed of before he found it, the sword with which he fought a dream-bout with Randolph and made but one mistake, answered for him.

This was not the cool, moon-silvered garden of his dream. He had neither moon nor sun in his eyes, but heard the roaring of the sea. The grass was not wet; it gave him good purchase. His feet and Randolph's did not squeak on the Dragon King's grass, but rushed and rustled. Their light blades did not hiss, but clanged as they came together, for this was neither a dream nor a session of practice. Ted's eyes stung with sweat. The clear, bright light of this southern morning seemed to be dimming; the roar, maybe, was a storm coming up. The air in the rose garden was still. He had no leisure to look up.

But he was fighting in the same way as he tied his shoes or rode a bicycle, easily and without thought. Somewhere in the back of his mind, the names of Randolph's moves and his own were flicking by, too quick and faint to catch. The crowd was quiet. Suddenly Ted knew he had Randolph. He did something with his wrist that swept Randolph's sword out of line; and lunged straight at Randolph with a force that should have put the sword through him. And froze, fully extended, his sword stretched foolishly in the empty air, three inches from Randolph.

He saw on Randolph's face not fear, not relief, but a sick disappointment. Randolph would go on standing there, and Ted could kill him. "Oh, no," he said, the harsh air rasping in and out of his aching throat. "No way, my lord." The crowd was making a great deal of noise now, but nobody had come out here to intervene. The roaring was louder.

Have at him now, said Edward. *He killed my father.* Your father forgave him! thought Ted furiously, which was a mistake; it let Edward further in, and Edward knew this sword, this body, and his own mind.

Dittany and Stephen were now holding on to Andrew. Ruth might not be strong enough to hold Edward, but he didn't trust anybody else. "Ruth!" he shouted at the top of his voice. "Come here!" He and Edward lifted the sword, and then Ted wrenched himself around so that it pointed nowhere. Randolph circled and placed himself before it again. Ruth came up behind Ted. "Grab my arms," gasped Ted. "Get the sword away."

Ruth promptly pinioned him as she had Andrew, but

made no move to take the sword. "Are you crazy?" she said in his ear. She smelled of lavender.

"It's Edward," panted Ted. "Say something soothing to him, can't you?" Edward was silent now, but Ted was afraid to move the sword, lest it call him back.

"Randolph," said Ruth, "put away thy sword."

"*No,*" said Ted, "don't make him disarm himself. Edward wants me to kill him." *Confusion now hath made his masterpiece,* said Edward, faintly. The roaring grew louder.

"Edward won't kill an unarmed man," said Ruth. Edward said nothing. "Randolph," said Ruth, as if she were talking to Patrick. "Drop the sword."

Randolph, the sweat running down his flushed face, his hair dripping, and every fold of his doublet limp as old lettuce, shook his head. His gaze, however, lingered on Ruth.

"Randolph," said Ted, in desperation, "by your oath to me, put down that sword."

Randolph's hand tightened visibly on the hilt of the sword; he brought it back into line; and then he curved up the corners of his mouth in the most mirthless smile Ted had ever seen, said, "I do obey you, both my lieges," and dropped it.

Ted uncramped his sword hand, and his own sword rolled on the grass with Randolph's. Ruth let go of him, and he walked unsteadily up to Randolph, a long, ordered, meticulous rebuke rising in his breast. Randolph reached out a shaking hand, probably meant for his shoulder, and bumped it against his collarbone with no more force than that of a falling leaf. "Look behind you, my prince," he said, in what was left of his voice.

Ted turned, thinking that Andrew was going to make trouble again. He found Andrew's gold velvet back, but Andrew was just standing there, as was everybody else. Ruth was making her way in their direction with great speed. Ten feet away stood what they were all looking at, a grimy and bedraggled group of people, every one of whom Ted knew; and a cluster of soberly dressed and nondescript people, whom he did not know, and a little apart from them, the man in red, and a unicorn, both unnaturally still.

The man in red held a sword that shone green as bottle-glass. Melanie's. Who had given him that? Ted took an incautious step forward, and one of his knees buckled. Randolph caught him under the arm, and then they were both on their knees in the grass.

"Just rest a moment," said Ted. He almost had his breath back, but his legs felt rubbery, and Randolph's arm was quivering. "Let them get settled down. Who are those weird people in brown? They look like a bunch of lawyers."

"Those are the Lords of the Dead," said Randolph, "as they commonly appear in drawings."

"And the man in red?"

"Him I know not."

"It's the man from the stark house, the one who asked us the riddles. He's not the Judge of the Dead, then?"

"There are no drawings of the Judge of the Dead," said Randolph.

"What's he doing with Melanie's sword? What have they been up to?"

"That is Chryse," said Randolph. "Beside Fence."

Ted had been counting heads. "They're all there," he said. "All of ours."

He and Randolph leaned together in the grass and listened to the vivid voice of the Dragon King greeting the Lords of the Dead as his dear cousins, and asking to what he owed this pleasure. One of them, in a lovely, lilting voice, answered, "To Fence the Wizard, King's Counselor of the Hidden Land."

"I might have known," said Randolph. His voice was less raveled.

Fence answered this assertion rather sharply, and in a louder voice than he usually employed. "Rather to the Princess Laura," he said. "I pray you pardon me." He pushed through the crowd and came swiftly across the trampled grass to Ted and Randolph, his tattered black robe floating behind him and no expression whatsoever on his round face. He dropped to his knees in front of them, squeezed Ted's shoulder in a grip that hurt, and said to Randolph, "Laura saw you fighting in a vision."

"It was Edward," said Ted. "He wanted to fight. What was Randolph supposed to do?"

Fence's hold slackened. His eyes were on Randolph, not Ted.

Randolph said, "It began with Andrew, who would have spewed the whole sorry tale all over the court of the Dragon King, and who moreover did muddy our dealings with offering Ruth and Ted in marriage to the children of the Dragon King. Ted did interfere in that bout, whereupon Edward did turn on me."

Fence still had no expression. He said, "There's other matter in thy face."

"Fence," said Ted, "when I rendered myself harmless and ordered him to drop his sword, he did it."

"Fence," said Randolph, "let be."

Fence looked at him; then, "With very great pleasure," he said, and taking his hand from Ted's shoulder he put both arms around Randolph. Randolph leaned his forehead on Fence's muddy robe and shut his eyes as if he never intended to look up again.

Ted got up in a hurry and walked over to his little sister. "We owe it all to you, huh?" he said.

"Somebody," said Laura, in an agonized whisper, "should apologize to the Dragon King; and somebody else should separate Chryse and the red man, because they were fighting."

"I think somebody should explain, not just apologize," said Ted, also in a whisper.

"Are these new statues for my garden?" inquired the Dragon King.

"My lord, no," said Laura, with more haste than courtesy. She cast a stricken glance in the direction of Fence, who was standing up now but still talking to Randolph. "These—we—" She stopped. Ted saw that the problem was not a failure to speak, but the fear that she would say too much. He launched into a series of elaborate introductions.

The Dragon King seemed to enjoy them. If Celia and Matthew disliked being presented to so fresh and elegant a monarch when they looked as if they had slept in a pile of leaves in the same clothes for a week, they managed not to sound like it. Ellen greeted the Dragon King sweetly and looked as if she were about to ask him a question. Ted hurriedly introduced Patrick, whom he had saved till last for fear of what he might say.

Patrick bowed and said, "We've brought you, your grace, a little exercise in sorcery."

"Patrick!" said Celia.

"Shan's Ring," said Patrick, disregarding her, "which we have just given to your good cousins there, hath rendered those two as statues. How, think you, might one best restore them?"

Fence and Randolph came across the grass in time to hear this. "Master You-are-a-wizard-do-something," said Fence to Patrick, "hold your tongue."

Patrick grinned at him, and was quiet. Ted looked at the Dragon King, who, mercifully, looked like somebody at the intermission of a good play. Maybe he would be patient.

"Forgive us," said Fence to him, "that we burst upon you unwashed and unannounced."

"The Hidden Land," said the Dragon King peacefully, "is full of surprises. What of your embassy?"

"Your grace, those two frozen there are our embassy," said Fence.

"Their forerunners were someways at cross purposes," said the Dragon King; the only note in his voice was one of inquiry.

"If they were," said Fence, "your perspicacity will discover the reason for't more readily than mine."

The Dragon King looked over Fence's shoulder at Andrew, and nodded. "You are gracious," he said to Fence. "So shall I be also. Do you take this garden and the servants therein, and the chairs, and what refreshment you will, till you have plucked out the heart of this mystery. When your embassy is prepared, send me word and I will receive it."

Fence bowed to him. The Dragon King lifted one ringed hand and beckoned. Andrew pushed between Fence and Randolph as if they had been a couple of trees, and went with the Dragon King and a great part of the crowd back toward the inner castle. The Lords of the Dead brought up the rear.

Chapter 30

The two parties from the Hidden Land milled around uncertainly, and the elegant minions of the Dragon King drifted out of his formal garden, leaving them alone.

"Fence!" said Ted, feeling irrationally that everything would be all right now. "What's he going to do to Andrew?"

"Give him his instructions," said Fence, very dryly. "Don't trouble yourself. Now. Is any part of your tale urgent?"

"Well, if you've got the Lords of the Dead—" began Ted.

Randolph interrupted. "Belaparthalion is im—"

"In that guise," said Fence, gesturing at the man in red.

"That's Belaparthalion?" said Ted. "But—"

"Who did destroy the dragon-shape?" said Randolph.

"Patrick," said Fence; and as Randolph made for Patrick he stepped in the way and added, "At Chryse's instigation."

"Why, what a guardian is this!" said Randolph, bitterly.

"It was not at Chryse's instigation, damn it," said Patrick, "except indirectly. Belaparthalion told me to do it. He said that he would get more power from Melanie's sword than he would lose by giving up the dragon-shape. Why the hell shouldn't I have let him out?"

"You couldn't help it," said Ruth. "It's this obsession you have with breaking large glowing globes."

"Shan," said Ted to Patrick, "told us to beware Melanie's sword, because it would show us our hearts in such a guise we'd cut them out."

"Well," said Ruth, hollowly, "that's what Belaparthalion did, isn't it?"

"Nobody warned *me,*" said Patrick.

"Randolph," said Fence. "What part of thy tale is urgent?"

"None, I think, beside this agitation of thine," said Randolph. "Sit down, and speak of it."

Fence folded himself to the ground, and the rest of them followed suit, forming a ragged circle. Fence said, "We are here for that Laura saw Ted and Randolph fighting, and did fear the outcome."

"You might have helped prevent it," said Ted, "if the Lords of the Dead took it into their heads to get Edward out of mine."

"But," said Fence, "we have now brought the two strongest guardians of the Hidden Land, helpless and at odds, into the very heart of the enemy."

"The enemy seems pretty harmless," said Patrick.

"He is indolent," said Fence, "and the workings of his heart are strange to us. But he is not harmless. Can we release Chryse and Belaparthalion, *and reform the cause of their quarrel,* then all will be well. They will perform their word to us, chastising the Dragon King; and we may depart in peace with all good protection. But do we release them merely to quarrel, it cannot come to good."

"All right," said Ted, "what's their quarrel?"

Fence explained it to him. Ted thought it sounded completely crazy; but he saw that Randolph took it seriously. "All right," said Ted. "If Belaparthalion is somehow half an Outside Power—is Chryse right? Would he have to give up the guardianship of the Hidden Land? Who gave it him, anyway?"

"Who did so transform him?" said Randolph. "For look you, an he did so himself, then he hath forfeited the terms of his guardianship. An it were done to him unknowing, then—"

"What we need," said Fence, "is the author of these disturbances."

"Melanie," said Ruth, flatly.

"What?" said Celia.

So Randolph explained that. Matthew was shocked. Celia looked grim. Ellen made an astonished mouth. Fence and Laura looked at each other as if they suddenly understood something; Ted wondered what that was about.

"Remember what the unicorn said, after the Hunt?" said Patrick to Ted. He, too, looked as if he understood something.

"We asked, who is Claudia, and it said, subtle, fair, and wise is she, but none of ours did send her."

There was a gloomy silence.

Patrick said at last, "Do you suppose, if we give the Dragon King two statues for his garden, he'll agree to leave us alone?"

Ellen sighed heavily; nobody else even looked up. Ted rubbed at his salt-encrusted eyes. His brain felt lamer than his body. They needed to find or fetch Claudia. Who and what was she, indeed? What did she want or care about; what shout would raise her? She was not dead; she was not in any of her houses they had been to in this country.

"Maybe we should go home," said Ted. "That's where we keep finding Claudia, in the Secret House in our own world."

"I thought you burned it down," said Ellen.

"That's a weary journey," said Fence, "during which we must leave these two hostage."

"Besides," said Laura, "if you use the swords, you wake up the Lords of the Dead, and they get nasty."

"Do it quick, then, before they go back to sleep," said Patrick.

"There are other Outside Powers," said Fence, rustily, "harder to wake, and harder to lay to rest again."

"Why a weary journey?" said Ted. "You got here fast enough."

"We paid the Lords of the Dead with Shan's Ring to bring us here," said Patrick. "We're running out of merchandise."

"We've got Cedric's flute," said Laura. She looked suddenly, below the filthy, tangled hair and the scratches, alert. "Is this the end it will save us at?"

"It's a pretty calm end," said Patrick.

"What music will call Claudia?" said Randolph.

"God knows," said Ruth. "Nobody *knows* her, that's the problem; we haven't the faintest idea what she's like." She looked up suddenly. "Randolph," she said. "You know her. Think. You were by her night and day, you said, for—"

"And I never divined what she was," said Randolph. He looked her squarely in the face. "That is what I said."

"You must have divined something," said Ruth, staring squarely back at him. Tears stood in her eyes, but her face was merely impatient. "Think, won't you? Good grief, if even a shape-shifter gives away his nature no matter what his outward form, surely she must have given away something to you?"

Randolph rubbed at his forehead, streaking all the dust and sweat in a new direction. He looked up and said painfully, "When we would meet, there was a tune I'd whistle, that she would know who approached. At least there can be no harm in Laura's playing it?"

"What was it?" said Ruth.

"'The Minstrel Boy,'" said Randolph.

Laura, disentangling the flute from her tunic, said, "She showed up once, when I whistled that."

"Randolph," said Fence. "Do you think on the historical layer of that song. One great harp will sing thy praise and one strong sword defend thee. The harp is Chryse, the sword Belaparthalion. And would it not suit Melanie's humor, that wished ill to the Hidden Land, to use that song as her emblem?"

Randolph looked sideways at him and smiled, not very successfully. "No doubt," he said.

"Okay," said Laura, "I'm ready."

"Play, then," said Fence, "as well as you are able."

She played it through once. Ted lay back in the cool grass and closed his eyes. The sound of the flute was very sweet, and all the dim noises of the Dragon King's castle died along the distances of the song. Laura played it through again, and Ruth, who had a pleasant voice, rather like Ted's mother's, began to sing. The others joined her, one by one. Ted had forgotten why they were doing this; but it was balm after the confused, stiff courtesies and pretended jollity of the evening before. He did not sit up, but he sang too. Laura played the song through for a third time, and the singers managed the second verse in something very like unison. And Ted looked idly through the green blur of the grass, past the still form of Chryse, around the bend of one of the drum towers, and saw a dark and slender woman in a red dress walking rapidly toward them over the grass. Ted thought she moved like an otter.

Ted sat up with a jolt. "Look," he said.

She seemed to be taking a long time to get there. Ted wondered if they should all loll on the grass like this and watch her come. He felt no impulse to go and greet her. The last time he had seen her, he had hit her in the stomach, and broken the magic windows of her house, and started a conflagration therein that he still hoped had reduced it to rubble. Claudia walked past Chryse as if Chryse were in fact some fanciful statue of the Dragon King's, and was within two feet of Laura when Randolph stood up and went toward her.

She smiled at him. "Oh, whistle," he said, "and I'll come to you, my lad."

Randolph neither smiled nor answered her; it seemed to be all he could do to sustain her cat-eyed gaze. She moved a little away from him and tilted her head at Chryse and Belaparthalion. The black hair fell down her back like water. "Your harp and your sword want mending," she said.

"How came they broken?" said Randolph.

"Wherefore should I tell thee?"

Randolph said, hardly above a whisper, "For the sake of what lay between us when we were innocent."

Her face did not change. "I am five hundred years old," she said. "When I was young, I had twelve fair lovers, the which I hated passing well. And lately in the summer, because my plans did draw to their conclusion, I did have you."

"To what conclusion," said Randolph, more strongly, "have they come?"

Claudia, who was Melanie, was silent for a very long time. Then she said, "That I should answer your question." She walked a few steps farther, surveyed the seated representatives of the Hidden Land, and sat herself down on the edge of the Dragon King's dais. Randolph came quietly around the outside of the circle and knelt in the grass behind Fence and Ruth.

"The twelfth of my fair lovers," said Melanie, "was Shan. And we did think to have the moon and the stars in our hands. But he did betray me, in every way that it was possible for him to do; and then he did escape me; for his betrayal was a joy to the Lords of the Dead, and they did admit him where I could not go. Now, while he lived, your little country was his dearest care; and he did almost refuse the great mercy of death granted him, for that it might leave you open to my malice. And he did therefore set safeguards over you. The royal family of the Hidden Land hath his blood; the libraries of the Hidden Land have his learning; the rivers of the Hidden Land run with his songs. I have taken from you every safeguard you possessed, save these two here. Between them I have set a quarrel shall harm one or both, when Shan's small meddling spell is removed."

"Can you remedy that quarrel?" said Randolph.

"Oh, aye," said Melanie. "Belaparthalion will not be as he was; but he'll guard you well still, an he be spared to't."

Randolph did not say, And will you spare him? He did not say anything. He knelt in the grass in his green doublet with tissue of gold, and laid one hand on Fence's shoulder, and looked at Melanie as Ted had seen his cousin Jennifer, who both adored and was allergic to strawberries, look at a bowl heaped full of them.

Ted swallowed. "How came Belaparthalion to this pass?"

Melanie had not, throughout her recitation, looked at anybody but Randolph. But now she turned her eyes on Ted, who felt as if he were being stared at by a basilisk.

"I gave him unicorn's blood," she said.

"No," said Fence.

"Oh, yes," said Melanie. "It killeth them not; that's a tale of the Blue Sorcerers. Over a mundane creature, the power of the unicorn's blood is to make it sorcerous, and that sorcery is expressed in immortality. Over an arcane creature, the power of the unicorn's blood is to make it otherworldly. Hence Belaparthalion became an Outside Power."

Matthew sat forward suddenly. "And the post of the Judge of the Dead was empty." He seemed to remember to whom he was speaking, and cut his historical enthusiasm short.

"It was," said Melanie.

"So," said Randolph to Fence, "Belaparthalion forfeits not his guardianship."

"It would like Chryse well, had she devised it, that he must protect the Hidden Land 'gainst himself also," said Melanie. "In a hundred years, or two, the thought will be pleasing to her."

"The thought that her fellow guardian hath taken unicorn's blood will not please her in ten thousand years," said Fence.

"She is too proud," said Melanie, shrugging.

Patrick said, "Why are you telling us all this?"

"There's another thing," said Melanie, looking at him briefly. Her voice altered and grew light, incredibly, with laughter. "All this I did in despite of Shan. How, do I complete my plots, I shall never say to Shan, 'Thus did I; thus didst thou'; for the Lords of the Dead will never let me in. An I desist, and they do let me in, for Shan I'll have no tale. You did swear me, my lad, many several sorts of aid and comfort. What remedy hast thou for this ill?"

She looked back at Randolph, who did not move. Into the charged, unnatural silence fell the ordinary sound of footsteps. Ted wrenched his head around, and saw three of the Lords of the Dead coming purposefully in their direction. Melanie saw them too. Her calm face, lightly etched with amusement at her own dilemma, set suddenly into fierce lines. But the Lords of the Dead, arriving at the edge of the circle, did not speak to her. "Lord Randolph," said the middle one, in its lilting voice.

Fence flinched under Randolph's tightened hand, and then laid his own hand over it. But Randolph stood up. "What would you?" he said.

"Your time of grace hath been long, and you have walked above the earth with the one whose life you bought," said the right-hand one, in its austere voice. "Since we have come hither, we thought to bring you back."

"I'm ready," said Randolph.

"You God damn well are not!" said Ruth, scrambling to her feet. Fence got up also, but said nothing.

"If there is dissent," said the left-hand Lord, in its rich voice, "we have a thing to suggest. Edward Fairchild, for whom you did in fact bargain to exchange your life, proveth troublesome under the earth. We will send him back also."

Ted in his turn got up. The sound of his heart in his ears was louder than it had been when he fought Randolph. His breath fought with his throat. He thought very carefully of Shan, with his quick perceptions and his wealth of strange tales. He thought of what changes might have happened, with the Lords of the Dead gone and Shan in possession of his brooch.

"Randolph," said Ted. "If you've got Edward, you don't need me. You stay; I'll go."

"You God damn well will not!" cried Laura, bounding up and letting Cedric's flute roll across the short grass.

"This won't serve," said Randolph to Ted.

"Neither will your departure," said Fence.

"Fence, a bargain was made. If any deserve this departure, I do so. Who shall go else? Will you lose Ted, whose crime is bright imagination?"

Fence's round face, as it had once or twice since Ted had known him, sharpened suddenly, so that you could see the bones of it. He opened his mouth.

"No," said Randolph. "Not thou."

"*I* know!" said Ruth, with an artificial brightness tinged with genuine hysteria. "Let's *all* go!"

"Oh, proud Death," said Patrick to the Lords of the Dead, not much more calmly. "What feast is toward in thine eternal cell?"

"None," said Melanie behind them.

They turned and looked at her. She had slid off the dais and now walked up to stand between Ruth and Randolph. Ruth shied away from her like a startled cat, and then moved closer again. Randolph stood still.

"Will you have me?" said Melanie to the Lord of the Dead.

There was another of those silences. Ruth looked sideways at Melanie, swallowed, and seemed to be about to speak. The rich-voiced Lord said, "Edward Fairchild must stay hence."

"That's naught to me," said Melanie.

"Is it not?" said Celia.

Ted remembered, with a shock almost as great as the original discovery had been, that Melanie, to whom it was naught if Edward stayed or went, had put him there in the first place.

"He is still troublesome," said the lilting voice.

The rich one said, "Let Melanie speak with him."

"Oh, *God*," said Ruth.

Melanie looked at her. "Vex not thy thoughts wi'that,"

she said. "Consider him." She inclined her head at Randolph, and looked around, picking out the five visitors. "You children," she said. "Have you a use, or a fondness, for this lord?"

She was looking at Ted. "I have," said Ted. "Both."

"Despite that he did murder William?"

"He didn't have any good choices," said Ted.

"Claudia," said Randolph.

"Who is she?" said Melanie, without looking at him. "Ruth Eleanora. Have you a use or a fondness for Lord Randolph?"

"Both," said Ruth, between her teeth.

"Laura Kimberly."

"Both," said Laura.

"Ellen Jennifer."

"A very great fondness," said Ellen, scowling. "What kind of a trick is this?"

"None," said Melanie. "I have misjudged my powers, or yours. I could not make you my creatures; you would not be my allies; you are caught in the web in a manner I did not mean, that is displeasing to me. Be quiet. Patrick Terrence. Have you a use or fondness for Lord Randolph?"

Oh, Lord, thought Ted. Edward said, quite clearly, *The players cannot keep counsel, they'll tell all.*

"I," said Patrick, "have neither use nor fondness for any of you; but keep in mind that the Lords of the Dead have much less of either for Randolph. I want him more than they do."

"You five," said Melanie, "I did wrong without cause. These others I did wrong with, it may be, insufficient cause; but cause there was. An Randolph will serve you better above the earth, I'll take his place below it."

Randolph stood up. "Melanie," he said.

"What you have done," said Melanie, smiling at him, "you may recompense by remembering it. Make this Edward a King. Be his Regent. An that's not suffering enough, tell all I have done to High Castle, and comfort what uproar followeth."

Randolph looked at Fence, and back at Melanie. He was extremely white. He said, "When two such warring teachers do bid me read in the same book, what may I do but obey?"

"Nothing," said Melanie, and she walked from between Ruth and Randolph to the Lords of the Dead.

The austere one said, "Desirest thou no preparation?"

Melanie looked back at the rest of them. "The voices of your others," she said. "How troublesome?"

"Edward was extremely so," said Ted.

"Lady Ruth gave me some bad moments," said Ruth. Ted heard in her voice an echo of his own tone, dazed and automatic.

"An I speak to them, will you keep them or let them go?"

"Keep them," said Ted. If this was the closest he could come to restoring Edward to life, then he would do it.

Ruth nodded; so did Laura. Patrick looked thoughtful, which was normal; but Ellen, too, hesitated and stared at the ground before she nodded.

"What else you would know," said Melanie, "seek in the house by the Gray Lake. I have writ a great part of my plans, if not of my accomplishments, therein." She hesitated; Ted had never seen her look anything like uncertain. "There are cats therein," she said.

"Are they more to you than those children were?" said Celia. Ted saw that she was so angry she could not even raise her voice; but very faintly, behind the fury, was a genuine desire to understand.

Melanie must have heard it too. Her tone was not placatory; but it was not scornful, either. "I had no children," she said.

Celia only looked at her. "Fence," she said. "Is this vengeance? Is this justice? She deserves—"

"Use every man after his desert," said Fence, "and who shall scape whipping?"

Celia began to say something; Randolph touched her arm and said, "He speaks of me."

Celia looked not at him but at Matthew. "Below the earth," said Matthew, "she will have what she deserves."

"Yes, she will," said Ted. "We saw those children, Celia. Edward will deal with her. He's changed."

Into something rich and strange, said Edward, and chuckled.

Melanie might have heard him too. She had been watching the discussion steadily, but now she turned away too quickly for a good dramatic effect, and said to the Lords of the Dead, "My preparations are done." They bowed to her; she did them a courtesy; they began to walk away. Against the bright roses and the brilliant grass, their sober brown dress looked darker.

Melanie spun suddenly and said to the gaping crowd of King Edward's court, "For your guardians, sing them a song. For yourselves—speak and write truly of me or you will be the worse for't."

"We will," said Randolph.

Melanie picked up her red skirts and ran lightly, like an otter, to catch up with the Lord of the Dead.

Chapter 31

In the Hidden Land, November came in with malicious winds and a downpour of icy rain that ticked against the windows like something trying to get in. The visitors to that country reacted to it each according to his nature. Ellen made friends with Celia and Matthew's children. Nobody had told them what was going on, but Ellen managed to get out of John, who was trusting and voluble, that while none of them really liked the Princess Laura, they thought her much improved of late.

"Except she's someways timid," said Margaret. "What hath made her so?"

"Looking on the Lords of the Dead," said Ellen; which was essentially true. It was her intention to make Margaret respect Laura, and not to take too much time over it.

She had less influence over the fates of the others. She had decided that Ruth should marry Randolph, but she knew better than to interfere. Ruth did not come sighing to her little sister with confidences; she just called herself names. Randolph would have to do something, that was all; and Ellen had had enough of even seeming to make Randolph do anything. As for Patrick, he should go home again. He didn't belong here. Ted did. So did Ruth and Laura. So did Ellen herself. Their parents wouldn't like it. Patrick was Mother's favorite, but her father, however vaguely, was going to miss his daughters. Patrick might miss his sisters, too; but that would serve him right.

Ellen thought over whom she would miss, and scowled.

* * *

Laura climbed the dusty steps of the North Tower at dusk on a day of cold rain. The door to the uppermost room was open this time. The gold light flooding out of it was kinder than sunshine. Laura stopped in the doorway, regarding the Crystal of Earth. Claudia, who had moved it hither and yon, preventing Patrick from breaking it, preserving it for the Hidden Land, could just as well have broken it herself and had done with it. Laura had read, slowly and painfully, muttering under her breath and applying frequently to Ted for the hard words, Melanie's account of what she had done with regard to this object.

The little globe Melanie had set here for Patrick to break had not held nothing. It had held their game, the Secret Country of their stubborn and flawed imaginations, the Secret Country into which no Claudia had ever stirred a meddling finger; the shallows to which the Hidden Land was a whole burgeoning ocean. Laura still sometimes thought she preferred the shallows. She had not asked Patrick what he thought; Patrick, who had fought a practice session with Melanie's sword, and had it taken away from him by an exasperated Fence and a horrified Randolph; and who had, perhaps, as Shan said, had his heart shown to him in such a guise that he wanted to cut it out. And yet he had never shown, in any way except his always being there to play with them, that the Secret Country had a place in his heart at all. He was harder to understand than Melanie. And he was going to be hard to live with, if they had to stay here.

Patrick was busy reading. He finished Shan's journals; and was not satisfied. He read as much of Melanie's voluminous writings as he could stand, filching them from Ted and Fence whenever those two gave up, as they did about once a day; and was not satisfied. He stayed up late making lists; he paced around the dusty corridors and the swept halls and the wet rose garden, thinking until his head hurt; and was not satisfied.

Some things he had figured out. Melanie had expected, when she brought Patrick and his relations into the Hidden Land, to be in almost complete control of them. She had intended to move them to do any of a number of things that would serve the double purpose of making Fence and Randolph unhappy and endangering the Hidden Land. She had also intended to merge them with the dead children, both so that the masquerade should not be discovered and so that it should be, in some measure, the real royal children who had committed whatever crimes she had in mind for them. She had had no control over the real children; she had expected to have more over their dead voices.

But both Shan's Ring and Melanie's own sword had awakened the Lords of the Dead, one by one; and while they were awake, however disgruntled, they would notice and retaliate if she tampered more than delicately with anyone in their domain. Melanie had not intended either Shan's Ring or the sword to have this property of waking the Outside Powers. Patrick could not discover where said property had come from, which was one of the things vexing him.

Another was that all these people and accounts contradicted one another. You might expect Melanie to lie of course; or perhaps just to have a very different idea of what had gone on than Shan had. You might expect the Outside Powers or the unicorns to sidestep the truth, or to have a viewpoint so different that nothing they said would ever make sense. But you would certainly expect the scholars of Heathwill Library to have made something of all these contradictions.

It also bothered him not to know why Melanie had been so far off in her estimation of how much control she would have over them all once she got them into the Hidden Land. Melanie herself seemed to think that the problem was a result of their having found the swords and stumbled in before she was ready for them; which had happened in Patrick's case because of a dog named Shan, and in Ted and Laura's because their cousins had been playing a game they loved as much as Ted and Laura loved the Secret Country. Fence and Randolph found these points significant. Patrick found them irritating. It seemed to him more likely that Melanie had failed because he and his relations had been stronger of imagination, or purer of heart, or just stubborner of spirit, than she had thought them. Or she might have been like Aristotle, possessed of a very fine mind and a set of erroneous assumptions about the universe. Maybe her philosophy of magic was as flawed, in its way, as Andrew's had been.

Andrew vexed Patrick too. He had been so besotted on his so-called sister that he had done anything she asked him to, even when he knew she thought it was magical and therefore should have thought it useless. He had hoped, Melanie thought, to win her from her false philosophies by slow degrees. And she had used this hope. Andrew had thought that he and she and Lady Ruth were engaged in secret negotiations with the Dragon King to bring about a sensible peace, instead of a disastrous magical battle. The details of this plot were not available to Patrick's questing mind.

He finally sought out Laura, who was the only one of his relations not constantly occupied, and asked her to help him go over his information, in case she knew anything he didn't.

"Why?" said Laura, sharply for her.

Patrick hesitated. It was irrational. But then, this country was irrational. "I said," he said, "that I wasn't going home again until I understood what was going on here. And having said it, I don't think I can, until I do."

"Oh?" said Laura. "So you aren't planning to break the Crystal of Earth any time soon?"

Patrick stared at her. He was not in fact planning to break it at all; but he was not, either, planning to disabuse anybody who had it of the notion that he might be dangerous. "No," he said. "Not any time soon."

Laura grinned. "I remember what you said in Australia," she said. "Princess Laura says, we should not pretend to understand the world only by the intellect; we apprehend it just as much by feeling."

"Carl Jung said that!" said Patrick, furiously.

"You might think about it anyway," said Laura.

The King of the Hidden Land received a letter from Lord Andrew. Andrew had stayed behind in the Court of the Dragon King. This, Ted had managed to figure out, counted as the vengeance with which Ted was supposed to reward oath-breaking. And certainly to leave a man who feared magic alone in a court of shape-shifters was punishment enough, whatever Andrew had done or contemplated doing. The letter said nothing of all this, but contained implicitly the assumption that Andrew had been left as a liaison and observer.

Nobody knew what Chryse and Belaparthalion had said to the Dragon King, but he looked far from benign when they finished saying it. Looking thus, he had made to Ted a speech so flowery and convoluted that Ted had not understood a word of it. Fence, consulted during the journey home, said it contained a promise of explicit treaties of peace, and the forwarding of damages for the late war.

Andrew's letter, opening with brisk formality, detailed the treaties. Ted would have to show them to Fence and Randolph. If they contained innuendos or double meanings, he could not find any. It might be that their language was so plain that it was subject to too many interpretations. It appeared that the Dragon King had agreed to leave the Hidden Land alone except in the case of three particular kinds of provocation, none of which sounded either possible or probable of occurrence, in return for nothing whatsoever.

He was also sending north a staggering amount in jewels and gold and fine cloth. Ted wondered uneasily if the shape-shifters of that court could turn themselves into emeralds.

Andrew's letter contained a postscript. "My lord Edward: My philosophy altereth daily in this place of shadows. My heart is as it was always; wherefore, my liege, I do humbly beg your leave to sojourn here yet a little time. If by my return your grace shall have departed to your other realms, take with you my good wishes for your safety and happiness."

That was clear enough. He hated it down there, and if he could possibly manage it he was going to stay there until Ted and the others had gone home. If they ever did. And that "If," of course, was the payment made by the Hidden Land. The Hidden Land had lost its royal children and received in return a motley and reluctant crew bent, if not on abandoning it, at least on making sure they had the means to do so. The Hidden Land had lost its dragon and received a patched-up composite capable of nobody knew what. None of these reverses had profited the Dragon King, but in that coin just the same the Hidden Land was paying for the Dragon King's friendship. And after all, the Dragon King had gotten an afternoon's amusement out of it.

Ted felt oppressed. The upper hierarchies of the Secret Country dismayed him. Everywhere you turned there were magical creatures of capricious ability whose power of distinguishing between right and wrong was less developed than a politician's. Recent events had shown that one was not exactly at their mercy; but one was always having to watch out for them. For the first time, he thought he understood how Patrick felt.

He presented this fact to Patrick later that day, at supper. Patrick heard him out gravely, but all he said was, "Consider the Second Law of Thermodynamics."

It came to Ted, with a more than minor shock, that he was going to miss Patrick. Not his part in the game; not even his genius for improvisation. Just Patrick. And if he felt like that, how would Patrick feel when he went home—if anybody could ever go home—and all the rest of them stayed?

If all the rest of them were staying. Ted did not know what he was going to do about his parents. He had thought of sending them a letter by Patrick, who was such an unlikely witness to all these events that they might believe him. Patrick's own parents would probably haul him off to a psychiatrist.

Ted took a savage bite of bread. He would worry about all this when they found the way out. *Tomorrow,* said Edward, not altogether approvingly, *is another day.*

On the sixteenth day of the awful weather, which had been broken twice, once by a day of watery sunshine and once by an inexplicable thunderstorm, Ruth took her courage in both hands and went looking for Randolph.

He was not in the Council Room, where Ted and Fence had buried the long table in books and grinned vaguely when she poked her head in the door. He was not in his own room, though the door stood open and a yellow dog thumped its tail from the hearth, where the fire was bright and new. He was, inevitably, in Fence's tower, so that by the time she knocked on the door her courage had leaked away with her breath but she was bolstered by the belief that he was not there, and as soon as he had failed to answer she could be comfortably irate and give up for the day.

"Come in," his voice called.

Ruth shoved her hair back and pushed the door open. Randolph, in two cloaks and a blue velvet hat and a pair of fingerless gloves, was also immersed in books. He looked up with the expression of pleased inquiry he reserved for Fence; it slid into blankness and then into a pleasant neutrality.

"I'm sorry to bother you," said Ruth. "But there's something I can't remember, and I'd rather ask you than Meredith."

Randolph put his pen back into the ink bottle and slid his hands into his sleeves. His breath made faint clouds in the air.

"For heaven's sake!" said Ruth. "You've got a splendid fire in your own room for the dog to get spoiled by." She made for the fireplace.

"It burneth not except by Fence's command," said Randolph. "There's a quilt, if you're cold."

"Never mind," said Ruth.

"What's the question?"

"Did you promise Meredith we'd be married before *the* year was out, or before *a* year was out?"

Randolph grinned. "A year," he said.

"All right. Now look. What are the choices?"

"To send thee home, can we contrive it," said Randolph. "To tell all to Meredith and beg her release us from this bond. To marry, and make the best of it."

"If you send me home," said Ruth, "I'll be safe, but as far as Meredith is concerned, you'll have broken your word."

Randolph looked blank, and then extremely uneasy. "We might marry first," he said. "Then send thee home. Thou wouldst be safe, as thou sayest."

"But I'd be *married,*" said Ruth. "To somebody I'd never see again. So would you."

Randolph shrugged. "For me, that makes no matter," he said. "'Twould keep me from the plague of marriage for policy."

"And you wouldn't, you think, when I was gone, ever want to marry anybody for any other reason?"

Randolph was silent. The rain clattered on the windows and the wind thumped the tower like an irate child kicking a locked door. Ruth was cold. The scolding she had given him for sitting here with the fire out replayed itself in the middle of her mind and sounded sillier every time it went by.

"No," said Randolph. He gestured at Fence's footstool. "Wilt thou sit down and recover from the staircase?"

Ruth sat, because she felt shaky.

"Now," said Randolph, "if thou thinkst to marry at home, I'd not prevent it. It was not what Meredith had in her mind when she did extract this promise; but 'tis possible to marry for a term only; for five years, or ten."

"Five," said Ruth, "would do me fine, and prevent my enacting some folly in my rash and splenitive youth."

"Well, then, we'll do't so," said Randolph.

"Not," said Ruth, "that I have anybody in mind at home." And that, of course, she ought not to have said. Randolph looked at her with a kind of thoughtful puzzlement.

"Have you not, then?" said Randolph. "And yet you said to the Dragon King that your heart was given already."

"Isn't it permissible to lie to one's enemies?"

"Did you so?"

She had done enough lying to Randolph to last her a lifetime. "No," said Ruth. "I didn't lie."

Randolph pushed back the chair and stood up. Ruth watched him with trepidation. He looked like somebody who was about to do something foolhardy for the sheer joy of it. His face was not happy, precisely, but held rather the beginnings of wildness: Ellen, aged seven, just before she threw her favorite doll into the pond because the thought of Patrick's face when she took up his dare held more attraction than the doll did. It was not a matter of spite, but the choice of a brief delight over a longer, settled content. Glory over length of days, thought Ruth suddenly, and pressed her hands together, hard.

Randolph walked over to the window and contemplated the darkness. Ruth could hear the little hiss of the torches burning. He was, no doubt, burying his crazy impulse, whatever it was. In the end, she couldn't stand it and spoke to him.

"What are you looking at?" she said.

Randolph turned and leaned on the window frame. Above his dark head the carved story of Shan gleamed dully. "Faintheartedness," he said. He walked across the room, and with no particular flourish, knelt on the floor a yard away from where she sat on the stool. "Let's put this matter on some better footing," he said. "Ruth. If I should ask thee, wouldst thou marry me?"

Ruth's breath clogged in her throat. "Faint heart," she said in a strangled voice, "never won fair lady."

Randolph smiled. "Wilt thou marry me?" he said.

"So much," said Ruth, "for the faint heart. Now."

"The fair lady," said Randolph, "is here."

"Wait," said Ruth. "I'm sure you can make pretty speeches. Don't do it yet. I'd hate them to go around and around in your head for weeks afterward. Randolph. I would love to marry you. *Don't say anything.* I am sixteen years old and I have a brain full of turnips. I don't know when people marry in this country, but in mine they do it at twenty, or later." She paused because she was out of breath.

Randolph had not moved. He said gravely, "I'm fond of turnips."

"Oh, go to!" said Ruth.

"I understand you," said Randolph. "It may be wise. Four years would settle many matters. We would marry, to fulfill our word; you must then do as you will."

"I could go to Heathwill Library and study something," said Ruth.

Randolph said, "An we do find the means to send you home?"

"I was thinking of staying," said Ruth, "anyway." There. She had said it. What would Patrick say? She added, "If they'll have me. I just wish you could meet my parents."

"So," said Randolph. "This rubble being cleared, what's thy answer, lady?"

"I'll marry you," said Ruth.

The fireplace bloomed suddenly with yellow light, and warmth flowed over them. "I am sorry I was so long," said Fence's mild voice. "Ted and I have found what we sought."

Ruth and Randolph looked at him. Fence, his arms full of books and a too-large blue cap on his head, peered at them from under it with a gaze as sharp as the Nightmare Grass. He said to Randolph, "She is too young."

Randolph said, "Four years."

Fence smiled, and dumped the books on the nearest chest, and looked at them again. Ruth couldn't have moved, but she thought Randolph's knees must be getting sore.

"Shall I give you solitude," said Fence, "or a celebratory glass of wine?"

Ruth looked at Randolph, and her bones turned to water. "Wine," she said, "an it please you."

It was the seventeenth of November, and still raining. The Council Room was full of books, but somebody had cleared enough chairs for the assembled company. They left Fence the chair at the head of the table, but he did not take it. He was blazing with excitement, as none of them had ever seen him. When they were seated, and almost before they were quiet, he began to speak, without preliminaries.

"Were any of us who sought this knowledge," he said, looking at Patrick, "of an experimental temper, we had had it long since. But we have burrowed this month in Shan's writings, and Melanie's, and then asked again for Ted and Laura's account of how they did arrive here, in the Mirror Room, sans any sword." He looked at Ted.

Ted said, "Purgos Aipos is an old name for High Castle."

"Oh, good grief!" said Ruth. "You put your hand on the mirror, and you say, 'Apsinthion'; and you come out in the stark man's house."

"And then," said Patrick, sourly, "you can just take the first flight to Australia. No problem."

"Hold a moment," said Fence. "Patrick; Ellen; Ruth. Hath your house any name?"

They looked at him blankly. Their parents didn't name things. Ted said, "My father calls it the Coriander Castle."

"What?" said Ruth.

"Coriander," said Ted, "stands for hidden merit."

"He would," said Patrick. "And it's going to work too; you know it."

"When shall we essay this?" said Fence. "Need you a few days' grace, to find if you will go or stay?"

Nobody answered him. Fence said, "You must know that you are, every one, most heartily welcome to stay."

"We will lose Patrick," said Randolph.

"I'm afraid you will," said Patrick. "I find I prefer the Second Law of Thermodynamics. It doesn't talk back."

"What about the civil war?" said Laura. "If Prince Patrick turns up missing?"

"It's time for truth," said Fence. "Andrew, mark you, who was to begin this war, is away, and hath had in the interim an education. Fear us not."

"I don't think," said Ellen, "that anybody needs time for cogitation."

"Wait just a moment," said Ruth. "Is all this glumness justified? Who says we can do this only once?"

"The Dragon King," said Fence.

Ted put his head in his hands. The three particular kinds of provocation, impossible of occurrence.

"The use of these mirrors," said Fence, "as the use of all of the magical artifacts of Melanie, doth awake the Outside Powers. The first use troubleth their sleep; the second maketh them to stir; and the third doth send them roaring."

Apsinthion had told them that, thought Ted; and they had not understood him.

"So," said Patrick, "we can all go to Australia, and everybody except me can say good-bye to parents. And then everybody except me can come back. And the Outside Powers will have but stirred in their sleep."

"One only," said Fence. "Three uses, to awaken one. But they have been so recently roused, 'twere folly to—"

"But the next time you use those mirrors," said Patrick, disregarding him, "be it in two years or two hundred, the Outside Powers will emerge roaring. Give me strength. You couldn't pay me to stay here."

"I don't hear anybody offering," said Ellen, absently.

"There aren't any magic mirrors in our house," said Patrick. "How do you propose to get there?"

"There will be," said Fence. "One magic mirror maketh another, by their property of reflection."

"Never mind," said Patrick. "Can we get this over? Can we just go and do it now?"

"Of a certainty," said Fence, and got up.

The five of them followed him along the drafty passages of High Castle, to the Mirror Room. Fence and Randolph would be coming to Australia with them, to lend what Ellen, or possibly Princess Ellen, called verisimilitude to an otherwise drab and unconvincing narrative. "Not drab," Patrick had remarked, "but about as unconvincing as you can get. Do you really think a short guy in a wizard's robe and a tall one got up like Hamlet are going to put any twentieth-century parent's mind at ease?" Ted thought of this, trailing behind his shorter cousin's vigorous stride; watching the way Ruth and Randolph walked close together without touching; and the way Ellen stuck next to Laura and talked incessantly at her. If they could *see* us come out of that mirror, it should help, he thought. He plunged forward and caught up with Patrick.

"Pat? Where *is* the mirror in your new house?"

"Well, there's one in the bathroom," said Patrick, as if he had been expecting the question. "But we wouldn't most of us fit through it. There's a full-length one on the back of my parents' closet door; and a mirrored wall in the dining room. And a full-length one in Ruthie's room. Take your pick."

In the Mirror Room, three black cats slept in an untidy heap on Agatha's sewing table. Ellen scratched them all behind the ears. Fence made for the Conrad tapestry, and twitched it aside.

"Fence?" said Ted. "Can we choose which mirror we come out?"

"Maybe," said Fence. "You might hold in your mind's eye the room you think best suited to't."

"The dining room, Ruth and Ellen," said Patrick.

"Join hands," said Fence. "Now." He laid his hand on the mirror. "Castle Coriander."

And he stepped through the mirror, drawing Ruth, Randolph, Patrick, Ted, Laura, and Ellen after him.

The surface of the mirror gave before Ted's hand like cloth. He stepped through, and the feel of cloth tattered and diminished. He saw a high-ceilinged, handsome room, flooded with early sunlight and furnished with a table and chairs he recognized. It was warm and smelled pleasantly of coffee and pancakes. The table was laid for four. Three of them sat there already: a tall abstracted man with dust-colored hair and a vague face, Ted's Uncle Alan; a little black-haired man with very blue eyes, his father. Ted's uncle had not noticed them yet. His aunt, who was sitting directly across the table from the mirrored wall they had walked out of, dropped her knife with a clatter and said, "Mother of God!"

"Angels and ministers of grace defend us!" said an ironic voice in the doorway; and there, in her old green bathrobe with her long brown hair falling over it in rats' tails, just like Laura's, stood their mother, her hands full of mugs and in her face a kind of horrified delight.

Laura ran at her, and she obligingly dropped the mugs, one of which broke, and hugged her daughter. "What are you *doing*—" she said, and stopped, and put Laura a little away from her. "Honey. You've grown too. What is going on here?" She looked over Laura's quivering head, found Ted unerringly, and grinned at him. Then she stood up. "I see two strangers here," she said. "Sirs? What does this mean?"

Ruth walked around the table and tapped her father on the shoulder. "Daddy," she said.

"Awake, are you?" said Ted's Uncle Alan. "I think there are some pancakes left."

"Alan, look at the mirror," said Aunt Kim.

He looked up. "Ted," he said, in a pleased tone. "And Laura. You didn't tell me they were coming," he said to his wife.

"Oh, God!" said Ruth, and burst out laughing.

"Oh, God, exactly," said Ted's father. "Teach me to call names. Mary Rose in triplicate, and Thomas the Rhymer in duplicate. And who are the rest of them? They look halfway responsible next to the bunch of you."

"Mother," said Ruth, in a shaking voice where laughter almost met tears, "this is Fence, and this is Randolph. This is my mother, Mistress Kimberly Carroll; and my aunt, Mistress Nora, and my father, Master Alan, and my uncle, Master Thomas."

Ruth's mother stood up. "Alan," she said, "I think we need some more chairs."

"I think," said Ted's father, standing up too, "that we need some more coffee."

"They drink tea," said Ted.

"They can drink coffee for once," said his father, eyeing him steadily. "Let them be a little off balance too." He held out a hand suddenly, and Ted bolted forward and fell on his neck, like a proper prodigal son.

There was a certain amount of sniveling all around, and an appalling amount of talk, and a staggering interrogation under which Fence and Randolph bore up very well. Ted's parents, he was relieved to see, believed the story, in the end. His aunt did not, but seemed willing, possibly through mere exhaustion, to let them continue to their conclusion. It was hard to tell with his Uncle Alan, who might not consider disbelief a barrier to, or belief a reason for, anybody's action. So Ruth explained that all of them except Patrick were going back to the Hidden Land; and the yelling started. Ruth and Ellen and Patrick's side of the family were great yellers.

Very few speeches into it, Ted and Laura's side of the family plunged precipitately into the living room, dragging a reluctant Fence, shut the door, fell into whatever chairs were nearest, and stared at one another in a worn-out silence.

"Now let's try again," said Ted's mother.

"No, wait," said Ted. "Fence. Have you got an immigration quota?"

"I beg your pardon?"

"Can they come too?" He had not been able to ask it in the other room. His aunt and uncle would never come.

There was another sort of silence. "Why not?" said Fence. He looked cautiously at Ted's father, who had been calling him a variety of names Ted had never heard before, and at Ted's mother, who had been steadily disregarding him, and said, "You'd be heartily welcome; heartily."

"I can't think why," said Ted's mother.

"If these were mine," said Fence, gently, "I'd fight as hard as this to keep them."

"Mom," said Laura. "They all talk like Shakespeare there."

"Well," said their mother, on a shaky laugh, "then there's no more to be said, surely?"

"Oh, Lord," said their father. "What time is it in Illinois? We'll have to call Kathy and Jim and tell them—something."

"Blame it on us," said Ted. "They'll believe anything about us."

"Do you think they're going to call the police in there?" said Ted's mother.

"They'll think of it," said his father, "and Randolph will point out that all seven of them can simply step back through the mirror before anybody so much as picks up the telephone."

"Tom," said their mother, "are we in fact going to do this?"

Ted's father put his head in his hands. "If we did," he said. "Power of attorney. Thank God we signed one before we left. We need to sell the house and most of the contents. Kim and Alan should have some of the good stuff. We'll have to make a list. Now. Why are we doing this?"

Ted's mother said, in a tone he recognized, "We've decided to emigrate. We're staying with Kim and Alan until we find a house."

"Postcards," said Ted's father. "We'd better write a series and have Kim mail them at intervals—if she will."

"Patrick will," said Laura.

"Yes, of course. You two had better write some too. Friends, relations, teachers."

"Another list," said their mother. "People you don't want to have worrying about you. We mustn't disappear. We must move to Australia and gradually lose touch. Will Patrick mail postcards for a year and a half? It would take that long, really."

"Patrick will follow a schedule until Armageddon," said Ted's father.

"What are we going to do down here to earn money?" said their mother.

"I could help Kim with the farm," said their father, dubiously.

The rest of the family burst out laughing.

"You're doing it wrong," said Ted. "What have you always wanted to do? Tell them you're doing it."

"Live where everybody talks like Shakespeare," said their mother, not laughing at all.

"What's your second choice?" said Ted.

"Cartography," said his mother, promptly.

"Does Australia need cartographers?" said her husband.

"The Hidden Land needs them," said Fence.

They had forgotten about him.

"Well, that's a relief," said Ted's mother. "I don't imagine being a parasite in a magical kingdom is any pleasanter than being one anywhere else."

"They're musicians, Fence," said Ted.

"That's well for us. Doth Australia need musicians?"

"Tell 'em you're taking some courses in computer programming," said Laura.

"They won't believe it," said her father.

"Sure they will. They'll say, well, finally, he's fulfilling his potential," said Laura, rolling the phrase on her tongue with a scorn Ted had not known she was capable of.

There was a great deal more to be said, but it was of a far less awful and enervating nature than what was going on in the next room. Ted was only surprised that somebody or other had not run out in a fit of hysteria or rage or both. But nobody did; and when Ted and Laura and their parents, trailed by Fence, cautiously opened the door and walked back into the dining room, the other half of the Carroll family was quiet, if tear-blotched, and actually looked at them inquiringly. Randolph was the only person present who had not, clearly, been crying; and he looked worse than those who had.

"We're all going back," said Ted into the stuffy air. "All four of us."

"And we are, all two," said Ruth, foggily.

"I'm staying," said Ellen, with great clarity.

Her father put out an arm and gathered her in; Ted's Aunt Kim closed her eyes with her fingers and leaned on the table, saying nothing.

"Somebody," said Ellen, "has to keep Patrick in line."

"Mother?" said Ruth, "I'd be going to college in a few years anyway."

"What you have to do," said Ellen, her cheerful voice beginning to clog up, "is figure out a way around this idiotic prohibition so everybody can come to the wedding."

"I don't see," said Ted's Aunt Kim, from under her hand, "that there's anything we can do or say that we haven't tried. If you're going, Ruth, you're going. You're too old to be ordered."

"Ellen," said Ruth, "don't do this for me."

"I'm not," said Ellen. "I liked it there; but I like it here."

And that, thought Ted, was perfectly true. Ellen made the best of whatever place received her. He looked at his sister, who was staring at Ellen, stricken.

"Margaret's nice," he said to her.

"Margaret's a demon," said Laura.

"So is Ellen a demon," said Ruth. "You're just used to her."

"I'm starting to get in your way, Laurie," said Ellen.

"That's stupid!" said Laura.

Ellen just looked at her. Ted didn't think it was stupid. As Laura became less of a mouse, Ellen wouldn't know what to do with her; Ellen had had eleven years of hauling around her terrified, clumsy cousin. No doubt they would have managed if they had stayed together; but there was no need to say that now.

"What," said Ruth's mother, with somewhat more energy, "are we going to tell people?"

"The four of us," said Ted's mother, in that same familiar tone, "are emigrating to Australia. Why don't we settle in Sydney, and take Ruth with us, Kim, because being stuck out in the middle of nowhere doesn't agree with her?"

"My English teacher'll worry," said Ruth, suddenly.

"Write her some postcards," said Ted's mother. "Though I don't know who's to mail them from Sydney."

"I will," said Ellen. "Mom can take me when she goes shopping. I can write some for you too, Ruthie; I can imitate your handwriting."

“Oh, yeah?” said Ruth, without much force.

“What are you doing about your house?” asked Ruth’s father, who had been hanging about the edges of this discussion with the expression of somebody who likes Bach but has been inveigled into attending a heavy-metal concert. Ted’s parents explained it to him, with relish, adding details as they went along, and finally got him occupied making a list of which of their books he wanted.

“Fence,” said Laura, “doesn’t this add up to an awful lot of lies?”

Both her parents looked around; they knew the force of that argument. Fence quirked the corner of his mouth, and then grinned. “Just this once,” he said, in excellent imitation of Ruth, “call it sorcery.”

There was a silence. Ted counted up the good-byes there were to be said, and was not sure he could manage it.

“Are you in a hurry,” said his Aunt Kim, rubbing her eyes, “or will you stay and eat something with us?”

“Yes,” said Ellen, looking over her father’s encircling arm at Laura with a very private and rather wavery smile, “have some cornflakes before you go.”